CRUEL Summer BOX SET

BY
RACHEL VAN DYKEN

Cruel Summer
by Rachel Van Dyken

Copyright © 2021 RACHEL VAN DYKEN

CRUEL SUMMER

Copyright © 2021 RACHEL VAN DYKEN
ISBN: 978-1-946061-99-7
Cover Design by Jena Brignola
Formatting by Jill Sava, Love Affair With Fiction

CRUEL Summer BOX SET

CRUEL
Summer
BOX SET

To hot summer nights,
to summer camps,
first loves,
loves lost,
and second chances.
Cheers.

PROLOGUE

Marlon

Senior Year 2014

I watched the princess in her glittery tower. My eyes burned with hatred, my anger was barely in check as I pushed the mower back and forth, back and forth.

One line.

Two lines.

Make the lines straight, Marlo.

Don't get grass on the cement statues, Marlo.

You smell like dirt, Marlo.

I gripped the push mower and let the sound of the engine fuel the blood pumping through my veins as a bead of sweat ran down my right cheek.

The door slammed.

Nya, my foster mom, held out a silver tray, the same one I imagined held the silver spoon that was stuck in the princess's mouth the day she was born. Mom made her way toward me, her gray hair curled with perspiration around her ears. Her black and white uniform looked crisp and ironed.

She probably did it herself.

The people she worked for didn't lift a finger. I imagined when they had to shit they just rang a silver bell, you know, to match the tray and spoon, and asked for a butler to carry them to the marble bathroom big enough to fit my entire house plus two cars.

"Do not frown," Nya scolded in a thick Ukrainian accent. Her hands shook a bit as she poured some lemonade into a tall shiny glass. I stopped mowing and walked over, grabbing the clean glass with my dirty hand and slamming back the cold liquid like it was life.

It dribbled down my chin at about the same time the princess walked out the door and stared.

I hated her stare almost as much as I hated everything else about her, from her polished toenails up her tan legs, past her slender hips and flat stomach, to the bored expression on her face, the perfect ice queen hair, and even to those crystal blue eyes. I hated it all. And my hate wasn't something that had just appeared. No, my hate had been tended, it had been watered, it had been pruned. My hate was four years of high school. Four years of her and her friends looking down on me. Four years of facing whispers behind my back. Four years of being shoved into lockers. Four years of random Facebook messages saying I should kill myself.

Four. Fucking. Years.

Things should have changed that night.

They didn't.

And now? Now that I could see freedom, college.

She took the last thing I had.

A drama scholarship to my school of choice.

She had the money.

So why apply?

I had to stay back one more year in order to afford school, I had to stay back and try for the same scholarship next year.

I got to mow lawns.

She opened her mouth like she was going to do something stupid and say sorry.

I shook my head in warning. Like any words wouldn't be good enough. After all, words from her mouth were just as empty as her head.

She'd had her chance last week.

She'd had her chance at school and looked away.

She sighed and then slowly walked across the lawn I'd just mowed and toward the garage.

The engine to her BMW flared to life.

And then she was gone in a plume of smoke and all my disappointments in life just felt that much worse.

"Try not to judge her too harshly." Nya patted my shoulder. "Things aren't always as we believe them to be."

I looked up at their twenty-two-bedroom house and snorted. "Really? Because from this angle it looks exactly how it's always looked."

I swallowed the knot in my throat and handed her back the lemonade.

"Don't be a blind fool." Nya slapped me on the back of the head. I winced and rubbed the spot. While she scowled.

"We are all human, we all feel pain, we all have emotions. Judge all you want, Marlon, but a shiny house doesn't mean we automatically have a happy heart."

Guilt gnawed uncomfortably at my chest. "She got my scholarship." Not just that, she got my dream. My escape. Self-worth. Identity.

Twenty-two fucking bedrooms.

"One day…" She chuckled under her breath. "One day you'll grow up, one day you'll see what I've seen ever since the first day we fostered you into our family, ever since you started working at this house."

"That life isn't fair?" I wondered out loud.

"The sparkle." She shrugged. "An old woman notices these things. The way she stares at you, the way you stare at her. One day you'll regret all this hate. One day she'll regret all hers."

"Is that also the day that zombies take over the planet? Cause I think I'm more prepared for that!"

"I will pray for the day to come!" She announced excitedly.

"The zombies?"

"No, you and Ray." She grinned. "I will pray hard."

"Please don't," I said through clenched teeth.

She started humming.

Great. Just great.

I started the lawnmower again. I would never be the princess's friend. I would never be anything more than a foster kid mowing her lawn and wishing for a better life.

Hoping for more was useless.

A kid like me knew that.

Abandoned at six.

Owned by the state for another month.
Hope and Disney were one in the same.
A fantasy.
An epic way to let yourself down.
Straight lines, Marlon.
Two lines.
Three lines.
Four lines.
Don't get grass on the cement, Marlon.
Ray and I? The princess and the pauper?
Unlikely.
I think we'd rather kill each other.

Chapter ONE

Ray

Four Years Later

I nervously drummed my fingernails against my denim-clad legs.

"I'm going to puke," I announced.

Nya, my nanny/maid since childhood laughed to herself and pulled the town car around the corner and put it in park. "Just breathe."

I hadn't seen her in a year. The closer it seemed I got to her, the more excuses my parents made that she was too busy to see me. I knew the truth. My stomach knotted as I closed my eyes and drew air between my lips, air that smelled like memories, air that tasted like him. Always him.

"Better?"

"No." I exhaled and opened my eyes. "But it was a nice try."

"You have nothing to be nervous about." Nya said with a smile. "It's summer camp not rocket science. Work for two months and then—"

I tried to keep the tears in.

It didn't work.

She was all I had.

Thinking about moving to LA without her just felt… wrong. On so many levels. She'd been the one to put Band-Aids over my scrapes when I was little. I still remember the song she used to sing to me when I was a baby and during college would use it as a way to keep my anxiety at bay. The Ukrainian words about protection and love.

Her precious baby.

Only I wasn't hers.

I was theirs.

My parents.

But thinking about them just put me in a bad mood and I was already stressed out enough as it was. I wanted to do a good job. I wanted to prove I was worthy of drama camp.

And most of all, I wanted to impress the producers, directors, and agents who would be at our camp finale, watching and waiting to see if the counselors were able to put together a show worthy of Hollywood.

Summer Heat, Camp to the Stars wasn't just a camp.

It was *the* camp you went to, to get seen.

And it wasn't just campers.

The counselors also performed in the production.

Twenty-two of them had gone on to win Academy

Awards later on in life, several others had won Emmy's. It was a big deal.

Getting hired had been a nightmare. I half expected them to ask for my first born and a spleen.

"You think too much," Nya said simply. "Just enjoy your two months. Oh, and could you do me a favor?"

"Sure." I unbuckled my seatbelt and reached for my brand-new Kate Spade, with the black and white polka dots and splashes of pink. It was a gift from my parents for graduating.

Well, it was the only one I would accept.

Since giving someone a brand-new G Wagon and a trip to Belize seemed like overkill.

Nya handed me a worn blue duffel bag. "Will you drop this off with Marlo?"

My ears started to ring as dread swept through my body. "Marlo? As in your Marlo?"

"Yours too." She grinned.

Yup, definitely going to puke.

Marlo. The same Marlo that mowed our lawn? The same Marlo half the senior class cheated off of in order to pass calculus?

Marlo. The guy everyone made fun of because they were just that unhappy with their own measly lives.

Marlo.

Marlo, the guy I beat out for a scholarship.

A scholarship I deserved.

A scholarship I needed, since my parents refused to pay for me to major in drama.

It was me or him!

I groaned into my hands.

The same Marlo who saw me for me. Who I touched…

Shit.

Shit.

Shit.

You know how people have enemies and then the people you know would drown you in a pool of your own blood if they had the chance? He was the latter. The one person who could ruin my day with a stare. The one person alive that could ruin my life by simply existing. The hate between us was thick.

And four years had probably done nothing but let it fester into this giant angry red boil that refused to pop.

"See you in two months!" Nya said cheerfully.

Wait, she was still here?

What had I been doing that whole time? Oh, right just envisioning this very uncomfortable situation where I'll most likely start off on the wrong foot because I always did with Marlo. No matter what I did, I earned a judgmental sneer.

Shit.

How many *shits* was that now?

"Right." I nodded numbly then opened my door and walked to the back of the car, Nya was out before I could tell her to stay in the driver's seat. Maybe it was out of habit that she helped me — a huge part of me hoped it was garnered from some love or affection she had for me.

Wishful thinking probably.

"You be good." She pinched my cheeks; her rouge lipstick made her lips stick out around her paper-thin skin and white long hair. "Make friends and try to enjoy life a little this summer."

"Yeah." I sighed. "I'll get right on that."

"Good girl." She turned. "Oh!" Her fingers snapped in the air like she almost forgot to tell me something. "You may not recognize Marlo. He's filled out a bit, spends his free time in the gym, says it feeds his rage."

Awesome.

Just. Awesome.

"Rage?"

"Who knows?" She laughed like it was funny.

It wasn't.

I was pretty sure I knew who said rage was directed at, but maybe he'd taken up hating other people? Dogs? Horses? Maybe another enemy had risen up and taken on the cause!

Maybe I was completely home free!

And exaggerating.

I frowned and waved Nya off as I took my bags and the small duffel down the sidewalk toward the main lodge for registration.

Honestly, four years is a long time to hold a grudge.

So what? Nya said he still managed to start school that same year and was in an even better program than I was at my college! According to her, he was a star, a regular Marlon Brando, considering his name was Marlon and that he'd had glasses and the skinniest body I'd ever seen, I highly doubted the physical comparison was the same, but still.

If my professors one state over even knew about him?

Then he was just fine.

Scholarship, schmolarship.

I was actually feeling better the more I walked.

Maybe it was the cramped car.

Or the emotional trauma of leaving Nya for two months after just reconnecting again after graduation.

I sucked in a breath of pine and dirt and grinned as my heels clicked against the hard surface of the lodge floor. High school kids were lounging everywhere. Immediately, I could see the cliques.

The cool drama kids were all wearing black and drinking lattes. Sigh.

The ones who were forced here by parents were huddled in a corner staring at their phones, probably flirting with the idea of calling 911 for rescue.

And another group of rich kids — like recognizes like — rested lazily across the three leather sofas nearest to the snack bar, wearing aviators and enough cologne or perfume to choke a person.

The registration desk was right behind them.

I quickly made my way over, dropped my bags, and straightened my tank over my leather leggings. I held out my hand to the first available guy with a black shirt that said staff. "Hi, I'm—"

He looked up.

His icy blue eyes locked on mine with such intensity my jaw went a little slack.

He. Was. Beautiful.

His stare was striking, like he was measuring me and found me wanting. His messy brown hair was tucked beneath a backward Yankees baseball cap, and his jaw was so thick and chiseled I wondered if he did one of those weird chin exercises to really pump up the veins in his neck because. Dayum.

He sighed like my breathing was his greatest disappointment — scratch that, my existence.

"Um..." I put my hand down. "I, um, my name's—"

"Ray, as in you have a ray of sunshine sticking out of your ass, De Lato. Graduated summa cum laude from Carnegie Mellon, you like pedicures, small useless things like spray tans, and I wouldn't be surprised if you stopped production because you broke a nail, am I missing anything?" He stood and placed his hands against the table. He towered over me by at least six inches.

"Okay I don't know who the hell you think you are—"

He smiled.

A beautifully cruel straight white toothed smile that had my girly parts doing a hoedown before I could tell them to shut the hell up and fight back. "Interesting."

I ignored his nice smile and massive body and the muscles contracting near his forearms, and sweet God, who knew triceps could stretch a shirt like that? Not this girl? Where did they make them like this? Iowa? How did I find more? Ones without severe personality flaws and chips on their shoulders like him.

"Look." I flashed my most confident smile. "I'm new this year. One of the counselors dropped out, and I was able to get in last minute as staff."

"I'm aware."

"Oh." I gulped. "Well, I wasn't sure, so I just thought—"

"Brax." Rude hot guy held a packet in the air. "Can you make sure Ray has her schedule and put her in the blue cabin?"

Brax's eyebrows shot all the way up to his black beanie. His reddish-brown hair curled near his shoulders, and his eyelashes were so long I was envious. He wasn't as tall or built as rude guy, but he was friendly looking and at least didn't scowl every time I looked in his direction. "Sure, boss."

"B-boss?" I just had to repeat.

"Director." He grinned. "Actually."

"For the summer?" I gulped.

Brax and the rest of the table snickered.

"Of the entire camp," he said politely. "I hope you enjoy your time here Ray — I know I for one... can't wait."

Brax walked around the table. "Here, let me help you with your bags."

"Brax, this isn't the Hilton. She can carry her own damn bags. Be quick about it, I need you both back at HQ for a meeting."

"On it." He nodded and strode out of the lodge. I could barely keep up with him as I teetered on my tall high heels.

"So, I don't know what you did to piss off one of the most cheerful guys I know, but I would figure out a way to fix it and fast," Brax said in a low tone.

"I wish I knew!" I was out of breath keeping up with him, and then he just stopped and pointed. "Wait, what's that?"

"Blue cabin. Your home for the next two months."

"It's on stilts." I gulped. "And it looks like it hasn't been lived in, in—"

"We call it the parent trap cabin because it looks identical to that creepy cabin in the movie where the girls are sent off away from all society and safety."

I clenched my teeth. "Well that's... not good."

"Like I said, whatever you did. Fix it." He patted me on the back and nodded to the ratty looking screen door that was halfway off its hinges. "We better hurry, wouldn't want to make it worse."

How could I make it better or worse if I didn't even know what I did in the first place?

Chapter TWO

Marlon

"That was rude," Jen said.

I didn't look up. I knew what was plastered all over her face. Disappointment. I felt it in my soul.

Four years.

I'd spent four years pouring my soul into drama, using it as my therapy, my muse. I ignored all the shit from high school. I honestly thought I was fine.

Completely fine.

And then suddenly *she* was there.

Wearing the same perfume, some sort of spicy candy scent that had my body involuntarily leaning in for more. And when I inhaled, the memories released right into the air.

With the hate.

With the rage that I thought I'd left on the punching bag. In the gym.

Then she just had to make it worse and smile.

Pretend not to know me.

Hell, maybe she just didn't recognize me.

I imagined this scenario a hundred times, a thousand times. She'd throw herself at me like every single woman had for the last three years, and then I'd confess who I was while giving her the best orgasm of her life, take her clothes, and leave her to wonder why they always say to be nice to everyone because, hey you never know, maybe the school nerd who mows lawns for a living turns out to be a ten instead of a four.

I ran my hands through my hair and put my baseball hat back on. "She can handle it, trust me, Jen," was all I said as I grabbed the stack of folders in front of me.

Jen sighed and handed me a green Red Bull and then shook her strawberry blonde hair. "I'm just saying you're the director this year, you're the example, the guy we all look to, your staff needs you to be focused, kind, logical, not an emotional train wreck who sees a pretty girl and loses his mind."

I smirked and then bit down on my lip. "She's not pretty."

"Are you drunk?"

"No."

"On a bender?"

I slapped her hand away. "I wish."

She scrunched up her nose, her freckles were a dominant and adorable part of her face. I'd always thought of her as more of a sister than anything. We'd worked together at the same camp for the past three years and now that it was almost over with, I almost felt sad that I wouldn't see her anymore.

Or the rest of my crew.

It was just an unfortunate accident that Darius couldn't return this year. And since I didn't do the hiring…

Well here we are!

Damn cruel universe.

"Look, I'm fine. I didn't get much sleep last night." I shrugged her off. "The sooner we start the staff meeting the sooner we can get set up for the opening campfire."

"Yeah." She glanced around the room. "Those millennials look positively thrilled."

I counted at least a hundred phones.

"Grab the bucket." I crossed my arms.

She side-eyed me. "So soon?"

"They look ready to start humping their own cell phones, so yeah, we're gonna take away technology this soon. They'll get them back every Saturday for two hours."

"Harsh. I like it." Jen winked and grabbed one of the black buckets labeled *Hell*.

"Listen up!" I yelled over the room. "We have a very strict no-technology policy." The door swung open revealing Brax and Ray. "And that includes staff. In case of an emergency, find a staff member and we'll get a call out on a landline. You're not here to tweet, or post an Insta story, and if I see any Facebook status updates with you doing a peace sign over your bunk partners missing eyebrow there will be hell to pay. We don't have a lot of rules, but the ones we do have are iron clad. Break one," I eyed Ray, "and you're gone."

Her nostrils flared.

I tried to ignore the way her body had changed.

When we had both gone our separate ways, she had been tall, a bit lanky, and hadn't quite filled out.

Now she looked like a woman.

Curves in all the right places.

The perfect sun-kissed skin.

And full lips that I remembered wanting to taste the first day I met her.

I quickly looked away. "You'll get your phones back every Saturday for two hours. Let's have 'em."

Groans and cursing followed as Jen passed around the bucket. I was used to complaining, if they didn't complain or wish death on my head, I'd be worried.

Jen stopped in front of Ray.

I waited for the spoiled princess to defy me, to look me in the eye and jut her chin out. Instead, she gritted her teeth and dropped her phone in the bucket with a light clunk then stared down at her shoes.

In what world did a camp counselor show up in spiky heels that could impale multiple humans at once?

I rolled my eyes as Jen kept passing the bucket. When the last cell phone was confiscated, I rubbed my hands together. "Our welcome barbecue starts in two hours. Get settled in your bunks." I walked to the center of the room. "Oh, also there's this thing called nature." Kids snickered. "Trees. Grass." I grinned as most the angry expressions left their faces. "And I know this one is really shocking, but there's, like, this thing called... talking to another human, you know, face to face. We adults like to call it a conversation. Try to have at least one without shitting yourself and you win a prize!"

"A prize?" some random person shouted. "What kind of prize?"

"Oh, we feed you." I grinned. "At the BBQ. Show up and isolate yourself, and we'll see how long you last without a hot dog."

"I'm a burger guy!" He shouted then stepped forward. I shook my head as Jackson, another staff member did a little dance and then winked over at Ray. "But I'll try to make new friends. I can be very friendly."

"Wasn't talking about you." I rolled my eyes. "All right guys, two hours. If you need help, find a staff member with a black shirt. Dismissed."

Jackson had the most incredible ability to swagger across a room, really it was an art form. And he did just that, all the way to Ray.

I clenched my fists. Partially out of anger that he would waste any breath on her, and well, another part that I completely denied and would deny until the day I died.

Was jealous.

"Jackson," I barked the minute he opened his mouth. "We need to get you a shirt."

"What about Ray?" Brax just had to ask.

"Yeah what about Ray?" Jackson grinned.

Bastard.

"Both of you, follow me." I crooked my fingers and marched toward the back room. I grabbed Jackson a large and then grinned menacingly as I grabbed Ray a large as well. "Here you go, your new uniforms for the day."

"Um, do they have any smalls or mediums?" Ray asked in a quiet voice. "It's totally fine if…" She gulped. Damn it she needed to stop being so pretty and annoying all at once.

I shrugged and crossed my arms. "This is all we have. We can't cater specifically to everyone's tastes. Next, you'll be asking for a track suit or a Starbucks run every morning. It's camping, not glamping, not spring break. We're here to make the best damn productions we can. Hopefully, the kids walk away knowing how to navigate the industry. We don't have time to play dress up."

Her face fell and then lit up. "No problem. Like I said, just a question."

Jackson let out a low whistle. "And on that note, Marlo, you need a cold beer? A shot of whiskey? Something to bring that blood pressure down?"

I jerked away from him. "I'm fine."

"Marlo?" Ray repeated. "Marlo?"

She looked horrified.

"Surprise," I whispered hoarsely as our eyes locked.

She didn't look away.

I didn't either.

I would win this war one way or another.

And then she did the strangest thing, she lowered her head in defeat turned around and walked out of the room, rubbing her cheek as if she had a tear.

But I knew the truth.

Princesses rarely cry.

It's the paupers that drown in tears.

That drown in hope.

She cried out of not getting her own way.

Guys like me? Cry out of devastation.

Chapter
THREE

Ray

I adjusted my black *Staff* shirt as best I could and finally just gave up and tied the bottom part of the material in a little knot so that it fit bitter.

"Looks nice." Jackson crossed his bulky arms over his chest and winked at me like we were sharing some secret between us. I narrowed my eyes and then turned around. I knew guys like that. I'd known them all my life. He oozed narcissism like a whore sweating in a church pew.

I wanted no part of that.

I had no room for repeat relationships where I'm told I'm lucky that a guy like that's with a girl who doesn't wear a double D.

God, my ex was a douche.

"Listen up!" Marlo blew a whistle loud enough to cause a ringing to hit my ears. I winced and waited.

At least Jackson wasn't talking to me anymore. Though he was still smirking like our conversation wasn't done. He had short buzzed hair and probably one brain cell that was so lonely it talked to itself at night.

I smiled to myself.

Bad timing.

Since that was when Marlon set his eyes on me.

I still couldn't believe he was the same guy who used to mow my lawn. The same guy one of my boyfriends from high school used to shove in the lockers. That guy had been so lanky he'd actually fit on multiple occasions and needed the principal to rescue him.

It was never funny.

Guys like that survived high school.

While girls like me thrived.

Though I'd hated every fake minute of it, it had been so important to me to find acceptance, an identity outside the life my parents gave me, the fake love they tried to shower me with.

So my friends had been my love.

It caused me to turn a blind eye to all the injustice to guys like Marlo. I wasn't that same person. Didn't matter though. He clearly still wanted to poison me as much as ever.

His eyes locked on mine as he started talking. "Staff hours are eight to eight. The main lodge is available for you guys to use to relax, gossip about the little shits that refuse to listen to your wisdom, and to party with all the confiscated alcohol we're about to take. Get high on your own watch and remember you guys are here for one reason and one reason only. I know I don't have to remind you why this is one of the best camps in the US. But I'm going to do it anyway. We've been around for twenty years, and in twenty years, we've had some of the biggest names in Hollywood grace our halls. You may be coaching the next Chris Pratt, so try to be patient. This is a place to make connections and it also looks incredible on your resumes. I know a lot of you are drama majors hoping to hit it big in an industry that crushes dreams almost as much as it crushes pills — try to use this as a learning experience. Network with one another." His gaze left mine. "This is your official Welcome to Summer Heat, Camp to the Stars." He handed a stack of papers to the girl standing next to him. "Memorize your itinerary for the week. We have seven days to decide on a show, make sure to put in your votes by Friday, we'll announce at the Saturday campfire. Your schedules will shift throughout the next two months, if you prove yourself in one area, then you may get upgraded to coach another. We've tried to place you in your specialties." His grin was more of a leer when he looked me over. Damn it, why did he have to suddenly look like Alexander Skaarsgard and Brad Pitt's long-lost love child. I blinked a few times like I was trying to take in the inches of muscle packed around his body. The sharp jawline, the veins running down his forearms.

"You should probably stop staring," Jackson said out of the corner of his mouth.

I jumped a foot. "What? No, I wasn't—"

"He can sense attraction, he smells it in the air like a shark during shark week who's been given a speck of blood." He grinned.

Heat flooded my cheeks.

"Don't worry my lips are sealed, but let's just say if you did nail him, you'd be the first to get through that rough exterior. He doesn't do girlfriends, he does one-night stands."

"You two must have that in common." I smiled sweetly at him then looked away.

He chuckled to himself. "Is that interest I hear in your voice?"

"Never." I rolled my eyes as Marlo kept talking about schedules and then Jackson handed me mine and whistled. I stared down at my name crossed out then scribbled in next to choreography and singing.

I felt myself pale.

I had severe stage fright when it came to singing.

And I'd barely passed my last dance class because I nearly fell off the stage. I had taken lessons because I wanted to be a triple threat, but acting was my jam — drama, not dancing, not music.

"That sucks," Jackson peered over my shoulder with a knowing grin. "He's fired at least four choreographers, and that was within the first week of camp. Good luck, you're going to need it." He smiled as if he knew something I didn't. Panic swept through my body.

"Great," I grumbled.

And then a warm arm was placed around me. I looked up into Jackson's green eyes and tried to be unaffected by his presence, but he was just like Marlo. It was like he sensed the chase and became more attractive by the second because of it. "I can coach you, you know. It's my specialty, voice of an angel right here, not to mention moves that would make you—"

I cupped my hand over his mouth and shook my head stern. "I'm going to ignore your obvious sexual innuendos for your own sake. I don't want a boyfriend. I don't want a one-night stand, and I sure as hell don't want you to coach me. I'm offering friendship because I'm severely lacking in that department right now. Take it or leave it."

His lips tickled my palm as he grinned against my hand.

I pulled it away, eyebrow arching. "Well?"

He held out his hand and widened his grin. "I'm a really good friend."

"Oh, I bet," I said sarcastically, taking his hand in mine.

"Ray," Marlon called from the front. "If you're done flirting I'd like to get back to the bathroom schedule and mess hall."

Flames licked at my face. "I wasn't…" I sighed. "Sorry, Marlo."

He just shook his head and kept talking about the mess hall and the bathrooms and how we needed to stick to our schedule otherwise things didn't work. Who died and made him director? The guy had a serious stick stuck up his ass.

Finally, he was done.

I'd heard about half of what he said.

"Dismissed." He nodded to us. Suddenly exhausted, I turned on my heel and started walking toward the door.

"Ray." It was Marlo. Damn it.

My steps faltered as I gulped and turned around. People shuffled out of the lodge, leaving us alone.

Marlo walked purposefully toward me. His ice blue eyes never left my face. And then suddenly he was in front of me. Every hard inch of him.

I tried to calm my erratic heartbeat.

The tension in the air could be tasted. It swirled around us as this tangible thing just like his anger. I felt waves of it hit me in the face, dance between us and around us, bringing my body closer.

I sucked in a breath when he leaned down like he was going to kiss me. My lips parted greedily trying to pull in the air between us, hoping it had pieces of him on it.

"You don't belong here," was what he said in a lethal tone. "Three strikes. I'm not afraid to fire people. And you and I both know you probably need this job more than anyone."

I flinched. "I'm sorry, what's that supposed to mean?"

His grin was evil as he held up his cell phone. "Shopping for an agent?"

"How'd you know that?" I hissed quietly. "Nobody knows that."

"First off, most of the staff members are." He shrugged. "Second, I heard you turned down Elliot Meyers, and he's trying to blacklist you."

My stomach dropped to my knees. "You don't know shit."

"I know he's one of the best, and he thinks you're a spoiled brat… he's not far off the mark is he?" Marlo shrugged and then lowered his gaze to my shoes. "I'd try harder if I were you…"

"Why do you hate me so much?" I asked in a pleading voice.

His eyebrows shot up. "If you really have to ask yourself that question than you're dumber than I thought. Must suck to lose all the power, hmm Ray?"

"The only power I ever had was the power you willingly gave, Marlo."

His eyes narrowed.

"Then again…" I reached up and caressed his cheek it held a bit of a five o'clock shadow. "That was just one night, right? One stupid drunken night?"

"You promised." He grabbed my wrist, his teeth clenched.

"Well, you just threatened me." We were chest to chest. "It goes both ways, Marlo…" I dragged out his name. I knew I was being a bitch, bringing up the past. Bringing up what was probably one of my favorite mistakes.

Finding myself in his room.

Finding myself in his arms.

Finding my mouth on his.

Skin against skin.

Tongue swirling around tongue.

It had been the best kiss of my life.

We'd both been wasted.

And I'd ignored him the next day.

"Hey! Ray!" Marlo ran toward me down the hall. He was wearing a baseball cap and looked so happy that I wanted to reach out and hug him. He'd been so sweet to me the night before, he'd taken his time, he'd kissed every inch of my body, he'd made me feel alive for the first time I could remember. And if I was being honest.

Loved.

He'd loved me, treasured me the only way a man with that much passion could.

I opened my mouth to say hi but was interrupted by Chels.

"No way!" Chels rolled her eyes. "Can you please disappear, nerd? Breathe in our direction again, and I'm telling a teacher you flashed us your tiny dick."

Hurt flashed in his expression avs he turned to me.

"Chels." I rolled my eyes. "Don't be a bitch."

"What? He's a lanky troll."

People around us laughed.

His eyes locked on mine.

Time stood still.

I chose myself.

Instead of him.

"Sorry, Marlo. Not now."

"But—"

"I said not now!" I roared. "God, can you just leave me alone?"

"What a loser." Chels laughed.

Everyone joined in.

And then my ex came toward us with a few guys from the football team. It all happened so fast, the fight. The blood. Marlo on the ground looking up at me like I was the devil.

And I walked away.

I walked away and didn't look back.

Tears welled in my eyes as Marlo looked down at me with that same expression, like I was the cause of all the pain the world — the major cause of his, when he was the only person who had ever kissed me like I mattered.

"Change your fucking shoes," he gritted through his teeth. "Try not to sleep with the first guy who smiles at you, and do your job or you're gone."

"Fine," I said with false cheer.

He shook his head and walked off, leaving me feeling nothing but shame and remorse.

Chapter FOUR

Marlon

"You look pissed," Jen pointed out at the bon fire that night. I shook my head and ignored her curious stare. It wasn't the first time she looked at me like I needed to be put in my place. But Jen grew up in the suburbs — not that I held it over her head, the biggest issue she had as a high school student was what to wear to prom, and if she should try out for cheerleading. Her college experience was much the same. No judgment, I loved her like a sister, but she didn't get it.

There would always be people who had it easy and were just too ignorant to realize it — she was one of those people.

"Sorry Jen, it's just one of those days…" I finally answered. "And just in case you were wondering, kinda hard not to be pissed on the first day of camp, right? Keeps the campers freaked a bit?" I tried for a smile.

She narrowed her eyes, she both saw too much and knew me too well.

Yeah, she wasn't buying shit.

Probably because I wasn't selling it worth shit.

The two hundred pushups had helped a little.

The quick two-mile sprint had done nothing.

"Is everything set up?" Gravel crunched beneath my Converses as I made my way over to the large fire that Jackson was struggling to set up. "Matches, bro, use matches." I tossed him a pack

He caught them with a wink then gave me a middle finger salute.

Some of the senior teens started making their way toward us. Everything felt like it was spiraling out of control. It was my last year directing before moving out West. I loved my job. I loved the teens. The camp. Teaching. I loved what it stood for. Why the hell was my last year going to be tainted with visions of the only girl I'd kissed in high school?

Was this some sort of punishment? And what had I ever done to piss off the universe that much?

I wiped my face with my hands and then threw my hat on the ground.

"Marlon?" One of the senior girls sashayed over to me, hands on hips, short as hell shorts and a wide come-hither grin that I was sure worked with every single boy in her class. Her dark hair was pulled back into a ponytail, and her smile promised secrets and heated kisses, I knew her type. I stayed far, far away. Besides, girls like that were trouble, and we had a very strict policy at camp. "Can we eat your hot dog now?"

People around her gasped. Oh, good. A blunt one.

"Oh, my gosh!" She covered her mouth with her hands. "I'm so sorry. I meant can we eat the hot dogs now?"

My ass.

I forced a smile, I didn't feel. *And so it begins!* "Sure thing…" I waited for her to offer me her name, which she would.

"Erika." She bit down on her lower lip. Yeah it was going to be a long two months.

"Great," I said with warmth and false affection. "Erika, why don't you grab some food? Jackson?"

I always made Jackson take on the flirty ones. He loved the attention and had no qualms about bluntly putting the girls in their place when they tried to flirt with me or any of the staff members. As much as he survived off sex and air, he knew what our rules were and found pleasure in making the girls think he wanted them when he was too busy with, in his words, a grown ass woman back at his cabin.

Basically, he was a creep.

But he handled it with more finesse, so I let him and stayed out of the way.

"Yeah?" He looked up glanced between us and grinned. "Hey there, sweetheart, need help with the hot dogs?"

She nodded.

He jumped to his feet and trailed after her.

"Don't forget our rules," I whispered under my breath.

He rolled his eyes and gave me a thumbs-up then trailed after her.

"He's going to be screwing her sideways by Friday," Brax's voice said behind me.

"Then he's going to get fired."

One could only hope. He was already sniffing around Ray more than I would like. Not that it was my problem; she could spread her legs for whoever she wanted.

Damn, when had I turned into such a prick?

"You should do something before he takes it too far and her rich family tries to sue the camp." Brax elbowed me.

"Her body her choice, besides, this is a safe place, maybe she'll learn that flirting with men is a hell of a lot more painful than sleeping with the boys in her class. I'll pull her aside after she comes to the lodge begging me to fire him for flirting with her, and I'll make sure that it doesn't happen again."

"Shit." Brax shook his head at me. "When did you turn into such a dick?"

Hah, it was like he read my mind. Fantastic. I looked up at him and saw Ray make her way toward us. She'd changed into tight skinny jeans, converse, and put a black beanie over her golden princess hair.

"Ah!" Brax snapped his fingers and whistled. "I see."

I grunted and threw a stick into the fire.

"Ex-girlfriend?"

"Hah." I felt the heaviness on my chest; it pressed down, it laughed just like she used to laugh at me with her friends and the entire fucking school. "Not in this lifetime."

"Revenge sex," Brax said under his breath.

"What?" I jerked my head to his so fast my neck almost cracked. "Explain?"

"Revenge sex is the best sex, or so I've heard. Play nice…" Brax lowered his voice. "Fuck her out of your system, then leave her. You're left satisfied, with the upper hand, and you prove to yourself and to her that it's nothing."

"I thought about it," I said, feeling like the lowest human being on the planet for even admitting it out loud. "But the thought of even pretending that she's anything other than a spoiled bitch really puts me in a bad mood."

"No. Shocker. You don't say?" Brax rolled his eyes just as Jen strolled up.

"What are we talking about?" Jen was way too cheerful. I didn't want her cheer. Or her smiles. At least she seemed to be over our little altercation.

"Nothing." I flashed a grin and wrapped my arm around her shoulders. "Have I ever told you I appreciate you?"

"Um, are you feeling okay?" Jen pressed the back of her hand to my forehead. "Because two hours ago I was afraid you were going to run someone over with the camp truck."

"Ah, that's still a very real possibility," I joked.

She and Brax burst out laughing while Ray grabbed a hot dog and sat next to a few girls who looked so lost it was almost laughable. They had no phone, ergo they had no direction.

Conversation?

Humans?

Holy shit.

How did one even begin?

She tried. She really did. I'd definitely give her an A for effort. She was animated, and her smile was friendly. But both girls got up, pale, and ran off, like they were ready to puke.

I snorted out a laugh earning her attention across the campfire.

The blaze roared to life like it was using our hate as its fuel.

And then she held the hot dog to her lips and parted them.

My breath hitched as she took in a huge bite, her eyes locked on mine like she had her mouth on me, her teeth, her tongue swirled around catching bits of ketchup that had hit the corners of her mouth, as she chewed she stuck a finger in her mouth and licked it.

What the hell kind of game was she playing?

"Like I said," Brax whispered under his breath and leaned closer to me so Jen couldn't hear. "Revenge sex."

"She'll think she won." I turned to him while Jen tended to the fire, oblivious to my dark thoughts. My pain. The sour direction my stomach had taken the minute I saw Ray walk up.

"So let her think she has the upper hand, then pull the rug out from underneath her. Easy."

"You need to stop hanging out with Jackson. Bastard's tainting your soul," I joked, toying with the idea more and more, tossing it around like a ball in the empty dangerous parts of my head. The ones where ideas were born or killed.

"I just hate seeing you like this," Brax said. "You're one of my best friends, plus it will keep all the teens from salivating over you if you have someone to focus on. It's a win-win."

Interesting.

It typically took the first month for the girls to realize that I wasn't interested, and it was annoying as hell.

It was a thought.

Sleep with her. Use her as a human shield. Then pretend like it never happened, like we never existed. Just the way she did four years ago.

She took another bite.

And then flipped me off.

I pressed my lips together to keep from smiling then turned to Brax and said. "Consider it done."

Chapter FIVE

Ray

One night down, a million more to go.

I was staff, so I didn't have a cabin of screaming girls that I had to watch over at night, which almost made it worse. I was lonely.

So lonely.

I wiped a tear from my eye as I grabbed the flashlight and the rest of my shower caddy and slowly left my spider-infested cabin and made my way toward the bathroom.

Any time after ten, the staff bathrooms were co-ed.

Which sucked for me, since the campfire had just ended, but I couldn't stand sitting in my cabin all by myself with my thoughts, plus I smelled like smoke.

I made a mental note to do a little sprucing up later that week, because my cabin looked like it was built in the twenties and had just had shitty updates until 2018. I was probably going to die in a fire, or it was going to just collapse on me while I slept in my bunk.

Yay!

With a shudder, I opened the bathroom door. Steam billowed out. Every shower was taken. I sighed in impatience and waited near the wall.

What kind of camp had only six showers for the staff anyways?

At least the room was clean. Stark white. It smelled like coconut body wash and Old Spice.

One of the showers turned off.

I pressed off the wall only to see Jackson pull open the curtain and grin at me. "Hey, friend."

I groaned.

"What? I thought we were doing this whole friends thing."

"Could you please not be naked during this conversation?" I pleaded turning away while he grabbed his towel.

"I can't help that I'm packing." He said with amusement. "Okay you can look now."

I turned back. The guy had a nice six pack, a V that would make any woman salivate, and enough muscles to make me slightly attracted. It was the personality that killed it.

"Like what you see?" He sauntered toward me.

I shrugged. "I've seen better."

"Doubtful." He nodded like I was cute for lying. "I didn't use all the hot water, but I may have fantasized a few times about a certain pretty girl."

"Ew!" I shoved him while he fell into hysterics.

"I'm kidding!" He nodded back. "But it was tempting."

"Oh, I'm sure it was, so many girls, only two hands and one dick. Poor guy!"

"Ha-ha!" He patted me on the shoulder. "I think this is the start of a beautiful friendship, don't you?"

"Undecided." I patted him right back, side stepped him, and turned the shower back on.

"Later, friend!" The door opened and closed, letting some steam out. I huffed out a breath and slipped off my flip flops just as the door opened again.

"Jackson, seriously—"

Not Jackson. Shit.

Marlo was standing there shirtless with a towel hanging over his shoulder, his caddy in his right hand, and wearing a pair of low slung shorts that made me drop my eyes to the impressive band of muscle around his midsection. Damn. What did he do to get abs like that? Just cut out all food that made a person want to live and survive off of dry chicken and beef jerky? Not an ounce of fat. It was almost disappointing, not being able to find a flaw on the outside when there were numerous ones on the inside.

"Disappointed?" Marlo tilted his head.

My first thought? Impossible. He was beautiful. The next thought was of our one night together, his mouth between my breasts, the way he clawed at me for more, the way I squeezed my thighs around him and begged him to go deeper.

"Uhhhhh," I had absolutely no non-sexual thoughts in my head. "No?"

"Is that a question?" He smirked.

I'd forgotten about his smirk.

The way it made him look dangerous, sexy, like the bad boy riding in on the motorcycle, the guy you don't bring home to Mom because he looks like his only goal in life is to live freely through the prison system and get a tattoo on his neck.

"Are you done?" He pointed to the empty shower.

"No, I was just getting in." I turned around, trying my best to ignore him. I had a plan, take the longest hottest shower known to mankind and leave him with nothing but cold water and pieces of my hair stuck to the walls just to disgust him and piss him off, maybe a strand would land on him and send him into fits of hysteria. One could only hope!

"Better hurry," he said with another smirk. "The other showers are taken, and they shut off the water at eleven."

I gawked. "Are you serious?"

"No, I'm shitting you." He grinned like we were friends capable of teasing one another, having a relationship that wasn't filled with hate. I didn't like how hopeful it made me feel. How dangerous that feeling was.

Friendship.

I'd never had real friends. Real people who cared about what happened to me. He'd been my friend that night.

Offered his shoulder to cry on.

And then his body.

I shuddered and let out a rough exhale. "My cabin's creepy. I really wanted a long shower."

Why had I just offered more ammunition? Information?

"I'll walk you back." He shrugged like it wasn't a favor. Just as another shower turned off. It was a staff member I didn't recognize. The shower was right next to mine. Marlo started stripping right in front of me while my hands were still on my own shirt waiting to peel it off. "Better hurry or I'll be done before you." That was the last phrase I was able to process before he slid his sweats down to his ankles and hung them up on the hook. Muscle, muscle everywhere. I was staring. I didn't mean to stare. I couldn't help it. His ass.

He had an ass.

My weakness in life was a guy who had an ass bigger than mine, hey a girl could dream!

I quickly turned away, stripped, and got into the shower. It was torture, the smell of his soap, the sounds of him slathering his body. Why was I being so stupid? My body was completely failing me with memories of our one night together over and over again.

"Let me love you," he whispered against my neck. I told him I was wasted. But I remembered everything. I nodded as he slipped my bra down my shoulders and tossed it to the floor like a pro. His mouth was hot and eager against mine. I could taste whiskey on his tongue, smell grass on his skin.

He was stronger than I imagined. Probably from all the hard labor.

We were in my room.

My parents were gone.

They were always gone.

I'd just broken up with my boyfriend at my own party. Marlo had checked on me out of drunken guilt.

And there we were.

Naked.

He ran his fingers down my stomach. I arched up. With every touch, he mesmerized me.

I shook the memories away just about the same time I heard Marlo's rough voice. "You tasted like candied rum and broken dreams."

I smiled despite myself. "You tasted like whiskey and smelled like fresh grass and mint tea."

"Your skin still as smooth as it felt against my tongue?" His voice lowered.

Holy shit.

I squeezed my eyes shut and ran my hands down my body. "Sure feels like it."

"Fuck." I could hear him bang something against the side of the shower and then. "Are you touching yourself?"

"Are you?"

"Guys, could you not?" Brax said from one of the showers. "I have a very vivid imagination, and I don't want to make it so that the only way I can get off is if I hear you guys discuss whiskey and fresh cut grass. That cool with you?"

I squeezed my eyes shut. What just happened?

"No problem!" Marlo laughed like it really wasn't, when my entire body felt like someone had just electrocuted me and put me back under water holding a blow drier.

The shower shut off.

I finished up, grabbed my towel, and then tried to dress myself in the small shower square. I ended up getting my sweatshirt a bit wet, but it still worked better than changing in front of Marlo.

He was already dressed and waiting for me by the door, same clothes, same smirk. As if our sexually charged conversation hadn't happened at all.

I sighed in relief when he didn't touch me or put his hand on my back on our walk to the cabin.

"It looks just as scary as I remember it." He grinned at the cabin like he was pleased with himself.

"Oh it is, I've made friends with at least seven spiders, and I think there's a rat." I leveled him with a glare.

He just shrugged. "I don't like surprises."

"And I take it I'm the surprise?"

"Pretty much."

"So I get to suffer because you aren't mentally prepared for my presence?"

"Exactly." He winked.

"What game are you playing?" I asked once we were at my front door. "Hours ago you wanted to murder me, and now you're having an adult conversation with me."

He leaned in, placing his hands on either side of my head against the cabin door. "Maybe this is a cease fire."

"You don't cease fire that much hatred," I said softly. "Though I wish it was true."

"Is that a polite way of saying you don't trust me?" He tilted his head like he was amused.

"Yeah. It is," I croaked.

"Smart girl," he whispered, his gaze lowering to my mouth.

I needed to escape.

Not to pull him into my cabin and ask him to get naked.

What was wrong with me?

All because he was the only guy to ever make me feel something other than lonely?

"I, um, have a bag or something for you from your mom."

"Foster mom," he corrected, his demeanor completely changed, like I'd somehow put division between our two positions in life, rich and poor.

"It's just… over here." I flipped on the lights and grabbed the small duffel for him and tossed it.

He caught it with one hand and then took a look around the small cabin. I wondered in that moment if he wanted to put me in this place because it was the way he'd lived his whole life.

A small room.

Nothing personal.

Enough food to go around, but nothing extra.

I knew what my parents paid them.

I knew the house was old, just like this room.

There were no pictures. Just two small twin-sized beds, a sink to wash up in, and numerous windows with a few shelves filled with dusty books and emergency equipment.

"There a reason you haven't decorated?" He pointed to the blank walls.

"I have nothing to put there," I admitted lamely.

"Family? Friends? Pictures of cats?" he offered.

"Not allowed to have any pets, I kept to myself in College, and I suck at decorating."

"That's… depressing." He crossed his arms.

Why was he still there?

The longer he stared at the walls the more it felt like he was staring into my soul, and I hated it. I hated that he saw all of my vulnerabilities without me even saying anything.

It wasn't fair.

"I should sleep," I blurted.

He stared at the walls a bit longer then back at me. "Me too."

Why was he not moving?

He reached into his duffel and pulled out something

small. It looked like a calendar of some sort.

"Grumpy Cat calendar." He shrugged and tossed it to me. "Two birds with one stone, you can decorate with the pictures, and you have a fake pet."

I caught it midair and gawked at him. "Stop being nice. It's weird."

"I've always been the nice one." He smiled.

"Um, no you've always been extremely rude unless drunk."

"And you've always been a spoiled princess with a stiletto up your ass... guess people don't really change, huh?"

I took in his massive appearance and lied. "Guess not."

"Sleep tight." He winked then left without another word. The screen door slammed behind him. I flipped him off and then grabbed the little calendar, held it to my chest as a tear slid down my cheeks.

"I just want one pet!" I told my mom. "A fish! An ant farm, something, anything!" I didn't tell her how scared I got at night. How I hated living in that giant house without any sort of warmth, how the fact that she was leaving for a girls' trip in Vegas over my birthday made me sick to my stomach. If I could just get something or someone to talk to. "Please?"

"Honey..." Mom rolled her eyes. "Pets smell. You don't need a smelly pet ruining your carpet."

"Fish don't do that!"

"Are you cleaning the fish tank? And ants can escape. Sorry but you don't need a pet, whatever happened to that rock collection!" She beamed. "Just name a rock!"

Name. A. Rock.

"But Mom—"

"I gotta catch my flight. Be good!" She blew me a kiss. The door slammed behind her.

And my second lonely tear fell.

Chapter
SIX

Marlon

The sound of Brax blowing the camp horn, signifying it was time to wake up, was the absolute last thing I wanted to hear. I'd slept like shit, tossed and turned so much that at one point had to get up and take some sleeping medication and then fell asleep for two more hours before I heard that damn horn.

It sounded happy.

I was anything but.

I quickly dressed in a new staff shirt, threw on a pair of ripped jeans, washed my face and brushed my teeth in the sink provided, and called it good. I had to be the first at breakfast and since it was our first official day at camp, it was imperative I be there to answer questions and help all the teens get to their classes.

I grabbed the main camp iPad and strolled out of my cabin in a hurry. My eyes focused on the gravel road ahead. I tried not to notice the outlier.

The cabin I'd put Ray in.

The one usually reserved for punishment.

I gritted my teeth. My heart and brain at war with each other.

Part of me realized it was ridiculous. I was twenty-two. Supposed to be a grown ass adult, and still I was fixated on making her life hell. Cease fire? It should be that easy. To just stop hating someone. But the minute you allow hate in, it sinks its talons into your soul and promises relief if you just let it stay.

So I did.

And now it demanded to be fed.

She was everything to me.

I'd been half obsessed with her throughout my life.

"You look funny," she said in a haughty voice even at six years old.

I self-consciously patted down my long hair and shrugged. "Well, you have ugly metal in your mouth. Metal mouth!"

"That the best you got?" She sneered.

"Yeah." I said with a laugh.

She joined in and then wrapped an arm around my scrawny body. "Do you like to swim?"

We were friends for one summer, the summer before everything changed, before everyone started caring about clothes, body types, cliques.

I shook my head in disgust and looked away from the cabin. I didn't have time to think about where things went wrong or how it was even fixable. Brax was right.

My best bet was to use her as a human shield while simultaneously getting my revenge. Maybe it would make the pain go away. The pain of rejection, of never being enough, of trying with everything in you, holding hope close to your chest, and then getting it ripped from you by the very person who gave it to you in the first place.

The more I thought about it the more the anger burned in my chest like a searing hot flame.

Teens were already starting to linger around the mess hall. I shoved the front door open and made my way toward the coffee. At this rate, I'd need at least two pots of coffee before I could even function without yelling at the first person who said his na—

"Marlon!" Jackson's voice rang through the nervous chatter from the campers. "Heard you had an invigorating shower last night."

Damn it, Brax. Was it that impossible to keep his mouth shut?

"It was hot." I filled my cup to the rim and then added three packets of sugar. "If that's what you mean."

Jackson followed suit and then leaned against the coffee counter. "So, she makes you hot and bothered, is that it?"

"Ah just bothered, actually," I pointed out as Ray made her way into the mess hall and then locked eyes with me.

"Sure…" Jackson let out a low whistle. "If that's the look of being bothered, you should go back for seconds. Lust looks good on you man. How long has it been?"

Too long.

A year.

I was tired of girls who wanted more commitment from me.

And to be honest nothing had ever compared to that one awkward night where I stared at her bra for a solid two minutes perplexed on how to get the hooks undone and get my palms on her breasts as fast as possible.

I hated that she smelled like sunshine as she made her way past me and to the coffee station. I tortured myself with memories of watching her walk to her car with coffee in hand. I'd take a breath only after she left, then walk to school savoring the flavor on my tongue.

I deserved to be shoved into lockers for the thoughts I had about her. On most days, it was a very critical balance between obsession and hate. Hate typically won out, especially when it was her boyfriend who was shoving me into said locker. She always looked away, like she couldn't handle my pain and my embarrassment, like she'd break if she said one word.

Stop. That's all I wanted someone to say.

Stop.

The thing is, people rarely think about saving the guy, guys are used to physical fighting. But all I ever wanted was the words, not even actions, just words. For someone to step in and say this is wrong.

Nobody ever did.

Maybe that's why being Camp Director was so important to me. Because I had the chance to make a difference with nerds everywhere.

God help us all if I was the role model.

"You look nice today." Jackson leaned way too close to Ray's coffee, basically heaving hot breaths into it as he watched her stir like it was the most interesting thing in the world, the way her bracelets clanged against each other, the way she gripped the stir stick.

Idiot.

And yet I was fixated by the same movement.

I wiped a hand over my face. "Jackson, when you're done being creepy can you go make sure that all the cabins are empty for morning announcements."

He winked at Ray and then stood to his full height. "You got it boss. See ya later, Sunshine."

I took a long sip of coffee and waited.

Waited for her to say something offensive.

Waited for the perfect timing where I could say something equally offensive back.

"You still drink it with three sugars," was what she said.

I almost spit out my coffee all over her face. Instead, I choked it down and then flashed her a confused look. "How the hell do you know how I drink my coffee?"

She shrugged. "Probably the same way you know how I take mine."

I rolled my eyes and smirked. It was impossible not to with the way she was grinning up at me like I meant something. "Oh yeah? And what makes you think I know that?"

"We're both perceptive." She offered a one-shoulder shrug. "Just because we were never friends didn't mean I never paid attention."

Some might say I paid too much.

I snorted out a noncommittal word that made no sense whatsoever and left her grinning at me.

Winning. Damn it. She was winning without even trying. Wasn't I supposed to be seducing her? Making her want me? Not thinking about her dimples or the way she grinned at me like fucking sunshine?

Well done, Marlo. Less than twenty-four hours with your high school crush, and you're going to go into obsessive mode again.

I clenched my jaw, Not happening.

I took another sip of the bittersweet coffee and grabbed a banana from one of the baskets we put in the middle of each table in an effort to encourage the students to eat something from a tree rather than coffee and pastries.

Jackson was taking a while. We didn't have a huge camp. Fifteen cabins total, and they all put up a white flag when they were out of their bunks, so all we really had to do was make sure they woke up in time to put up their flag and we were good to go. Plus the mess hall looked like its name, messy with nervous sweaty teens. I sniffed way too many tears — and way too much cologne.

Jackson finally made his way in the door followed by six guys and six girls, who looked like they'd stayed up all night. Wrinkled clothes, messy hair, and broken dreams were painted on their faces.

Hungover as hell was what they looked like.

Jackson was carrying a box and grinning at me like he just won the lottery, which he probably had when it came to alcohol.

It was the popular kids.

One look at their expensive yet wrinkled clothes and good looks, and I knew they were sent here from money, and lots of it, which usually meant underage drinking.

Jackson deposited the box on the table in front of me. A few gallons of alcohol greeted me along with enough pot to last the entire two months.

Nice.

I crooked my fingers to the twelve seniors.

They slowly made their way to the front of the room.

"Listen up!" I yelled.

The room quieted down.

"Break the rules and suffer the consequences." I shook my head at the twelve in front of me. "You guys get kitchen cleanup for the next month. Jackson, can you grab some aprons?"

Jackson saluted me and went off in search of the aprons.

"I'll just be keeping this." I pointed to the box. "You're dismissed."

They all shuffled toward a table and sat. Two of them just lay their heads down and closed their eyes.

It brought me great pleasure to pull out the air horn and give it a little squeeze.

The two with their eyes closed jumped a foot and then pressed hands to their temples like someone was slowly chipping away at their brains.

Good.

"We have a three-strike rule for every camper and staff member," I reminded them. "Alcohol and drug use will not be tolerated. This is your future. It's only two months — you can do anything for two months. And if you find that you can't, maybe this camp isn't the place for you. Ten minutes and you need to report to your first classes."

I handed the box over to Jackson, who had found our aprons. They were a mixture of ugly oranges and pinks, meant to stand out so people knew that the campers weren't working to pay for camp and were under disciplinary action.

I checked my watch as tired campers shoveled food into their mouths and chatted with one another. Ray walked to one of the staff tables and sat far away from everyone.

Was she isolating herself purpose? Did she really think she was better than everyone? It was just proof yet again that people didn't really change, no matter how badly you wanted them to.

I hung my head in disgust and if I were being honest, a bit of disappointment as the chatter of campers filled the room.

Ten minutes crept by.

And then everyone was gone including Ray.

It was better this way.

Better to just get her out of my system, better to show her that the world didn't revolve around her — not anymore.

Chapter SEVEN

Ray

I was completely desperate.

I didn't know anyone.

The one guy I did know probably dreamed about running me over with his lawnmower on a nightly basis.

I hugged myself as I made my way to choreography. At least all lesson plans were done in advance for staff. I'd taken one look at my binder and almost puked. Today I was supposed to go over the syllabus and then do a quick and effective jazz class, which in theory sounded easy but it was the Chicago style jazz with very slow-quick movements that made a person sore for days — if you messed anything up, people noticed.

It was also one of the only C's I ever got in college.

It was like he knew.

It should be a happy day. Part of me expected my parents to stop by or at least send flowers or something.

I was almost afraid to hold out hope.

Last year they had completely forgotten my birthday and then tried to make it up to me by flying me to Disneyland with all of my nonexistent friends. I'd cried even harder.

I didn't know how to make real friends who wanted something other than my money. Guys in general only wanted me for my face — one had even told me that to my face. He liked what I looked like on his arm. Gross.

I exhaled a rough breath then opened the door to the dance studio and walked to the front of the room. My class clustered in each person still in their weird cliques and groups. Their success was my success.

Because Marlo was right. I needed an agent. My parents said the only way I could move to LA was if I already had an agent — basically the impossible. Though I'd at one point had one.

I shook the thought away.

Creep.

"Listen up," I rubbed my hands together as nerves assaulted me. I wasn't the type of person that liked public speaking let alone teaching something I wasn't good at. Thanks Marlo. "I'm going to go over the choreography syllabus for the first month of camp and then we're going to do some stretching before starting in on Jazz."

Groans were heard throughout the group making me smile. "I know, I know, it's not the easiest to start with — it's no hip hop or contemporary but this is Broadway not So You Think You Can Dance, all right."

Teens shrugged.

Some nodded.

Others looked at the glass behind me and primped their hair. Nice.

I went through the syllabus as fast as possible and then plugged in the class iPad and put on the Chicago soundtrack. I had to teach everyone Fosse moves of Jazz. Fantastic.

All That Jazz started in the background. I remembered the steps from the year previous when we did a compilation of the most popular Broadway dances for our senior project.

At least whoever assigned me to this knew that I could battle my way through it.

I breezed through the steps on the iPad and then turned to face the class. "I want you guys to listen to the entire song before we start on the steps. It's not a normal eight count the way you guys are used to, so close your eyes and envision, then I'll show you the entire thing. We'll work on the first few steps starting with learning how to snap your fingers and flick your wrists." There, that sounded good, right?

And cue the crickets.

And boredom.

Great. I could almost feel the strike against me.

And as luck would have it, the minute the end of the song came, Marlo walked in. Just in time to see my performance.

He leaned against the door and nodded to me as if I needed permission to continue with my own class.

I gritted my teeth, ready to start, and then an evil idea hit me. It's not like I wanted him to suffer, okay so maybe a little bit. "Marlon! What an honor that you'd visit our class first!"

His eyes narrowed as he looked between me and my slack jawed pale teens. "You can continue, Ray."

"Oh but wouldn't it be super fun to demonstrate… together?" I could have sworn he flinched when I said together.

I could barely suppress my smile as the teens started to clap.

"See?" I spread my arms wide. "Marlon, Marlon, Marlon!" I was so going to Hell for this. His look said he was daydreaming about strangling me.

I expected him to say no.

Expected him to ask "for a word" with me.

Instead, he dropped the iPad onto the ground along with his ball cap and then ran his hands through his thick silky hair.

I gulped.

His shirt was so tight I could see his eight-pack.

Did the guy even enjoy food anymore or just survive off of air, protein shakes, and the tears of people who defied him?

"Sounds good." He nodded.

A few of the girls in the front row gasped. One was lamenting about not having her phone so she could stare at the pictures later. I made a mental note to protect Marlo from the little creeper in pink.

Not that it was my job or anything.

"Ready?" I was still waiting for him to back down, please let him back down from this very intense and somewhat sexually explicit dance. Please. God. Please not on this day. Not today! My hand hovered over the play button.

"If you are." Was it my imagination or had his voice always been that deep and raspy? My girly parts cheered. I told them it was a false alarm. It wasn't real. He wasn't real.

"Great," I said with fake vibrato. Well, shit. I pressed play and faced the class and tried not to tense when he stood next to me.

Within seconds, we started the beginning of the dance, snapping fingers, twisting wrists. I fought to keep his timing — because of course, it was impeccable.

It was like he was born to dance.

Damn him.

He turned to me, braced my hips as I bent completely backward, then he spun me around so my ass was pressed against him. I could feel every inch of him. My body buzzed while my mouth went dry, his hand ran down my cheek, down my breast and to my hip as he pushed me into the next movement with his body. I was cocooned in his sexual web and I wanted to stay there forever.

My breaths came out in gasps as I tried to focus on the music and not his warmth. He dipped me back again, his hand slowly running between my breasts as we made our way into the next part of the dance.

Sweat ran down my temples.

It was completely brought on by him.

His touch was driving me insane. His nostrils flared as he twirled me in his arms. We were to the floor part of the routine. I crawled toward the crowd as he crawled toward me and then spun me onto my back in a straddle. Holy mother of God I was having sex with my clothes on in front of eighteen-year-olds, most of whom had absolutely no social life and probably hadn't even had their first kiss.

Yup, hell was waiting for me.

I probably had a table with my name on it.

Right next to Marlo's.

He pulled me to my feet as we completed the dance, me in his arms, his mouth pressed against my neck. Both of our chests heaving.

Of all the bad ideas I'd had in my life.

This took the cake.

The music stopped.

And the entire class erupted in applause. Applause I wasn't expecting. We both bowed. Hoots and hollers brought my students alive, their faces were all excitement and smiles as they continued to clap, completely relaxing me and making me realize that it wasn't about me — and as long as I could get that through my brain I would be okay. I was there for them, to put that smile on their face.

"Good job, Ray." Marlon's smile didn't reach his eyes. "Guys, looks like you're in good hands, so I'm off to check in on the rest of the classes."

I didn't miss the funny way he was walking.

Or the way his entire body tensed when he bent over to pick up his hat and iPad. When the screen door slammed behind him, I let out a rough exhale.

"Miss Ray?" One of the shy girls raised her hand.

"Yeah?"

"Is that why my mom says dancing gets you pregnant?"

The entire room fell into fits of laughter.

My face felt red and hot. Great. I rolled my eyes. "Dancing doesn't get you pregnant. Though it used to be believed it leads to sex." Sex, sex, sex, my body cheered. With Marlo!

No!

I gulped and shoved the thought out of my brain. "At any rate, this dance — in fact this entire musical — was believed to promote sexuality but it's realistic of the time, and I think that just adds to the magical effect of the entire musical. Now, let me teach you how to snap and twist your wrists."

I was a snapping and twisting zombie for the next twenty minutes.

My body was present.

My brain and heart were still stuck in that dance, twirling around, and around that room in my enemy's arms.

Chapter
EIGHT

Marlon

I put my hat on my head then jerked it off, then threw it on the ground and kicked it a few times before picking it up and dusting it off and clenching it between my fingertips.

The same fingertips that had just been all over her body, touching her curves, caressing her skin.

"Damn it," I muttered under my breath. I should never have touched her, it unleashed all those repressed memories the way alcohol loosens someone's tongue and inhibitions.

Suddenly I couldn't escape her scent.

Memories of her tongue tangled with mine.

Her ass had pressed so firm against me — my dick had developed other ideas during that dance. Ideas with no clothes, grinding bodies, skin on skin.

"I've never looked at a hat like that before. And I like hats." Jackson's voice interrupted my fantasy like getting doused with cold water.

"Shut up." Yeah that's all I had. Shut up? Really?

He grinned. "You're sweating."

"I was dancing." I started walking toward the next class. "Aren't you supposed to be teaching?"

"Next hour. I was going to go see how Ray was handling the shy kids and choreography, but considering the way you're looking at that hat, and the way you're walking like you got a beanpole stuck in the front of your pants and don't know how to shove it back where it belongs…" He fell into a fit of laughter again.

"Was there a point to this visit?" I wondered out loud.

"I just told you my point, I was going to check in on her. Someone should. Choreography duty sucks, and it was in her file that she doesn't do public speaking and that her only C was in dance."

"You read her employee file? Unbelievable! That's against policy, Jackson, not to mention it's an invasion of privacy." I put my hat back on and pulled the brim hard enough to give myself a headache.

"First off, I helped Jen with all the placements this year and knew it would be tough for the new girl since she had a C in that class, but she came on so last-minute Jen didn't know where else to place her." He shrugged.

While I fixated on the fact that she got a C. In dance? That girl? She'd basically seduced me without speaking, and she'd gotten a C? God help us all if she had gotten an A.

"She did fine." I didn't mean for it to come out defensive or like I was snapping at him, but my nerves were already shot. I shouldn't have had that much coffee.

Shouldn't have touched her.

Shouldn't have liked it.

She'd challenged me.

And I took her up on it, hoping she was horrible at dance so I had one more thing hanging over her head.

Instead, it had been… I shook my head.

"Well fine." Jackson smirked. "I'm going to go grab some more coffee before my class on the smolder."

I almost threw my hat at him. "It's not the smolder, stop calling it that. It's a class on facial expression."

"Quick what's my facial expression now?" He tried his smolder and then lifted a middle finger.

"Real nice, Jackson, and your smolder's broken — you look more pissed than sexy, hate to break it to you."

"Crusher of souls and dreams," he yelled at me and then ran in the other direction, only to stop and turn around. "Does this conversation constitute as sexual harassment? Should I go to HR and tell them you don't think I'm sexy?"

"Go." I pointed to the mess hall. "Now."

He lifted his hands into the air and jogged away.

And I was left sitting there listening to the music pumping from the dance studio. Imagining my hands on her, her hands on me.

Yeah, day two.

And already I felt out of control.

I ignored the arousal I felt for her.

That's all it was.

Chemical.

Any guy would feel ready to rip her clothes off after having her ass kiss his body that way.

I cleared my throat and made my way to the script writing group.

Brax had everyone in a circle. They were brainstorming ideas of what we could do for the camp production.

We had done Hamlet last year.

A few requested the Twelfth Night.

I listened as Brax wrote everything down then instructed the campers to write out character descriptions. He was a natural. Teens loved him. He didn't need me babysitting him.

I gave him a little wave and left.

I repeated the same process the entire day, checking in with every class to make sure we had no issues. It was my job to make sure things ran smoothly. To make sure the campers were happy and the staff felt like they were a part of something important.

I was almost late to the staff bonfire because of all the check ins I had done. It was the first staff event of the summer. A way for us to bond outside of the actual camp-run activities.

I hated that my eyes roamed over the group of people in a greedy search for Ray.

And when I came up empty.

I was pissed.

Livid, actually.

"Brax," I yelled him over.

He jogged toward me and stopped. "What's up?"

"Ray. Where is she?"

He shrugged. "I think Jackson said she went back to her cabin or something."

I grit my teeth. "The bonfire's mandatory."

Brax gave me a look of complete amusement all at my expense. "I don't think I've ever seen you so irritated with another human. Normally you're all about no yelling, no bullying, world peace. The sooner you sleep with her the better."

"I still can't decide why that sounds offensive when you say it out loud," I muttered.

"It sounds less offensive when you think it, and you know you are thinking it, you can't stop thinking about it, and I'm sure your little dance number didn't help things." He chuckled.

I shot him a dark look. "How did you find out about that?"

He shoved his hands in his pockets, "Really, bro? By the time I had those students this afternoon the story had gone from a very magical moment between you two, to Ray pregnant with your twins."

"Fuck." I wiped my hand down my face. "Just what I need."

"Kids?"

"Rumors," I clarified. "And the dance was…" I didn't deny I could still feel her body between my hands. "We're getting off track. She doesn't get preferential treatment just because she's pretty. I'll be right back. Hold the fort down."

"Yes sir." He smirked.

I rolled my eyes and focused on the path leading back up to the cabins. She was pretty. She was rich.

She was spoiled.

And I wasn't going to stand for it no matter how good she used to taste or how bad I wanted to taste her again.

Chapter NINE

Ray

It was stupid.

Stupid that I was staring at the cat calendar in my shaking hands. Stupid that I was crying.

They forgot again.

As soon as I knew Marlo was on the war path toward another class, I ran into the main lodge and swiped my phone to double check. Maybe they left a voice mail?

I would have even been fine with a text.

Nothing.

I wanted to blame them so badly, but a part of me had always blamed myself, maybe because whenever my mom looked at me, I knew she saw him too. We'd had the same nose.

Funny, how my nose is a reason that my parents can't be bothered with me, can't be bothered to look at me or even celebrate my twenty-second birthday with me.

I wiped a tear under my eye and tried to think about something happy something that would make the tears ago away. I was already late for the staff campfire. I needed a distraction in a huge way and I figured at least being with other people was healthier than staring at the stupid cat calendar.

At least I now had three uses for it. Decorations. Pet. Birthday present.

Something loud banged on my door.

I jumped up, dropping the cat calendar on the bed like a hot potato and almost screamed when the knock came again. "Ray? I know you're in there."

"Marlo?" I took a few steps toward the door and jerked it open. He was bracing his massive body against the frame, his eyes were wild, his breaths came out in short gasps like he sprinted all the way there passing several hills on the way. "What's wrong?"

"What's. Wrong." He repeated in that condescending rasp. My body shivered while my mind wanted to fight. "What's wrong is you're pushing me too far, that's what's wrong."

"I'm pushing you…" I narrowed my eyes. "How exactly?"

"Do you play dumb on purpose? Do people fall for this bullshit? Really I'd like to know."

I normally had my armor on.

Every day was war wasn't it?

Especially for me.

But he'd caught me at a bad time.

He'd caught me sad.

And I wasn't good at fighting the sad. I never had been.

A tear streamed down my cheek, leaving a trail of wetness. I tried to stop it, but another one just followed it, and another, until I stopped counting.

I sucked in a breath. "I'm sorry for whatever I did. I was just… getting ready to come down to the campfire, but I needed a minute."

His face softened a fraction of an inch. "A minute to cry?"

"A minute to celebrate." I shrugged stupidly. "It's my birthday, I thought maybe my parents…" I shook my head as a ball lodged itself in my throat. "Don't worry about it. I'll just grab a sweatshirt."

"Ray—"

"It's fine, I'm not pushing you on purpose."

He sighed. "Listen—"

"Where did I put that sweatshirt anyway?" I did a small circle.

"Damn it, Ray, just listen to me!" He was in the doorway, and then suddenly he was gripping my arms, holding me steady, staring into my soul, feeding me with his warmth. "I'm sorry."

"Don't." I couldn't handle his pity. It felt like an itchy sweater. I wanted out. I needed out or I'd do something worse and collapse in his arms or something. "Don't do this." I looked away.

He gripped my chin between his thumb and forefinger forcing me to look at him, to see his beauty up close. Even with my blurry eyes I could see the blue flecks in his, I could smell the aftershave he wore, the cologne that reminded me of hot summer nights when he'd be mowing the lawn while I lay out by the pool.

The tension between us was enough to scald the pool — and the smell was always the same, as was the look of hatred he sent my way.

It was always like that after.

After we touched.

After we kissed.

Like our hearts decided that if we couldn't have one another, they'd choose something just as passionate, something just as wonderful and horrible all at once — hate.

He watched me then. Holding my face tenderly.

While tears dried on my cheeks.

While I waited for his sneer.

Hoped for it to replace the pity in his eyes.

The truth that followed.

The fact that he'd always had a reason to pity me. He just didn't realize it because it was the only armor I'd had left when it came to him — my social status, my money.

Smokescreens and more smokescreens.

I tried jerking away.

"Stop," he hissed.

I licked my lips.

He lowered his head.

This wasn't happening, was it?

He stopped inches from my mouth, right where I could taste him. All I needed to do was lean my head up, move closer to his heat, to the smell of spearmint on his breath.

"Twenty-two," he breathed out, and then his mouth lowered to my right cheek. "One." He moved to the left cheek. "Two." I sucked in a breath as he pressed a kiss to my forehead. "Three." He kissed my neck next, and then lower. He grabbed my right hand and kissed the back of it, and then my wrist, he repeated the process with my left hand. He kissed me everywhere.

I was too stunned to say anything.

"Twenty-one." He kissed my fingertip and then pulled me against his chest so hard my breath hitched.

I didn't have time to prepare myself for what it would feel like to be wanted by him, touched by him.

So when he lowered his head and brushed a petal soft kiss against my mouth, his tongue traveling along my lower lip as if he needed to sneak a taste, I didn't know what to do.

"Twenty-two." He stood back, his eyes hooded, his posture strained like he was having a hard time not shoving me against something. My chest heaved as he rasped, "Happy Birthday."

Stunned, I stood there while he walked over to my suitcase and the chair next to it, and grabbed the hoody I'd been searching for as if he had laser vision, tossed it to me, and said, "Staff camp fires are mandatory."

The screen door slammed after him.

I pressed my fingertips to my lips in stunned silence.

And then jumped when he yelled out. "Ray!"

"Coming." I stumbled toward the door and pulled the hoody over my head just in time to see his disappearing form heading toward the staff lodge and huge campfire.

I must have looked wide-eyed, because the first thing that Brax said to me with a knowing smirk was, "So… heard Marlo and you were dirty dancing. I'd ask for details, but the students' memories were very thorough."

I glared and then flipped him off, much to Jackson's

amusement as he walked over with a plastic cup and handed it to me. "Compliments of all the kids currently doing KP duty." He grinned. "Cheers!"

"Ch-cheers." I gulped down something sweet and heavily laden with what tasted like vodka and locked eyes with Marlo across the fire.

The flames rose higher and higher until all I saw were his icy blue eyes.

I shivered.

While his gaze fanned the flames.

I'd always wanted to be looked at like that.

And now that I was.

I wanted to run.

Because there was possession in his eyes, and I belonged to no one but myself.

He smirked.

Yeah… just keep telling yourself that, my blood roared.

And then the damn man winked.

Chapter
TEN

Marlon

I shouldn't have kissed her.

My body wouldn't stop flashing me with images of her tears, and if that wasn't bad enough, I was starting to get concerned that I would never forget the way she felt against my mouth.

But nobody should spend their birthday alone, and I truly couldn't conjure up much hate. Part of me wanted to shout "Karma" from the rooftops, while the little boy inside me, the one abandoned by his parents at age three, cried out.

He rebelled.

Beat against my chest and demanded I do something kind.

Something that would make her feel less alone.

Less angry.

Less afraid.

Because I wasn't a fool — loneliness was one thing, but fear almost always followed it, they were, in a way, partners, weren't they? Because loneliness caused us to doubt our own humanity.

And as much as I wanted to get even with her.

As much as I felt like I deserved it.

I couldn't bring myself to do anything except touch her, comfort her, kiss her twenty-two times.

I sighed as the flames of the fire died out.

She was still there, talking with some of the other staff members, but always with her arms crossed, always with a polite smile that basically said, *please don't ask me questions.*

Hell, she was just as bad as some of our technology-obsessed students, wasn't she?

Clearly, if my social skills suddenly surpassed her — the sky had indeed fallen.

I smiled at that.

And gave my head a shake.

"You have that look again." Next to me, Jackson whistled, stoking the fire a bit before tossing the stick in. "The one where I'm afraid you're going to maul the nearest object with your dick."

"So in this case…" I pointed to the flames.

"Hell, no!" Jackson shuddered. "I was thinking more along the lines of…" His voice trailed off as his eyes fell to Ray.

"Hilarious."

"Am I laughing?" He snorted. "Girl pretty much shut me down on day one. Maybe you'll have more luck since you got all down and dirty with her."

"Dancing." I rolled my eyes. "Big deal. We're actors — it's what we do, pretend."

"Ohhhhhh…" He snapped his fingers. "So all this sexual tension is pretend? Why didn't you just say so, man?" He winked and sauntered over to her.

The hell was wrong with me?

I watched him wrap an arm around her shoulder.

I felt her stiffen as if I was touching her.

And then she very politely stepped away from him and rolled her eyes as if he was the annoying best friend.

Best moment of my life.

Because I knew what that was like.

Friendzoned so hard you get bruises on your heart.

Feels awesome.

He looked back at me and shrugged then wrapped his arm around Jen, the guy moved fast, but he'd already done a stellar job of dating and dumping several of the staff members to the point of earning himself a reputation. So unless he could get Ray to fall for his shit — it was going to be a really lonely summer with his right hand.

Ray was alone again.

Sometimes I hated my conscience. Hated that I wanted to comfort her when for years all I ever wanted to do was seek justice for the way she tossed me aside in high school, for how she beat me for the scholarship I needed more than her.

No matter how many times I tried to bring up logical arguments, my brain just pointed to my heart and shut down.

Before I knew it, I was next to her. "Walk with me?"

Her eyes narrowed — so much mistrust between us, so many reasons why it would never go away no matter what we did. "Are you going to murder me then bury my body in the woods?"

I let out a deep laugh. "If I was going to kill you, I wouldn't prepare you for it, Ray. I'd just do it. What sort of murderer do you take me for?"

"This isn't helping your argument." Her lips pressed into a smirk. God, I'd forgotten how obsessed I'd been about her mouth until now. It caused many a guy to lust in high school, and I knew if I could just taste them again I'd be swimming in my own damn sin.

"I promise I won't attempt murder on your birthday. You did just turn twenty-two..." I held out my hand.

She stared down at it and then finally gave in.

I squeezed it.

I didn't let go.

The plan was to hold her hand for a few brief seconds.

And now I was holding it as if it belonged pressed against mine.

Jackson stretched is arms overhead and then did a double take, and his smirk was as big as a house, bastard.

"*Eff you,*" I mouthed.

It just made him grin harder.

With a sigh, I squeezed her hand and tugged her with me toward the mess hall. We walked in silence, the only real noise coming from our shoes as they crunched gravel with each step.

I stopped at the rear entrance, grabbed my set of keys, opened the door for her, and pointed inside. "Ladies first."

"So you're burying me in the mess hall? Huh, have to say I didn't see that one coming." She sashayed by me, giving me a full whiff of her perfume.

I gulped and barely regained my composure before firing back. "Were you always such a smart ass or is this new?"

"I don't know, were you always such an arrogant dick?"

I bit down on my lip and smiled. "I'm pretty sure you know the answer to that question, SP."

"SP?" She repeated in confusion.

I leaned in and winked. "Short for spoiled princess."

"Is there a point to this little trek?" She put her hands on her hips and tossed her head. Her light hair, piled in a ponytail at the top of her head, swished, and she licked her lips.

"You mean other than the murder?" I asked in confusion, earning a punch to the shoulder.

"Ouch! Shit!" She shook out her hand. "What the hell do you eat now? Steel?"

"Naturally." I really tried not to take it as a compliment, but warmth spread across my chest uncontrollably. "I mean when I'm not feeding off small children and protein shakes at the gym with my bros getting all…" I made air quotes. "…swoll."

"Ah, still a nerd I see." She smiled like she was glad.

I smiled back. "The day I start talking about PRs and how CrossFit changed my life, I'm handing you a knife and letting you throw at will."

"Did it, though?" She tilted her head. "Because you never really…" The tension in the room wasn't helping. "I mean you never really."

"I was tall and had one ab that I was so fucking proud of I think I took a picture," I admitted, twisting my lips into a grimace. "But we're getting off track."

"From what?"

"This." I walked over to the fridge and pulled it open. We were having cupcakes later that week for dessert. They were pre-made, and since we often celebrated campers' birthdays if they were with us, I knew where our candle and match stash was.

I quickly set the pink cupcake on a plate and then grabbed the lighter from one drawer over as well as one green candle.

I'd like to think that when she saw the color green she thought of her grass, and when she thought of her grass, she thought of me.

It was stupid.

Just the delirious daydreams from a heartbroken nerd, who'd had one night with the most popular girl in school and was thrown in a locker the next day.

"This." I lit the candle and held it out. "This is why we're here."

Her eyes filled with tears as she stared at the cupcake in wonderment, like nobody had ever taken time to give her something so precious when all I did was steal it from the fridge.

Ray swallowed slowly and whispered, "So that's what it feels like."

"What?" I blinked in confusion.

She flashed me a warm smile. "Blowing out candles on your birthday."

I almost dropped the cupcake. "You mean you've never—"

"Never." She licked her lips. "It was just another reminder to them, that I was alive — that he was dead."

"He?" The story was getting weirder by the second. "Who's he?"

"Do you think that maybe I can just blow out this candle and keep this birthday to myself? For once? I know that sounds selfish and you already think the worst of me, but I really, really want my first candle to be for me."

I felt my throat clog up, and I had no idea why. I finally settled with, "You're not selfish."

"SP." She repeated my nickname for her. "All right, I'm going to blow."

My body responded in all the worst ways. "Make a wish, Ray."

Her eyes flew open when she pursed her lips together and blew, and I could have sworn as the flame snuffed out…

A tingling ran down my spine.

Of awareness.

Of warning.

I ignored it all, though.

I ignored it, and I handed her the cupcake. "Happy Birthday, Ray."

"Celebrating my birthday with my high school arch enemy, nice."

"You have to be on the same playing field to be an enemy." I shrugged and then reached for the door so we could get back to our cabins. It was getting late.

And my self-control was almost completely used up.

"Funny." She dipped her finger in the frosting and brought it to her lips. "Because I was always under the impression we were." She held the cupcake up. "Thanks Marlo. I won't forget this."

I wasn't sure if I was relieved.

Or even more infatuated with the girl who had it all.

But who'd never blown out a candle on her birthday cake.

Chapter ELEVEN

Ray

I didn't eat the cupcake.

It seemed wrong.

So that night, I put it on my desk and stared at it like it meant more than it did. The first real cake I'd ever had. The first candle. It felt wrong destroying what was my first. I fell asleep staring at the pink frosting with a smile on my face.

And when I woke up, things didn't seem as daunting.

Oh, I still had to teach choreography, but at least the vote for whatever musical we were going to do was happening sometime this week. Come to think of it, I wasn't sure how they even narrowed down all the options. Every camper had a different idea about what they wanted to do.

I quickly got ready, pulled on my staff shirt, a pair of jeans, and then grabbed my beanie and wrapped a sweatshirt around my waist. I dabbed on some lip gloss and put on a little bit of mascara, but other than that, I was going all natural.

The brisk morning air chilled my body as I made my way to the loud mess hall. The lights were bright from the inside, and campers were sprinting toward the doors like the food was going to run out.

Ah, to be eighteen again and have the metabolism of a toddler.

Nobody was at the coffee station, so I lucked out there and quickly made myself a cup of coffee that would hopefully wake me up. Amid the chaos and the loudness, I had to smile into my searing cup.

There was something about the energy here.

The excitement.

Like the day before school gets out or maybe even the first day of school when everyone has something to say about summer. I smiled briefly to myself and made my way through the buffet line in search of something that looked edible.

I settled on blueberry oatmeal and some bacon that looked charred but still worth saving and sat down at the only empty table.

"That bacon looks like it's been killed twice." Jackson pointed his fork, his mouth full.

Brax was to my right. "Well at least she got some bacon, I had to help put out the newest fire with Marlo and then lost the good fight over the past batch before they put that one out."

"Here." I handed Brax two pieces.

He clutched them to his chest while Jackson rolled his eyes.

"What?" Brax shoved a piece in his mouth.

"She didn't ask you to marry her, bro, take it down a notch," Jackson said in a bored tone and then grinned at something behind me. "Looks like he's on the war path, and only two days in, one of us should monitor his blood pressure."

I bit down on my lip to keep from laughing or encouraging Jackson more when I knew it would only make him think I found him funny and, oh my gosh, we should totally have sex.

He might be funny.

But guys like Jackson wielded their humor like a weapon to get a girl's clothes off, and I knew from experience — it worked better than it should.

"Fuuuuuuuuuuuck." Marlo plopped down on the bench next to Brax took one look at the bacon in his hand, jerked it out, and shoved it in his mouth.

"And now I'm in mourning..." Brax announced. "What the hell, man?"

"Your students, ergo I steal your bacon. Your class is supposed to help other campers choose the musical, and today I woke up to at least ten different campers at my table arguing why we should do the musical they either just starred in or went and saw on Broadway. One smart ass said anything but Hamilton is beneath us."

"Hamilton." Jackson's eyebrows shot up giving him more of a boyish and less of a I wanna sex you up look. "They do realize that Hamilton is—"

"Don't." Marlo held up his hand. "The point is, we have until Friday, it's Tuesday, and I'm ready to pull all my hair out. And I don't know my parentage — this could be as good as it gets." He pointed to his head.

I remembered running my hands through that hair.

I knew its length.

The way it curled around my fingertips like it had a mind of its own or like it was just telling me that he wanted to stay.

"Why don't you just choose?" I offered in a soft voice. "Pull your trump card as director, give a stupid reason that makes sense to an eighteen-year-old who has way too many hormones to actually make a logical decision outside of what to wear, and there you have it." I bit off a piece of bacon while Brax did a slow clap.

Jackson sighed. "Your prettier half has a point."

"She's not my half." Marlo said through clenched teeth at the same time I said. "We're not together."

All of this, of course, just made Jackson grin wider like he knew a secret we weren't in on yet. "Sure…"

I rolled my eyes and tried to tamp down the heat rushing to my cheeks, while Marlo jumped to his feet and walked toward the front of the room.

"Listen up!" he roared in a loud voice, catching the attention of every camper and every staff member in the place.

Even the kitchen staff stopped working and moved toward the door to see what the fuss was about.

Marlon gazed over the campers like they were his friggin kingdom and he was the ruler, which wasn't far from the truth I guessed.

He threw his hat onto a nearby table and ran his fingers through his dark hair. I licked my lips and imagined my hands were his, like a freak.

He inhaled. A few girls up front giggled.

I rolled my eyes even though I knew why they were reacting that way. The man wasn't just beautiful to look at. He had perfectly toned muscles to match, strong hands, nice hair. And a megawatt smile that put his scowl to shame. Damn it. I was cataloging his scowls and smiles now?

"I'm pulling rank," he finally said. "By the end of the week, we're just going to have more and more arguments over what we should do for the musical, so I'm going to pick."

Everyone seemed to hold their breath.

Even me.

He scanned the room, his eyes landing on mine. And then, he sucked in his lower lip and smirked down at the ground and back up. "Dirty Dancing."

A sliver of excitement ran down my body.

Brax elbowed me while Jackson coughed out, "Ray's fault."

I almost threw what remaining bacon I had at him.

He grinned from across the table. "Smile any wider, and it's going to freeze on your face."

I stuck my tongue out at him.

"Mature," he rasped. "Also, don't tempt me, I'm already waiting for the day our friend Marlo screws this up and you come running."

"Not happening," I said quickly. "You remind me too much of my ex."

"You mean drop dead sexy? Hilarious? Gives multiple orgasms in multiple positions, that kind of reminder?"

"Oh, my ex?" I said in a flirty voice. "Nah, he had limp dick and often referred to sex as let's get some." I stood and did a little bow while next to me, Brax clapped.

Jackson's smile didn't fall. Instead, he just nodded as if he was accepting some invisible challenge and winked.

While I dumped my trash and walked on wobbly legs out of the mess hall and stared out at the lake.

Dirty Dancing.

I'd seen the movie.

I'd been in the musical once.

I hadn't played the role of Baby.

I'd been cast as her sister.

Didn't matter though, I knew the choreography, and from what I didn't know, I could learn every night before I taught the sessions to the campers. It wouldn't be too bad.

As long as I could reserve one of the studios.

"What do you think?" Marlo's deep voice washed over me.

I didn't turn around, just stared straight ahead. "I have a lot of work to do, that's what I think."

"You'll be fine." He said it so casually I turned and looked at him with disbelief. "What?"

"Was that a semi-compliment?"

He pulled the rim down on his hat and smirked. "Maybe, maybe not."

"How very non-committal of you," I mused.

"That's me, the very face of vague conversation." He shrugged. "Let me know if you need any extra help." He turned and walked off.

I narrowed my eyes after his disappearing body. "Wait, why would I come to you in the first place?"

"Because," he called over his shoulder. "Senior year of college I was the lead..." He turned and started walking backward. I prayed for a root to jump to attention so I'd have a reason to focus on the nerd I used to know not the sexy man smirking back at me. "Off Broadway."

Son of a…

"Great." It was a faint great. An *oh shit* great. An *I'm totally going to mess this up* great.

He had more experience than me.

He'd been the darling of the theatre.

And now it was coming back to bite me in the ass.

In what world would I ever be better than him?

In what world did I even stand the chance of getting an agent with someone like that standing in my way?

One thing was certain. I should have never danced with him in the first place, because now it felt personal.

Now it felt like a story of us.

When it was just him yet again trying to prove me wrong, like I wasn't good enough, like I didn't belong.

"We'll see, Marlo," I said to myself. "Watch me."

Chapter

TWELVE

Marlon

It wasn't a proud moment.

Standing by the window, watching her excitement, feeling it wash over me while it washed over all the campers in that room. Had she always been so animated? I turned away. It wasn't my place to keep checking up on her. Plus, I had another class I needed to teach.

I was just walking away as class was ending.

Campers shuffled out in fits of laughter.

I waited and listened in.

"This is gonna be interesting. Our choreographer isn't even familiar with the lead roles, except for Baby crawling on the damn floor."

"Classic," another camper said. "And our chances at Hollywood go up in flames!"

"Hey guys, she said to trust her. She's our choreographer for this, we trust her," a nice girl added to the noise.

They all passed me by wide-eyed, like they'd just noticed I was standing there. One of them stopped and crossed his arms. "Sorry, but it's all true." It was a tall lean guy who looked like he needed multiple cookies and maybe an orgasm for good measure. "She's not the most experienced teacher here. You are."

Shit.

It had never been my intention.

Yes, I typically taught this class, but since she had some experience it freed me up to do other things that, being Director for the first time, weighed on me. Like making sure nobody got drunk or drowned in the lake, that sort of thing.

"Guys, trust the process, all right?" I shrugged. "We have the best staff in the world, that's why you're here, right?"

Nobody said anything.

Finally, tall guy sighed. "I still wish you were choreographing."

Such shitty timing that she would round the corner and hear our conversation. Her face paled as she forced a smile at me and then walked off.

Fuck my life.

Two steps forward, one step back.

Then again, the steps forward, were they even genuine? Or based on this insane need to fuck her and make her feel like shit? I wasn't even sure anymore.

All I knew was that her birthday had given me a different view.

A different perspective

Like maybe the monster in the tower was a princess all along.

"SP," I yelled. "Hold up."

I jogged past the campers and stood in front of her. "They're just kids, they whine, it's what they do."

"Right." She sneered.

"What the hell is your problem?" I threw my hands in the air and then grabbed her elbow and pulled her behind the nearest cabin so we had some privacy. Her chest rose and fell while her beanie did a good job of covering part of her face and forcing her pretty hair to drape by her pink cheeks and full lips, damn it those lips.

"My problem?"

What was I saying about those lips again? Those violent tumultuous lips with promises of pain and pleasure all in one? Perfect. That's what I was saying. What I was thinking.

"My problem, Marlo, is that you're undermining me at every freaking step! You put me in this position to fail, admit it!"

I shook my head. "Believe what you want."

"Why can't you just say it out loud? Ray I screwed you so I could prove a point. I'm better. I'll always be better!"

I took a step, plastering her body against the wood of the cabin. "Oh if I screwed you, you'd know, Ray. Then again… you always were good at denying the truth, right?"

She shoved at my chest. "How dare you!"

"How dare I?" I laughed. "Really? How dare I? Tell the truth?"

"You wouldn't know the truth if it slapped you in the ass."

It was one of my pressure points, the places a person could press that would cause me to snap. I hated liars. I'd grown up watching all the pretty people around me lie, believe in the lie. I was insulted to my core and hurt. Part of me was hurt that she would believe the worst in someone like me — a guy who, when he was at his most vulnerable and naked moment, had told her how he hated liars.

"Says the sad drunk girl who sleeps with guys and forgets about them the next day," I spat.

Tears filled her eyes. "Take it back."

"You first." I gritted my teeth.

"Unbelievable. You're even a bigger dick than before, and that's saying something… and here I thought…" She shook her head. "I'm not quitting."

"Then don't fail," I said to her back as she stomped off.

And part of me, the part that loved her fire, smiled and craved the challenge that she would bring.

The fire that she hid beneath that pretty exterior.

The fire just begging to be freed from its pretty prison.

And maybe, that was the problem.

She'd lived her life in a prison of her parents' making.

And only knew how to survive — by taking that prison with her.

Chapter
THIRTEEN

Ray

I went to the stupid campfire that night because I knew if I didn't go, Marlo would start a witch hunt, and I could kiss my chances goodbye. It's like the guy knew every hot button I had and vice versa. I clenched my fists and made my way to an empty log to pout and was intercepted, of course, by Jackson, who had two drinks in hand.

"What?" I said in a bored voice.

"Word on the street is that you need this… maybe more than one cup, but we'll start you off slow because I'm such a gentleman." He grinned.

I took the cup and shook my head slowly. "It's weird that you actually believe the crap that comes from your mouth."

"Speak it so you believe it, sweetheart."

I made a face.

"What? Am I not boring enough for you like our friend Marlo?" He nodded his head to Marlo, who was sitting on a log talking to Jen and helping her roast a marshmallow. She was all smiles, and he seemed the most relaxed I'd seen him... ever.

Probably because he knew I would be gone soon and all his childhood rage wouldn't be for naught.

I grabbed a nearby stick, shoved a marshmallow on and put it directly in the fire and sat.

"You look like you wished the marshmallow was Marlo's head." Jackson chuckled, grabbing one of the nearby sticks and doing the same thing. "Can't say I blame you."

"He's setting me up," I said through clenched teeth.

"Hmm..." Jackson rolled his stick near the bottom of the fire, not in the flames where mine was currently burning hotter and hotter. "What makes you think that? Is it the sexual tension? The hate? Are you confused on why they feel the same? Or is it the fact that he keeps staring at you?"

"What?" I pulled my stick out of the fire and blew on the marshmallow. "He put me in choreography. I got a C in choreography."

"I know." Jackson grinned. "I helped Jen build the classes, and that was the one that he normally teaches, since they kept getting fired, but since he's Director this year." Jackson shrugged. "You were the next logical choice, plus your professors all said what you didn't know, you'd bust ass learning, though they left out the word ass. Added that in because I can't find it in myself to use the word 'rear' that dear old Professor Locke used."

I stared at him slack jawed. "You did this to me?"

"Hey!" He grabbed my stick. "Let's remove all weapons first," With a flick of his fingers the marshmallow was off and on the graham cracker with chocolate and pressed together in a sandwich. "Here, this will make it better."

I took the gooey sandwich and glared. "Speak."

"I wouldn't be all commanding and shit, just gets me hard." He ran a hand over his buzzed head.

"Gross!" I almost threw my s'more at his face and kicked some dirt for good measure.

"What?" He fell over laughing his green eyes sparkling with mischief. "I'm all about the honesty. I like a bossy woman, so just be polite and we can still be friends with benefits."

"We aren't—"

"Just making sure you're paying attention. Yes, I put you in that class, and yes, it was the only option. And you're going to be fine." He sighed and glanced over at Marlo. "You're a lot like him, you know."

"Do you want me to hit you?" I took a bite and moaned a bit then wiped the stickiness from my lips.

"Are you trying to continuously turn me on? I love a good hit, and no." Jackson's easy smile was making me at least feel better. He was nice to talk to, as long as he kept his hands to himself and his penis inside his pants with the zipper shut up nice and tight. "I'm just saying Marlo's fucking focused… and you're the same way. You both would have been generals in another life, and that's probably why you fight all the time."

"Well…" I took another bite and looked down at the dirt. "We don't fight all the time… he's just easily provoked."

"And you're what? A tame little de-clawed kitten?" Jackson wrapped an arm around me and squeezed, I could feel the warm tight muscles beneath his shirt. "Marlo doesn't set people up to fail... he sets them up to succeed."

Defeated, I hung my head in shame. "He's still an asshole."

"And you're... perfect?" Jackson whispered so only I could hear. I looked up into his bright green eyes. "Mmm, thought so."

He pulled his arm back and grabbed his drink from the ground then took a nice long sip.

The fire felt good, soothing in a way.

We both drank and ate in silence.

I could feel Marlo's stare.

I shivered.

And then someone sat down next to me.

"Hi!" Jen held out her hand. "I mean we met earlier, but I wanted to formally introduce myself to the woman who makes Marlo growl in his sleep."

"Most animals do." I laughed taking her hand in mine. She was cute, like the girl next door who makes homemade cookies for her crush and falls in love with the first boy to give her a Band-Aid for her scraped-up knee at the age of six.

"So." Her freckles were cute, her strawberry blonde hair had the perfect bounce. A sliver of jealousy stabbed me in the chest. She was with Marlo a lot.

I suddenly felt sick to my stomach. The marshmallows were clearly too rich.

"A bunch of us are headed to the lake to skinny-dip since it's such a nice night, wanna come?"

"Skinny-dip!" Jackson jumped to his feet and peeled off

his shirt. A glaring six-pack met me at eye level, and then he touched the top button of his jeans.

"The only way you're going to keep your dick safe is to keep it tucked away, Jackson," I said in a warning voice.

He just laughed and started sprinting toward the water, followed by another ten or so people, Marlo included.

My heart caught in my throat as he threw the shirt over his head and disappeared into darkness.

"Come on! Only a few girls are going, the others are too nervous." She winked. "I'll be with you, we'll change on the other side of the dock and get in that way so Jackson can't see any nakedness for his nighttime daily recap."

I burst out laughing. "Yeah, you won me over with that one."

"He's just…" We both stood, she looped her arm in mine like we were best friends. "Complicated. Jackson's…" Her face fell a bit.

"No way!" I gasped. "You and Jackson?"

"Once." Her blush was pretty; it transformed her face into something from girl next door to underground sexpot within seconds. Interesting. "It was… amazing, but he's just…"

"A player?" I finished for her.

"Yeah," she admitted, tucking her cropped hair behind her ears. "And I'm such a tomboy, I have more guy friends than girls because A, girls are mean, and B, girls are mean."

I laughed at that. "They're the worst. I would know. I used to be one of the mean ones."

"I figured."

Her honesty surprised me. I wasn't really sure what to say.

"Don't take that the wrong way, it's just… you're too pretty, too confident not to be, plus that and I kind of heard a few things from Marlo that made me wonder if you were one of the girls he pined after during high school."

"I want you," he whispered against my neck. "Please…"

"Marlo…" My shirt was off. His was on the floor somewhere. We locked eyes. "This is a bad idea."

"I'm sure of it," he agreed.

I ran my hands through my hair.

And he just let me touch him.

Explore him.

I tugged his lower lip with my teeth, measured his kiss against my tongue, and then I lost myself in the feel of his warmth. In the tender way he kissed me. In the way he treasured me, while the party was going on downstairs. For minutes, we were locked in my tower.

For minutes, I felt like a princess.

And my knight in shining armor had ridden in to rescue me from the demons that haunted me.

"Yes." I said between kisses. "Yes."

"All I've ever wanted from you…" He stole kiss after kiss, and then he was pulling my jeans down my legs slowly. "Was a yes."

"Hellloooo?" Jen waved in front of my face.

"Sorry!" I covered my face with my hands. "Sorry, I totally spaced out."

"Visions of Marlo naked do that to a girl."

"I wasn't!" I was ready to defend myself when I noticed what she was staring at. Brax, Marlo, and Jackson's bare asses as they jumped off the dock. Damn, what did they feed those boys? Marlo stood out amongst them the most, but it was an impressive view.

"Wow," was all I had.

"Trust me, with Jackson it only gets better the longer you stare, honestly all those guys are nice to look at, I just wish they thought with more of their brain cells than their D's." She winked, "Come on, this way."

We walked around the dock. There was a few trees and a nice bush that gave us enough cover, and the one tree went all the way up to the shoreline. It was perfect.

"Nice!" I laughed then pulled off my shirt and sports bra.

We both stumbled a bit in the sand to get our clothes off, and then naked, crashed into the water and swam toward the dock.

Male laughter filled the night sky.

I looked up, breathed in the fresh air. It was the perfect night. So many stars I couldn't count, and the perfect warm breeze that made me want to swim all night until I was exhausted.

"The fun has arrived!" Jen announced from next to me as we joined the rest of the group.

You'd think she'd just yelled shark.

Jackson did a double take and then glared at her like she had no right to be naked in front of others, while Brax's wide eyes looked like he wasn't sure if he should hold Marlo back from charging toward me and demanding I put my clothes back on, or toward Jackson.

Interesting.

I gulped while Jen just rolled her eyes. "Feminism. It's a thing. Equal rights. Voting." She said voting super slow, eliciting a glare from Jackson. "So that means we're allowed to skinny-dip too."

That's when I noticed.

We were the only girls.

Literally.

I splashed her with water. "You said there were more girls!"

She burst out laughing. "You wouldn't have come! I refuse to apologize for the amazing water and night."

I grinned as warmth spread across my chest. It had been a while since I'd met another girl who seemed genuinely nice. "That's fair, I guess."

The closer we got to the guys, the more everyone relaxed. Even Jackson finally relented, but Marlo? Marlo had his eyes locked on me with such intensity I almost felt like I needed to dive under the water to cool down.

So I did.

I dove under the water and realized that even with the darkness, the lake was pretty crystal clear. Almost like glacier water but not quite as nice.

I could kind of see feet and some legs that were close but that was it, and even then everything was blurry.

I blinked under water.

And then a face appeared in front of me.

I screamed and soared to the top gasping for air at the same time as a laughing Marlo.

"You ass!" I splashed him with water. "I could have drowned!"

"Doubtful." He was a foot away from me, his wet hair slicked back over his head, his massive shoulders just floating like they could help him tread water all day. "You used to be on swim team."

"Right, but on swim team, heads don't just magically float in the water."

"The head was attached to a body." He leaned in. "Both of them."

"What do you mean—" Realization dawned, and I splashed him again.

Jackson burst out lugging. "Good one, Marlo."

Marlo saluted him and swam toward the dock. "Who wants to play Marco Polo?"

Cheers erupted. Oh yay, getting chased by naked guys with grabby hands, every girl's dream, right?

I shared a look with Jen.

"Only if we can be it first!" Jen announced. "Girls against guys."

"Oh, so you want to start off knowing you'll lose, that's cool." Brax laughed just as someone ran down the dock and held up a half gallon bottle of tequila. "Bro, you saved a life tonight, I commend you." Brax said as he swam over and opened his mouth. All the guys followed, everyone but Marlo.

I wondered why.

I didn't voice my question.

But Jackson must have read my face because he pointed to me and Jen. "Before you Marco, you must drink. It's tradition."

"Since last year." Jen rolled her eyes. "Whatever, one shot won't kill us. Come on, Ray."

I tilted my head as an evil grin spread across my face. "I'm in, as long as Marlo puts his big boy — was it boxers or briefs? — back on and joins us."

He stared me down, then swam toward the dock and

tilted his head back, whoever it was poured a heavy shot down Marlo's throat.

Marlo wiped the tequila from his neck. "I'm waiting."

Shit.

I swam over with Jen and followed suit.

And just as the first part of the Tequila fell into my mouth, making me wince, Marlo whispered in my right ear. "Neither."

I choked a bit and wiped my mouth as the gross tequila traveled into my gut like lead. "What do you mean?"

"Neither." He said it louder this time. "I don't like boxers or briefs."

"Can't tame his python," Brax, obviously drunk, shouted sending all the guys into fits of laughter.

All but Marlo.

Who was looking at me like he was ready to say, *she should know.*

He didn't though.

I breathed a sigh of relief as Jen grabbed my hand and shouted, "Marco!"

The guys all scattered.

I closed my eyes and moved through the water toward all the voices of "Polo!"

Every time I thought I got close to someone, he swam off. The liquor was hitting me a bit harder than I would have liked, which was making it hard to focus on swimming.

Finally, I heard laughter and a faint Marco.

I reached out and grabbed.

Ankle.

Good enough.

"Hah!" I opened my eyes. "And looks like the girls are

already ahead!"

"YES!" Jen splashed the water with her hands.

Brax gave me a very buzzed smile. "I'm a slow swimmer, what can I say?"

"Bullshit!" Marlo yelled from far away. "You wanted her to touch you."

"I admit nothing!" Brax fired back and then moved toward the dock and started yelling Marco.

I dove under water and swam hard in the other direction in an effort to get away from most of the group, but when I got above water, I bumped into another hard body.

Marlo's hard body.

I'd somehow managed to get to the other side of the dock.

"Marco!" Brax shouted.

"Polo!" everyone answered.

Everyone but us.

I sucked in a breath as Marlo leaned down and whispered, "Are you cheating?"

"Are you?" I fired back.

His lips turned into a smile, blinding me with the attractiveness of his face, of the way the moon kissed his skin and made him look almost inhumanly beautiful. Straight white teeth, I focused on the teeth.

The eyes were too much.

The hair.

The broad shoulders.

The way I was basically pinned against the dock with Marlo's body as my only way of escape.

"Marco!" Brax shouted.

"Po—"

Marlo clapped a hand over my mouth and then slowly his gaze lowered to the top of the water where I was aware he could almost make out my naked breasts.

I gulped.

"Marco!"

He leaned in his head, tilting near my neck, and then he pressed his mouth to my shoulder like he was inhaling me, memorizing me. And then he pulled back and shook his head. "Fucking hate tequila."

And that was it.

He swam off yelling. "Polo!"

While I treaded water and wondered why my teeth were chattering.

And why I wanted to ask my enemy to come back and finish whatever he had been about to start.

I was asking for trouble.

And heartache all in one.

But his eyes.

Those eyes, they haunted me.

They made me hate and want both at the same time. I just hoped the right one would win out in the end, because I discovered something about myself in that lake.

With Marlo staring me down.

I had no self-control when it came to him.

Maybe I never did.

Because even all those years ago.

I'd always wanted him to want me.

To tell me he saw me for me.

I did everything in my power to try to make something real, something tangible, and then I made the biggest mistake of my life by saying yes.

Because once you experience that sort of desire.

Everything else pales in comparison.

Ruining your future.

Ruining it all.

I slowly rejoined the crowd and kept my distance from Marlo the rest of the night, and when I closed my eyes in my cabin, I grabbed the cat calendar and tucked it under my arm and imagined it was him.

Chapter
FOURTEEN

Marlon

The minute we'd decided to do Dirty Dancing, I'd put in an order for all the things we'd need and expedited it to the camp. We luckily had the script and some of the main music, but we lacked the behind-the-scenes instructions, including props which made me a bit nervous considering how much time we had to make everything. The set team was going to be a pain in my ass this summer, I could feel it already.

Luckily, the shipment came two days later.

Two days after skinny-dipping.

Two nights after dreaming of her lips in my sleep.

I was bordering on having a sleeping disorder because of

the way she smelled, and it pissed me the hell off — why? Why couldn't I just let it go? Why did I have to constantly look for her in a room?

Why did I have this constant hunger?

This need to rip down her walls and ask her to trust me, to trust her back and believe that maybe humans were inherently good, not evil like I'd always believed.

I saw flickers of it, her goodness, her smile. All of it.

And the more I saw, the greedier I became for more.

Like the day of her birthday.

Four nights ago, when we teased each other and didn't rip each other's throats out in the process.

I smiled to myself as campers made their way into the mess hall, yelling about starving to death and the horrible conditions.

I took one look at the coffee bar along with its espresso machine and gave a heavy shake of my head.

Teenagers.

I felt her then.

Maybe I smelled her first.

Like the worst sort of sin I could commit in this lifetime — like both my enemy and my friend.

"Marlo." Her voice was soft, it floated around me like perfume. And then she was pouring black coffee into her cup.

"RAY!" Jackson's voice boomed so loud, the coffee jolted out of her hand sending scalding liquid splashing over her thumb.

"Shit," she hissed, shaking her hand.

Already I could see the angry red skin bubbling up, they made the coffee searing, it's why most people added a shit ton of creamer to it so you could actually drink it right away.

"Nice one, jackass." I shook my head at Jackson then gently wrapped an arm around her. "Let's get that taken care of."

"It's fine, I—"

Maybe my look was more pissed off than gentle because Ray just pressed her lips together and let me lead her to the back of the kitchen where we kept a med kit.

"Up you go." I lifted her effortlessly onto the counter and then set the med kit right next to her.

"Did you really just lift me onto the counter like a toddler?" She huffed.

I didn't even look at her when I responded. "Did you really just like it?"

And nothing.

I smirked down at the burn cream and then held out my hand. Gingerly, she placed her hand on top of mine, while I slowly rubbed cream across the ugly red mark.

"That hurts," she said through clenched teeth.

"A bit of pain now." I kept softly rubbing and locked eyes with her. "Means no searing pain later."

"I think my hands already been seared," she joked.

My lips twitched as I grabbed a bandage and wrapped it around her thumb then taped it in place so the burn cream wouldn't be exposed to the sun.

"Just take it easy." I had both hands on the counter, one on either side of her body. I moved to grip her hips and pull her down.

Instead, what happened was a freak accident caused by idiots in the kitchen. Someone bumped into me from behind, meaning I bumped into her causing her to wrap her arms around my neck and her legs around my waist to keep from falling on her ass.

Fuck, it would be easy to slam her against the freezer to my right. Or even lay her down on the cutting board to my left — because nothing screamed sexy quite like a cutting board or raw meat.

Her breath hitched as her breathing shallowed. I focused in on those blue eyes, that blonde hair that I'd dreamt about pulling more times than I could count.

And then her bandaged hand touched my face.

I exhaled slowly like I needed time to process.

And then with the self-restraint of a god, I set her on her feet and whispered, "Just be careful today, all right? If you want me to take over your class I can—"

"And yet again life makes sense." Hurt flashed in her eyes. "Are you seriously taking advantage of the fact that I burned myself?"

I rolled my eyes. "Are you seriously assuming I'm that big of a dick?"

She said nothing.

"Wow." I threw my hands in the air. "I was just trying to be nice. Then again, you probably don't know what that means do you? Girls like you—"

"Girls like me?" she repeated. "What the hell is that supposed to mean?"

"You tell me, SP." I smirked. "Girls born in castles with gold shoes and silver spoons, brand new BMWs and enough friends to fill this entire campground."

She paled. "Funny how you think you know so much about my life now, funny how the only information you have is based on the past. They say it takes a while for guys to grow up, shouldn't you have been at least halfway by now?"

It hit a hot button. That she was making me feel like the immature one.

"Don't be a bitch." That's what I went with.

"Um, guys?" Brax poked his head in the kitchen.

"What!" we yelled in unison.

"Campers can hear you. I can hear you. God, he hears all, so maybe just... use inside voices and stop cursing?" He smiled. "Thanks!"

"Shit." I wiped my hands down my face. "Do you have to be so damn provoking?"

"Do you have to be such a giant asshole?" she asked sweetly.

I just clenched my teeth and turned on my heel. "If you need help, don't ask. And for the record, I was trying to be nice."

She didn't say anything.

I didn't give her a chance to, not really. I was already pushing my way back into the mess hall cursing myself to hell.

Why did she have to make everything so difficult?

It was like trying to mix oil and water, peanut butter and pepper. Nothing mixed, nothing worked. She was like this beat-down dog that refused to believe anyone had anything good to offer her.

And that's when it hit me.

Maybe.

She truly believed there wasn't.

Maybe the flaw wasn't me.

Maybe it was just humans in general.

It haunted me the rest of the day, that thought, that

pathetically sad thought, that in a world full of hatred —
she never saw the light and truly believed that goodness was
dead.

And that I wasn't one of the ones who could change her
opinion, since my only goal had been to sleep with her and
walk away.

Well fucking done Marlo.

Chapter
FIFTEEN

Ray

I slammed my hands down on the table. Sweat from my forehead dripped down my cheeks, off my chin — I was a complete mess. The studio was a nice ninety degrees. I had every freakin' window open so I could get a breeze to blow through.

And I was pissed.

Still berating myself for how I'd acted with Marlo.

I knew he was trying to be nice.

But then he'd called me a bitch.

And I'd just reacted, reacted out of a need to keep my job, I thought he had been threatening me again and then it was too late.

Always too late with him.

I hung my head as the music poured over the system.

The dance moves weren't necessarily hard, I just needed a partner, and I had too much pride to ask the one person who could probably do most of the numbers in his sleep.

"Penny for your thoughts?" Jackson's deep voice reverberated through the room.

I groaned and wiped my face off with a towel. "I have no energy for your bullshit."

"Aw, tuckered yourself all out getting pissed at Marlo during breakfast or have you just been dancing for the last four hours since your class ended." Yeah, he wasn't leaving. I heard no door shut.

With a sigh, I turned around and crossed my arms over my tight black tank top. "Both."

He nodded, his smile reaching his eyes like he found amusement in my pain. And then he peeled off his shirt and tossed it on the ground.

I held up my hands. "That seriously wasn't an invite, Jackson."

"And as sad as I am about said circumstances between us…" He sauntered over to me, his jeans slung low on his hips. "…I'm actually here to save your tight ass."

I gritted my teeth. "Compliment me in that way again, and I'm going to be shoving my equally tight foot up yours."

He grinned. "Fair."

I re-did my ponytail and grabbed the iPad, pressing play again for the song between Johnny and Baby, it was the epic Lover Boy song where she was crawling all around the floor and— "Aghhhh!" I tugged at my hair.

The music kept going.

And then hands were on my shoulders.

I jerked in surprise.

"Calm down…" Jackson laughed. "Again, I come in peace, walk me through the steps and I'll adjust where necessary."

"I must be desperate." I hung my shoulders in defeat.

"Just tired," he said in a soft voice that held no humor whatsoever.

I turned and stared into his green eyes. "I'm not sleeping with you."

"I'm not offering my services." His grin was back.

"Services." I rolled my eyes. "You would call it that, like you're just servicing a car engine, or checking the oil."

He just shrugged as if it was all the same.

Men.

"Fine." I closed my eyes and then opened them as I gripped his outstretched hands and started the cha-cha like they'd performed in the musical.

As his character had done, Jackson kept trying to throw me off, to grab me and pull me into his arms.

So basically, he was playing himself only better.

I laughed and pulled away then went to the corner of the room and started lip syncing. He lay back on the floor while I got on my hands and knees and crawled toward him, both of us lip-synching.

I found myself smiling more than once.

And then he abruptly stood and pressed stop on the iPad and crossed his arms. "Your soul is missing."

"Excuse me?" I jumped to my feet and dusted off my clothes. "What the hell does that even mean?"

"It means," he said with a sly smile. "That you don't give two shits about me — in real life, that is — and when you act through the choreography you're so focused on the next step, anticipating your next movement, that you lose that moment, that feeling when your soul tethers to the song, and by doing that, you join with your co-star in this fucking amazing threesome that makes you feel alive." He grinned and then lowered his voice into a whisper. "Which means... I actually can't help you, because you will never trust me enough to let go. Maybe that's why you got a C, Ray... because you only trust in yourself when it comes to the dancing, and forget about trusting in the music, in your partner, in the joining of souls."

With that, he grabbed his shirt and walked out of the room.

The screen slammed behind him.

Tears welled in my eyes as I hit my water bottle off the table.

Why was I even ready to cry?

Why did it matter?

A few tears slid down my cheeks. I wiped them away quickly. He was right.

God, I hated so much to say that in my head let alone out loud.

He was right.

I wasn't feeling it.

I was afraid to.

Afraid of what letting go would feel like. I only trusted myself because nobody else in my life had ever been reliable.

Not my parents.

Nya was the closest thing I had, but I wasn't allowed to visit her as often as I got older because my parents said it looked bad.

I crumpled to the ground and hugged my knees to my chest just as the mess hall bell rang for dinner.

With a sigh, I stood, grabbed my stuff, and walked at a turtle's pace back to the mess hall to carb up since I had a big night ahead of me.

When I walked in, Jackson was already there, deep in conversation with a pissed-off looking Marlo.

Fantastic.

Was he tattling on me?

I couldn't tell.

But when Marlo looked up, it was concern marring his features. I narrowed my eyes at both of them then went to the buffet line to grab some food.

I couldn't even remember what I grabbed, just that I had food and I had a seat.

I numbly shoveled the food into my mouth and chewed.

Was there something wrong with me?

Maybe I really was a worthless bitch.

I had one job, and I couldn't even get it right enough to show my campers. What made me think I could make it in Hollywood if I couldn't even teach a few stupid routines without crying?

"Ray." Marlo tapped my shoulder.

Slowly, I turned. "What?"

He nodded to the door. "Come with me, bring your food."

"I'm done." I'd had maybe five bites, but everything tasted like lead, I was too stressed to eat, plus I had some snacks back at my cabin. I tossed my food into the trash and followed him on wobbly legs.

I shouldn't have worked out for four hours.

I just… I was trying to do my best.

It was still pretty light outside. We walked in silence. And then we were back at the HQ lodge for staff.

"Am I in trouble?" I stopped walking.

"Why would you think that?" he asked in confusion, holding open the door for me.

"Because you hate me. Because we like to yell at each other. This morning… There's way too much to choose from at this point." I exhaled roughly and followed him down the hall and into a bathroom with three huge trough-looking metal tubs.

Marlo smirked and walked over to the wall.

Two ice machines were placed there with bags.

"Noooooooo." I groaned. "You're not serious."

"Dead serious." He grabbed a bag and started filling it with ice. "You won't be able to walk tomorrow let alone teach."

"It's not bad."

"It's worse than bad." He tossed the full back of ice into the tub and repeated the process four more times.

I shivered just thinking about it.

"All right," He pointed to the tub. "Get in."

"Now?"

"No, after the ice melts. Yes now."

"But I'm—"

"Ray," he said softly. "Believe it or not, I really am trying to save your ass. Get down to your bra and underwear and crawl in, I'll time it for you and come back in when it's over."

I clamped my jaw and peeled my shirt over my head. I figured the faster I did it, the faster he would leave me alone. I tugged down my sweat-slicked shorts and then kicked off my flip flops.

"Hate you, hate you, hate you, hate you," I chanted as I lowered myself into the ice bath.

For some reason more tears came.

Along with Jackson's words.

"Do I have a soul?" I asked in a weak voice. Utter silence. "Never mind, forget I asked."

I looked up. Marlo's blue eyes blazed with fury. "Who the hell told you that you had no soul?"

"Doesn't matter. Is it true?"

Marlo sat at the edge of the trough. "No," he whispered. "You have a soul."

Without looking away from my gaze, he reached into the frigid water and pulled up my leg onto his lap and started massaging the arch in my right foot.

I cried out and stiffened.

"Better it hurt now than later in bed." He pressed his palm down on my arch and rubbed.

I squeezed my eyes shut. "Does this torture have an end time?"

He chuckled. "Ten minutes, and then I'm walking you back to your cabin and giving you the night off."

My eyes jolted open, "I don't need the night off, I still have things I need to work on and—"

"Take the night off, or you're fired." He shrugged.

"How is that fair?"

He dropped my leg back in and grabbed the other. "I don't want you hurting yourself. Take it easy, the dancing will come, so will the rest of the show. We don't need to rush the process, Ray."

"But—"

"Promise me?"

I nodded while he kept kneading my foot.

And then, once the prickling sensation of the cold water simmered to a numbing icy bath, he grabbed a nearby towel and handed it to me. "Have a good night, Ray."

With that, he left.

He left me alone.

With a towel in my right hand, and my body buzzing with excitement and pleasure.

He'd touched my feet.

He'd massaged them.

Why?

Why was he being nice?

Chapter
SIXTEEN

Marlon

I stared up at the ceiling. I adjusted my pillow. I checked my phone. It was past midnight, and I couldn't get her face out of my head.

Pissed at myself, I decided to go for a run to see if I could mentally and physically exhaust myself. I quickly put on a pair of shorts and Nikes, then grabbed my pods and phone and ran out of my cabin.

The trail around the lake was about five miles. I sprinted. I pushed my body so hard that everything hurt. Sweat ran down my chest as I neared the mess hall and noticed that the dance studio lights were still on.

I clenched my teeth, irritated that Ray had spaced and

left them on. Then again, she'd been so exhausted I could almost understand how it slipped her mind.

Almost.

I jogged over and took the stairs two at a time then yanked open the screen door.

One lamp was lit in the corner.

And there was Ray dancing.

Swiveling her hips to the main theme song of the movie as if Johnny was holding her close, dipping her body backward.

Fuck me, she was dancing the sex scene.

And I was watching.

I gulped.

I didn't let her know I was there.

I wanted to see what she would do.

I wanted to see how far she would take it, how much she would dedicate her body to each movement, each erotic dip of her hips.

Her eyes were closed as she bent backward, lifting her foot as if she was hooking it around a body.

My breath hitched as she turned quickly, and then parted her lips like she was letting some invisible bastard run his hands between her breasts, and then lower, she touched herself like they were his hands.

Not mine.

She kept touching.

And I watched.

A warm breeze pushed through the windows and wrapped itself around my body. I couldn't look away from her as she danced, as she pushed her exhausted body past the point of coming back.

She twirled.

I watched each step.

I counted.

Her black crop top fell over one shoulder, and her white shorts showed off her lean, tan legs. My mouth went completely dry.

One, two, three, spin, dip backward. I knew the musical by heart, I imagined my hands on her neck, my lips replacing my hands, gripping her thigh and pulling it against me while she hungrily clawed at my neck.

Abruptly, she spun and spun like she was purposely trying to make herself dizzy, and that's when I noticed the tears.

She was a fucking ballerina.

I don't know how I never noticed it before.

The way she twirled.

She had perfect feet.

But Jackson was right. He'd said something was missing. He'd been cryptic as hell.

More tears fell as she spun, and then she collapsed to the floor in a heap of tears and so much sorrow it hurt to look at her.

I should walk away.

But instead, I walked over to her.

I knelt down and tilted her chin toward me.

If she was surprised, she didn't show it.

She just looked up at me with hopeless empty eyes. I wondered what sort of soulless human would be so cruel as to stare at her — knowing that they were responsible for that look — and walk away as if it didn't matter.

I didn't speak.

I just walked over to the lamp and turned the small black knob.

Blanketed in darkness, the music started another loop, obviously on repeat. I reached for her hands and pulled her into my arms.

"Don't close your eyes," I whispered.

Tears continued to stream down her face as I gently pulled her body against mine. Her expression turned numb.

Like she was purposefully shutting down.

Like it would hurt too much to feel more than she was already feeling.

"See me," I whispered. I knew the risk. I jumped anyway.

She startled and turned her head.

"See me." I gently gripped her chin and pulled it back toward me, and then our foreheads touched, I pressed a kiss to her cheek, wiped her tears with my lips, licked the saltiness with my tongue, and then very slowly braced her body and let her fall back. "Trust me."

She stiffened.

"It's just us," I encouraged.

She didn't let go.

It was one of the most disappointing moments of my life.

I was both afraid to break her and afraid to let her live that same hollow existence through the music.

Music set souls free.

It didn't trap them.

The sadness choked me.

I pulled her against my chest, harder this time, then threw her body back, forcing her to arch against my hand as I thrust her against my chest. I gripped her thigh with my fingers, so hard it would leave a mark, and then I spun her back. She let out a little gasp as I swiveled my hips against hers showing her the correct rhythm, how to feel it, how to breathe it in.

The tension built as the music shifted from straight up dancing to something more sexual. I touched her then. I ran my hand down the middle of her breasts, I cupped her ass and forced her to watch me do it. I forced her attention on me, on the music, on us and what it built between us.

She bit down on her bottom lip as her eyes filled with more tears. I spun her out from me and then jerked her back and gripped her hips lifting her effortlessly into the air as she wrapped her arms around me.

I pressed her against the wall, holding her there as the music built around us. She locked eyes with me; it was like watching scales fall in rapid succession to the floor.

Her mouth met mine in a frenzy of heat and sweat.

My body roared to life as I kept her there.

Kept her safe from my reaction.

I kissed her back because I had no other choice.

And she clung to me like I'd always been her first.

The music ended, ready to loop again, breaking the moment between us. I slowly dropped her back down to the floor, her body slid roughly against mine, it was so painful I hissed out a curse. I wanted her. I wanted her. I wanted her.

Her face transformed into a small smile. "Thank you."

"Ray." My voice came out raspy. "You need to learn to trust the music."

"I can't." She gave her head a shake.

I gripped her face with my palms. "Ray, you must. Or what the hell are you doing here? You give yourself completely to it. To your art. You sell your soul to the notes."

"I've only ever given myself completely to one person,"

was her cryptic answer. "And I let him down before he could."

I jerked away from her.

She shook her head and walked out of the room, leaving me wondering if it was me she'd given herself to.

And if that was her way of saying sorry.

Chapter
SEVENTEEN

Ray

I tried to pretend like it didn't happen.

Like he didn't just see me at my worst.

Like I didn't just steal the best kiss of my life so that I would feel better about what Jackson said, about what everyone always saw.

My inability to fully commit to my craft.

Out of fear of rejection.

Out of fear that once committed, once denied, I wouldn't have any parts of me left for me.

What if they love you?

What if they hate you over and over again?

What if in the end, after I give everything, I'm still found wanting?

I didn't know how to separate myself from dancing, I never had. Acting was one thing, but dancing? Music? It had been our thing.

"Dance with me!" He let out a funny laugh that made me warm all over as we pressed our sticky palms together and started to dance.

"I'm going to be a dancer one day." He twirled me.

I knew it was true.

Because he was so good.

Not his dancing.

His soul.

His soul was good — his dancing would be great.

I woke up in the same position I had gone to sleep in. I hadn't showered the night before, something about washing Marlo off my body — off my mouth — only made my eyes sting with unshed tears.

With a groan, I checked the little digital clock near the cat calendar. Six a.m.

Great.

I still had a few hours to mentally prepare for my first class of the day. There wasn't enough coffee in the world.

I got to my feet and almost swore.

My body hurt in places I didn't know a body could hurt.

I limped over to my shower caddy, grabbed a towel and slid my feet into a pair of Uggs then made the trek down to the showers.

The lights were on.

But no showers were running.

I started the one on the far right; it was in the corner so

it was the largest. At least I could stand under the hot water.

I turned up the radio station that was on so that I would have a distraction that would hopefully wake me up before coffee, and then started to strip.

"Sore?" A voice came from the door.

I almost stumbled into the wall. Thankfully, I at least still had my shirt and underwear on.

I turned.

Marlo was leaning against the wall, shirtless — just my luck.

And sweaty like he'd just gotten done running fifty million miles.

The guy's abs heaved.

Sweat slid down each perfect muscle.

I gulped and looked away. "Yeah, I'm pretty sure I wouldn't be able to move, though, had I not done the ice bath, thanks."

He didn't say anything.

I looked up.

He tilted his head and stared me down with those crystal blue eyes like he was trying to read my mind.

And then he approached, stopped right in front of me, and pressed his hands down on my shoulders.

I exhaled slowly.

He gripped them with his fingertips then turned my body around and started massaging.

I closed my eyes and fell back against him in a heap of pain as he kneaded my muscles, as he worked down my arms, down my back.

His breathing deepened.

Or maybe it was mine.

He was all hot, sweat sliding against my skin, pulling up my T-shirt, with each movement of our bodies melting together, like my clothes didn't want to stay on anymore.

Like they had no choice.

"Fuck." He stopped massaging.

I didn't want him to stop.

I just — I wanted.

That was it.

I wanted.

He made me want.

It was a dangerous game we played.

One where hearts were involved more than bodies.

He pulled his hand back. I reached behind me, as he breathed into my neck. I grabbed that perfect hand and placed it on my stomach. His fingertips clutched my T-shirt and fisted it.

I sucked in a breath as he slowly peeled it off my body and then tossed it onto a nearby bench. My bare back was against his stomach, his chest. He was a fortress of heat and sex. My legs trembled as his mouth pressed against my shoulder.

I rocked back against him, pressing my ass into his body feeling his hard length beneath his shorts.

He was so hard, searing hot.

I let out a little gasp when he bit the skin he'd just kissed.

The sound of laughter filled the air.

We both froze.

And then I was under the hot water with him. The curtain pulled. Just us in that corner. Just us in that universe.

His eyes searched mine.

I didn't give myself time to think, I cupped his face with both hands and jerked him forward, meeting his mouth for a kiss that would eventually ruin me.

The thing about Marlo? He was so unapologetic about the way he kissed me, almost like he knew it was part punishment, part uncontrollable lust and fire like it had always been.

There would always be that sliver of anger between us, that underlying hatred that fueled our passion, added kerosene to the sparks that flew between our mouths like ammo.

More showers turned on around us.

It didn't matter did it?

Not anymore.

Water dripped between our hungry kisses as he devoured each and every word that should be said between us.

I gripped his hair with my fingertips while he hooked his thumbs in my wet underwear and jerked them down to the ground. I stepped out of them without breaking the kiss and did the same to his shorts, they floated in a puddle at our feet as he lazily kissed down my throat.

In a way, he was more experienced. He knew how to kiss, how to drive a girl crazy. He knew how to create a frenzy, a slow burning fire that made it impossible to think straight.

My thighs trembled as my core pulsed for more of him.

His length pressed against me, hot, needy.

Marlo broke the kiss, chest heaving, and locked eyes with me again just as more talking ensued around us. More laughter.

The other staff members had no idea.

No idea.

Jackson's laugh was easy to pick out.

"And then I told her, look, if you can't even look at it

while it's all erect, do you think you should ask to suck it?" Male laughter ensued.

Marlo lowered his head, brushed a kiss to my mouth, and then whispered in my ear, "How quiet can you be SP?"

I smiled at my nickname. He would be the guy to still call me out seconds away from moving inside me.

"Can you?" I hissed back.

That. Damn. Smirk.

He didn't answer. He just picked me up with both hands on my bare ass and pressed me against the wall. I wrapped an arm around his neck to hold on while my body rocked against his.

I expected him to go fast, to enter, to get off, to get us both off.

I should have known with Marlo things were never that easy.

He slid down to his knees until my legs were hooked around his neck, and with that smirk still in place, he thrust his tongue inside me.

I held onto his hair and let out a little gasp.

"Shhhh…" He flicked his tongue.

My thighs trembled as he worked me into a frenzy so damn fast that I couldn't help but squeeze his head between my thighs.

He suddenly stopped and stood, letting my body slide down his until I couldn't slide anymore, until he stopped me and with one movement, was inside me. I gasped, tried not to cry out, and was treated to his hand covering my mouth while he slowed his thrusts, driving me crazy.

I couldn't take it anymore. I hooked my heels together and pulled him in as deep as I could. He swore against my neck and pumped faster and harder.

"Don't stop," I begged, biting down on his ear lobe.

"Can't." His mouth moved down my chest in tiny kisses until he was sucking on one of my breasts. I held him between my thighs. I wished for him to stay there. I found my soul in that moment.

Tethered to his.

Like I knew it had always been.

And when I chased my release and felt him pump into me one last time.

I mourned the loss as if someone had died.

The loss of him inside me.

The loss of the only thing between us that had ever made sense.

We stared at each other.

He opened his mouths to say something.

And then I heard Brax's voice in the background... "If you ask me, it's a brilliant as hell idea! He wants revenge. What better way than to fuck the girl who fucked you over before she can do it again? The guy's been in such a shit mood, a little sex will do him good, plus you know Marlo, one-night stands, never two." They all fell into fits of laughter.

And the remaining pieces of my heart crashed to the ground between the guy who had only ever seen me... and the stupid, stupid girl who thought she could trust anyone other than herself.

ACKNOWLEDGEMENTS

I'm so thankful to God that I get to wake up and do what I love. This book was no exception. It was such a fun journey that brought me back to my times at summer camp though let's be honest my camp experience was never like this haha. I was a more nerdy camper and had our counselors or directors looked like Marlo that would have probably been something I would have written home about haha.

Thank you so much to iBooks for this incredible opportunity to write an exclusive for you guys! Thanks to Ian for being so incredible through this experience. Nina thank you for being the best publicist ever, this was such a fun project to work with you on! To Becca, Jill, Katherine, Paula--everyone involved in the editing and formatting. To my beta readers Jill, Krista, Tracy, Stephanie, you guys were so amazing with all of your input and I could not have done this without you.

I'm so thankful to the rockin' readers and the rest of my readers for being so gracious with this project. I really do feel like I went to summer camp this year, only I went there in my head, though I still smell the campfires and marshmallows. I hope this book transported you as much as it did me, and I hope that it brings a smile to your face.

To my family, Nate and Thor, thank you for being so incredible during this deadline process. As always Nate was there so that I could have extra time to write. You are my soul mate, I love you.

If you want to follow me on social media, head over to Facebook and add Rachels New Rockin' Readers (friendliest group on Facebook I swear!), or you can follow me on insta/ Twitter @RachVD until next time, HUGS! RVD

Summer
SEDUCTION

To summer crushes
and the way they make us feel,
to sunshine and first kisses
and everything in between.

Chapter ONE

Marlon

My body was stiff.

My breathing heavy.

I could still feel her thighs clenching around me. The girl who had gotten away. The spoiled princess I used to hate. Now a woman with swollen lips staring at me as if I'd just pulled her heart from her body and ripped it to pieces — smiling at me all the while.

I lifted my hands to cup her face. "Ray—"

"Don't you fucking touch me," she said in a harsh whisper as more male laughter sounded around us.

We couldn't leave.

If I left, people would assume the shower was empty. They would know.

If she left, the same thing would happen.

We were trapped in a wet sex-filled Hell.

I couldn't tell if the moisture on her face was tears or water from the shower spray. All I knew was I had to fix it. I had to fix that look. I had to make it better.

Because as much as I wanted to be that guy — the one who used revenge sex to make the girl who'd hurt him in high school feel like shit — I wasn't.

Not with her.

She was…

She had been…

Would always be…

Everything to me.

All it had taken was a succession of vulnerable moments followed by vulnerable moments where I saw the girl I used to know shadowed by the girl she was forced to be, and I was lost.

"Ray," I tried again, lowering my voice. She let me touch her this time, but she refused to look at me. "It's not what you think."

She shook her head and then covered her breasts with her arms. Her eyes zeroed in on her lacy black underwear floating by my feet. They probably cost more than my entire wardrobe, those underwear. It was a weird thing to fixate on.

"It's fine," she whispered. "We both wanted it. We both got it. End of story."

I clenched my jaw and cornered her against the wall. "Don't fucking say that, Ray."

She jerked her head to attention; her face was indifferent, her pretty blonde hair was wet and sticking to her cheeks. She'd never been more beautiful than after we were together.

It was why she'd broken me, because she'd allowed me to let her bloom then closed up minutes later.

And they said history repeated itself.

"What?" She shrugged a shoulder. "It's just sex, right?"

I narrowed my eyes. "You're better than that, and you know it."

"You aren't," she snapped. "What's this about revenge sex and one-night stands? You know what? You wanted your revenge." Her lips trembled. "Congratulations, you just got it."

"Ray—"

"Fingers crossed you got me pregnant!" she shouted over her shoulder, picking up her wet underwear and tugging them on. "Bonus points if you tell the entire staff that you fucked me in the shower!"

I didn't want to say they probably already knew since she was yelling so loud.

"Ray, stop…" I reached for her.

She jerked away from me, yanked open the curtain, and grabbed her shirt. She pulled it backward over her head. Leaving her caddy and everything but her flip-flops, she ran out past a wide-eyed Jackson and Brax.

The door to the bathroom closed.

I slammed my hand against the tile again and again.

"Dude…" Jackson looked between me and Brax. "What the hell, man?"

"I didn't know she was in here." Brax looked pale. "I swear, I had no idea, but hey, at least you finally did the deed. Now you can move on and—"

I punched him before he could say more, nabbing him in the right eye at least twice before Jackson pulled me off him.

"Chill the fuck out, Marlo!" he roared. "You can't just punch your staff members. You're the director!"

"I'm murdering him!" I seethed as visions of Ray's face played on repeat in my head. Her pleasure. Her soft moans and gasps while I filled her. And then her pain. So much pain.

"Whoa." Brax held his hands to his face. "Shit, that hurts. Marlo, I didn't know, and even then, why the hell do you even care? You just got the best revenge possible, and you have witnesses. Need I remind you that this is the girl who broke your heart and embarrassed you in front of the entire student body after sleeping with you in high school? So what. At least it's a drama camp for high schoolers, and you guys are college graduates. You only have six more weeks of this hell anyway. Just leave it."

I wiped my face with my bare hands and grabbed my towel, wrapped it around my waist, and then shook out my right hand.

"What's done is done," Jackson said in a calm voice. "It doesn't leave this room, all right?"

"Yeah." I exhaled a pissed-off breath that did nothing to calm me down. I could still feel her on my skin, taste her on my tongue, and no sane part of me wanted to keep quiet about how good it was between us.

About how good it could have been if I hadn't let my anger rule my emotions.

I didn't look back as I made my way outside the bathroom. Every muscle was taut as I angrily shoved the door open to my cabin and dropped my towel to get dressed.

It was going to be a hell of a long day.

Chapter TWO

Ray

My hands shook as I tried to grab myself a cup of coffee. I hadn't really showered, not the way a human is supposed to. And because of that, I smelled the sex between us.

No matter how many times I sipped the searing coffee in an effort to burn away his taste from my tongue, it existed. It was there.

I squeezed my eyes shut.

I closed off my mind to the way he'd looked at me — as if I was special.

The world was a cruel monster. I knew this. I just didn't expect his hatred to run that deep for me, that he would pretend to care and then just strip away one of the only things I kept close to myself. He didn't know that, though.

He didn't know that the only other guy I'd ever given myself to...

Had been him.

Willingly.

I'd gone willingly twice.

And both times had been burned for different reasons.

It was the universe telling me it was wrong. All of it.

I wiped a fallen tear that decided to make its presence known all over my makeup-free face. My skin felt hot to the touch, as if he'd somehow managed to bruise the outside as well as the inside. I wiped another tear, then another.

This was the time when a girl normally called her best friend, someone who cared about her, who wouldn't judge her despite her bad choices. Or at the very least, went to her mom and proclaimed that all men should burn in Hell while said mom gave her ice cream and a hug.

I had no one to hug.

And I'd never felt so alone.

Not even when *he* had died.

Not even then.

Because at least that day my parents had hugged me.

It was the only time I'd ever felt truly close to them.

The best twenty-four hours of my life — when I had felt like I was a part of a family, where it was okay to grieve and shout how unfair the world was.

My stomach revolted as if preparing to puke.

He had touched me.

He'd made me feel alive.

Wanted.

Cherished.

And now I was used. Dirty. Just a game.

A revenge plot gone wrong. Or maybe for him, horribly right.

I couldn't stop the shaking as my teeth started to chatter. Maybe it was possible to go into shock from heartache. Maybe that pain would get so severe I would just collapse against the coffee machine.

Would anyone even care if I did?

Would my parents even answer their phones?

"Hey…" Jen touched my arm. How long had she been standing there? "Are you okay?"

"Great," I lied. "Just… fantastic."

"Yeah, I cry when I'm feeling fantastic too," she joked.

A warm summer breeze picked up as the door to the mess hall opened. It seduced me with its smell, with its promise of good things.

And then trampled all over me when I realized it was Marlo walking through those doors.

Our eyes locked.

His appeared just as sad as mine felt.

But that was impossible.

I was his revenge.

Cheers, asshole.

"Uh-oh…" Jen grabbed my free hand. "Tell me you guys didn't…"

Tears. So many tears filled my eyes I couldn't see her.

"Crap." She took the coffee from my hand and pulled me toward the farthest corner of the room. "What happened?"

"The usual…" I sniffed. "So much sexual tension that you're sick with it, so sick that the only thing you convince yourself will make you well is…" I shrugged. "I went to take a shower, he was there, one thing led to another, and…"

Jen winced. "At the risk of telling you something you already know, Marlo doesn't have girlfriends. I mean, he's really great at one-night stands. Let's just say I've heard stories. He's no Jackson — in that he'll sleep with anything that looks fun — but he isn't a saint either."

I choked out a laugh. "Yeah, trust me. I know."

"What am I missing?" She lowered her voice as Marlo walked by us to grab a cup of coffee. My damn body was betraying me just like my eyes. I refused to be that girl, the one who pined after the guy who wanted nothing more than to get his rocks off and talk about it to his friends.

He'd never been that guy.

I'd done that to *him*.

High school had ruined him; college had refined him.

My fault.

All my fault.

"Look, Marlo!" I hissed, slamming my hand on the locker door. "I don't know what the hell you want from me! Do you want me to just admit to all of my friends we had sex?"

He glared. "It's a start. Don't you think?"

"It just… happened." I lied through my teeth, already at risk of leaning toward him and begging for a kiss. "Plus, you know we can't be seen together like this. You'll just get thrown into another locker, and I'll have to stand by and watch while you just let them make fun of you."

"Watching's just as bad as participating, princess," he sneered. "And I don't fight back because it proves nothing and gets me expelled, and I need scholarships. I'm a foster kid. I don't have fucking options."

I sighed. "Marlo, I'm sorry. Maybe we can hang out after school?"

"Oh my God, so I can maybe be like your secret fuck-buddy? Yeah, sign me up. Let me just go ask my foster mom if it's cool that I'm going into prostitution for the richest family in town. There's one way to pay for college!"

I slapped him so hard my palm stung. Then I gasped. "I'm sorry. I just reacted."

"I hate you," he whispered before walking off.

I knew he didn't hear me say, "Sometimes, I hate me too."

"Hey!" Jen waved a hand in front of my face. "Are you still with me?"

"Yeah." No, I had been transported to five years ago when I'd made my first mistake in a long line of mistakes between me and Marlo.

He'd changed on the outside. Almost as if he had set out to prove to the world that he was its equal. And he did well. Too well. He was every girl's walking dream. And my current nightmare.

"I'll be fine." I sighed. "I just need to process. That's all."

"What's to process? He took you to O-land in the shower, and it looks like he's ready to start a fight with anyone who looks in his direction. Must have either been really good or really bad." She winked.

It was everything.

I squeezed my eyes shut as one last tear leaked out.

And when I opened them again, it was to see Marlo watching me with an equal amount of pain, laced with the ever-present hatred that would exist between us. Never to be eradicated.

Because pain is allowed residency for that long, it refuses to be ignored. It must be felt, it must be dealt with. And we'd only made it worse by letting our bodies talk and keeping our hearts out of the discussion completely.

Chapter THREE

Marlon

An eerie calm washed over me as I made my way back to my office that morning. I stared at all the perfect folders stacked on my desk, all the pictures of campers lining the walls.

The blue duffel, that my foster mom had sent with Ray to give me, was sitting on the chair in the corner.

I grabbed it and tugged at the worn zipper until it growled its way open.

I'd only glanced inside.

I moved some of the PowerBars around that she'd tossed in there, in search of something — anything — to anchor my thoughts to make my chest stop hurting. To keep me from running over to Ray's cabin and demanding that she listen to my explanation.

Even when I had nothing.

Because what would I say?

"The plan was to hurt you."

Mission accomplished?

I hadn't been thinking of hurting her this morning. All I'd thought was, *my God that woman is too pretty for words.*

It hurt to look at her.

I'd seen all the wasted years in her eyes.

And I'd wanted her sadness to go away.

I still wanted to know who'd put it there in the first place.

Most of all, I wanted to make sure it was eradicated by my touch if it had been me. If I'd been the guilty party.

Fuck.

A sick feeling washed over me as I threw the duffel against the wall. PowerBars scattered out of it along with what looked like a photo album.

With a grunt, I knelt and swiped across the album's cover. It didn't say anything on the outside, and it was dirty as if it had been in storage for a long time.

I opened the first page.

And there we were.

Me and Ray.

Laughing.

We were maybe ten.

It was *the before.*

Before middle school.

Before we'd known that social classes were decided by looks and name brands, by how a person talked and if you were considered cool.

She had an ice cream cone in her hand. Little drops of vanilla ice cream ran down her skin, and I was leaning in, trying to lick them off.

Damn, even at ten, I was trying to up my game with her.

I looked... happy.

And the shitty part was that I didn't remember ever being truly happy when I was little. I was too busy being worried that I was going to get taken away from my foster mom. Too worried that my real mom would come searching for me and make me live with her.

Worried sick to my stomach that she would take me from Ray.

My first real friend.

My first real heartache.

We had sat together at school.

We'd eaten lunch together.

And then... we'd grown up.

And our childhood had shattered.

One day I'd been sharing my carrots.

The next day she'd flaunted lipstick.

That was how fast it had happened in my head.

And the days following that became harder and harder as I'd tried to stay friends with someone who was on the top rung of the social ladder while I still had holes in the only pair of Nikes that my foster mom could afford at the time.

I flipped through the rest of the pictures without a clue of what I was searching for. Justification maybe? Something that proved I was in the right and she was in the wrong.

The very last picture was high school graduation.

In the picture, I was surrounded by my foster mom and dad and the few fellow outcast friends that I'd had.

And then there was Ray, off in the corner.

No parents.

No friends.

She was staring down at her shoes, the ones with red soles.

Her fucking shoes that cost more than my parents' rent.

I dropped the album back onto my desk as the guilt descended. Happy moments deserved to be filled with friends, with family.

I wondered how many happy moments in her life had been filled with silence.

And that damn thought haunted me the rest of the day.

Chapter FOUR

Ray

Class had been complete crap.

Who was I kidding? It wasn't going to get any better because I was refusing to allow myself to look at the dance choreography as more than just steps with numbers.

And every time I would try to teach a new move, it was as if I felt the ghost of Marlo all over my body, as if my skin couldn't help but recount how his heat had felt against it. I was so emotional that by the time the class was over, I didn't even say goodbye to the students. I just ran out of the studio and let my legs lead me.

I stopped when I made it to the dock on the lake.

It was a hot, peaceful day, hardly any ripples in the water. I inhaled through my nose, exhaled through my mouth, and watched.

I watched the wild ducks quack at one another.

And I felt a buildup of tears when a few little tiny ducks fell in a row behind their mama, and I wondered what had brought me to such a horrible place that I was jealous of such an innocent tiny animal.

What I wouldn't give, I thought, to be in that little line without a care in the world.

I'd believed that high school had been the deep black sea.

And then college taught me to dream.

And camp… well, camp was supposed to be a stepping stone to that dream. Instead, it felt like everywhere I looked I was given nothing but reminders that I was alone and always would be.

That the universe for one reason or another didn't want to play fair when it came to Ray De Lato.

"So, the great mystery's solved," came a familiar voice. "Ducks make you cry."

I snorted out a stupid laugh and didn't turn around. "What do you want, Jackson?"

"Not just Jackson," came another voice I recognized as Brax.

"Ah, fantastic." I hung my head. "You guys here to shove me in the lake and hold my head under water? I'm taking volunteers. So far the ducks have it…"

They both walked up to me, flanking me on each side. Without looking at me, Brax handed me my T-shirt from the bathroom, while Jackson dropped the caddy at my feet.

"It's peaceful out here" was all I could manage to get out.

"Water always looks peaceful…" Jackson said in a rough voice. "…until you see what lurks underneath. Who's to say we don't have a giant-ass shark out there just waiting to chomp on a camper who never learned the breast stroke?"

Brax crossed his arms. "It's always wild beneath water. We just like to pretend that it's peaceful so that we have peace. Most of nature's a smokescreen."

"Bees…" Jackson let out a sigh. "They make honey, they're fuzzy, and they sting the shit out of you if you aren't careful."

"Geese eat their young," Brax pointed out. "And swan dads drown theirs."

"Is this conversation supposed to make me feel better?" I muttered.

"The real question is, why do you feel bad?" Jackson asked.

I gulped and looked down. "Why ask a question you know the answer to?"

A hand touched my shoulder. I wanted to slap it away. It was Brax, and as much as I wanted to shove him into the water for what he'd said, part of me knew that it had been based in truth, however bad it hurt.

"Ray…" Brax gripped my shoulder. "…I fucked up. I'm sorry. Had I known you were in there…"

I jerked away from him. "You did me a favor. At least now I know."

"But I don't think you do. I mean, maybe in the beginning it was this revenge—"

"I can't talk about this," I said with a wobbly voice. "Thanks for my shirt."

His sigh was heavy, and then footsteps thumped on the wooden dock.

Jackson, however, was still there.

I looked up into his green eyes. "You should go too."

"I know." He shrugged. "But I figured you already had the girl talk with Jen this morning, at least if my suspicions are correct, so now it's time for phase two."

"Phase two?" I asked dumbly.

He moved before I could stop him.

He wrapped his bulky arms around me and squeezed tight.

I had no fight left. I let him hold me.

And then I started to cry.

He kissed the top of my head and whispered, "Take it from a manwhore who knows his faults. Marlo may get caught up in bad intentions but it's because he feels... everything."

"So that excuses him for using me?"

"Nah, I'm not saying it's ever okay for a guy to use sex as a way to gain revenge, and I'm not saying that I haven't done my fair share of shitty things when it comes to the opposite sex. What I am saying is that Marlo isn't the type of guy who has sex to have sex. He has to feel. If my one-night stands are to get off, his are to create a symphony. It was like that all through college. He'd date girls, get bored, move on, and it was never *them* he fell in love with. It was their talent. It was the way they sang, danced... It was the way they created."

I pulled back and narrowed my eyes at him. "Are you saying I was a pity-lay?"

He smirked. "You mean because you refuse to feel the music and suck at dancing?"

I swatted him with my hand, but at least I was smiling again.

And then he did something unexpected, and it unarmed me. He smiled as if he had a secret he wanted to tell.

I waited.

Pondering with expectation.

Tell me I'm different.

Tell me something.

Anything.

"With you..." he started, paused for a beat, then continued. "...it's never been about the talent, has it?" He leaned in. "It's you he fell for first. Not what you could offer the world through your acting, your dancing, your voice — but through what you could offer the world by simply being you."

I stumbled backward.

He nodded once as if his job was done and then started walking off. When he got about halfway down the dock, he stopped and called over his shoulder. "Use it, Ray."

"Use what?"

"Your pain." And off he went, in his tight blue staff shirt and his skinny jeans and Air Jordans.

I wasn't sure how long I watched the empty dock.

How long I listened to the ducks.

Or how long I tossed around what Brax and Jackson had both said. They'd made me rethink what I didn't want to question. Because it was easier to hurt. It was easier to be angry at Marlo than to believe there was another reason other than his ultimate revenge on my coldhearted soul.

And as if the universe was still against me, the wind picked up, and Marlo started walking toward the lake.

Chapter
FIVE

Marlon

I needed space.

I needed to think.

I needed to dance.

And every damn studio was taken.

I needed the music. I needed it to consume me, so she wouldn't. The more I thought about her, the more it hurt, the more I felt like this rope was choking my neck, threatening to pop my head off.

I hated feeling out of control.

I hated that every fucking second I was wondering if she was still crying, if she was still pissed, while still trying to control my own anger that history was repeating itself. As if

I stood up in front of God and everyone and said, *"I choose her."*

She would laugh.

Wouldn't she?

I'd grabbed one of the extra iPads from the office and made it down to one of the beaches on the lake, then peeled my shirt over my head. I kicked the sand and sank to my haunches. The water was too quiet.

I needed something loud.

I needed an escape so damn bad.

How did it take one incident to bring me back to all the fears of not having food on the table? The fears of going to school in the morning and wondering if I would get bullied again. If I'd get texts from random numbers saying I should just kill myself and get it over with.

Or worse, the online chat room for our high school that almost always had something to say about my claiming to be with Ray the night after we were together. As if I was a lying piece of shit who didn't deserve life.

I squeezed my eyes closed as memories surfaced. Memories of prom night, where all I'd wanted was to just go and be a part of something.

Where I'd watched her dance as prom queen.

Where I had watched him kiss her as the prom king.

Where I'd wished I had something more to give her than a name that had been given to me by a stranger.

And a wallet with exactly ten dollars in it.

I loathed her in that moment.

With her glittering crown and sparkly dress. With her fake smile and fake friends, and the fake fan club that clapped and shouted for her.

Where had they been on graduation day?

Where had they been on her birthday?

Nonexistent.

Smokescreens.

Shadows.

And yet, I'd been pushed away. The only real thing.

I stood and kicked the sand again.

With a sigh, I grabbed the iPad, hit one of the first songs, slipped off my shoes, and closed my eyes.

Chapter SIX

Ray

I hid behind one of the trees.

I watched him kick dirt.

I watched a war rage on his face, a battle in his muscles, flexing all around his body as he turned in a small circle.

And then his shoes went flying.

His shirt was gone.

I sucked in a shallow breath at the sight of him.

Of his beauty.

Marlo was like this barely restrained animal; every muscle flexed without warning, even his jaw seemed to be cut from steel. He clenched it as if he needed to feel physical pain.

And then he turned on some music. It only took a

second before I recognized "Zombie" by Bad Wolves. He blared it loud enough to consume my thoughts and scare every animal within a five-mile radius.

He moved his hands, so slight, so purposeful that it drew me in, sucked me away from my pity party and invited me to watch.

And I lost all sense of reality as I followed him on a journey I knew there would be no coming back from.

Contemporary dance was my favorite to watch. I knew the biggest fault I had with dancing was the obvious — I couldn't let go. I couldn't trust the audience to see my pain, to feel it with me, to experience it again and again with its crippling agony.

I wasn't that brave.

Marlo was.

He thrust his right foot into the air and twisted his entire body then came down and kicked up more dirt, the movement so natural it was hard to tell if the plume of dirt was accidental or part of his performance. He flipped back onto his hands and then collapsed to his knees as sand flew around his body. His hands sank into the grains, and he gripped the earth as if it was his only tether, as if it was both fighting him and grounding him. When he pulled his hands back, he roughly rubbed the sand up and down his arms and stood. Grit now coated his face, his entire body as the music slowed. He lifted his hands into the air and let them hang as though in suspension. His fists clenched. Then he brought his hands down and beat his chest. Another spin had him flying in the air, the dirt coming with him, and he landed again on his knees in the sand. Sand exploded around him, covering his face and body again as he moved with the music, swaying back and forth, gripping his head like the melody was torturing him, as if it threatened to release his demons — as if he wanted it to.

Mouth dry, I stood watching as tears welled in my eyes. On the next verse, he stood, his body trembling as the music slowed. Each line he made with his body was perfection.

Another spin, and he was on the ground again, rolling around with the sand, one with both the earth and the music.

I couldn't see where he began, where the beach ended.

All I saw was music.

All I heard was his body crying out with the feel of it, with the need to tell a story in such a violent way that he couldn't hold back even if he'd tried.

And as the song neared its end, he collapsed onto his knees, hands uplifted, then he jumped to his feet and did an aerial before falling back onto the beach and bouncing into a backflip. Sand spun around and around his body until it was like a tornado of grit and emotion.

And like that, it was over. The song ended. Only the gentle lapping of waves on the shore broke the silence. Marlo's chest heaved, but otherwise he didn't move.

And I knew.

I had seen not just a dance.

But a man expressing his emotions in a way I'd never experienced before.

He hadn't held back.

Because men like Marlo didn't know how.

And as I quietly walked back to the privacy of my cabin, I wondered if what Brax and Jackson had shared was true.

Had he fallen for the woman first?

didn't necessarily want to go to the late-night staff get-together, mainly because I imagined it would be about as uncomfortable as showing up at a party naked.

But Jen had convinced me.

Plus, apparently, it was *Greased Lightning* night.

Who knew?

I hadn't brought a ton, but I did still have my leather leggings, so I threw them on with a pair of flat sandals — so I didn't trip on a tree branch and meet my untimely death — and then grabbed a white crop tank. My hair was a raging mess on account of this morning I'd been under the shower without conditioner and hadn't had time to really do anything with it except stare at the tangles in the mirror and be reminded of what it had felt like to have Marlo pull it.

Great.

By the time Jen knocked on my cabin door with a giant grin on her face, I was hot and bothered and pissed all at the same time. How dare he still have control over me hours later!

How dare you spy on his special dance and imagine another nighttime routine.

Right.

I was going to lose my mind before the summer was over.

The soundtrack to *Grease* filled the night air as we walked in silence toward the giant bonfire.

Campers were supposed to be in their cabins by nine.

It was our only time to decompress, to be stupid college kids before joining the work force by taking on three jobs at three different restaurants while trying to support ourselves as starving artists.

Jackson was standing on one of the stumps combing his hair back, jiggling his leg. "I got chills, they're multiplying, and I'm losing control…" He winked over at us.

"He can sing," I said dumbly, a bit awestruck.

Jen sighed in annoyance. "It's how he gets so much ass. He's like a black widow that lures you into his Justin-Timberlake-themed web only to wrap you like a fly with each verse."

"Graphic." I nodded with a small smile. "Does that mean he Justin Timberlaked you right into bed?"

She scrunched up her nose. "That, paired with his ability to talk any human out of all clothing… yup, pretty much!"

Jackson held out his hands as a few of the guys jumped behind him and started dancing. That was the thing about theater camp — we were all cut from the same cloth. We lived to perform, to act, to sing. Most of the staff members were triple threats. Broadway? No problem. Choreography? Easy. Golden Globe? Nailed it.

We couldn't be hired for this camp and not have talent.

Nerves erupted in my belly.

I had to make this work.

Then again, it wasn't like my parents were supportive anyway. What if I just did it? What if I just moved without the agent? Without any sort of security from them?

All they had to offer me was money.

And even that was given only when they deemed it reasonable or felt guilty.

I let out a sigh, not realizing I'd walked all the way up to Jackson until he grabbed my arm and pulled me up on the stump with him. "You got second verse."

That was all he said before wrapping me around his arms and thrusting me into a dance — body roll, body roll, hip swivel.

My eyes widened as Jen grinned and lifted her hands into the air. "Justin Timberlake web!"

Hmm.

I hopped off the log and shoved Jen toward Jackson. His smile fell a bit as he pulled her onto the log and repeated his movements, but this time... this time I noticed something.

When I'd been up there, he had touched my hips.

With Jen up there — it was like he was afraid to touch.

Interesting.

His movements slowed as she sang, and then with a laugh, she finished the second verse and shoved him off the log. "Where my pink ladies at?"

A few of the girls ran over to me and suddenly I was in my own version of hell as the girls started snapping their fingers and then falling into choreography around me.

I either had to join or run.

I eyed Marlo on the other side of the fire, watching the dancing, watching us.

His look made my decision easy.

I fell into step with the rest of the girls and let myself believe nobody was noticing as we danced around Jen and sang the rest of "Summer Lovin'" while the guys circled us, snapping their fingers and twirling around, and then someone grabbed me by the waist and flipped me 180.

Every girl was paired off.

Unfortunately, my other half was Marlo.

And he was touching me again.

He twirled me and then picked me up and swung me around his back.

I didn't want to crack my neck, so I let him lead and prayed I could remember how to swing dance without meeting an untimely death against the campfire or nearest rock.

He flipped me backward over his arm.

He gave me no choice but to trust him.

And as the music ended, and everyone erupted into cheers, his hand lingered on my waist, pretending to belong there.

His eyes locked on mine as if they couldn't look away.

This morning, he'd been moving inside me.

And right now, we couldn't even use words.

I was afraid if I spoke, I'd yell.

I was afraid I would scream my truth.

Afraid I would cry.

Worried the last parts of me that I kept safe would be unlocked, and he'd throw away the key, laughing.

Revenge sex, revenge sex.

I jerked away from him.

He let me.

And as staff around us started dancing and singing again, I made my way over to a log and sat by myself.

I wasn't there for long.

Soon Jackson joined me.

Wordlessly, he handed me a cup of something that smelled strong and then whispered under his breath, "I may know a few things about mistakes."

"Oh?" I turned my head.

But he wasn't looking at me. He was looking at Jen, and his usual smirk or arrogant smile wasn't there.

No, it was raw.

It was this insatiable hunger.

"You could fix it, you know." I elbowed him. "She's right there."

"That's the thing about people like us, Ray."

I frowned. "Excuse me?"

"People like us, we don't let people in. We're too afraid they'll run away screaming. A girl like Jen... she wouldn't stay long enough, and I don't think I could survive being abandoned or finally having to look at myself in the mirror and ask the question..."

My throat went dry, my stomach heaved. "What question?"

"What if she saw me — and it still wasn't enough?"

"Jackson—"

"Don't *Jackson* me." Now the arrogance was back as he leaned in. "You do the exact same thing. You've got a fucking wall built around you. The best thing for people like us is to find someone who forces us to question why the hell we're so afraid in the first place."

"You're afraid?" I found my voice.

"We all have our things." He shrugged and then smiled. "Isn't she pretty?"

My heart broke a bit. "She's beautiful."

"Yeah. I'd like her to stay that way. Beautiful. Unobtainable. Untainted by my baggage. I think I'll keep her on that shelf, where I can look but tell myself I'll just shatter her if I touch her with my grimy hands."

"Sounds like you're making that decision for the both of you."

He let out a snort. "Sex confuses girls. Trust me. She'll tell me she's fine, and then one day there will be tears. There are always tears. And then I'll feel like shit because I'll start stacking my baggage around me, and then she'll feel like she has to break through it, and then I'll have to tell her that it's a crutch, that I need it there to survive. And then she'll go back to that shelf worse than before. No, I'll keep her there. She's safe. Pretty and safe." He leaned forward and then shook his head as if it was foggy. Some of the liquid in his red cup spilled out onto the dirt.

I frowned. "How drunk are you?" I finally asked a few minutes later.

He'd started to sing under his breath about unrequited love and then had cussed out a mosquito.

"Oh, I'm completely fucked." He nodded seriously. "How'd you know?"

I bit down on my lower lip and patted him on the back. "Yeah, let's get you some water, champ."

"What's that?"

"Water?"

"I don't know what water is."

"Yeah, a lot of water." I helped him to his feet only to have him stumble, putting his entire weight down onto my body. "Whoa, there…"

"He okay?" Marlo grabbed his other arm and put it around his neck.

We started walking toward Jackson's cabin as if we'd planned on the arrangement, when all I wanted to do was let Marlo carry Jackson while I ran in the opposite direction.

"He's completely tanked," I said in a calm voice, despite the hammering of my heart. "Does he do this a lot?"

"Only when he needs to forget."

"And he needed to forget today?"

Marlo's jaw tightened. "He'll be fine."

"What aren't you telling me?" I asked as we made our way up the stairs into the small cabin.

"It's not my story to tell, Ray." He grunted and flipped Jackson onto his bed.

Jackson burst out laughing. "Marlo!"

"Hey, man." Marlo smiled. "We're gonna get you some water and aspirin, all right?"

"She's dead still, huh?" Jackson asked.

"Shit," Marlo said under his breath. "Yeah, she is."

"I loved her."

"I know." Marlo sighed. "I know you did."

"I fucking hate aspirin." He shook his head. "No aspirin. Reminds me of how she left. She left me."

"She was sick," Marlo said in a soft voice. "Remember?"

"It was my fault, wasn't it?" Jackson grabbed a pillow, hugged it, and then started snoring.

I was too stunned to do anything.

Marlo grabbed my arm and basically dragged me out of the cabin. "Not a word to anyone."

"What would I even say?" I threw my hands in the air. "Someone needs to stay with him!"

Marlo pinched the bridge of his nose. "Look, he's going to wake up really pissed. He hates hangovers and hates being drunk, but it's his weird way of honoring her death."

"Her death," I repeated, my mind going a million miles a minute. "Someone he loved died on this day…?"

"Three years ago." Marlo shoved his hands into his pockets and looked away. "She committed suicide. She was on staff at camp."

"They were friends." I nodded in understanding.

Marlo let out a harsh laugh. "No, Ray, they weren't friends. They were siblings."

I covered my mouth with my hand as my heart thudded against my ribs. I felt as if I couldn't suck in enough air to survive the next minute.

All I wanted to say was *"Me too."*

He hadn't committed suicide.

But he was dead.

And when someone you love dies, it doesn't just leave you empty…

It leaves the world worse than before.

"Everyone has their demons." He put his hands on his head and then slammed his hand against the door.

"And who was she to you?" I whispered, almost afraid to find out.

He looked back over his shoulder. His eyes were wild, and then he said. "She was my replacement for you."

Chapter SEVEN

Marlon

I hadn't meant to admit that. Both Jackson's sister and I had come to camp that year lost, needing to bury ourselves in someone else. She'd just broken up with her boyfriend and was two years older than I, and it had been easy.

Too easy to fall into this sexual relationship over the summer that made me forget Ray.

It had been fake.

Like going tanning because you miss the sunshine but not knowing how else to get the Vitamin D your body needs.

I hated that I even admitted it out loud.

Hated that Ray looked so horrified that I would stoop so low as to use another girl because I couldn't have the one I really wanted.

But I knew that I would never stand a chance with Ray if I wasn't honest. If I didn't show her ugly with good.

Because I wasn't a good guy.

Not anymore.

I was jaded.

Bitter.

Resentful.

And the pathetic thing was that I'd felt justified in all of it until I had seen Ray again, and then I'd realized I was in the wrong, but it had been too late.

The seed was planted.

Ray took a step toward me, then another.

I waited for the slap.

For the judgement.

"Can I ask you something?" Her eyes didn't leave mine.

"Yes," I rasped.

"This morning… when you came into the bathroom…" Her voice shook. "…what's the first thing you thought?"

"First thing…" I sighed and shook my head, "My first thought was *God she's beautiful, like sunshine. Like my own personal Ray of light after a lifetime of hell.*"

Tears filled her eyes, shining in the dim light, lending her a wide-eyed waif-quality.

"What was the first thing you thought?" I countered, needing to get the attention away from me before I grabbed her and kissed her, before I told Jackson to get the hell out of his own cabin while I peeled her clothes off one by one.

I bet her leggings would stick against her legs.

I bet I could take my time moving them down with my teeth.

I bet she would like it.

I bet I could die with her taste on my lips.

Ray smiled and looked away. Pink teased her cheeks as she tucked a stray hair behind her ears. "First thought."

"Play fair." I smirked.

"Damn, that guy must like his protein shakes if his muscles have muscles."

"Ah, so she likes muscles."

"Meh." She took a step away from me.

I didn't reach for her.

Tension swirled between us. I knew if I inhaled deeply, it would smell like her shampoo.

It would smell like sex.

Like us.

"Are we at a ceasefire?" I asked, crossing my arms.

"You're still an asshole." She narrowed her eyes.

I chuckled. "Yeah, I'm aware."

"A buff asshole," she grumbled.

"A buff asshole and sunshine." I nodded. "Perfectly unmatched in every way."

"Prove you aren't just going to pick me up so you can drown me in the lake the minute I tell you I trust you," she said in parting, leaving me alone on the stairs as she sauntered off toward the raging fire.

She didn't hear me speak it across the wind. She didn't hear my heart slam against my chest.

I smiled and inclined my head, whispering. "Watch me."

Chapter EIGHT

Ray

I stayed at the campfire long after everyone went to bed. The embers were dying down. I didn't know why I'd stayed.

It wasn't as if I was deep in thought.

Just the idea of going back to my cabin felt… lonely. So lonely.

And after this morning… this afternoon…

What Marlo said…

I honestly just wanted a hug, wanted someone to tell me everything was going to be fine. I needed a friend.

"Still up?" Marlo's voice had me jumping a foot, nearly into the embers.

I put my hand to my chest in a vain attempt to comfort my racing heart. "Could you walk louder?"

"I called your name twice before I sat down." He stoked the fire from his seat next to me.

The warmth of his body reached out to me.

The way he restrained himself as if he was seconds away from snapping, perhaps out of anger, lust, or just all of the above.

Campfire smell filled the air, smoke billowing in my line of vision as we sat in tense silence.

"Why?" he asked. One word. No further explanation.

"Why what?" I licked my lips and watched as the smoke grew tiny tendrils that wrapped themselves around the charred wood.

He dropped the stick and rubbed his hands together. "Why are you still up?"

"I—" My voice caught. It caught with things left unsaid. Things I couldn't say. Things that were real when spoken out loud because when you say words out loud, your ears hear, your heart believes them. It's like manifesting your truth.

And I wasn't ready to do that with mine.

"You have no reason to trust me," he began.

His deep voice caused goose bumps to erupt all over my skin. I rubbed my arms back and forth with my palms and waited for whatever else he was going to confess. I was an addict for his truth, scrambling with my hands, digging through the dirt to seek it out, to uncover the treasure. Because I knew there was nothing more beautiful than a person's truth.

It was why I was petrified of mine.

Because it was ugly.

It was so damn ugly.

Alone.

Afraid.
Alone.
Afraid.
Worthless.
Unlovable.

I shook as the words bounced around in my head, quivering with the need to get them out, to tell Marlo I couldn't remember a time when I hadn't been afraid.

To tell him that my favorite place — even if it was just for revenge — had been in his arms.

"It's getting late." He stood and held out his hand.

I took it.

He was director, after all.

And the staff had a curfew too. I mean that curfew was two a.m., but still I knew I had to get up early and attempt to teach choreography without baring my soul.

I almost laughed at the thought.

That was a little bit like saying I was going to act without emotion, wasn't it?

He dropped my hand when I stood.

He moved it to my back.

I took a few steps, and then the pressure on my back forced me to turn. I gave him a sideways glance as we kept walking away from my cabin.

Toward his.

I almost dug my heels in.

Almost laughed at the same time.

Did he really think that, after this morning, I was going to get naked with him? I was ready to yell at him, to scream at myself.

To throw rocks into the fire and run away when he

opened the cabin door and ushered me inside.

A lamp was lit in the corner.

He had two beds.

I frowned.

Both were made.

Two. Beds.

Why was I fixating on the number of beds?

He pulled his shirt over his head, kicked off his pants. I tried not to stare at every inch of sinewy muscle that flexed in my direction, but the only way not to stare was to poke my own eyes out, and I enjoyed what I saw too much to look away.

He ran his hands through his thick hair and then nodded to the other bed. "Sleep."

"In here?" I gaped at him. The guy was crazy.

He yawned as if I bored him. "Yeah, Ray, in here, in your own bed. At least then you won't be alone."

"How did you know I didn't want to be alone?"

Now the smirk was back. "Because you chose sitting around a dying campfire and possible bear attacks over going back to your cabin at one in the morning."

Valid point. "Wait, there are bears?"

"Nature." He spread his arms wide.

My mouth went dry at the sight of his tight eight-pack and low *V* that I hadn't even had time to process yet as it dipped into tight briefs that made his ass look amazing.

My God, I am sexually harassing him in my head!

I am just as bad as Jackson!

Worse!

"Right." I cleared my throat and did a small circle. I was about ready to jump in with my clothes on when a fresh-smelling cotton shirt was tossed onto my bed.

"Sleep, Ray." He crawled into bed and lay on his back.

I quickly stripped out of my clothes, kept my bra and underwear on, and pulled his white shirt over my head.

It smelled good.

Like him.

Fresh.

I hadn't realized I was still smelling it until I heard a chuckle from his bed. I grabbed a stray pillow and slammed it down onto his face.

It just made him laugh harder.

So, I hit him again.

And again.

"That's it." He jumped up, gripped me by the waist and threw me over his shoulder, stood and walked me back to the twin bed, then threw me onto it.

I bounced up and nearly knocked him in the head before I was pinned to the mattress.

My breathing slowed.

His eyes flickered to my mouth.

Then away.

"Sleep," he said, his voice cracking. "I'll just be over here taking care of all the pillows in case you decide to hold one over my mouth mid-sleep."

I rolled my eyes. "You wouldn't even know you were dead."

"Good to know. I'm thrilled I invited you into my cabin. Make sure the cops know I was a giant dick so they don't put you in prison. I mean, you have a legitimate reason to want to murder me."

"I do." I turned on my side as he crawled into bed.

Moonlight flickered through the window near his feet.

"Hey, Marlo?" It was almost too quiet.

"Yeah, Ray."

"Are you on human-growth hormone?"

He burst out laughing. I decided that I liked that laugh so much more than the sexy scowl. I liked every angle I saw. From the angsty drama kid to the guy who ran because he genuinely enjoyed it to the dancer who wore his heart on his sleeve. I loved it all.

I loved his layers.

I loved his voice.

I needed someone to put the pillow over *my* face. Immediately.

"Can't say anyone's ever accused me of HGH." He turned to face me. "No. I'm just the product of what happens when you don't peak in high school."

"I peaked in high school," I said more to myself than anyone.

"No." He said it as if it was true. "You haven't peaked yet."

"Excuse me?"

"You haven't peaked yet," he said slowly. "Trust me, when you do, you'll be unstoppable."

"I have boobs," I said dumbly.

"Yeah, nice ones too," he said in a sing-song voice. "Many a man would sell their souls just to drown between them, but not what I was talking about, Ray, and you know it. You've always been beautiful."

"Thank you… I think." I frowned and lay back down.

"Night, Ray. Try not to overthink this conversation to the point where you look like hell in the morning and can't teach your class."

"Ah, asshole's back."

"Asshole never left." He put a pillow over his head as if I annoyed him.

And I smiled because I found great satisfaction in the fact that I probably did.

Chapter

NINE

Marlon

I never thought I'd live to see the day that little spoiled princess woke up in the same room as I, with her bare legs on top of the comforter and her long icy hair spread out on the pillow like a fucking feast.

I tried not to stare.

Too much.

But I was a man.

And when a beautiful woman was just lying there, mere feet from you, it was hard not to take notice, to take inventory of all the tiny things you couldn't do when they were awake.

Like the tiny freckles on her knee. The scar near her right ankle. Rollerblading. We hadn't been friends then, but

I remembered her limping home and giving me a dirty look while I washed her dad's car.

He'd often done that. If the lawn had been done, he'd given me other jobs. Paying jobs. As if he knew I needed more purpose outside of school.

And maybe more purpose outside of his daughter, my ex-friend.

"SP…" I kicked her bed. "…time to get up."

She moaned and then shot me a death glare. "Did you just kick my bed?"

I smiled and kicked it again. "Think of me as your personal alarm clock, slightly less annoying and better looking."

"We sure about the less-annoying part?" Her voice was heavy with sleep. She moved to a sitting position and hugged her knees to her chest. "Tell me you have perks as director. Tell me you have an espresso machine or instant coffee. I'll chew beans, Marlo."

"Wow, desperation looks good on you." I ruffled her hair.

Then got slapped.

And realized that even though we were at ceasefire…

Even though I knew she was off limits for now…

I hadn't woken up that happy in a really long time.

She would never trust me if I tried anything.

I wanted her to come to me.

I wanted her to tell me she couldn't take this thing between us.

Most of all, I didn't just want her to bare her heart.

I wanted her fucking soul.

And I refused to settle for the parts she gave others when I knew there were parts she kept for herself. I saw glimpses of it that morning.

And like all good addicts, I needed a bigger hit.

I flipped the switch on my Keurig and grabbed a pod, only to feel her breathing heavily behind me as if she'd just run a race.

"I've been suffering for a week, and you have a Keurig!" she yelled, shoving my back and then jumping onto me like a monkey ready to kill its own young.

"The hell, Ray!" I tried peeling her off, but she looked minutes away from tearing a piece of skin from my ear. "Do you always wake up like this?"

"Coffee." Her right eye twitched.

Smirking, I held her body with my left arm and then grabbed the pod with my right hand and shoved it in the Keurig and pressed the blue button. "Almost ready. You're welcome, princes. How else can I serve you this morning?"

Her breath hitched.

I zeroed in on her mouth.

It was as if she just now realized that she was wrapped around me, her ankles hooked, her body flush against mine.

"Y-you're strong" was what came out of her mouth.

I leaned in and whispered, "It's the HGH."

"I knew it!" She slapped me on the chest.

I laughed and sat her down on her feet then handed her a black coffee. "I'm kidding. I like weights, and I eat a lot of beef jerky."

"Beef jerky doesn't do that." She motioned at me with her hand and then sipped the steaming drink slowly. A smile spread across her face. "That's all I need in life."

I peeled my shirt over my head and went in search of a new one. I felt her eyes on me like a laser beam.

I grabbed my shower caddy and instantly felt guilt.

I was pretty sure I'd just reminded her of the elephant. Of the sex.

Of us together.

Of how good it had felt.

Shit! I was going to die for wanting to be inside her again.

It consumed me.

Holding her.

Kissing her.

I braced my hand against the wall and took a deep breath then grabbed a nearby towel. "See ya at breakfast."

That was what I ended with.

And when I finally made it into the bathroom and pulled the curtain, I was so hard I could probably re-hammer every nail in that sad cabin with my dick and have more strength to spare.

I gripped myself just as I heard Jackson's loud shout. "My head. I'm dying. Ray, stop yelling, damn it!"

The doors opened.

I was still gripping myself.

And then a shower started.

Ray laughed.

I looked down at the bottom of the curtain.

I saw her walk by and heard the shower behind me turn on.

"Marlo?" she called.

"Yup." God, I was going to burn in Hell, wasn't I?

"Can I borrow soap?"

"Doesn't she have soap?" Jackson called.

"No!" I yelled, not wanting him to know why she didn't have her caddy and why she needed my soap and not his.

I leaned down and grabbed some body soap and then

poked my head outside the shower just as Jackson yelled. "Fuck this. It's making my headache worse. I'm out. See you guys at breakfast. I need grease."

The door slammed.

Just us.

The temptation to step inside...

To repeat yesterday morning...

Was so strong that my dick pulsed.

I'd had no idea what torture was.

No clue.

Until that moment.

I was ready to scratch my fingernails down the tile, to rip it to shreds with my teeth.

"Ray?" I waved the body wash midair between us, using the shower curtain to cover my raging hard-on.

She pulled the curtain back, water dripping down her face as she gripped the bottle. Our fingers grazed. "Thank you."

I nodded.

She let out a sigh.

And I jerked the curtain back so hard it almost came off the rod.

And then I imagined her rubbing the creamy body wash all over herself.

I imagined my hands doing it for her.

I sucked in a breath when I heard her moan.

Was she?

No.

It was my very vivid imagination, wasn't it?

"Hey, Marlo?" Her voice made it worse.

My breathing was strained. "Yeah, Ray?"

"Do you really think I have nice boobs?"

Really? Now? I gripped myself, pumped once, twice. "Yeah, Ray… I do."

"I'm touching them," she whispered.

Fu-u-u-ck. "Are you trying to kill me?"

"It seems fair." Her voice sounded amused. "It may even go toward making us even…"

"Ray…" I said in warning.

"I'm squeezing them between my hands… My nipples feel really hard."

I slammed one palm against the tile, the other pumping harder. "Yeah?"

"Mmm…" She moaned. "…my hands moved."

Where? Where the hell did they move?

"You still there, Marlo?"

"Yes." I bit back another curse as my dick throbbed in my hand.

"I'm touching where you kissed me. I'm trying to decide why your tongue felt so much better…"

I turned my shower to cold and cursed. "Ray… seriously… this isn't funny."

"It isn't funny," she agreed. "It's revenge."

I cursed under my breath.

"You can't touch yourself while I'm touching myself," she said in a sweet voice. "It's cheating, Marlo."

"Is it though?" I wondered out loud with a humorless laugh.

"Show me your hands, Marlo."

"You've got to be shitting me," I muttered.

"Now."

I held my hands high, so she could see over the tile barrier.

And then she moaned.

Moaned so fucking loud and sweet that my hips pumped air. Shit, she was turning me into an animal.

"Mmm… that feels so-o-o good." She moaned again and again.

I got dizzy with the moans, with the slight breaths and then the scream as something hit the tile wall. A hand? My body wash?

And then the shower was off.

And my curtain was being jerked back.

I didn't have time to cover myself.

And as luck would have it, my hands were still high in the air as if I was getting arrested.

Her eyes lowered, smug satisfaction crossing her face before she held out the body wash.

"Were you really…?" I took the bottle, fully aware that I looked ready to impale anything that got too close.

She shrugged and patted me on the face. *Let's be honest… it was more of a rough slap.* "Guess you'll never know."

I saw nothing but towel and thigh as she gave me her back and left the bathroom, and like an idiot, all it had taken was one sniff of body wash, one slight touch of my hand. Hell, maybe the air conditioning had turned on, and I was so aroused a light breeze did it.

But I spent in the shower as if I was a fucking middle schooler who had just noticed that girls make him feel nice.

"Touché," I muttered with a smile. "Well played, Ray. Well-fucking-played."

Is it a game now?

She'd said revenge.

And since we'd both gotten ours…

I wondered if the pieces had shifted, and if they had, did that mean they were back in my power?

You wanna play, princess?

I'm game.

Chapter
TEN

Ray

Fire burned in my cheeks the entire walk back to the mess hall, and when I sat down next to Jackson and Brax, I earned two throat clears before I finally looked up. "What? You boys getting sick?"

Brax narrowed his eyes then took a bite out of his breakfast burrito, pointing it at me as he finished chewing. "It wasn't sex but something equally as... invigorating."

"Go for a morning swim in the chilly lake?" Jackson grinned, leaning forward.

I just rolled my eyes. "You guys are impossible. I showered. I'm here. The end."

"By yourself." Brax apparently had felt the need to point out.

I threw a hot-sauce packet at him then followed it with two more when he laughed as if it was funny.

I'd only halfway forgiven him.

And Jackson? Well, Jackson was just… a puzzle of angst and arrogance, wasn't he?

"So…" Jackson slid his tray out of the way and clapped his hands on the table. "…I was thinking…"

"Always a dangerous thing when you have one remaining brain cell, but I'm listening." I grinned.

The air behind me shifted just as the smell of lawn and cedar and something else sexy blew by me and then planted in the seat next to me.

"Marlo." Brax grinned at him.

"Brax, look at me like that again, and I'm cutting your dick off."

"Whoa! Someone needs to get laid."

Marlo groaned while Jackson just shrugged and waved him off. "So, you know how you were struggling with letting go…"

The table fell silent.

Fantastic. My favorite subject, me and my inability to be a good choreographer in front of one of the best in the room.

My smile felt forced. "Um, yes."

"Jackson…" Marlo's voice had a warning protective edge to it.

I realized I liked it. I loved it. I loved that even after hearing his labored breathing and knowing he was enjoying the show and feeling tortured that he would jump to protect me, even when I didn't deserve it, when he deserved my attention even less.

After last night.

Something had shifted.

And I liked it.

I really. Liked it.

Too damn much.

Jackson met my eyes. "It's the musical."

"What's the musical?" I deadpanned.

"The reason you can't connect. You don't really know the musical well enough to connect with the character. If I was a guessing man, I'd say you're all logic when it comes to choreography, afraid of the passion, afraid of the emotion, afraid it—"

"That's enough, Jackson."

"What?" Jackson shrugged. "I'm just trying to be helpful."

"Be helpful over there." Marlo nodded to the breakfast bar. "And grab your new best friend a coffee."

"New best friend?" He frowned.

I raised my hand.

He high-fived it and shook his head. "This discussion isn't over."

Marlo eyed Brax.

Brax let out a low whistle, grabbed his tray, and walked off in the general direction of Jackson.

"He gets… inspired." Marlo shook his head at his tray, his expression pensive. "I just didn't want him saying anything that would make you uncomfortable."

I crossed my arms. "And how would you know what he was about to say?"

His smile was sad. "Because I sense it in every breath you take."

"Excuse me?"

"Jackson was going to say, 'afraid of the emotion, afraid it will never be the same again — once you let go.'"

"Oh, really?" I was skeptical.

With an arrogant flip of my hand, I motioned Jackson back over.

He sat and exhaled. "All right, so what I was so clearly trying to explain before he got all protective and weird, is that you're afraid you won't be the same again, like the emotional toll won't just tax you but change you. You're afraid you won't be you again."

Marlo stood, put his hand on my shoulder, and smiled. "And I rest my case."

"What?" Jackson frowned. "What case? What did you say to her?"

Tremors raced through my body and became full shakes as I stared straight ahead, my posture perfect, eyes unblinking.

"Don't be a robot, Ray. Even robots learn to feel. It's science." Jackson kissed the top of my head and ran off leaving me more determined to own the choreography, to teach the crap out of it.

To gain the trust of my students.

To be the best.

I grabbed my breakfast burrito, shoved it into my mouth, and dropped my tray off, then walked with purposeful steps out of the mess hall.

"Walk hard, SP, walk hard." Marlo winked at me as I passed.

And my stomach fell. My heart skipped.

And I knew.

There was so much danger in letting myself feel.

In letting go.

Yes, I would be changed.

Altered.

And the parts I had saved just for me, the parts of my heart I'd had to protect growing up in a family where love was just a topic never an action — they would fall at his feet.

And then what?

He'd make a choice.

And when in my life had anyone ever chosen me?

Chapter ELEVEN

Marlon

I checked in on every class. Brax's class was easily doing the best; the brains behind the scriptwriting were already pouring over all the lines along with the music. The set crew was excited about the way they could frame in the dance scenes with a lot of people while still using part of the audience as the actual audience during some of the dances to give it an inclusive effect.

The first two weeks were always chaos at camp.

We had to decide what musical the campers would do since the counselors had to join them on the final production, organize within our different classes, and then we had auditions.

Saturday.

Followed by a party on the beach where we had races across the lake to our nemesis, hip-hop camp.

They thought we were rich kids with nothing better to do.

And most of them hadn't even studied dance — let alone hip hop — long enough to know anything beyond how to crump. It was filled with white kids who wanted to dance without having to put their hands over their head and clap.

And instructors who probably hated their lives trying to teach high schoolers with no rhythm how to magically find it in two months.

I shook my head at my clipboard and eyed her name.

Ray.

May as well say, "Laser beam. Use extreme caution."

I tapped my pencil against the board and then slowly walked toward the dance studio. The music was blaring as it was most days. The windows were pulled open, the curtains waving in the breeze.

She wasn't dancing.

Her class had been dismissed for at least two hours.

She was lying on her back staring up at the ceiling, balancing a pencil on her forehead.

I frowned and made my way into the studio then knocked on the door. "Solving world hunger?"

"World peace, actually," she said in a dry tone without moving.

I dropped my clipboard onto the nearest chair and joined her on the floor. I laid my hands at my sides and stared up at the boring white ceiling as the smell of cedar and campfire filtered into the room.

It was a mixture of outdoors.

Of life.

Adventure.

I inhaled and closed my eyes.

"How do you do that?" she asked in a small voice.

"What?" I turned my head.

Her shoulders were hunched by her ears, her face tense. "Just… exhale and exist. How do you relax, shut your brain off?"

"Turn your other organs on?" I offered with a smug smile.

"Very funny."

I smirked and moved my hand and lightly tapped two fingers across her chest. "I meant this…" *Tap, tap.* My fingers grazed her collarbone then lowered. Her skin felt like velvet, and even through her flimsy staff shirt, I felt her heat. I felt her heartbeat, and I wanted. "…your heart. Get your head out of the gutter, SP."

"Fine." She squeezed her eyes shut as the music started again the song from the *Phantom of the Opera* soundtrack.

"Good choice." I cleared my throat as the driving, throbbing beat of the main title took on its own presence in the room. "One of my favorites."

"I saw it three times," she confessed. "Twice in London, once in New York."

"Must have been nice," I said as politely as I could. I'd seen it once, and I'd sat in the balcony and been so stunned that my jaw had come unhinged two minutes in.

She had probably been in a box seat.

Or backstage shaking hands with the actors and actresses.

"The first time," she began, "was so I wouldn't be angry with my parents for missing my high school graduation."

A thousand knives dug into my chest. Rage poured over me as I clenched my teeth. "Well, that's bullshit."

"They forgot."

"Your graduation?"

"It was my fault. I didn't sync my calendar with theirs."

I bit my tongue to keep from calling them names that were very deserving.

"The second time was a date, college. I was so excited. It was our third date, and he was… charming. Another theater major. He left halfway through because he was personally offended over their casting choice."

I snorted out a laugh. "Yeah, sounds like an actor."

She turned and smiled at me.

"And the third time?"

Her face paled. She jerked her gaze back to the ceiling. "He was powerful…"

"And?"

"…and…" She let out a long painful sight that made me want to pull her into my arms and kiss her lips, whisper against her mouth that I'd protect her, that I'd been wrong, that I'd do anything to take back the hurt I felt from her whenever she was near.

The music built toward a crescendo as the artists sang of dreams and the power exerted over a person.

"He wasn't a good man."

Man. She'd said man.

I stored that away for later as the music shifted yet again into "Music of the Night." I grinned. "Close your eyes."

"Why?"

"You know, we could probably be better friends if you didn't question everything I asked you to do."

"You know, Marlo, we could probably be better friends if you didn't get me naked in order to satisfy a revenge plot you've had against me since high school."

My eyebrows shot up. "Not since high school. Don't flatter yourself."

An elbow came down on my stomach. Hard.

"Fuck!" I heaved out a painful breath then grabbed the elbow and the person it belonged to and pulled her to my side, locking her next to me, pinning her arms at her sides. "It wasn't revenge until I saw you. Until I saw…" I stared down at her mouth. "Ray, it's never really been about revenge."

"Could have fooled me." She wiggled in my arms and glared.

"It's been a lot of things." I leaned in until my lips were inches from her neck. "It's been war. It's been chaos. But it started with want. Revenge doesn't just happen. You have to lose something first, something so pivotal in your life that the only way you think you can ever truly exist is if you get it back in any way possible."

She stopped struggling and relaxed against me. I kissed her bare shoulder. "And what did you so desperately need back?"

"Other than my pride?" I joked.

She wiggled again.

I pulled my hands away. "It's not so hard to figure out."

She sucked in a breath, drew it between her lips as she zeroed in on my mouth. "Other than your pride?"

"Come on." I held out my hand and stood. "And remember, close your eyes."

"So, that's it?"

"Until you figure it out, absolutely. Now let me help you."

"No."

"Yes."

"I don't like your kind of help." She crossed her arms. At least her eyes were still closed as she stood there. Even her damn body swayed toward me as if it didn't want to believe the words coming out of her mouth.

With a sigh, I gripped her hand and squeezed her fingers. "Listen to the 'Music of the Night…'"

Chapter

TWELVE

Ray

I gulped as he squeezed my hand harder. I tried to focus on the song, but all I felt was him, his massive presence, his cologne, the faint smell of outside on his body as if he'd been rolling around in pinecones, and it smelled so masculine I wanted to lean in.

I cleared my throat.

Once.

Twice.

"Focus!" he snapped.

I let out a sigh as the music shifted. My heart wanted to soar with it, but it was like my soul, my emotions were trapped inside my body, fighting for release. But my soul needed a map.

Directions.

A bridge.

Anything.

"How do you feel about crickets?" Marlo asked.

"Random much?" I opened my eyes.

He pulled me to my feet, grabbed the iPad, and nodded to the door. "Fieldtrip time."

I hesitated.

He ran a hand through his hair and exhaled as if *I* was the difficult one. "This is about you finding something inside and releasing it. This isn't about our past, revenge shit, or anything. When was the last time anyone ever truly did something for you?"

Tears filled my eyes.

I wanted to snap at him.

To say *"All the time."*

To snort and cross my arms because I had everything, right?

Wrong.

I had a nice car.

I had a bedroom back home.

A credit card with no limit.

But I was empty.

My soul was sad.

And it was the most depressing thought, the fact that my soul — what made me... *me* — felt trapped behind plastic things and money.

In order to survive, the soul needed to breathe.

And I'd been suffocating all my life.

Marlo pushed open the door, and it felt bigger than that. Bigger than just a door I had to walk through. Bigger than him helping me with my class.

Maybe because I knew the minute I walked over that threshold out into nature, I was giving a piece of myself to him.

And I didn't exactly have a load of pieces to hand out.

If I wasn't careful, he would take them all.

And I didn't trust him.

Not anymore.

I wanted to.

Maybe it wasn't just him.

Maybe it was just humans in general.

"It's just a door, Ray." he said softly, his eyes sparkling a bit as if he was excited about what was coming next, when all I really wanted to do was lash out at him. I was officially defaulting to what I'd done in high school when he made me sad. When I'd thought about our friendship and how it had all gone sideways.

But that was the thing about regret — it was so much easier to blame every single thing around you than to admit that maybe you'd had a part in the decision-making too. Maybe the other person wasn't the problem.

Maybe it was you.

With a golf ball stuck in my throat and lead in my legs, I followed him out of the studio and down the stairs, each step harder than the next.

I didn't speak.

I didn't trust myself not to say something stupid, or worse, cry.

We walked until we were at his cabin.

I gulped as he took the steps two at a time, and then opened yet another door I would have to walk through.

That made two doors.

Two instances when I had to blindly trust the same guy who knew what I looked like naked and what moans I made when I orgasmed.

All this before finding out I was nothing more than... nothing.

I shook my head.

Nothing.

I am nothing.

Legs even heavier, I walked up the stairs and quickly sat on the bed where I'd slept the night before. It felt scarier in the light.

The darkness had a way of covering things you didn't want seen.

But the light? It demanded you see it all.

"Watch," it said.

Marlo placed the iPad on the bed; he didn't speak, just moved around the room as if he was looking for something. He rummaged through a bag like a squirrel hellbent on finding the last nut before winter, and then he thrust something black into the air.

"A tie?" I asked in confusion.

"A tie." He winked.

My stomach dipped.

My heart thudded.

This guy.

This guy was not safe.

I needed safe.

Someone who wasn't so good-looking it stole my breath away.

Someone who wasn't so talented I just wanted to bask in

his shadow.

"Stand." He snapped his fingers.

I crossed my arms.

He just rolled his eyes and brushed more of that perfect hair away from his chiseled face. "I have to go meet up with Brax about auditions in a half hour, so we have a half hour to practice."

"To practice…" I nodded to the tie. "…how to properly tie your tie without hanging yourself?"

He crooked his finger.

I sighed and moved toward him only to have him grab my elbow, turn me around, and start tying the stupid thing around my head, completely covering my eyes.

"Hey—!" I grabbed the tie in an effort to pull it down.

"Nope." He swatted my hand and tied it so tight I lunged backward. "This is going to help. I promise."

"It's the same thing as closing my eyes, genius!"

"No, it's not."

Wait, did he move? I rotated in a small circle and put my hand out, effectively colliding with at least one eighth of the pack banded around his midsection. My heart sped up as I swallowed against a very dry throat.

"This is sensory deprivation. It awakens the senses. When you take one away, the others have to step in, right?"

I swallowed. "Right."

"And when you choose to close your eyes, you can choose to cheat and open them."

"You calling me a cheater, Marlo?"

"If the shoe fits, SP." He'd moved behind me.

I grinned despite the fact that I wanted to clobber him with the closest shoe I could find.

"Now..." He was distant again, the music started up. "...*Phantom of the Opera* is all about the senses. He covers his face so that she can't see him, but she never falls in love with his face..." He moved behind me. "What did Christine fall in love with?"

I gulped. "His voice."

"His voice," he agreed. "His magnetism, the way he moved, the way he sang, the way he wrote. She fell for his soul."

I sucked in a breath and waited as the music played on, the rise and fall of the lyrics, the captivating sway of the rhythm taking on its own life, gripping me in its spell, creating a subtle longing to let my guard down.

"He's obsessed with her," Marlo murmured. "He wants her, but he wants every part of her, not just her beauty, but her soul. He wants her to follow him to the depths of Hell and never look back. No regrets. Complete submission."

I shook my head. "I don't understand. I mean, I do understand. I just... I don't understand how a person can do that to someone else without losing everything."

"You lose in order to gain," Marlo said in a soft voice. "Trust me, I've never had it all. I never had anything to lose but my pride, and it's in those moments where I've been emotionally and physically bankrupt that I've found myself. Your problem, Ray..."

The way my name fell from his lips brought tears to my eyes. He hadn't said it like a curse. No, it was worse. He'd said it like a prayer.

"...is that you've never lost everything."

"You don't know me!" I lashed out, ready to punch him in the face. "I've lost more than you could possibly—"

He cupped a hand over my mouth. "Good. You've lost. Now use that loss as a way to live. A loss imprisons you, or it sets you free. Your choice."

He moved his hand.

The music was halfway finished.

I knew the scene. The moment when they were walking around the Phantom's underground cave, the candles lit, the Phantom dying to touch her as his addicting song fell from his lips. As she yearned to live in his voice forever.

Marlo placed his hands on my waist and started to sing the Phantom's part. "'Softly, deftly…'"

I leaned back against him.

I don't know how long I stayed there.

Long enough that the song started again.

"'Nighttime…'" he began, singing about sharpening sensation and darkness stirring in the mind and waking up every single part of the soul.

And Marlo sang.

He sang better than the guy on the soundtrack.

The orchestra was beautiful.

Marlo was more so.

And then his voice was at my ear. He lifted my right arm and wrapped it back around his neck as he sang against my skin.

Stillness settled my nerves, and I drank in every word as if it was meant for me.

I wished for once it was.

That it wasn't just sexual attraction,

Revenge sex.

That it was more.

Us in this moment.

I bit down on my lip as he talked about surrender and my dark dreams.

And when he asked me to purge my thoughts of my life. I did it.

I squeezed my eyes shut.

And I gave myself away.

I turned in his arms and clung to him, keeping him there, scared to ask for more. It was like his voice was caressing me, making love to me. His hands were barely touching me, and I felt so alive from the words that I was almost panting.

The music ended too soon.

The blindfold was pulled off and tossed onto the bed. "I have to go check in with Brax," he said, taking a step back. "You can keep practicing."

"Without you?" I asked in a hoarse voice.

His lips twitched. "I figured that it would be best for you to do this alone, since the last time you trusted me, I had my mouth between your thighs."

My entire body seized while my heart slammed against my chest. Heat filled my body until I felt like I was going to sway onto the bed in a sweaty puddle of need. "Right."

"Right." He nodded slowly, his eyes hooded as he raked his gaze over my body as if he had a right to, and then he was gone.

My heart raced inside my ribs.

"Ugh, stupid." I threw a pillow against the wall, grabbed the offending tie, and turned up the music.

Chapter
THIRTEEN

Marlon

I'd had to leave.

If I hadn't left, well...I was having very vivid fantasies of tying her hands up and then wrapping that same tie around the bedposts.

Her body had responded well; her mind kept her trapped.

But those few moments when she'd let herself go, she was so fucking beautiful I wanted to keep them forever, so I could watch them over and over again on repeat.

My head and my heart were at war.

My head said she was going to screw me over again.

My heart said that nobody had ever once been on her side.

I wiped my hands down my face and made my way back over to Brax.

He was alone in the studio with a shit-ton of papers strewn before him and an irritated look on his face.

"Problem?" I pulled out a chair.

"Not really." He yawned. "Script is already done. Obviously."

"So?"

"So, the creative-writing scripts for the audition are shit."

"How bad?"

He let out a snort and shoved a paper toward me. I read about halfway down. It wasn't bad. It wasn't good either.

"So…" I cleared my throat. "…we have them act out a scene from the musical."

"The point…" Brax leaned forward. "…is to make them uncomfortable with something original so we can see what we're working with. We need them to write their own monologue. It's tradition. And it makes them vulnerable. We need to see the raw vulnerability, or we're going to be like every single *Dirty Dancing* musical out there with Baby and her little tank tops and Johnny with his angst."

I barked out a laugh. "You sound thrilled with this year's choice."

He shrugged. "They'll get there. We just need a few more days, and auditions are Saturday."

I checked my watch and stood. "Well, I'll help you edit."

"No shit?" He looked ready to kiss me. "I was going to be in here all night!"

"Yeah, looks like it." I started collecting papers. "Let's at least get them all started off on the right foot, offer positive criticism." Should only take another six hours.

Well, one thing was for certain.

I was officially missing a staff bonfire for the first time.

My mind flashed to Ray.

It was probably a good thing.

Because I wasn't sure how much longer I could be next to her and not touch.

And the last time I'd acted on instinct…

I'd broken her.

Chapter
FOURTEEN

Ray

I couldn't sleep.

I hadn't seen Marlo the rest of the day.

And I was worried.

About bears mainly.

Bears mauling me in his cabin.

Someone finding out that I'd snuck back into said cabin.

Cougars.

The bears again.

Where the hell is he?

I checked the alarm clock. Two a.m. He was director. The job had a lot of responsibility. It was not as if he was still at the staff bonfire, right? Plus, Jackson had made it sound like Marlo was arms-deep in camp work.

So why help me today?

I chewed my lower lip.

Part of me felt guilty that he was even spending time helping me while the other, more rational part felt like he owed me after everything.

Except, he'd been trying.

He'd been… nice.

More than nice.

He'd smiled.

I pulled the pillow over my face and screamed then tossed it behind my head and let out a huff.

It had to have been ten minutes.

But the red digits on the clock stated the obvious — less than one minute had passed, and I was still obsessing. And to make matters worse, the entire cabin smelled like him.

The thought of going back to my cabin made my skin itch and my chest feel hollow. No. Even if he hated me and told me he was going to put peanut butter on my face and leave the cabin door open, I was staying.

Because I was afraid.

And the more he tried to help me unlock everything that was safely tucked inside my head…

The more fearful I became of everything around me.

As if I wasn't aware until now of how dangerous the world was, how scary. And how much the world wanted to devour every last vulnerable inch of me.

I snuck another glance at the clock.

Two minutes. Really? How was that possible!

I glanced over at his bed.

He had a really nice down comforter.

It was white.

What guy had a white down comforter? Dirty boys and white comforters did not mix.

Not that he was dirty.

I gulped.

Well, kind of dirty. I mean, his mouth…

"Stop it," I hissed at myself.

His sheets looked nice too.

In fact, his entire bed looked inviting.

I am officially hallucinating, aren't I?

With a shrug, I tossed off the covers and padded over to his side, looked left and right as if I was about to commit a crime, then tucked myself right into his bed.

I was Goldilocks.

He was my bear.

And he was going to have to burn down the cabin to get me to move. Bastard had a feather mattress! No wonder it looked so inviting. I shimmied myself into a comfortable position. The sheets were a high thread-count.

I let out a breathy moan and turned to face the wall. I fell asleep so fast that the last thing I remembered was the smell of fresh grass.

"Comfortable?" A male voice rumbled behind me.

My eyes jerked open.

I didn't turn.

I was frozen in place. "Y-yes."

"Something wrong with your bed? The one I so generously loaned you?" I could feel him hovering over mine, casting a shadow from the moonlight; even my body buzzed with awareness.

"You mean after giving me the scary *Parent Trap* cabin?"

He cleared his throat. "Ray..."

If that wasn't a warning. Shoot. "You have a feather mattress."

"I can't like nice things?"

"And your pillows..." I gulped and inwardly rolled my eyes. "...are, um... fluffy?"

"Fluffy?" he repeated.

I couldn't tell by his tone if he was pissed or just exhausted.

"Right." He didn't say anything else.

I was just about to get up and apologize profusely because I couldn't take the static-sounding silence.

But when I turned to speak the words...

I almost swallowed my tongue.

People needed their tongues!

He was in black boxer briefs.

He was also only inches from my face.

Not really his body.

His... just... package.

I was afraid to move.

Sudden movements cause things to go away, right?

Is that how it worked?

He licked his lips. "Scoot over."

"Huh?"

"If you're going to steal my bed, then I'm going to steal it back. Sleep here, sleep on the floor— Hey, here's a thought. Sleep outside with the bears or go back to your own cabin..."

"Did you say sleep here?" I asked in a weak voice.

He let out a long sigh, and that was when I noticed the dark circles under his eyes, the exhaustion in his tone. "Yes. Just. Sleep."

I was not sure why I did it. And even as I moved toward him, I knew I'd regret it, but I couldn't help myself.

I ran my hands down his face and then moved to his shoulders. I dug in massaging down his arms as he leaned toward me, and then a little snore escaped his lips.

I smiled at that. I loved it more than a girl who had nobody should, because it made me want more.

It gave me hope I could have it.

I helped him lie down, and I pulled the covers over his body, and when I turned on my side back toward the wall, Marlo pulled me against him as if it was normal.

He claimed me as small spoon.

And a tiny tear of happiness found its way down my cheek.

Chapter
FIFTEEN

Marlon

A gentleman wouldn't notice how tight her ass felt against his cock; he also wouldn't be thinking of the elderly naked in order to get rid of every straining inch of himself, but there it was.

Her hair fell in a curtain over her face. One ear peeked out, and that one ear held my attention for longer than it should. I noticed its curve. I noticed the smooth neck connected to that curvy ear.

And I wanted to lick my way down so desperately that I was frozen in place, afraid to move. Afraid that the alarm clock would go off too soon.

I wanted to keep her there forever.

Because I'd never gotten the chance to.

Guys weren't supposed to have dreams of waking up with girls, and for the most part, I never had.

I sent them packing. Every time.

But with Ray, it had been different. We'd smelled like sweat, like each other, like horny teenagers with way too much alcohol pumping through their veins.

And it had been perfect.

For an hour.

For one hour, the foster kid from the wrong side of the tracks, the unwanted hired help, had held the princess in his arms.

I sighed and pinched my nose as I recalled all of the memories that I hated thinking about.

The stiffening of her body.

The way she gasped as if she had no recollection of what had transpired between us. She tugged the sheet and covered her breasts, the ones my mouth had just been all over.

And then the horrified look in her face.

The look a princess gave a monster when she woke up from her deep sleep only to find her prince missing and someone like me in his place.

Rejection stung.

Rejection from the one girl who I'd waited for...

Was excruciating.

"Marlo." Tears filled her eyes. "The party's over... You could probably go home now."

I heard the real meaning.

Leave.

My throat felt swollen as rejection and hatred fused their hands together, twisting my insides, stabbing my chest repeatedly until it felt as if I would bleed out. "Right."

"I mean…" She offered a sweet smile while I snorted, turned around, and started to dress. "…it was fun."

"Fun," I repeated in a weak voice. "Yeah, a blast. I owe you one."

"Marlo, stop. It's not…"

"Not what? Like that?"

"No, I just mean… we don't want to get caught." Her face softened.

But I also caught the lie; it was evident in her eyes, in the way they darted from left to right before finally settling back onto me. And then she smiled.

So, I trusted the lie.

I trusted the smile.

And I smiled back and kissed her cheek. "I'll see you at school."

"Yeah, sure." She grinned wide.

And I walked out of her house a man.

Or so I thought…

My alarm clock chose that awesome moment to spring to life, making me nearly fall out of my bed.

And the sick part of the whole situation…

I was petrified that she'd give me that same look.

And because I'd let her in…

Because I had no choice…

I knew it would hurt.

God, it would hurt so fucking bad.

I waited for her to say something.

The alarm kept ringing.

I frowned to my right.

"Marlo…" Her voice was deep with sleep. "…if you don't turn that damn thing off, I'm going to choke you to death, not in a sexy way, in a you-will-not-survive sort of way."

A smile spread across my face. "Morning, SP. Anything else I can get you? Coffee? A massage? Bacon?"

Her head jolted up, matted blonde hair covering part of her face. "Are you just being a jackass, or do you really have bacon hidden somewhere in here?"

"Why don't you just sniff it out." I winked.

A pillow came crashing down on me before I could get out of the way.

"Hey!" I grabbed it from her hands, or at least tried to, but she was feisty in the morning. She slammed the pillow onto me three more times and then straddled me and jerked the one out from under my head. She clearly used the element of shock and awe against me and looked ready to smother me.

"Truce." I held up my hands. "I'll grab you coffee."

"Promise?" She held the pillows high.

"Pinky promise." I held up my hand.

Her eyes flickered to my pinky, and then she hooked hers around mine. I used that as an opportunity to jerk her against my chest. Because I couldn't face the rest of the day without knowing what it would feel like to have her on top of me, legs on either side of my body, chest to chest, face to face. Matted hair and all.

"I like you in the mornings," I whispered softly, cupping her face with my free hand.

She gulped. "Because I yell at you?"

"That…" I nodded. "…and because you haven't had time to put your guard up. It's when you're most free."

She quickly looked away and moved off me.

And I let her.

Shit. Another moment ruined.

The room fell silent.

Good job, Marlo. Well done!

"Hey, Marlo?" Her back was turned to me; she was fidgeting with the Keurig as if she didn't know where the power button was.

With a sigh, I walked over to it, grabbed a pod, and started making her coffee. A week ago, I would have called her spoiled; today, I just wanted her to smile at me again. Hell, I'd even take the pillow pummeling.

As long as I survived it.

And I'd survived it all when it came to her.

"Yeah?" The coffee was brewing. I crossed my arms around my bare chest and waited.

Her tongue darted out, licking her lips.

I tried to focus on what words would be coming out from them, but all I wanted to do was capture them between mine and make promises I had no business making against them.

"How do you do it without being afraid?"

"Drink coffee?" I joked.

She scowled. "How do you let go?"

So many things to say.

Admit.

Confess.

"We all have our shit, princess." I shrugged. "I let some of mine go because if I hold onto it, it just destroys me, destroys my creative process, but that doesn't mean I'm perfect obviously."

She smiled at that. "You let go because it hurts you more when you hold on to it than it does the person that you want to punish. And that's the truth."

She sucked in a breath, her eyes filling with tears. "What if I want people I should love to suffer?"

I let out a sigh and tilted her chin toward me. "Punish them with the music." I pulled her in for a hug. "And raise hell."

"That's just another way of saying to let it go, be vulnerable, give everything, jump without a parachute."

I released her and handed her the hot cup of coffee. "You know you never jump by yourself the first time."

She frowned. "What?"

"You jump with an instructor." I shrugged. "I'm just saying... nobody ever said you had to do this alone."

"But—" She shook her head. "—I'm on staff."

"Yup."

"And everyone has their jobs."

"Absolutely."

"And—"

"Ask me what I did last night."

She took a sip of coffee, her eyes narrowing. "Went for another stupid run where you got birds to wave at your eight-pack and squirrels to chant your name?"

I leaned in. "Close." I grabbed the cup from her hands, took a sip, and handed it back. "I helped edit all of the auditions with Brax. My point being... you don't do this alone. And as much as I hate to even say this out loud, if you need someone to help you who isn't me, ask them. We're a team here."

I couldn't look at her anymore.

Because I wanted it to be me.

I wanted her to ask me to wait while she jumped in my arms.

I would take anything I could get. I needed to make it up to her. To take a chance on something that she had no clue of scared the ever-loving hell out of me.

"So, you think Jackson would be good then?" she called behind me.

I gripped my shower caddy so hard I was surprised it didn't just crumble into dust between my fingertips. Every muscle tensed. I didn't turn around. "Yeah, he's... a triple threat. He'd be great..."

No, he'll be trying to get her naked within minutes, and he'll take advantage of that fucking beautiful face she gets when she feels her body relax into the music. He'll see her beauty in a way that was otherworldly, and I'll have to hit him over the head with a shovel and toss his body into the lake.

"...just... great."

"Hmm, all right."

Was that it?

I gritted my teeth and took another step when something hit me in the back of my head and fell to the floor. I turned.

"You forgot your towel. Distracted?" She took another slurp of coffee then winked at me over it. "And why would I ask Jackson when I have the best choreographer at camp in my cabin?"

I jerked my towel off the floor and pointed at her. "My cabin."

"I'm taking over."

"You have one side, just stay on it." A smile tugged at my lips.

She sat down on my bed and stretched an arm over her head. "You sure you want that?"

"I can guarantee that if you don't stop testing me, you're going to be naked on your back in my bed, and then where will that leave us?"

"Where... indeed?" she repeated.

Our eyes locked.

The tension went from zero to five hundred.

The shower caddy slipped from my fingers and landed on floor with a thud. Her eyes raked over my body as if she wanted breakfast early, and I was the bacon.

In two steps, I was taking her coffee from her unresisting grip and setting it on the nearby table.

And then she was wrapping her legs around my waist as I leaned in. Our foreheads touched. Her scent wrapped around me, her warmth drawing me in.

And naturally, a knock sounded at my screen door.

"Interrupting?" Brax's annoying voice had very much interrupted whatever had been about to happen.

Ray's chest rose and fell, her nipples hard beneath her white tank top. Never mind Jackson. I was throwing Brax in the lake and praying that a released pet piranha who had a taste for human flesh found him immediately.

"What..." I said through clenched teeth. "...is it?"

"Figured you'd want to announce auditions, and I just got back from HQ. We have all the signups..." He grinned at us. "So, you guys—"

I stomped over to him, grabbed the stack of papers from his hand, then my shower caddy and my towel, and let the door slam behind me.

With hurried footsteps on gravel, he quickly caught up

to me. "Did you guys…?"

"No," I barked then squeezed my eyes shut. "Maybe. I don't know."

"It looked like she was ready to suck your face off."

"Romantic," I said dryly. "Go be anywhere but here."

"Why?"

"Because I want to tie you to the shower, fill every drain with cement, and leave you there to see if you'd drown!"

"Well, that's weird. Why not just throw me in the lake and tie cement around my feet? Way more effective, bro."

"Go!" I roared.

He held up his hands. "Interesting first two weeks, huh? Just try not to get caught in the shower again with your dick in your hand and no place to stick it!"

My eyes widened. "Who told you?"

"Jackson, after he told everyone else. Is it true? Did she really get you all hot and bothered then leave you high and dry? Revenge for revenge, tit for tat — I like it."

"It was like I took Viagra and needed to call 911. You should be more concerned for my sexual health."

He shook his head. "No, bro. You need to be concerned. That ain't right."

"Yeah, well…" I jerked the bathroom door open. "… neither is fucking her and having my friends talk about my revenge sex plot."

"Touché." He squinted. "I'll just leave you to it then. Don't think of me when you're in there. I want no part in your sexual fantasies!"

"You wish." I rolled my eyes.

"Don't make it weird!" he called just as the door slammed behind me.

And because I knew suffering so fucking well, I walked into the shower I'd shared with Ray, and I let myself relive every single moment. As the water slid down my body, I remembered hers.

And I burned more than I'd ever burned in my life.

Chapter
SIXTEEN

Ray

It felt as if he was avoiding me. Either that, or I was just used to seeing him now, and when I didn't see him, I assumed something was wrong. I was overanalyzing everything.

Ever since two mornings ago.

It was Saturday, and we were still in the same cabin, but he hadn't made another move, and it was slowly killing me.

I understood why.

To an extent.

He was acting like my friend.

Offering advice.

Making me coffee.

Being so damn nice I wanted to slap the coffee out of his hand and ask him if I could touch his eight-pack.

Or bulging arms.

Or bulging anything really.

He'd let me sleep in his bed every night.

Technically, I'd let myself sleep in his bed, and he had begrudgingly put up with it, but he always ended up wrapping his arms around me, pulling me against his body as if I was his own personal teddy bear. And my shorts were thin so I felt him pressed against me. I felt every stupid throbbing inch in the morning.

He was searing hot.

And then cold.

Because he'd pull away, grip his hair so tight I wondered if he was trying to pull it out, then walk over to the Keurig and asked how I slept.

After forty-eight hours, I was ready to wait for him naked in his cabin with a rose between my teeth.

And then the sick part of me wondered if it was a trick. If he was doing this just to sleep with me again, driving me to the brink of sexual insanity, only to see if he could have one more shot and then abandon me in the end.

My trust issues were more than severe. They were paralyzing.

I sucked it up and made my way into the main outdoor theater It seated three hundred and faced away from the lake, giving it the perfect backdrop for *Dirty Dancing*.

It was beautiful.

I was one of the staff judges.

Along with Jackson.

He waved me over and handed me a clipboard. "If they suck, write that they suck. Constructive criticism isn't necessary. They either nail it, or they walk on by. Easy." He handed me a pen and sat.

With an exhale, I plopped down next to him. "How many tryouts for the leads?"

He whistled. "Ten for Johnny, forty for Baby."

"Forty!" I repeated loudly.

He cupped a hand over my mouth. "Don't make them more nervous with the shouting."

"That's a ton of auditions!"

"You're telling me." He reached into the staff bag at his feet and pulled out a silver flask. "It's also why I came prepared."

I rolled my eyes. "You're going to be wasted in minutes."

"I plan on it." He gulped and flashed me a playful grin then completely sobered when Jen made her way over.

Wordlessly, he handed her a clipboard.

She gave me a sad smile, glared at him, and walked off.

"Jackson!" I poked him with my pen. "What the hell did you do?"

"What I always do." He shrugged. "Fucked up. Saw something pretty, told myself it would make me feel better. Same ol', same ol'."

"You slept with Jen?"

"No, I slept with DeeDee. Not that any sleeping was really involved."

I smacked him and then smacked him again. "You asshole! Who the hell is DeeDee? And furthermore, who sleeps with a DeeDee?"

"It's weird how well you know my thoughts because all I kept thinking as I slid in and out was just that. *Why the fuck am I fucking a DeeDee?*"

I hit him again. Because I could.

Another staff member approached. She had pretty cropped black hair and short jean shorts. He handed her a clipboard. She hit him over the head with it and walked off.

"Ah," I nodded in understanding. "Would that be DeeDee?"

"Isn't she a gem?" He rubbed his head.

"Well!" I threw my hands into the air. "What did you expect? That you'd sleep with DeeDee, and she'd thank you for screaming Jen's name while you climaxed!"

His eyes got wide. "Who told?"

I covered my face with my hands. "You didn't. Oh God, tell me you didn't."

"I was… confused?" He frowned.

"Don't make me hit you again. You need to go apologize to Jen. NOW."

"And say what? 'Sorry that I slept with yet another staff member that wasn't you, but hey, bonus points for imagining you while I plundered her cave. We cool?'"

I groaned. "Don't say plunder, or cave, ever… *ever* again."

"It's for the best. Trust me, the last girl I even— Whatever. It doesn't matter. I'm not good for her. She knows it. I know it. The universe with its cruel tricks knows it."

"Why not just be the better guy, be deserving of her?" I wondered aloud as the lights hit the stage.

"Why not just tell Marlo you're scared, and that you've been in love with him since high school?" he countered smoothly.

I froze. My entire body went stiff.

"Uh-huh," he whispered as Marlo made his way onto the stage.

God, he was too masculine and pretty for his own good.

"That's what I thought. Easy to hand out advice. Hard to take it."

"At least…" I ignored the choking sensation around my throat. "…at least try with Jen. Why can't you try?"

"Why can't you?"

"Stop deflecting!" I hissed under my breath, earning a dark chuckle from him as Marlo glared at us from his spot on stage.

I flashed him a smile and straightened.

He didn't smile back.

My resolve crumbled a bit.

My fault.

I'd done something wrong.

And yet, I still wanted to lash out and say *"You started it!"*

But I knew that would accomplish nothing.

Were we always going to be at odds? Enemies or friends?

"Welcome to auditions!" Marlo said in a happy tone that was in no way because of me. "This is how things are going to go. You'll come up, read your own audition to the best of your ability. We'll pick the best candidates and post results in the morning. Immediately following, we have our annual cookout near the water where we attempt to steal the seal from the other side of the lake!"

Cheers erupted.

"Wait, the seal?" I whispered under my breath.

"It's plastic. Chill out," Jackson drank from his flask and hid it back in his bag. "And it's attached to the main mess hall at the camp across the lake. We steal it then bring it back in special decorations. Last year was mafia. We gave it blood, knuckles, and a cigar. The powers that be were not amused with our choice."

I smiled to myself. "And what do you get if you steal it?"

"Duh, honor." He scoffed. "And you get a favor from the camp director."

I froze. "A favor?"

"Not that kind of favor." He barked out a laugh. "I mean, unless you steal it. Then I guess anything goes. But for anyone else, more like *'Hey, can I have a private audition with such and such agent or producer?'* But if that's not important to you, you can always steal the seal and ask Marlo for something more... personal."

My thoughts wandered more than they should have.

And then the first auditionee was walking onto stage.

I had a brief flashback to watching *Pitch Perfect* the first time as she sat cross-legged and started her performance. She was cute, angsty, and had some great lines about high school that made my chest ache. When her music turned on, she danced a contemporary that took my breath away. When she was finished, I was ready to stand and clap.

"She was amazing," I whispered under my breath.

Jackson sighed. "She's also blown half the guys here already. Rumor is, that's how she gets her dancing ability." His face wrinkled in a grimace of distaste. "Meh. Next."

Every audition was better than the last until I sat there slack-jawed like an idiot.

Three hours of entertainment later.

I was side-eyeing Jackson's flask as if it was the last piece of chocolate cake. Marlo made his way back on the stage amidst all the claps.

"All right! And to finish, we have our staff auditions."

I tilted my head at Jackson and mouthed, *"Say what?"*

He just grinned and stared down at his clipboard, letting out a low whistle.

"Nominations were taken at lunch today."

I'd missed lunch. I had been practicing.

Shit. Shit. Shit. Is that why Marlo looked so pissed?

"And…" He gritted his teeth, his eyes landing on me. "It looks like you guys voted for both Ray and myself to show you how it's done."

My eyes widened. *HOW WHAT'S DONE?*

I elbowed Jackson, who was laughing so hard I was ready to strangle him with my bare hands. "What the hell!"

He stood and started clapping. "Woohoo, yeah, Ray! Marlo-o-o!"

People followed suit.

I officially had no friends.

I shoved him out of the way as I nervously walked toward the stage and stared daggers through Marlo.

When I got to his side all I said was "Hate you."

"Ah, feeling's entirely mutual. Believe me," he said through a frozen smile.

"I'm suffocating you in your sleep tonight." I grinned up at him.

He just gave me a bored expression and said. "I dipped your toothbrush in the toilet."

I gasped.

"Twice."

"You have a tiny dick."

"Small tits."

"Skinny legs."

"No ass."

The clapping stopped.

He held up the microphone to his mouth. "You guys voted, and it seems as if the people who weren't in choreography when we showed the original duet felt left out…"

"Get it, MARLON!" Jackson shouted.

I mouthed, *"Dead to me."*

It just made him grin harder.

"That is, unless Ray isn't feeling up to it?" Marlo turned to me.

I was ready to hyperventilate.

And his eyes heated, as if he knew he was better than me, as if he knew that I would bail because I was afraid.

So, I took the microphone from him and said, "Try to keep up."

"Oh-h-h!" The crowd loved it.

Meanwhile, I was having an internal meltdown.

I had major stage fright.

Marlo knew this!

My hands started to sweat, my blood pressure spiked, and I could taste fear on my own tongue, like bitter metal.

And then the lights on the stage darkened just enough to give it a sensual effect as Marlo took the microphone and put it back in the stand then handed me a freaking watermelon.

No-o-o-o.

Music erupted around me, and all of the teens watching jumped to their feet and literally re-created the *Dirty Dancing* scene perfectly, as if they'd been studying the musical since the womb.

Jackson hopped on stage and elbowed me. "That's my cousin Johnny…"

And all I could think of was I carried the watermelon.

I gulped and then watched as Jen jumped on stage and started dancing to Odis Redding with Marlo.

Damn it, they looked surreal.

She was… amazing.

The song faded in order to make it possible for people to hear the dialogue. Everyone clapped and cheered, and that was when I lost every ounce of pride I had, which wasn't mine.

Marlo approached, his hips swiveling. *Why the hell is he channeling Patrick Swayze while I am holding a watermelon?*

The lines flew by on stage and then my "I carried a watermelon" just spilled forth, earning laughter from the crowd while I squeezed my eyes shut in embarrassment, real embarrassment.

Marlo moved back to Jen. They danced down the line of people, and then his eyes were on me again as he crooked his finger, wearing a show-me-your-stuff smirk.

Watermelon gone, I walked over to him and stiffened as he placed his hands on my hips. "Move them this way. All right, that's good…"

I sucked in a breath as he grinned down at me. God, he made me feel as if it was real. I didn't want to leave his arms. I forgot about the arguing, about the constant push and pull, and just let him — for once — lead me without me objecting or crying or yelling.

"Watch me. Watch my eyes," he encouraged. "Good, that's better."

He grabbed me, and I pretended as if I didn't want to curl my body into his and let his hips thrust me wherever the hell they wanted to. He backed up and then slid his leg between mine as we moved back and forth.

I didn't take my eyes away from his.

And I was one-hundred-percent sure he wouldn't have let me.

I allowed him to lead me.

I was helpless against the power of his hips. *Dear God, what is happening to me?*

Hands on my hips, he ground against me.

In front of everyone. The. Entire. Camp.

My eyes widened a fraction as he leaned forward and thrust against me again. I knew it was part of the dance, but still, I felt vulnerable as every hard inch of him pressed against me, heated, hungry. I shuddered as the music ended.

And stumbled a bit as he released me.

Applause.

And I stood there stunned, eyes wide as Jackson released everyone to the cookout by the lake.

Of course, that was the time Marlo walked by with his judgmental eyes and whispered, "D-plus."

I jumped after him.

Jackson caught me by the waist and spun me around. "I was thinking more C-minus, but who am I to judge?"

I gritted my teeth. "I was caught off guard!"

"It should have made you better." He stared me down. "Instead, it made you worse. He'll crack you. He always does."

My heart sank. "So, he does this to all the staff members that suck?"

Jackson burst out laughing. "I was talking about his students. He doesn't… well, since—" He paled. "Let's just say it's been a while since he's been with a staff member here." He looked ready to puke. "Go enjoy the cookout, yeah?"

"Where are you going?"

He grinned. "Refill!"

Right. Refill. The guy was going to drink himself into a

stupor. Part of me wanted to help, but the other part of my heart that needed protecting said if I helped even more, he'd want to help me, and I didn't want help. Not yet. I wanted protection.

And every person I turned to wanted me to jump off the cliff.

As if they weren't completely damaged.

I snorted and walked slowly to the lake and watched as teens jumped into canoes and paddled across.

My eyes narrowed.

A favor.

One favor.

As dumb girls did, I daydreamed about asking Marlo a favor. *"Kiss me, make sweet love to me under the stars."*

My body heated.

One favor.

One seal.

No revenge sex.

This time it would be all on my terms.

I slowly grinned and ran after the last canoe.

I was just pushing it off when Jen jumped in after me. "Oh no, you don't. You need two to paddle."

"I've never paddled a canoe."

"Dip it in the water and pray we go straight." She handed me the oar, and off we went.

Chapter
SEVENTEEN

Marlon

"Jackson, you seen Ray?" I yelled over the bonfire on the beach. His eyes were glassy. Shit, the guy had been spiraling ever since the anniversary of her death. It was always hard on him, this time of year, but he'd never been this bad, drinking during the day, missing teaching some of his voice lessons with the students.

He shook his head no then jumped to his feet. "Shit!"

"What?"

"I think she's going to try to steal the seal." He ran toward me. Well, at least he had coordination under the influence, or maybe he wasn't as drunk as he looked.

"Why the hell would she do that?"

"Because I may have told her about the favor thing…" He gave me a *"whoops"* look. "If she's not in her cabin…"

"She's not in her cabin period," I said, not explaining further. Most her stuff was at mine, so she wouldn't be in her cabin. She loved my coffee too much.

Hell, am I really getting used for my comfortable bed and coffee?

Do I care?

Not really, as long as she is beside me.

Two of the canoes made their way back to camp; another three were visible. Meaning, we were missing one.

"Let's go." I ran toward the canoe while Jackson jumped in. We had enough staff watching things, but still it made me nervous leaving everyone.

"Could you paddle any slower?" Jackson complained.

"Could you be any drunker?" I snapped right back.

He sobered and put his back into it. "I'm fine."

"Yeah, you look fine. You'd probably drown in your own vomit if I left you by the campfire."

He rowed harder. "It's been a shit week. It's always a shit week during these seven days," he said softly.

He didn't meet my eyes. "I know you miss her."

"She was a great human. You remember that. She just had… demons."

"Don't we all," I said without humor.

And then silence enveloped us along with the inky black darkness of the sky, the stars shining over us, and the irritation that Ray had paddled across into enemy territory without saying anything.

It was not like anything could really happen to her. It was just that Jackson had neglected to tell her one specific detail.

The other camp fucking captured prospective thieves and staff members and then asked for something in order to return them.

The last time someone got kidnapped he'd been forced to swim across the lake naked, all the while being subjected to harmless hazing that still left him traumatized every time he heard the word pineapple.

Needless to say, it had been harmless. But I didn't want to take any chances.

Screaming erupted from hip-hop camp.

Jackson gave me a wide-eyed look as we both started paddling in sync as if we were about to lose the Olympic gold.

We reached the beach just as the girls came running toward us, fucking seal in hand and legit pitchforks and torches chasing them — well, not just the objects, but the hands attached to bodies that were screaming and—

Holy shit, do they have war paint on?

Jen and Ray jumped into their canoe and started paddling toward us.

"Reverse!" Jackson roared.

We quickly changed directions and fell into sync with the girls as teens shouted profanities from the beach and some threw their torches onto the sand.

"Holy shit!" Ray yelled from her canoe. "That was intense! They have guard chickens!"

"You're shitting us!" Jackson yelled. "You can't train fucking chickens!"

"YOU CAN'T TRAIN FUCKING CHICKENS!" Jen repeated, flashing her arm.

"Are those peck marks?" Jackson looked ready to puke

and then turned to me. "Dude, you know how I feel about chickens."

"You got chased *once,* as a child!" I scoffed.

"IT WANTED MY SOUL!" he yelled, clearly drunk. "JEN!" More yelling. "YOU LIVED TO TELL YOUR STORY!"

Ray fell into fits of laughter. "Oh, we lived all right. We got the seal, and I got a pet!" She pulled something out of her jacket.

"SATAN!" Jackson screamed, dropping his oar and then scrambling for it and rowing away from them. "Marlo, tell her! Drown the thing or we're sending her back!"

"No!" She held the chicken close. "It's mine now!"

"And so is the seal!" Jen raised it in triumph.

But I was too focused on the way Ray held the possessed chicken as if it was the best thing she'd ever accomplished.

Stolen a pet chicken — guard chicken? — from the enemy camp and paddled it across the lake.

"That's not staying with us." I shook my head. "Not a chance in hell."

"We'll see." She glared at me.

"Us?" Jen asked.

Jackson tilted his head at me.

"Let's get back to camp!" I changed the subject.

And by the time I made it to the campfire, I was wiped.

Teens yelled and cheered with Jen as she lifted the seal into the air, and naturally, that was when Ray managed to hold the chicken out as if it was our annual sacrifice.

Jackson gave the chicken a wide berth. At one point, he made a cross over his chest and then mouthed what appeared to be a prayer.

And I was stuck watching the joy on Ray's face as she truly held her first pet in her hands and showed everyone as if she was in first grade during show and tell.

And I fell more in love with her then.

When she showed people her chicken.

And smiled as if it was the most beautiful pet in the world.

I went to sleep that night with a grin on my face — one that mirrored hers — and a possessed chicken nesting on her bed, while I held her in mine.

Chapter
EIGHTEEN

Ray

Something was touching me.

Or pecking me?

What was that?

I jolted awake and stared straight into the eyes of Johnny. My new chicken.

"Don't. Move," Marlo whispered. "He doesn't like it when we move.

I turned, and the bird just fluttered off the bed then hopped on ours.

"Fuck, he doesn't even blink, Ray. What do we do with a chicken that doesn't blink?"

I cautiously grabbed Marlo's hand. "He's just scared."

"I'm scared!" he hissed. "He won't stop giving me side-eye!"

"He's very protective." I shrugged.

Marlo exhaled.

Johnny didn't like the movement. He hopped onto Marlo's head, making Marlo freak the hell out as he jumped off the bed and shoved Johnny to the floor amid a lot of squawking.

I scrambled after my frazzled pet, picked him up, and put him back on my bed. I tucked blankets around him gently. "There, see?"

Marlo's look was incredulous.

"What?" I yawned and climbed back into bed. "Go to sleep."

"And have Johnny kill me? No thanks."

"He's not a killer. He's a guard." I rolled my eyes. "And he's just a chicken."

"Chicken that knows things..." Marlo slowly crawled in next to me, Johnny didn't move as he scooted so close I was almost plastered against the wall.

"What are you doing?" I whispered.

His body pinned me tight. "Protecting you?"

"Try again."

"Hiding from the chicken?"

"He's friendly."

"Sure, he's plotting my demise, but yeah, totally friendly," he grumbled.

The blank white wall an inch from my nose, I stared at it with Marlo's arms around me, tension swirling in my belly. "Why were you pissed today?"

He exhaled a curse.

"The truth." I squeezed my eyes shut.

"The truth," he repeated softly, moving his hand from my hips, inching up past my ribs until his thumb grazed my nipple. "I'm not pissed."

I leaned back into him, thrusting my ass against him while he breathed against my neck. "Felt like it."

"I broke your trust because you broke mine. Break my heart… I break yours. Hurt me… I hurt you. Love me… I'll love you back harder." He cupped that same breast. I gasped as he massaged. "We'll never be at peace, you and me — always war, always fighting and fucking — maybe because it's all we know, maybe because we're both untrusting. It's a tragedy. We're our own tragedy. Because I can feel you. I can taste you. I can want you all I want… but you'll never really be mine."

He turned away from me then.

And I felt the walls I had long ago erected around my heart crack.

And when his heavy breathing filled the room…

A tear slid down my cheek. For him. For us.

Because neither one of us wanted to give in. Our comfort was brought out of our hate.

And we'd defaulted every single time.

Because it was all we knew.

And that was the saddest realization I'd had.

That Marlo and I might not ever be on the same page because we were so busy fighting to get to the next one first.

I felt his sadness like my own.

His frustration too.

And I hated it just as much.

But I didn't know how to unstick us without putting myself out there and asking him to jump with me.

And the what-ifs destroyed my sanity.

They told me it wouldn't work.

They promised me safety if I lashed out.

They reminded me of the times I would jump for my parents, and they wouldn't show up.

I'd be broken and bloody on the ground. And they'd apologize with a new car when what I really needed was a bandage and a hug.

What if I jumped, and Marlo just responded with a laugh?

Or worse?

What if he jumped with me.

And then walked away.

Chapter
NINETEEN

Marlon

I woke up and nearly rammed my face into a coffee mug. A coffee mug that Ray was holding out to me like a peace offering.

I narrowed my eyes. "What's this?"

"Coffee," she said slowly. "You drink it, or in your case, just IV it right into your veins and then ask for some more."

"Thanks."

I tried not to be skeptical. We fought. We hadn't exactly gotten along to the extent where I made her breakfast in the morning and we poured over our feelings and mistakes.

"The chicken had to use the restroom, so I took it—" She frowned. "Why are you giving me that look?"

"It's… trained?" I said in a hoarse voice.

"Clearly!" Now she was giving me a crazy look. "I swear they trained it. It stayed up all night watching us—" Nice, not the scariest sentence I'd heard in my life but a close second. "—and now it's completely crashed!" She pointed to her bed. The chicken was tucked into itself looking innocent as hell while I was rubbing my burning, probably red-rimmed eyes and willing the caffeine to work faster.

"So…" I nodded at the chicken. "…it's like a guard dog we can eat?"

"You will do no such thing!" She stood and put her hands on her hips. "He's useful, plus, now we won't have anyone interrupting…" Her voice trailed off, and she pinned her gaze on the floor.

My eyebrows shot up. "Sleep?"

"Yup. Sleep. Right. Of course." She started chewing on her thumbnail, did a slow circle, and then grabbed her shower caddy.

I kicked myself when she left.

And waited for the chicken to attack.

When it didn't, I lay back on the bed and wondered what I could do to make things easier, how I could help her.

And came up empty.

Ten hours later, we were just starting the staff bonfire, and I still had nothing. I'd seen her a handful of times.

She was polite.

I was polite.

I wanted to either get drunk or punch a wall.

It wasn't supposed to be like this!

We were fire and ice.

Oil and water.

I wanted her passion, her fighting, her screaming. I

wanted her at odds with me so I could convince her with my tongue how good it would feel to be even.

Jackson handed me a beer.

I chugged it.

Waited for her.

Held out my hand and magically got another cup placed in it.

"Just fuck her," Jackson said.

Brax sat down on my other side. "But this time not for revenge. You know, do it because you look miserable, she looks miserable. She took home a chicken, dude. No girl should ever replace a guy with a fucking chicken."

I smiled down into my beer, feeling a warm buzz in my blood. "It's her pet. Johnny stays."

"Hell, she named it?" Jackson shuddered while Brax burst out laughing.

Ray and Jen rounded the corner of HQ with linked arms. Campers and staff members ran up to them to talk, and I saw Ray's face light up, as if she was a part of a team, and I wondered how much better her life would have been had she felt like that during high school. Had we both just ignored our immature shit and bonded. Stayed friends.

Enemies.

Anything was better than what had happened.

And now?

Now I felt like I was at square one.

If I seduced her, she'd think I had ulterior motives.

So, I left the ball in her court.

Her very skittish, untrusting, spooked-up court.

I took another long sip.

"You know…" Brax cleared his throat. "…not that I'm as

good at all of this as you guys, but girls, they like attention."

"Spare me," Jackson said sourly, taking another draw from his red cup.

"Hear me out." Brax stood and shouted, "I'm IN LOVE!"

"How much alcohol has he had?" Jackson said under his breath.

"'I'm in LOVE...'" Brax sang and then dropped to his knees. "'...with a stripper...'" And like any nerdy drama camp with musicians and actors, and everything in between, suddenly it was as if *Camp Rock* puked all over us. People harmonized, added in instruments with their voices, sticks, buckets.

It was impossible not to grin.

"'She poppin', she rollin'.'" Brax moved his hips.

"Not bad for a redhead!" Jackson shouted and jumped to his feet and joined him.

Jen lit up when Jackson danced toward her and pulled her into his arms, and Ray stood there with a frozen smile on her face.

And it hit me like a dagger to the chest.

That smile, the reason it bothered me, irritated me, made me angry...

Was because it was the same smile she had worn through high school. The same smile she gave me after I kissed her real smile.

Livid, I marched over to her, grabbed her hand, and basically dragged her away from the campground like a caveman.

I walked.

She followed.

No words were spoken.

And I was beginning to realize that when it came to us? No words were really needed. Because our bodies just bled our emotions all over the place without really needing to say anything at all, didn't they?

Me walking: *I'm pissed.*

Her following: *Get in line.*

My grip on her hand: *I'm terrified of losing you.*

Her grip back: *I'm petrified of letting go.*

And on and on the conversation went, with each of our bodies warring against our minds, both of our souls fighting to be set free, and two broken hearts trying to mend themselves with shards of glass that continued to pierce them over and over again.

I stopped at the lake, chest heaving.

I couldn't control my own feelings over the situation. Fight her or kiss her? Yell at her or gently take her hand and ask what was wrong? The inner nerd, the foster boy who'd been abused in high school wanted justification. He wanted revenge. He wanted so many fucking things.

Ignoring him meant ignoring a wronged part of myself when she turned me away, when she treated me like shit.

And yet acknowledging him meant I wasn't able to be what she needed right now in this moment.

The wind blew against my face.

I clenched my jaw. "If you could take anything back, what would it be?"

Ray didn't let go of my hand. "Nothing."

I tried to pull away.

She squeezed my fingers so tight it felt as if they were going to fall off my hand. "Mistakes don't break us. They refine us. I wouldn't take anything away because I'd like to think I'm smarter now."

"No regrets, huh?"

"A ton of regrets," she said quickly. "My biggest regret being that I never told Marlon Brandon how I felt about him. Furthermore, when he stood bravely in front of a group of seniors and claimed me as his, I looked away."

I closed my eyes. "I wanted to go to prom with you. I made this ridiculous flower out of paper, thinking that if I had something different, something that didn't die…" I gulped. "…something you could keep forever, that you'd say yes." I turned, dropped her hand, and glared. "I hated you."

"Not as much as I hated myself," she said faintly.

"I loved you." I cupped her face with my hands.

"You were the only one who did." Tears filled her eyes.

I crashed my mouth onto hers without warning, and she pressed her body against mine without an apparent care.

Our tongues tangled in a frenzy that said more than any more words would. I winced in pain when she dug her nails into my forearms, and when I gripped her ass with my fingers, digging in and jerking her against me, her whimper was all I needed.

Everything.

"Jump with me," I whispered against her mouth, pulling away.

Her eyes darted from the lake back to me. "I don't think—"

I pushed her in.

And jumped in after her.

"What the hell, Marlo!" she roared when she surfaced, splashing all over the place then shoving my chest.

I pulled her against me, even as she banged her fists onto

my body, and when she started to cry, I spoke against her neck. "I figured it was less scary when you have no choice but to jump... and let me follow."

"I hate you." She raised her hand to hit me.

I grabbed her wrist, wrapped her arm around my neck, and shook my head. "Love and hate... hand in hand." I pressed a kiss to the side of her mouth while she gasped, as if she wanted more. "We'll always have both."

I swam us backward and grabbed onto the pier then jerked off my shirt, followed by my wet shorts and everything else.

"Wh-what are you doing?" Her eyes widened.

"Loving you." I shrugged, tugging her shirt over her head, and unhooking her bra, cupping her breasts and straining toward her. "Hating you."

She fell against me then unbuttoned her shorts and pulled them down her hips; she chucked them up on the pier and stared at me with still-wide eyes and puffy lips. "So, hate me."

"With pleasure." I pulled her into my arms and gripped her panties in my right hand then slowly pulled them down her thighs. I dipped my hand between her legs, and my fingers found her core.

She hissed out a curse.

"With fucking pleasure," I murmured.

"Marlo..."

Her head fell forward; she rested it in the crook of my neck as I sank my fingers into her heat and played. She bit down on the tender skin beneath my ear.

"...more... I need you more."

"I know you do." I teased her relentlessly, lying to myself, claiming it was physical, but it was the exact opposite. This was how we had conversations, wasn't it? When words weren't enough? When all we did was throw barbs at one another and seethe with hatred? Our bodies were the only honest thing we had going for us. This impenetrable tension, this heat pulsing between us like a heartbeat, like a living, breathing thing.

She dug her heels around me, and I gripped onto the metal ladder that would take us to the dock, but I didn't haul us up. Water sloshed around us, and I let out a curse when she angled her head and slammed her mouth against mine just as I dipped my fingers into chaotic angry perfection and told myself that I would come back without any scars.

My tongue slipped past her lips. I sucked hard as I moved my fingers back and forth, and when I retreated, she grabbed my fucking wrist and held me there, rocking her body against my hand with wild abandon.

I jerked away and flipped her around so that she was facing the ladder, and then placed her hands around the metal. "Hold on," I rasped, verbally anchoring her there. She twisted, but I pressed against her ass, pushing her into the ladder's rungs, and she gasped as I reached around her, once again finding my favorite playground. The sight of her skin in the moonlight as water trickled down her bare back was the most erotic sight I'd ever had the pleasure of seeing. Her moving with me, soft gasps between swollen lips, excited me beyond measure.

She arched her back against me and squeezed her legs together, the slight movement capturing me between her thighs. Closing my eyes, I reveled in the sensation of searing heat there while the cool water surrounded the rest of me. But if I stayed there too long…

A groan slipped past my lips as I drew back and turned her around, pinning her back against the ladder as I pressed my body into her from the front. Time seemed to slow, and we hung there, suspended in the moment, as the lake lapped at us in a lazy rhythm. Water dripped from my hair, running over my forehead and into my eyes, and I shook my head, breaking the spell.

Our gazes collided, and my brain had trouble focusing as her eyes searched mine, so many questions, too many words, words that would cut, leaving us bloody and broken, more pissed-off than before.

"Tell me something true," I whispered against her mouth, teasing her entrance with my tip.

Heat exploded between us, and she let out a shaky breath. I shouldn't have spoken, shouldn't have introduced conversation when our bodies were doing just fine.

"I will always hate you as much as I love you," she said sadly, "because you made me hope after a lifetime full of letdown. And you did it twice."

My chest snapped, my heart stuttering to a stop and then rebounding painfully against my ribs as her hurt expression met mine. "And I'm hoping…" Tears filled her eyes. "…that this won't end badly because I seem to lose all sense of reality around you. All I see is you. Can you handle your truth, Marlo?"

I sighed and pulled away.

Tears spilled over her cheeks. I wiped them with my thumbs. "The problem with words that are true— They make you think. They stop you from acting. And as much as I want to act right this very second, I think the spoiled princess deserves more than a hate fuck in a lake."

She lowered her eyes as red stained her cheeks.

I tilted her chin up. "So, ask me…"

"What?"

"Ask me for something true."

"I'm afraid of the answer."

"Don't be."

She bit down on her lower lip. "Fine, tell me something true."

"Being with you… wasn't just a favorite moment of my life, a blip in high school you brag about to your friends. It was everything to me. Everything I didn't realize I'd missed. It was my first introduction to true love. And that is why I will both always love you and hate you."

"Guys!" Jackson's voice sounded from the dock. "The chicken — or Johnny or whatever the hell you're calling it — escaped and chased a camper. I ran, and maybe you can't hear me, or maybe you've gotten over your shit, and you're hiding under the bushes dry-humping, but you should probably take care of that."

"This isn't over." I brushed a kiss across her lips.

"Has it ever been over?" she asked while I reached up to the dock for my shorts, only for Jackson to toss them over.

Great.

I smiled at Ray and then cupped her head and kissed her once more, tasting her again, loving her again, hating her again. "No."

She smiled against my mouth. It felt so damn good that I wanted her smile pressed against my lips forever.

But Jackson was clearly aware of where we were and what we were doing, and I didn't want him staring at her underwear for longer than a few seconds… or at all.

I growled and pulled myself away from her. "Tonight."

"Same time, same place?" Her smile didn't quite reach her eyes.

I hated it.

"As long as the cock doesn't interfere."

She rolled her eyes. "Which one?"

I barked out a laugh.

"I can hear you guys…" Jackson let out an irritated sigh. "I was trying to be a gentleman."

"And that would be a first," I grumbled, tugging on my wet shorts and taking the ladder rungs two at a time to reach the dock. I gently tossed down Ray's clothes and crooked my finger at Jackson. "Turn around and walk. Look back, and I drown you."

"Think you could manage it?" He flexed.

I flicked his bicep.

"Ouchie!" He laughed and then jogged off.

I waited for Ray.

I kept my back turned.

Because I wanted her all to myself.

No more sharing with nature.

With stolen nights away from parents.

Showers.

Mine. All mine. Which meant the chicken was either going to have to wear a blindfold or get traumatized for life.

Either way, tough shit.

Ray's steps interrupted my thoughts.

And then she interlocked our fingers.

We walked hand in hand back to the camp. Completely drenched.

And somehow, I felt calmer than I had in years.

Chapter
TWENTY

Ray

I rescued Johnny and put him back in the cabin. He looked disappointed in himself, or maybe he just always looked disappointed. Then again, what did I know about chickens? He'd jumped from my bed and perched himself in the far corner, sitting near a pile of clothes that I was pretty sure Marlo would never see again.

My heart was heavy in my chest, and my brain felt like it was going to explode.

I couldn't match up my thoughts with my racing heart, with the way my body roared Marlo's name every single time he looked at me.

I would not survive him walking away with the very last piece of me.

And I knew that he didn't trust me not to do the same damn thing.

How do you build trust when you have this sort of attraction? This buzzing awareness that makes you want to devour every inch of the other person and come back for seconds.

I grabbed a nearby stick, tossed it in the fire, and yawned. It was getting late anyway, but Marlo was busy talking to an upset DeeDee. I only hoped it wasn't because of Jackson. The guy could use a break.

Plus, he was already passed out back at his cabin. Jen had stayed with him for reasons beyond my comprehension.

Leaving me...

And Brax, who kept trying to show me how to roast the perfect marshmallow. I let out a defeated sigh.

I had six more weeks of this.

Six more weeks to prove myself, to get the attention of an agent who wouldn't...

I shuddered.

It was worth it. It would always be worth it.

I just wished I had the confidence in myself to believe that I was worth it, that I could make it on my own, that I was worth fighting for, worth loving. And that was the worst part. What guy wanted to be with a girl who looked at herself in the mirror and counted her flaws? Both inward and outward.

Because if I had something to offer...

Then wouldn't my parents care?

Wouldn't they be at least a little bit affected by me?

I thought back to my senior musical. I had earned a big role — not starring — but still, it was something to be excited about. I could remember seeing the *Reserved* signs on their seats.

Ray's Parents!

Would Marlo have come? If we had stayed in touch? Would he have clapped for me? Cheered?

Or just thrown popcorn and booed?

Brax handed me a piece of chocolate and plopped down on the log next to me. "So, you know about DeeDee, right?"

"About her and Jackson, and him screaming Jen's name during? Yeah, I know all about it…" I was actually thankful for someone else's drama.

"So…" Brax grabbed a graham cracker and chomped down on it. His red hair was tucked behind a black UW baseball cap. "…apparently, it gets worse than that."

"How exactly does it get worse?"

"Well… word on the street—"

I elbowed him.

He rubbed his arm. "Fine, word amongst the staff members — mainly DeeDee, who confessed to Cassandra—"

Ah, Cassandra, the pretty blonde with a bob haircut and wing-tipped eyeliner that was drawn to perfection; she helped with all the costumes and makeup.

"—is that he didn't even get off. He went like completely limp and then grabbed his clothes and bailed."

My jaw dropped. "Like mid—" I used my hands to finish the statement with a clap.

"Yeah, I don't know what you mean by clapping just now." He grinned. "But yes, mid—" He clapped, and I pushed him. "Apparently his dick and heart are not in sync. Bummer for him."

I rolled my eyes. "No, not a bummer for him. He doesn't even like her!" I pointed at DeeDee just as Marlo glanced over at us.

"He looks pissed again. What'd you do?" Brax said in a low tone.

Oh, you know, we both got hot and bothered and then said words, and the words felt funny because our bodies wanted to do something different, but the words were more important so, nothing. Just confessions and confusion. Next.

"We talked," I finally managed to get out, quickly taking a bite of chocolate and chewing so I wouldn't have to say anything else for a minute or two, or ten.

Brax snorted. "Is that code for screwed?"

Sadly, no. I twisted my lips into what I hoped was a smile. "Not this time. Disappointed you weren't there to ruin it?"

He sighed. "I said I was sorry."

I pulled his hat off his head, ruffled his hair, and shoved it back on. "Yeah, yeah…"

"Hey! Nobody touches the hair."

Marlo made his way over to us and sat on my right then held out his hand. I put chocolate in it, and he frowned before slowly lifting it to his lips. I sucked in a breath and zeroed in on his mouth.

Words. We still needed words.

Brax cleared his throat. "I'll take care of the fire. Why don't you guys go have some deep… conversations… about politics, religion, and the state of the economy."

"Sounds riveting," Marlo said in a bored tone, flipping him off.

I reached for Marlo's hand, nervous he wouldn't want me to, that he'd tell me not in front of the staff members, but he gripped it back and in front of the last few remaining campers, walked with me back to his cabin and closed the door behind us.

"Everyone saw," I said, throat dry.

He was behind me. He hadn't turned the light on yet, keeping us blanketed in inky black darkness and moonlight. And then his hands were on my shoulders. "Let them see."

I laid my head back against his chest. "We should talk."

He let out a laugh and then sobered. "Wait, you're actually serious?"

I spun around and poked him in the chest. "Everything else just makes me more terrified and confused and—" I put my hands on my hips. "Hey, I want my favor."

His eyebrows shot up as he crossed his arms and towered over me. "Oh, yeah?"

"I stole the seal." I grinned. "So, I get my favor."

He squinted. "Shouldn't the favor be taking in a chicken? I'll do you one better, taking in… you?"

"Nope." I rocked back on my heels. "The chicken just comes with the territory, and… well, you took me in…" I gulped as insecurity slammed against my chest. "…you took me in because…"

He tilted my chin toward him. I couldn't look away from his icy-blue eyes and wanted nothing more than to tug on his silky hair and pull him down to my face.

"Because you were lonely," he finished.

My nostrils flared as anger swirled around my mind, trying to choke out the way my heart thudded with pain — pain from the honesty of his words, pain that he would notice the loneliness, pain that my enemy would be my safety.

"So…" My voice wavered right along with my confidence. I was too focused on the fact that I'd needed him again, and he'd offered himself just like he had in high school. And I hated the truth of the situation. That if I had told him I'd needed him at any point in high school, he would have been the first to sacrifice for my happiness, for my safety. And I'd just taken advantage of him, like any spoiled princess would. "My favor…" I stared down at my feet. "Each truth equals a piece of clothing. If you lie, you put on clothes. If you tell the truth, you take something off."

"And what happens when we're both naked?" he asked, voice thick with lust.

"Hopefully, by then…" I let out a sigh. "…we'll be on the same page. If not…"

"If not, I'm sleeping with the chicken?" he offered with humor lacing his tone.

I laughed. "Maybe, you never know. Johnny may rock your world."

Marlo drew his brows together in a scowl. "Never say that again. Not even to repeat it to Jackson." He grabbed my hand and sat me down on the bed then strolled to his mini-fridge in the corner and pulled something out of it.

Tequila.

I glared. "Do you have everything in here?"

"Probably." He didn't even look guilty as he smirked at me and walked over then handed me the bottle. "Figured courage was needed."

"For you, maybe." I elbowed him.

He rolled his eyes. "Right…" He opened the bottle, tilted it back, swallowed, and winced. "Cheers, SP."

"Ah, the nickname's back. Nice. Wanna know what I call you?"

"Perfect?" he offered with a completely cocky expression.

"Lawn-boy," I said in a snotty voice.

He flinched.

"What?" I grabbed the tequila and chugged some back then wiped my mouth. "It's like I'm calling you farm-boy, and we're in *The Princess Bride.*"

"And yet..." He narrowed his eyes on me. "...it doesn't feel like it."

"Ready... lawn-boy?" I grinned.

He smirked and leaned closer to me. I could smell his cologne and was dying to touch the bristles on his cheeks, the shadow that would be gone tomorrow after he shaved. I wondered if it would burn my face after hours of making out. I wondered how much I would like it as I clenched my thighs together to stall the growing pressure and tried to focus. "As. You. Wish."

Well, that backfired quickly, didn't it?

I licked my lips, tasting the tequila there, wishing I was tasting his mouth, and then I lost all train of thought. Was I supposed to be asking a question? Answering one?

"Apparently..." He chuckled low in his throat. "...I get to ask first, since I've rendered you speechless."

I scowled as I scooted back against the headboard and waited with arms crossed while Johnny slept in the corner — or at least appeared to be sleeping, I wasn't exactly an expert on the nocturnal behavior of chickens.

"Why did you let me kiss you?"

My scowl quickly turned into a glare. "You mean a few hours ago?"

"No..." He turned to me. "...in high school. Why did you let me kiss you?"

I didn't want to answer.

Answering that simple question meant that he would

know more than he should. It meant pain, possible rejection; it meant I was a fraud. And worse of all, he would know that his torment in high school really was all my fault because I wasn't brave enough to stop it.

I grabbed a beanie from the desk next to me and pulled it over my head. "My turn."

"Wow," he said bitterly, "one question in, and you're already not answering. Why am I not surprised?"

I ignored him, grabbed another swig of tequila, and after the burn faded, asked, "Why did you come?"

He squinted at me then flashed a sexy grin.

"Be mature, Marlo. Why did you come that night?" I sighed. "No matter how I say it, it sounds bad. Why did you come to my house?" I grumbled and waited for his answer.

He grabbed a nearby hoody and held it in his hands.

I waited an eternity in that cabin while he held the sweatshirt. If we could never talk, we would never get beyond this moment, beyond just wanting to let our bodies take over and protect our hearts from further harm.

And I knew I'd set a bad example.

Out of fear.

Because what if I asked him to love me? Really love me?

And he turned the other way?

"Shit." Marlo threw the sweatshirt onto the ground and turned to face me. "Would you believe me if I told you I'd just wanted to make sure you were okay?"

I frowned. "What do you mean? We were neighbors?"

"I heard you fighting with your douche of an ex, and then I heard tears, followed by something breaking."

"Ah, because I threw my phone at the mirror."

"That." He nodded and tilted his head as if he was trying

to figure me out like a complicated math problem, which was true. I was complicated, but I wasn't born this way. I wasn't born stuck in a geometry field. I truly thought I was simply born simple.

Love me.

And with every year, my circumstances complicated my simplicity so much that even I didn't know how to get out of the field, out of the maze.

"So," he said and sighed, "I went to your room to make sure you weren't bleeding and to make sure that if he *was*, you had help burying the body."

I snorted out a laugh. "So, really what you're saying is you wanted to be my partner in crime?"

"I've always wanted to live a life of crime. Why not start with the spoiled rich girl who had tears on her face and blood under her fingernails?"

I smiled at the thought of us joining forces.

The world wasn't ready for peace talks between Marlo and me, not yet.

I wasn't ready either.

That would mean I had no more excuses.

No more walls.

"So, you were worried." I nodded. "That makes sense."

"Yeah, I'm not finished."

I lifted my head. "What?"

"I said…" He grabbed both of my hands in his.

Why am I shaking? Why is he so warm? And why does this feel bigger than me, bigger than us? Furthermore, why do I feel like crying?

"…I figured you needed a friend. A real friend, not one of the plastic shadow-hunter friends you hung out with who told you how pretty you were to your face then gossiped about how fat your ass was behind your back — and for the record, you've always had the best ass."

I gulped, smiled a watery smile, and searched his eyes. "Sometimes, I think you know me better than I know myself. I needed a friend that night."

He smirked. "Yeah, in hindsight, I wasn't exactly emotionally stable enough to be walking into your room after downing a few shots with my fellow nerds, but there it is."

"You weren't that drunk."

"I wasn't that drunk," he admitted.

"I want to change my answer." I stared down at my hands. I focused on my perfect fingernails, the pink gel polish that covered them, the way they dug into my palm. "I let you kiss me because I wanted to know what it would be like—"

He swore.

I gripped his hand keeping him in place. "I wanted to know what it was like to kiss someone I actually liked. Who cared more for me than he did himself. I wanted love so badly..." Tears filled my eyes. "...and I knew you would give it to me with all of your heart." I choked on a sob. "So, I took it from you because I was so sick—" I put my hands over my face and cried. "—so sick of being unwanted. Ignored. I just wanted someone to see me." I wiped under my eyes, too afraid to look at him.

Had he ceased breathing?

Had my heart stopped?

Had the world ended?

I looked up through a blur of tears.

His eyes blazed, raked over me like a thousand heated

kisses. "That," he whispered, "is the nicest and truest thing anyone has ever said to me." He leaned in and pressed a kiss to the falling tear on my right cheek then cradled my head. "It would have been an honor to kiss your tears then, to hold your hand and tell you how much you were worth, but since I didn't, since we hated each other…" He smiled. "…I'll just tell you now. You are beautiful."

I sighed against the pain that felt as if he was stabbing my heart with a sharp arrow.

"You are talented."

I tried to look away. It hurt. It hurt too much. *Why does it hurt?*

"You're funny. You're caring. You are everything that's right with this world, and anyone who says otherwise is clearly everything that's wrong with humanity." His gaze gentled. "I've always seen you, Ray. The problem is, you've never seen yourself the way I do. The way others do. And I can't wait until you're able to love yourself enough to accept love — real love — and look in the mirror and actually smile."

I threw my arms around his neck and held on so tight I probably scared him, but he didn't say anything else.

He didn't push me away.

More tears streamed down my cheeks as a heaviness released from my body. And slowly, very slowly, Marlo lifted his hand and pulled the beanie off.

Then whispered in my ear, "Next question."

Chapter
TWENTY-ONE

Marlon

'd never thought tears were beautiful. Until now. Until I was the one who'd caused them, until I saw how they released her from a prison of sadness. And then I was addicted to them, just like that. I wanted to free her. I wanted to be the guy who told her all the things that nobody had ever said to her. And I wanted to do it because she deserved it, but also because I knew what it was like to be unloved, unwanted. Until my foster parents, I hadn't known love.

Only rejection.

We lay on the bed, and she pressed her head against my chest. "Tell me something sad."

I exhaled while she ran her hand up and down my shirt as if I wasn't already struggling to keep my self-control in check. We were different. One conversation, and we were different, and I was done letting things stand in the way of us.

The way we were always supposed to be before life rose up against us.

"I hate Disney Channel."

She laughed. "How can you hate Disney Channel?"

I shrugged. "When you're a little boy with no parents, or at least parents who don't want you, and you're put in front of Disney Channel as a way of babysitting, you learn to hate it. You hate the love you see between the families. You hate the perfection. You resent the lives you see played out in front of you. It's like this huge tease. *This is what everyone else has, Marlo, but you'll never have it. Nobody will ever love you enough to give it to you.'"

She sucked in a harsh breath and then leaned up on her elbow, her eyes searching mine. "You don't still think that, do you?"

I smiled sadly. "Not usually, but sometimes my six-year-old self reminds me of my roots, and I default to a complete asshole who shuts out the world out of fear, fear that one day I'm going to be happy, then someone's going to pull the rug out from underneath me."

"You deserve to be happy. You're good. Plus, you're only an asshole ninety percent of the time."

"I pour my heart out to you, and you still call me an asshole?" I asked, smiling hard enough to crack my own face.

She reached for my shirt and tugged it up over my head.

I let her. Because it was a game, wasn't it? And in the morning, all of our clothes would be back on, our secrets locked back down.

I squeezed my eyes shut and opened them just in time to see her pull off her own shirt. We'd already dealt with socks, shoes, hats… All we had left were our jeans and shirts. She'd already unhooked her bra and dropped it in my lap an hour ago.

And like an idiot, I'd stared at it a bit too long, earning a shove from her as if I was back in high school seeing my first Victoria Secret tag.

"I'm just preparing to answer my next question." And she was topless. No bra, no shirt, just topless with her platinum hair hanging over her tan shoulders, and she was staring at me.

And I was…

What the hell am I doing? Going into a fucking coma?

I licked my lips and reached for her, gripping her hips between my palms as I asked the next question. "No backing out."

"'Kay." Her voice wavered.

"Will you dance with me?"

Her eyes widened. "You want me to dance? Naked?"

"Right. Don't freak out… but I want you to dance naked."

"In front of the chicken?"

I frowned. "It's not like we fed him KFC. He'll be fine. Besides, the moonlight looks perfect on you, and I think… I think you may just surprise yourself."

"And if I don't?"

"How about you just trust me?"

"Easier said than done."

I sighed. "I believe in you."

She gasped as if nobody had ever said those words to her. And I hated…

I raged…

At anyone and everyone in her life that had been put on this damn earth to love her — and hadn't.

And I hated myself the most.

Because I'd selfishly thrown that love back in her face to protect myself. That was what monsters did.

Not men.

"Please?" I stood and held out my hand.

She gave me a small nod, one that could have been mistaken for a flinch, and I was off my bed, turning on the first music I could find.

Black Sea.

She twirled in front of me, the cadence a lot of stop go, stop go, which made the song extremely hard to dance to, but if anyone could do it…

She could.

She put her hands over her head and then twirled into my arms, eyes closed, and then she was dipping forward, and I was going with her on the journey of whatever story she wanted to tell me.

She rose onto her tiptoes as I turned her on one foot, grabbing her leg and snaking it backward around me.

She jerked away and turned.

I nearly bit off my tongue when she did a body roll and jumped in the air, just trusting me to catch her, and then she slid down my body, moving her hips against mine in a way that set every part of me on fire, my blood roaring. Moving perfectly with the beat, she bent completely backward, her hands following her as she arched at the most elegant angle and then thrust forward, throwing herself against me.

I repeated the movement, and when she came toward me

again, I twisted her in my arms and flipped her over my back in the air, letting her slide behind me. Her palms ran down my face as she used her hands to move my head around with the music, and then she splayed them across my chest.

I gripped her by the wrists, the music completely forgotten as we played off one another. I pulled her to her feet and pushed her boundaries, asked for complete surrender from her body, fucking demanded she dance her truth for me, for us.

Tears streamed down her face, and it felt like more than dancing, as if we were living our love, our hate, and everything in between as we pushed at one another then pulled, only to dance as one and repeat the process.

She turned again. I tugged her against my chest and locked my arms around her waist as we swayed in sync, eyes penetrating, breathing labored.

"I figured it out," she whispered.

"What did you figure out?" I smiled down at her excited expression, expecting her to say something about finding herself through dancing, through letting go.

"I couldn't let go…" She was up on her tiptoes, gripping my face as if she had something important to say. "…because I was always meant to dance with you."

Her mouth opened to say something else.

I devoured her next word with my tongue and swore I would never look back. She wrapped her arms around my neck as I lifted her off the ground and carried her over to the bed.

She fisted the front of my jeans with her hand while I pressed into her, my erection straining against her. She trembled and arched toward me for more.

I kissed down her tear-stained cheeks.

It had never been infatuation with her.

Never.

It had been a lot of things.

Hate. Love.

Love will always win out, won't it? Despite the hate I had thrown her way… love had always won.

I stopped kissing her tan skin. The smell of sunscreen brought on a smile. She was a Ray of sunshine and didn't even know it.

"No revenge," I murmured tenderly.

Her smile was dazzling as she looked up at me. "No revenge."

I leaned over and kissed her forehead then reached for her jeans and unbuttoned them slowly, savoring every movement as if it was my last. I unzipped and tugged.

She wiggled out of them, and I tossed them to the floor and braced my hands on either side of her hips. And then I hooked my fingers into her lacy underwear and slid them down her thighs, fascinated with the violet color of them against her skin, obsessed with the way her hips lifted like she was giving me permission to love her.

The ethereal look of her hair spread across my pillow, on my bed, was something I knew I would never forget, the way she reached for me once she was naked, as if she couldn't wait one more minute to touch me again, to kiss me.

Our mouths fused. She tasted like my sunshine, like light. She tasted like she was finally free. My head swam with possibilities while my heart pounded against my chest.

Finally.

Fucking… finally.

I pinned her hands above her head and pressed a teasing kiss on her neck — one, two kisses, three, four. My tongue met the sweetest skin, and I inhaled deeply, wanting it to last forever.

"My turn." She hooked her feet around me. I let her press me onto my back as she took over. I was one-part insecurity and helplessness and one-part completely turned on that she was taking the lead, that the spoiled princess who I'd wanted to both kiss and make cry, was straddling me as if I was hers.

Dear God, please let me have her forever.

"You're smiling?" I cupped her breasts because I could and because the view from flat on my back was the best I'd ever seen. Mouthwatering, forbidden, shameless.

"Well…" She rocked her hips against me, against my straining cock and jeans. The friction was almost painful. "…I was thinking…" She was officially Wonder Woman in another life as my jeans all but disappeared along with my briefs, leaving me vulnerable and naked in front of the only woman capable of breaking me.

She could ridicule.

She could run away.

She could tell me this was all in my head.

She had the power to reach inside and laugh the foster kid out of the room.

I didn't realize how much my insecurity was still there until I let out a relieved breath as she crawled back up the bed and lay against me, skin on skin, and pressed her cheek against my chest.

I played with her hair. "So, now we're sleeping?"

She yawned.

I pinched her ass.

Dying.

I was dying.

"I just wanted to feel you, Marlo."

"You are feeling me."

"I wanted to hear your heart too."

"Why?"

"So, I could remember the way it raced when I told you… I love you."

I exhaled a shaky breath.

"There it is." She sighed happily. "So…" She gazed up at me with a drugged look on her face, her eyes shining with unshed tears, with happiness I'd like to think I had put there. "…that's what love sounds like?"

I nodded, afraid to trust my voice, then pulled her down so I could kiss her and whispered against her lips. "Now let me show you what it feels like."

Chapter
TWENTY-TWO

Ray

He was hard heat.

He was perfect.

He was staring up at me as if I was the most important part of his life, as if he wasn't sure he could take another breath without doing it in sync with me, and I wanted more.

I was drugged by each kiss.

Needy for more of his touch.

I pressed my palms against his chest and slid them down, letting them slowly graze each part of an eight-pack I would most definitely dream about later.

We linked fingers, and then he shifted beneath me and lifted me into the air. I wrapped my legs around his hips and sank down onto him, slowly, inch by inch, feeling each pulse from his body, clenching each one between my thighs as he filled me not quite to the hilt, never once taking his mouth from mine. His tongue slid against my lips while I clung to him for dear life, while he moved in and out creating the most aching tension between our bodies. A thrill shot through me when he pulled away his eyes and locked on mine as we moved together.

He kissed down my breasts. I couldn't breathe, couldn't focus on sucking air between my lips as he found new places to kiss, new places to explore that made my body shudder with the need for a release so intense I wasn't sure I would survive it. My breath hitched when he groaned, his head between my breasts, his body trembling as if he was trying to hold back, when all I wanted him to do was let go.

He hissed when I pulled him deeper, farther inside me, when I took him all the way and held him there, when our bodies pulsed on the brink of free-falling from a cliff. I squeezed my pelvic muscles, clenching around him.

An explosive sigh blasted from his lips, and a sense of power rocketed through me.

"So fucking greedy for more of you, all of you, now." His lips moved against my skin. "I want this moment forever."

"Me too." I tugged his hair and leaned down to press a kiss to his mouth.

He surged forward then. I gasped against his lips as he thrust faster, so deep I couldn't stop the moans coming from my mouth, the desperate gasps.

"Marlo, I'm so close I can't—"

"You will," he said with authority. "You're beautiful when you let go, so let go."

"But—"

He kissed away the next words I had.

I was consumed by the feel of him inside me, by the feel of us together. The rightness of it all.

He tore down my walls, peeled back my defenses.

"Marlo…" I couldn't hold on any longer. "…I'm yours…"

Shock waves of pleasure exploded between us as I let go. Skin sliding against skin, I absorbed every hard inch of him as I felt his release, his taut muscles, the way his chest heaved against mine.

"You think," he asked, out of breath, "we could just… stay like this for a few years?"

"Wouldn't be weird." I laughed as he kissed me again. "Totally normal for campers to see their director naked with the choreographer, just wrapped around each other like really horny pretzels."

He laughed against my mouth then indulged in more kissing.

I wanted him again, and again, as many times as he would let me, as many hours as were in the night.

"You're not sleeping tonight." He said it like a threat.

The best kind. So, I smiled and replied, "Neither are you."

Chapter
TWENTY-THREE

Marlon

"Hell, you two look rough." Brax stood next to the coffee bar and eyed us both up and down — well, inspected was more like it. "If that's what titillating conversation looks like, I want some."

I narrowed my eyes and gave him the finger. "Shouldn't say titillating if you can't even spell it, dumbass."

Ray swayed a bit on her feet. And then stumbled toward the breakfast table, walking a bit gingerly the entire way.

Brax's eyebrows shot up to his hairline as he watched her carefully sit, and then he eyed me with such wide eyes I thought they were going to pop out of his head. He slapped me on the chest. "It was the politics talk, am I right? She got all horny when you said, *'I'll be your Mr. President,'* then pulled your dick out?"

I gave him a sidelong stare. "And it's suddenly so apparent why you don't have a girlfriend and are going to die alone."

He smirked and handed me a cup of coffee then made another. "Well, clearly you know you did it right if she's walking funny."

I grabbed him by the back of the shirt. "Notice her walk again, and I'm going to run you over with the camp truck. Got it?"

He spread his arms wide and chuckled. "Uh-huh, must have been a titillating night."

"You need a new word."

"I find this one very tit—"

"Seriously, Brax, I'm not against punching you, and I got less than one hour of sleep last night. Try me."

"Oh, boo-hoo, go complain to someone who isn't having all the sex. Oh wait…" He rolled his eyes. "I'll just go hang out with my right hand."

"You're left-handed."

"Stop noticing weird shit." He shook his head. "I'll use my right if I damn well please."

I laughed and shook my head and started making a coffee for Ray. "Do me a favor? Go grab cook's meal plan for today so you can write it on the board."

"Is this my punishment?"

"No, it's your job," I said slowly. "But if it feels like punishment, then we all win, don't we?"

"I see how it is. You have a naked girl screaming in your arms, and you're still an asshole. Good to know!"

I saluted him with my middle finger then picked up Ray's coffee and took it over to her.

"Yes-s-s." She lifted it to her lips then blew across it.

I cleared my throat just as Jackson sat down. Dark circles rimmed his eyes. Jen sat next to him, though not close. "If I steal your coffee, can we still be friends?"

He directed the question at Ray. I opened my mouth to tell him to get his own coffee when Ray handed her cup over to him then dropped her hands into her lap.

"Really, Jackson? You can't get your own cof— Fuck!" My hips jerked against her hand as she palmed me over my jeans, my tight jeans.

My very tight jeans.

Jackson shot me an odd look, his features twisted in confusion. "Coffuck? What the hell is that? Is it some new kinky shit where you bring coffee in on everything and then, I don't know… like throw it between your bodies while you slide your hand in their—"

"Yes." I swore under my breath. "I mean, no." *Air. Get air. Focus.* "Can we not talk about this right now?" I braced my hands against the table while a perfectly innocent Ray sat next to me.

I was going to murder her later.

After more sex.

And after I got her naked.

And had my mouth between her thighs.

Twice.

Twice sounded good, because, damn, I loved her taste.

Jackson narrowed his eyes at me, and then a stupid grin crossed his lips. "You guys put your differences behind you or something?"

"Nah…" Giving an exaggerated wink, Ray was the first to answer. "…I still hate him."

And my smile was back. Yeah, she hated me all right, all

night long, at least five times, and each time had been better than the last.

"Must be nice to be hated," Jen piped up.

Jackson let out a sigh and stared down at his hands as if he didn't know what to say, and the entire table went from comical and witty to tense and awkward.

"Oh, Camp Director?" Brax made his way back over to us. "Got the menus, and rumor has it a few campers stole some fireworks last night. Should you take care of this, or should I?"

Ray jerked her hand away.

And I suddenly wanted to kill every single camper I saw.

I adjusted myself as best I good, jumped to my feet and stomped after him, making my way past the kitchen and out of the mess hall.

Gravel crunched beneath my feet as Brax followed, iPad in hand. "If rumors are to be believed, they stole them from HQ. Want me to head over there and double-check first?"

I stopped and chewed my lower lip, "Nah, let's just—"

"Let's just… stand here and hold our cocks or…?"

"Do you smell that?" I frowned and looked up. "Shit!" I ran down the path toward Cabin 6 just in time to see one of the campers stumble out followed by another two. "Brax, go get help!"

"But—"

I grabbed him by the front of the shirt. "Brax, call 911. Get HELP!"

He stumbled off while I ran toward the sobbing girl. "How many are in there?"

"W-we fell asleep. There were a few candles. It wasn't serious and—"

I grasped her shoulders and steered her off to the side. "Stay here." I ran into the slow blaze, covering my face with my shirt as screaming assaulted me on all sides.

Something exploded next to me.

What the hell?

The smoke cleared enough for me to see some scattered fireworks in the corner, and the three terrified looking girls and one guy all giving me petrified looks.

"Let's go!"

They didn't move.

Shit. "NOW!" I roared.

They jumped to their feet, and as I pushed them toward the door, they tried grabbing stuff. Did they know nothing about emergencies? Fire safety?

"Leave your crap!" I shoved two of them through the door.

"My photo album!" one girl wailed. "You don't understand! It's all I have left from her. It's all I have!"

I sighed as I persuaded her closer to the door. It was going to be one of those days, wasn't it? "What color is your bag?"

"Blue." Tears streamed down her cheeks. "It has a yellow sun on it."

"I'll get it. Just go." I propelled her over the threshold and down the stairs and turned. The smoke was black now. What the hell did they build these cabins with? I covered my mouth and ducked onto my hands and knees, the whole time keeping my eyes on the flames that were getting closer and closer to the bed as they climbed up the walls and floated over the ceiling above me in one giant *whoosh*.

Finally, I spotted the bag in the corner and grabbed it, muttering a prayer of thanks as I turned to make my way back out.

I'd heard it was a sixth sense.

That crawling-down-your-back feeling when your hair stands on end, and the universal clock of life slowly ticks toward your doom. I'd always thought it was bullshit. Until a wall of fire fell between me and my exit.

One of the curtains had fallen next to the open door.

A wall of fire.

With fucking fireworks behind me.

Time stood still as the first sound of a Roman candle went off.

Chapter
TWENTY-FOUR

Ray

"Your cheeks have color," Jackson commented once Marlo was gone and Jen was off grabbing her own cup of coffee.

I narrowed my eyes. "Maybe I got some sun yesterday."

"Or just got some… yesterday." He chuckled and then sobered. "I'm happy for you. Marlo's—"

"FIRE!" A camper ran into the mess hall. "There's a fire!"

I jumped to my feet and started running as sickness pierced through my stomach, my thoughts carrying my heavy legs toward the smoke now billowing up above the trees.

The sound of sirens filled the air as I made it in front of the small cabin and greedily searched for Marlo.

Where the hell is he?

A loud sound popped as glass shattered from every window.

"Marlo!" Brax shouted. "Marlo!"

"He's still in there!" One of the girls sobbed. "I shouldn't have asked him to go back." She fell into a heap of tears against Brax while I waited for Marlo to come through.

He always came through.

This was Marlo.

Marlo, the foster kid who mowed the lawns and always did the right thing.

My Marlo.

Another blast from inside had everyone covering their ears and me taking a step toward the door just in time to see something slide down the stairs.

"My bag!" The girl ran toward it.

"Marlo!" I yelled. "MARLO!"

I started running, pumping my legs as I made it to the first step and looked beneath the fiery piece of fabric, to see Marlo looking back at me, his face black, his eyes fiercely white.

Apologetic.

Twenty-two years' worth of confessions.

Twenty-two years' worth of love.

Friendship.

And hate.

"Marlo!" I reached for him.

And was sent reeling backward as a blast of heat assaulted my body. I heard the screams.

I felt glass against my body.

And for the first time in my short life…

I wanted to close my eyes and never wake up.

Because I knew.

He was gone.

I felt it in my soul.

I felt it in the ripped shreds of my heart.

I had heard about life flashing before your eyes when you die. What they don't talk about is what happened when you're the one left living.

All I saw was his face.

And I knew it would haunt me for the rest of my life.

His smell.

His touch.

His kiss.

Him.

Marlo.

Lawn-boy.

And I could have sworn the wind carried his last words to my ears. "As you wish…"

ACKNOWLEDGEMENTS

I'm so thankful to God that I'm able to do what I love and this book, man this book, was a lot of happiness and tears! I'm so happy that people have been enjoying it and it would not even be possible without Nina and Ian, the team at iBooks have been amazing and I'm so thankful that I get to work with them on this project. Thank you to my wonderful husband Nate and beautiful son Thor, I've had to sacrifice a lot of my summer to get this done but you guys are the inspiration behind it. From the bonfires, to the swimming at night, you guys are and always will be my inspiration! Thank you to my beta readers, Jill, Georgia, Krista, Tracey, and Stephanie, you guys have been so helpful and I actually look forward to your feedback every time I send something! Jill thank you for another amazing format and making it so pretty and Jena again I love you hard for your covers! Nina, thanks for the peer pressure on these cliffhangers, and to my entire time with Rockin' Readers and my reader group you guys are the best. I adore all the bloggers and readers who make writing books possible.

Thank you so much from the bottom of my heart and as always if you want to connect you can find me trolling Instagram @RachVD or you can connect with me on Facebook Rachel's New Rockin Readers, blood in no out ;)

HUGS! And thank you for reading!

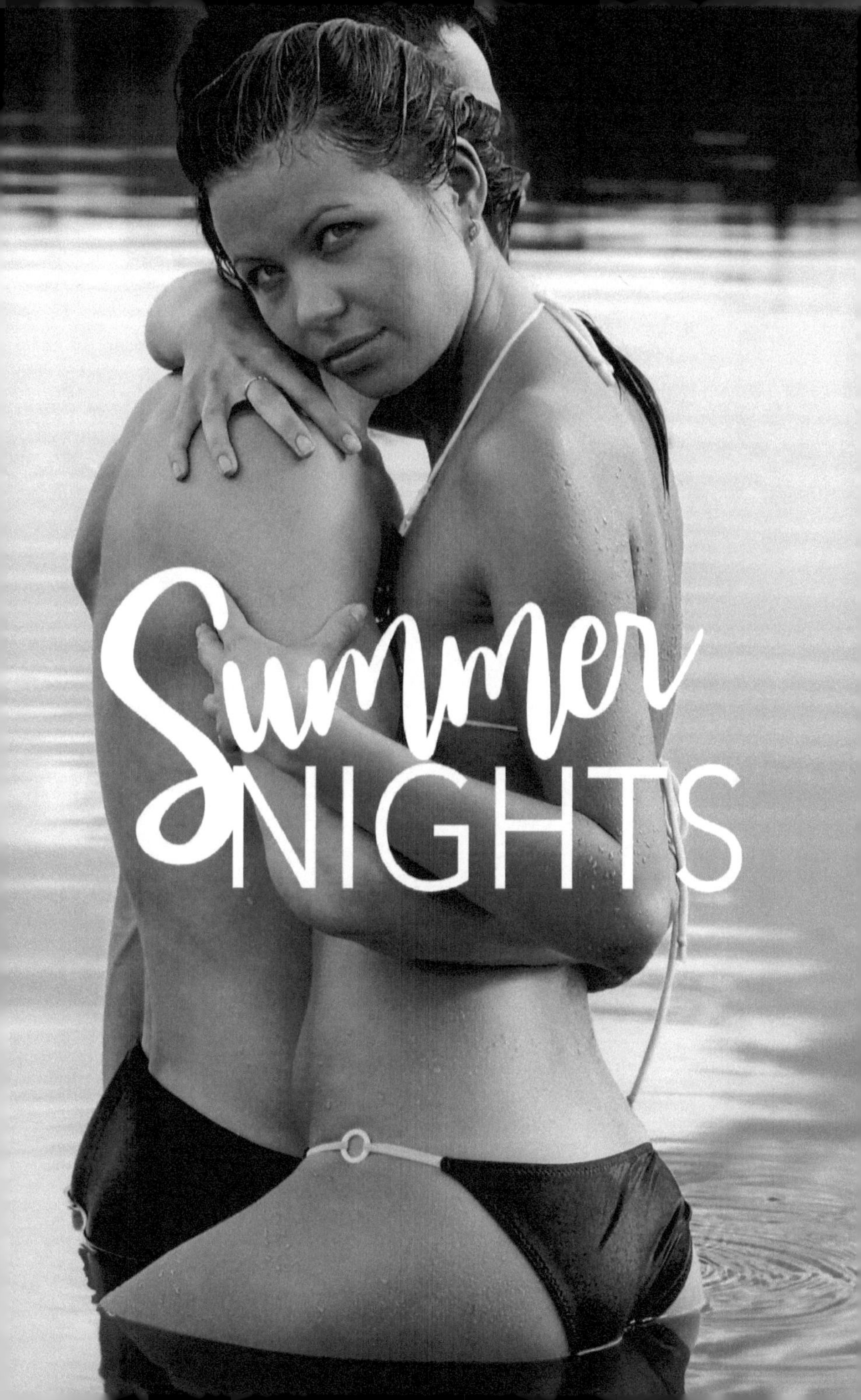
Summer
NIGHTS

To Dirty Dancing
and
hot Summer Nights.

Chapter ONE

Ray

Gravel pierced my hands as I tried to stand.

Tears cascaded down my cheeks.

I hung my head as the world continued around me in a frenzy of firefighters and crying campers.

I wasn't strong enough to do this.

I couldn't.

I fell in love.

I lost it.

I lost my heart.

I lost my soul to a burning building.

To a blue duffel bag.

I moved to my knees as a paramedic tried to help me to my feet.

"I got her." Jackson's rough voice sounded like alarms in

my ears, or maybe they were just ringing from the blast. All I knew was that his arms felt all wrong.

His smell. Wrong.

He was just wrong.

I tried to pull away from him, but he wouldn't let me as we walked toward an ambulance.

"You need to get checked out," he whispered.

I shook my head no, but the paramedic didn't listen, maybe because I couldn't find my voice.

Maybe because I couldn't feel my heart.

It had died with him.

Burned.

The way I burned for him.

Tear after tear streamed down my cheeks in rapid succession. I tasted salt on my lips as my heartbeat picked up for no reason, shock? Devastation?

And then.

"We got him!" A male voice yelled.

I turned as they pulled Marlo out of the cabin on a stretcher. I stumbled over to him just as he opened his eyes.

"Hey there, SP." His voice was hoarse, his words punctuated by several coughs. It was the most beautiful thing I'd ever heard.

I burst into tears over his body while paramedics tried to move him.

"Holy fuck," Jackson said from behind me. "Could you not ever do that to us again?"

Marlo didn't even look at him, just stared me down like he couldn't believe I was real.

I clung to his wet hand and then frowned.

"They sprayed the building with water the minute it

exploded, I got hit with a shit ton of water shoving me back against the closet." He winced. "When the fireball from the explosion hit, I was behind a fallen bed frame and the only part of the cabin that wasn't burning."

I cried harder.

He tried to sit up, but the paramedic gently pushed him back down. "Look, I'm fine!"

"You were just in an exploding building, sir, you're not fine," He made air quotes with his fingers, then grabbed an oxygen mask. "Now let me do my job and examine you."

Marlo smirked, looking sexier than ever with smoke caking his face, against his white teeth and perfect smile. He nodded to me. "Can she do it instead?"

The paramedic looked less than amused while Jackson chuckled under his breath.

And then Jen was suddenly airborne.

Jackson caught her and stumbled back. "What? What's wrong?"

She kissed him so hard everyone with girly parts got pregnant with twins.

"Damn." Marlo wrinkled his face as though in pain. "I think she broke him with that kiss."

Jackson set her on her feet, wrapped his arms around her body, and pulled her so close my chest ached, in a happy way, for them. It was like once he was unleashed he couldn't help but love her back.

The paramedic flashed a penlight in one of Marlo's eyes and then the other.

I smiled as Marlo reached for my hand and squeezed it.

"Mild concussion." That same paramedic said as he took his blood pressure and did a hundred other things while staff members kept the campers back. "You have someone who can stay with you tonight?"

"I'm the someone." I raised my hand. "What do I need to know?"

"Not to let him fall asleep for one," the paramedic said in a stern tone.

"Don't worry, sir, we've got that covered." Marlo rasped while my cheeks flashed red.

"Uh-huh," the paramedic looked between us like he was doubtful Marlo was in good hands. "And you're going to need to take it easy the next few days."

"Wait!" Marlo tried jumping to his feet and stumbled against me instead, I steadied him. "I can't just take it fucking easy I'm the camp director. I have—"

"Look, I don't care what you have to do, you were just in both a burning and exploding building where little things like humans go splat. Who's your second in charge?"

We both looked to Jackson, who was currently pulling at Jen's clothes in such a frenzy that I almost covered my eyes.

"Her." Marlo cleared his throat and pointed to me. "She'll take over."

I gave him a wide-eyed look, ready to strangle him and send him back into the building.

"Great, all settled." Mr. Happy Paramedic finished checking out his unhappy patient while I sent seething thoughts Marlo's way.

All of which, he just deflected with his perfect smile and, well, the fact that he was alive. When the paramedics finally left, I helped him back toward his cabin where I forced him to change so I would never have to look at a burnt staff shirt again.

Marlo peeled the staff T-shirt over his head.

And that's when I lost it.

Just completely lost it.

I fell into a heap of tears and hiccups.

"Whoa, whoa, whoa," Marlo gripped my head between his palms. "What's wrong, princess?"

"You!" I smacked his chest. "How dare you think you can just run into a burning building and save someone's life! You're mine! You're mine, damn it! MINE!"

With each shouted word, his smile grew, and then he gave me a smug look. "Are you done?"

"No!" I fisted my hands. "I'm not done! I'm pissed! I'm terrified! I love you! I don't love people, Marlo! I didn't even have a pet to love! I have you! I need to always have you don't you get it? You can't just bare your soul, ask me to bare mine, and then leave me broken! You can't! You. Are. Mine!"

"I'm yours." He agreed with a hitch in his voice. "I've always been yours, even when you didn't want me." His eyes darkened. "But we can't control the universe so I need to know that if the worst ever happened, if for some reason I drown in the lake tomorrow and you can't follow me… you'll be okay."

"No. You just have to live forever."

"Right." He snorted out a laugh. "Well thank you, for loving me so much you control my life, my death, my every waking moment. Thank you, Ray. I don't think anyone has ever loved me that much. I don't think I'll ever deserve that sort of love."

"Just…" I swiped my cheeks. "Take off your clothes already!"

"Huh?"

I tugged his charred jeans down, kissed each bandage on his chest, and then grabbed his shower caddy, a pair of shorts and tossed them at him. "Let's get the smoke off."

"All right…" he slowly got into his shorts and followed me to the bathroom.

We stopped in front of the same stall we'd had sex in.

I turned on the water.

He stood behind me.

I could feel his heat.

Feel his need.

It almost covered the choking fear still wrapping itself around me.

I leaned my head back onto his chest while he gripped my hips and pulled me against him. He was hard, hot, perfect.

Alive.

"If I go in there, I'm not just showering."

"If you go in there I'm going to put my mouth on you." I shrugged, peeled off my clothes, and stepped in.

Chapter TWO

Marlon

I was trying to be strong for her, for us, but every time I lost focus, I saw her face. Her terrified gaze as she reached for me, as the explosion sent me reeling backward so hard that the next thing I remembered was getting pulled out by the firefighters.

It hit me in those brief moments that felt like forever, while we stared at one another, I would do anything for her. And I'd be lying if I didn't at least admit that I was petrified it wasn't real, that she'd consider this a summer fling and move on.

With a sigh, I wrapped my arms around her waist. She flipped around so fast I stumbled back and then she fell to her knees, taking my shorts down with her.

We weren't even in the shower yet.

I still smelled like smoke, had it all over my face and hair.

And she was on her knees in front of me like a fucking dream.

Maybe I did die.

Maybe this was Heaven.

She wrapped a hand around me.

I jerked toward her, bracing my hands against the white tile, my fingers digging in while she lowered her head. Her hair spilled over her cheek, grazing my dick like a caress right before I felt the warmth of her mouth surround me.

I gritted my teeth against hot, tingling sensations that ricocheted through me, weakening my knees and leaving me short of breath. "I'm not going to last that long." Or at all. Not in my current state, not with the vision of her on her knees, taking me in, sucking me dry.

The sound of talking had her pulling away with a smirk. I pressed her against the wall, our mouths met in a burst of pent up passion and fear as I turned on the shower and spiraled into an oblivion of pleasure with her rubbing her body against me like she was going to go insane if she didn't have me. A heady craving drummed through me as her breasts slid against my chest. I wanted her there forever in my arms, under that shower, anywhere I could have her.

"We seem to have a thing for sex in the wrong places." She laughed against my mouth and deepened the kiss. Her tongue tasted so sweet I wanted to keep sucking it.

Another shower turned on.

We both laughed mid-kiss. I stopped laughing when she reached between us, grasping me so hard that I saw stars, and pumped into her hand.

"Don't stop," I saw a dizzying amount of stars as she moved back and forth. I growled against her mouth and slapped her hand away then slid inside her in one thrust that had her thighs clenching around me as her fingernails dug into my shoulders, shooting sharp, exquisite pain down my arms and into my neck.

I rocked into her, each thrust deeper than the last, faster. "Princess I can't—I want—" My thoughts jumbled together. My body wanted one thing, my brain said to slow down and savor it. My body was winning the argument.

"You're mine, Marlo." She pushed me against the tile while I gripped her ass and lifted her, deepening my angle. "That feels so good."

I groaned. "It feels better than good."

Her body went taut along with mine as I moved her against me. And then I was pushing her up against the wall, impaling her, with each thrust I swore I'd love her forever. And with each moan that erupted from her lips, I knew I would have her.

Mine. She was mine.

"Marlo…" Her head fell back against the wall as she found her release. I followed soon after, spent, exhausted, ready for the longest nap in the history of naps.

I kissed up her body as she slid down mine, and met her lips, sucking the water droplets from the shower as she grinned against my mouth.

"Glad you're feeling better," came Brax's tight, traumatized voice from one of the other stalls. "Also, good to know your dick didn't burn off. I was worried."

"Damn, Brax!" I yelled back. "Could you at least cough next time?"

"Like a cough would have stopped you two going at it like hyenas." He shut off his shower while I mouthed at Ray, *"Hyenas?"*

"Don't you mean bunnies?" Ray asked.

I shot her a look of please don't encourage his crazy.

"That too." He sighed. "Also, I feel like it needs to be addressed, that was a three-minute shower, all right then! See you soon! Get some rest, Marlo!"

"I almost died!" I yelled after him. "Stop judging my sexual performance, this isn't the Olympics!"

"Good because you wouldn't have even medaled!" he yelled back just as the door slammed.

I was seconds from chasing after him.

Probably would have just because I wasn't thinking straight.

But I heard sniffling.

When I turned, it was to see tears streaming down Ray's face. She'd always been beautiful to me, but when she cried, it made her eyes almost glow. It was impossible to look away, and I knew in that moment, there would never be a time in my life where I would be able to let her go. Where I could be able to walk away without a fight.

"Ray, look at me." I tilted her chin toward me. Tears dripped off of it, her lower lip trembled. "It's going to be okay. I promise."

She nodded her head, though her eyes said she didn't believe me.

"What are you afraid of?" I whispered, slowly grabbing some soap and washing up and down her legs. I looked up, waited.

She gave her head a shake. "I didn't stand up for you."

"What?" I frowned and ran my soapy hands up her stomach, around her breasts; she sighed and leaned into me. "What do you mean?"

"I mean, I didn't stand up for you. I deserve bad things, not good things. I laughed when they made fun of you, I called you a nerd behind your back while secretly watching you from my bedroom window. I did all of those things. For four years, I did those things, so why would the universe let me have you now? When I've done nothing to earn you?"

"You're right." I rinsed off my hands. "I should probably go."

She looked down at her feet, a tear dripped from her chin.

"I mean, I'm perfect right? I should just… go find someone who can last three minutes too… Someone who likes revenge sex in bathroom stalls and likes to play the part of the asshole ninety percent of the time…"

"It's not working…" She wiped under her eyes. "I know what you're doing."

"Oh yeah? What's that?"

"You're saying you're just as bad…" She shook her head. "You don't know what I've done, the things I've done."

"Nothing will ever make me stop loving you." I pulled her into my arms, "All right?"

"Don't say things you don't mean," she whispered and then grabbed some soap. She didn't say anything more, and maybe it was my concussion but I felt her pull away.

I felt her do what she swore she would never do.

Only this time, out of guilt, out of a past that no longer mattered.

I pulled her into my arms and kissed her head. "Let me see you."

With a sigh, she lifted her chin, our eyes met. "I'm right here."

"Good, because you have a long day ahead of you as director." I slapped her ass. "Better carb up."

She scowled and then somehow, I was kissing her again.

And her hands were tangled in my hair.

And I thought, *this is what I was missing out on, every summer night I saw her swim at her parents, every summer night she stared me down like she wanted me to watch.*

This.

And I vowed, never again.

Chapter THREE

Ray

"**B**rax, seriously!" I threw my hands up in the air. "Just get the menu so you can write it down and find me the damn whistle!"

He grinned. "Aw, you want Marlo's whistle? Is that what the kids are calling it these days?"

I glared.

I'd had exactly zero sleep.

So freaked out that the concussion Marlo suffered was going to kill him that I made his Keurig my bitch and literally sat up all night waking him up every few hours and asking him stupid questions like how old are you, who do you love?

"Twenty-two, and you. I love you. Sleep, Ray… my Ray of sunshine…" He turned on his side and pulled me next to him.

God he was so warm.

So strong.

Just everything that I wasn't, everything that I needed so desperately I hungered to just touch him, and soak him in.

The guilt over the way I treated him kept creeping back into my consciousness ruining the dopey grin on my face when he said my name in his sleep.

He was mine.

I wasn't giving him back.

To anyone.

I just had to learn how to deal with the guilt and move on with him, right? Together?

I just had this horrible feeling that because of what I'd done, the way I'd treated him, the universe was going to punish me.

Punish me for not being strong enough to earn him.

Punish me for being so weak that I chose to hate him instead of love him.

When the alarm went off, I tried to gently wake him up, and when he didn't open his eyes, full on panic set in. "Marlo! MARLO!"

His eyes flashed open. "Holy shit, SP, are you trying to kill me?"

I smacked him in the arm. "You weren't waking up!"

"So you yelled an inch from my face?" He winced and rubbed his eyes.

Yeah, maybe I'd been hopped up on caffeine a bit much. "Uh, yes… I did."

"Oh I know you did, my ears are still ringing, careful or you're going to turn me into an asshole again where I yell right back." He smirked.

I rolled my eyes. "Once an asshole, always an—"

He grabbed me by the waist, tossed me onto the bed and straddled me. "Are you sure you're up for it today?"

I was too busy staring at his growing erection and licking my lips wondering if I could have another taste.

"Hey, eyes up here, we're not animals." He snapped his fingers in front of my face.

"The hell we aren't." I jerked down his briefs, and as he sprang free, I let out a happy sigh. "For good luck?"

With a groan, he was already rolling onto his back pulling me with him. "Wasn't I supposed to take things easy today?"

"Absolutely." I clawed down his perfect naked chest, avoiding the band-aids the paramedic had applied to the small cuts from flying glass. "So, let me take care of you."

His eyes hooded as I peeled my shirt over my head.

"For a spoiled princess you sure have fantastic ideas."

"For an asshole you sure have a nice cock."

He licked his lips and looked away. "You trying to make it hard for me to think about anything but pounding inside that perfect body?"

"Uh, yeah?" I winked and then we were together, perfectly in sync, perfectly us.

"YO!" Jackson waved a clipboard in front of my face. "Just check in on all the classes make sure everyone's happy, and don't forget you have to teach in an hour. Brax and I split Marlo's responsibilities. Brax is bringing him lunch, I'm bringing dinner, and you, baby girl, get to bring dessert, rawr."

"Oh… he already had that this morning." I winked.

"I've never hated him more." Jackson sighed and crossed his arms just as Jen walked up and gave me a forced smile.

"Everything okay?" I asked.

"Yup!" She sounded way too happy with my question and way too happy with her one word answer. "I was just going to see if you needed anything. I've got a lot of free time on my hands now that the guy I like decided to reject me."

Jackson groaned.

"After sex," she added.

Another groan from Jackson.

"Twice."

Now a curse.

I glared at him while he just stared down at the ground.

"Actually…" I cleared my throat. "If you could just check on Marlo in the next hour that would be great, I'm sure he's fine, but…"

"She worries," Jackson added.

Jen didn't even look at him, just flashed me a warm smile. "Absolutely. See you later, Ray."

"I'm standing right here!" Jackson yelled.

"Ohhhhhh," Jen turned around, "And Ray, you may want to get rid of the tiny dick standing next to you." She flipped him off and kept walking.

I whistled. "Really? Really Jackson?" And then I was shoving him while he shoved me back. Apparently Marlo was the only real adult among us.

I pinched his arm.

"Ouch!" Jackson swore. "I have sensitive skin!"

"Bullshit! You need to stop poking your sensitive dick into other people who prefer your heart over your—" I sputtered. "Go apologize!"

"I did." He hung his head. "You know… after."

"What every girl dreams of, apologies after sex. Good job."

Campers mulled around us, grabbing food and coffee, and there was Jackson staring after Jen, who wasn't even in the room anymore.

He let out a rough sigh. "I think I love her."

"Someone needs to muzzle you," I grumbled. "You don't tell a girl you THINK you love her. You either do or you don't. Furthermore, why would you push her away if you love her?"

He shot me a glare. "Oh, gee I don't know, why would I do that? Any clues Miss Perfect, oh wait, you and Marlo…"

I pinched him again. "We're fine now."

"Bullshit." He snorted. "Sex ruins it, doesn't fix it, so you had what? A conversation and now everything is perfect? No skeletons in the closet? No crazy banging down your door? Yeah, I say a hell no to that. Relationships take work and time, I would know, because I despise both of those things, but the truth of the matter is this. Marlo's never been in one, and I'm guessing you haven't either, so if you think everything is peachy, you're crazy."

The blood drained from my head, leaving me lightheaded.

"Chin up, buttercup." He patted my head. "At least you guys are on speaking terms. And at least you didn't wake up with honey on your dick."

I covered my mouth with my hands "You didn't."

"I may be unable to perform sexually until all the honey's gone, I haven't Googled it yet, but it doesn't exactly…" He frowned. "It doesn't slide the same, it's like someone threw sticky paint on the slip and slide, and I'm afraid I'm going to get stuck and just — snap in half." He winced. "She's a joy, my Jen."

I burst out laughing. "Well, while you're dealing with that, I'm going to go eat before choreography."

"You do that." He saluted me, and I was off. Only I wasn't off.

I was stopped a million times with questions from anxious campers and staff members, so my breakfast turned into a muffin and a small cup of coffee with a banana to go before my first class.

And I was still five minutes late.

Luckily, I was just teaching the background, later that afternoon I'd be practicing with the leads.

"All right!" I clapped my hands. "Let's start at the beginning."

I hated that my focus was on Marlo and not the students.

But I'd spent a lifetime without what he had to offer, without this feeling in my chest, this sickening yet incredible feeling.

And I was so worried that one day, it would be gone.

How do you keep a feeling anyway?

How do you hold it in your hands?

I wish I knew how.

For now, I'd just hold him.

My head throbbed as the last of my class dismissed themselves. I sat down on the chair and pressed my fingertips into my temples then decided the only thing that was going to make me feel better was drinking my body weight in either coffee or red bull. Who knew being director was so difficult? It wasn't just that, it was balancing everyone's needs while still trying to make sure you did a good job at teaching.

Legs heavy, I made my way from the studio all the way over to the mess hall to grab something to drink. When I opened the door and stepped in, I narrowed my eyes at a guilty looking Marlo who was standing in front of the coffee bar.

"Aren't you supposed to be in bed?" I yawned as I made my way over to him.

He smirked into his coffee, but I could see his hooded eyes over the rim, filled with lust and delicious promises that made me want to peel my shirt over my head and lay down on the nearest table. "Aren't you supposed to be with me?"

"Hah." I wagged my finger at him. "He's got jokes and a concussion, nice."

"I'm fine…" He didn't look fine. He looked exhausted, though still gorgeous, his tanned skin was still rippling with too many muscles, and his smile still made me want to do dirty things to him.

Why did he have to be the sort of guy you wanted to piss off and make smile? It was almost the gut instinct to lash out just so I could feel his penetrative gaze on my skin.

Yeah, I needed a nap, a long nap.

"Loser!" A girl shouted and then started laughing as she poured milk over another teen's head. He was pretty scrawny and had his head ducked into a book. Milk dripped down his lips as he started to shake.

"And no, the answer is no, I'm not interested." She sneered while her friends rolled their eyes at each other. A few nearby teens started laughing.

I blew my whistle, outrage seeping out of me. "Hey, you two, here, now!"

The girl flashed me a pretty smile, but not before tossing a napkin at the teen and muttering. "Clean yourself up, milk man."

"Out of line." I pointed my finger at her. "That's one strike, two more and I'm calling your parents to come pick you up!"

"Like they would care, do you know who my parents are?"

"Do you know who I am?" Marlo moved to stand next to me. "Listen carefully, I have the power to destroy whatever pathetic career you may or may not have depending on the end of the summer. You want an agent? I'll make sure you're so far in the background that nobody even sees the hair on your head, are we clear?"

She lifted her chin. "Yes."

"Good." He grinned, looking exhausted and pissed again. "Now apologize, using his real name. Not milk man, lawn boy—" I jerked my head to attention when he stopped himself, clenched his fingers into angry fists, and exhaled. "Have some human decency. That's all I'm asking."

Marlo turned to me, his face unreadable, and then he shook his head. "I'm sorry, you're right, I should have stayed in bed, I'm going to go lie down."

I frowned and reached for his hand. He took it and stared down at our interlocked fingers like he wasn't sure what to make of it.

Panic seized my lungs.

He leaned in and kissed my cheek then walked away.

I stared after him as the world faded around me.

Fear crept into my chest at the thought of seeing his back and for some horrible reason, it just reminded me of my childhood that much more, of my parents turning their backs on me.

Always their backs.

Never their faces.

What if he did that to me too?

What did I possibly have to capture his attention once the summer was over? Was I just the challenge he could never win?

And what type of person thinks that after confessing love? After saying this was forever?

Me. The type of broken person who can't even function on their own without hating themselves.

The type of person who bullies a broken high school boy in order to fit in with her friends, so they accept her.

The type of person so desperate for any sort of love, that she'd cling to just about anything and mark it as hers.

I hung my head.

Physically everything was perfect wasn't it?

But about emotionally? What about the words? The painful ones I kept to myself? The hard confessions I'd rather forget?

What about the truth?

That he was coming to me completely whole.

And I was only giving him the best part of myself because I was so ashamed of the other half.

I moved toward the door, bumping into Brax before righting myself.

He steadied me. "You all right?"

"I'm—" I frowned. "Fine?"

"Are you asking me if you're fine?" His eyes narrowed.

"Here." I handed him the whistle. "I'm going to take a walk then go down to the beach can you cover?"

"Sure." He drew out the word.

"Good." I turned and walked.

I walked and walked.

And when my legs felt shaky, I finally went to the beach and prayed that for once in my life the dancing would set me free.

Because I'd just realized.

Nobody could do that, but me.

Chapter FOUR

Marlo

I was bored out of my mind.

My head throbbed at my temples, but I figured it had more to do with Jackson's voice than anything.

"So then I was all, I think I love you." Jackson sighed. "Was that wrong?"

I squeezed my eyes shut. "Man you lost me when you said you slept with her and then said you were sorry."

"Shit!" He kicked a pillow toward me. I dodged it and let out a sigh.

"Wow, I finally know what it's like to have a slumber party. Fucking hate it."

Jackson flipped me off and then lay back on the other bed, the one I'd had Ray sleep in, the one I never wanted her in again.

Mine.

All mine.

My body buzzed with awareness at the thought of her, of pressing my mouth to hers, gripping those hips, thrusting into that perfect heat. She was my sunset, my dawn.

Shit you know it's bad when you write lousy poetry in your head.

A knock sounded on the screen door. Finally. Rescue!

Brax made his way inside without me saying anything. "Sure, come on in…" I muttered. Not exactly the rescue I had in mind.

"Huh?" He looked genuinely confused. "So, anyway, as I was saying…" What the hell? "Ray's doing great, she looks a bit stressed but she's checked up on all the classes, the only problem is that we don't have any understudies for the main roles, and the campers who want to be understudies look ready to shit themselves when you put them on stage."

"Nice." Jackson chuckled.

"We'll do what we always do." I shrugged. "The staff members are understudies, and extras. That way the staff still gets seen by scouts."

"Uh-huh." Brax grinned at me. "That's what I thought you'd say."

"You're confusing the hell out of me," I muttered.

"Campers voted, you lose. Both you and Ray get to be understudies for Johnny and Baby, congrats bro!"

I nearly fell off my bed. "I'm the director. I'm the only one who *doesn't* get on stage."

"Not this year." Brax offered a half-assed shrug. "Campers said that if the worst happens they want you guys up there, something about making babies with your dancing?"

Jackson snorted out a laugh while I squeezed my eyes shut. "Fine."

"Hey, no worries, you'll probably just end up being in the background like the rest of the staff, but I'd polish up on your lines just in case." Brax held up his hand.

"What am I supposed to do with that?" I pointed at his palm.

"Bro, high five, as in you hit this with your hand? Do I not get a high five for delivering good news?"

Jackson kicked him in the ass.

"Son of a bitch!" Brax rubbed his ass and jogged toward the door at the same time. "Fine, I'll let you girls gossip, but before I leave, I thought you should know…" He grinned. "Ray's at the lake."

"Okay?"

"She's dancing."

I narrowed my eyes. "By herself?"

He nodded and then whispered. "It's fucking beautiful."

I was out the door before he could say more, running as fast as I could, concussion or not, toward the beach. Thankful that I was a runner, that I hadn't inhaled too much smoke, that my lungs weren't seizing with each long stride.

A cloud of dirt went up around my feet when I stopped, my jaw nearly came unhinged from my face as I watched her body move.

She was dancing on the beach.

To no music.

My eyes burned, but I barely blinked, just watching the sunset over her body as she lifted her hands into the air and twisted her body around.

Our gazes locked.

And I could have sworn my heart stopped in order to hear the cadence of hers and join in — I'd never wanted to touch another human so desperately in my entire life.

I took a step toward her.

Lips parting, she dropped her hands and then crooked her finger.

My blood heated as I finally reached her.

But I didn't touch her.

I knew if I did, I'd combust on the spot.

So I stood inches from her face and read every expression in her eyes, loss, sadness, anger, joy.

With each blink, she showed me her truth.

With each exhale, she showed me her soul.

Our foreheads touched as I whispered. "Dance with me."

Chapter FIVE

Ray

My chest rose and fell with each touch of his fingertips on my body, like I was fragile, like he knew I was falling apart.

I had every reason in the world to be happy.

I had him.

And yet, I was a mess.

Every time I thought of us, a choking sensation from my past rose up and wrapped its hands around my throat.

So I danced.

I danced it away.

Because I danced better than I talked.

He twirled me in his arms.

I sucked in a breath as he whispered against my neck. "What's your truth…"

"More of this?" I said a bit breathless.

"Until I have all of you," he promised.

Another twirl.

And then like a waterfall of words, I confessed. "My friends came over, we laughed while you mowed the lawn. I threw—" My stomach rolled as my foot caught in the sand, he kept me upright. I couldn't even look at his face. "I threw skittles at you and called you stupid." Oh God, was that me? Had I been that person? "And then I told them you tasted like grass."

"I probably did," came his quick answer.

A tear slid down my cheek. "I used to walk by your locker and scowl, but it was because I knew I wasn't good enough for you, and after that night, all I wanted to do was find a way to crawl into it and stay there forever."

"I wouldn't have minded," he whispered against my neck as we found our steps around one another, like a choreographed dance we both had memorized. What was happening?

My chest lightened as he smiled against my neck and pressed a kiss there, still holding me in his arms as we moved. "You were naked, and I laughed." I squeezed my eyes shut as a tear fell. "I laughed and I pointed, and you looked so angry, and I knew I deserved your anger, but I also knew if I didn't point, if I didn't laugh when I walked by the pool house, I'd ask you to kiss me again, so I laughed to keep myself from you. I knew my friends wouldn't let me and they — they were all I had."

"They weren't friends."

"They weren't friends." I sighed. "But they were all I had."

"That's not true," he said in a gruff voice. "Because you could have had me. And did have me, every single time you pointed, every single time you laughed, every single time you sighed. You've never been able to hide your eyes from me, and even then, when I hated you and dreamed about running you over with my lawnmower—" I laughed at that. "I knew that if I touched you again I would take you forever, and you'd never forgive me for it."

"You would have taken away my only friends, my only solace."

"And your parents?"

I went still in his arms. "I thrived off your hate because at least it was something, it was passion, it was so closely tied with what I thought love was, that I thought maybe, just maybe, it would sustain me."

"Did it?"

"It made me want you more..." I turned to face him. "My last confession... you're the only person who has ever said they loved me out loud."

His eyes softened.

And I hated myself for what I was about to do.

"Are you ready for the final truth?"

"No." His voice cracked as he swallowed, his eyes never leaving mine.

"I don't think I can fully love you the way you deserve... unless I love myself first... and I don't know how." I sniffled and wiped the tears falling under my eyes.

I thought he'd yell at me.

He was, after all, a self-proclaimed asshole.

"Are you saying — a day after I nearly died — that we're through?"

"I'm saying..." My throat caught, tightening my voice. "...that I'm broken, and as much as I wish it, your love can't fix me. Only I can fix me."

He dropped his arms and took a step back.

I wanted him to hold me forever.

I wanted him to say he would wait for me.

I wanted him to say he understood.

Instead, his expression was unreadable.

And then pain.

So much pain I wished for a swift death.

"Marlo?"

"No." He shook his head. "No."

"No what? Say something!"

"You want me to say something?" He gritted his teeth.

I jerked at his angry tone.

"I think you're weak," he said in a cold voice. "I think you're running because it's easy. I think you want a road without pain, and that road doesn't exist. Life is pleasure and pain over and over again. It's sick chaos. And the worst part? You've believed the lie that one day you'll wake up whole, when you already are, you just refuse to accept it." He did a small circle and then wiped his hands down his face. "You need space? You need to find yourself?"

I gulped.

"Do it without me then, but remember this point in your life when I offered you everything and you didn't trust yourself enough to take it."

"Marlo—" I reached for him, touched him.

He jerked back. "Get the fuck away from me."

"Marlo!"

He turned around.

And walked away.

He'd asked for my truth.

He'd asked for my confession.

He wasn't ready.

Then again, neither was I.

I crumpled to my knees and sobbed.

I cursed my parents.

My life.

My past.

And for the first time since his death — I said my brother's name.

"Kieren."

It burned my throat.

It was as if the universe had a knife pressed into my chest.

Kieren.

Marlo didn't know.

He didn't know that I wasn't whole.

I haven't been since we'd buried my other half.

Since my parents blamed me for his death.

Since my twin's bedroom had been locked away from the world as if he was going to come back some day.

I wasn't whole.

Because I was born as a half.

Chapter SIX

Marlo

Two weeks ago, I had everything.

Two weeks ago, despite being caught in a firestorm caused by a fucking firework — I was happy.

Deliriously happy.

Now? Now I wanted to day drink and punch anyone who looked at me sideways.

"You going over your lines?" Jackson elbowed me, then grabbed a cup and started filling it to the brim with black coffee.

I scrolled through the first act on my iPad and shrugged. "Seemed to be the only thing to keep me from throwing coffee at everyone who said hi."

He whistled. "Is this what happens when you go without sex? Gotta admit, it's a bad look on you. When was the last time you shaved?"

"When was the last time you had honey on your dick?" I countered.

"Bastard," he muttered under his breath. "I'll be surprised if I could ever get it up again after that traumatic experience, thanks."

I looked up at him in confusion. "Wait, you've been... celibate?"

He narrowed his eyes. "You know it is possible for me to keep it in my pants, thank you very much."

"Right," I nodded slowly, "But last time we had this discussion you just replied with, why would I do something like that?"

"Why, indeed..." He swore as he took a long swig of coffee. Jen and Ray had found solidarity in one another.

Jen was pissed because Jackson was actually trying to do the right thing, just with poor execution.

And Ray?

Well, Ray still looked beautiful.

She also looked lost again.

The circles under her eyes concerned me, but not enough to go over and pull her into my arms.

Because I was an addict for her.

And I knew it would cause an explosion of hatred, rage, love, anger, and everything in between.

It would be a catastrophic explosion.

And we'd be back at square one.

She looked up at me.

I scowled and looked away.

"So, things with Ray are progressing, at least you're looking in her direction without yelling."

"I hate her. I love her," I admitted. "I want to strangle her then kiss her senseless, it's a problem."

"Maybe leave out the strangling," Jackson suggested helpfully.

I shot him an evil look and found a seat far, far away from the girls, he followed, Brax, dirty traitor, winked at us then went and joined the girls.

I heard them laugh.

And it suddenly felt like high school all over again.

Only this time it was worse.

Because I knew she loved me.

I knew she cared.

And yet she wasn't willing to give me everything, was she?

She wasn't willing to let go of it all.

She held on to her pain the way people hang on to their loved ones, almost like it was so familiar she wasn't sure she could survive without it, not realizing that the very thing that made her feel safe was killing her.

The words on the screen in front of me blurred a bit before I just shoved the iPad down and rubbed my eyes with the heels of my hands.

When I looked up it was to see Jen staring me down with a worried look on her face.

"Spill." I crossed my arms.

She jerked her head to the side. "Make him go away and I will."

"You have her doing recon?" Jackson snapped his fingers in the air. "And I'm right here, have I told you yet how much I miss your wet—"

Jen clapped a hand over his mouth.

He grinned behind her hand.

Hey, at least him teasing her kept them in physical contact.

I would do anything to touch Ray.

My fingers itched.

My chest ached.

And nothing took the pain away.

Jackson stared up at Jen.

Jen stared at me.

I cleared my throat.

With a grunt, Jackson stood, then leaned toward Jen and whispered, "I smell you on my skin, every damn night… just thought you should know, you're driving me crazy."

"Good." She didn't look at him, but I saw her falter, saw her clench her hands into tiny fists to keep from reaching out.

Yeah, give it a week and he was going to be bringing Gatorade to his cabin and ordering condoms in bulk.

Lucky him.

Jackson gave me a middle finger salute and walked off while Jen sat opposite me, her face impossible to read. "She misses you."

"Good." My voice came out sounding bitter, angry.

Jen leaned forward and reached out her hands. I grabbed them both and squeezed. "How are you Jen, really?"

"Bad." Tears filled her eyes. "I love him, and he thinks he loves me, what if this all ends and he goes back to being Jackson? I want to punish him but I don't know how long I can stay away. I've always loved him."

"Jackson is…" I let out a sigh. "He's complicated. Ever since his sister died, things haven't been right. We were all altered when she killed herself. You do remember when you had to wake my drunken ass up for breakfast for a solid month right along with his right?"

She nodded. "Does Ray know?"

"About?"

"Her."

"She knows enough."

"I doubt it." Jen angled her head like she was examining me. "There's a lot you don't know about her. I know you grew up gazing at her window and sighing like a girl every afternoon hoping to see a flash of boob, but the shit with her parents, it's deeper than you could possibly imagine."

"Her parents." I drummed my fingertips against the table.

"Oh no, I know that look. What are you thinking?"

"I'm thinking it's time for an impromptu parent visit day. We'll use it as a dress rehearsal." I grinned.

"That could very easily blow up in your face, you know that right?"

"Look, I'm the director, and what I say goes, right? Plus, it's good practice for the campers and they get to see Mommy and Daddy, what could go wrong?"

"Only everything." She groaned. "Plus, if my parents get wind…"

"Your parents are awesome."

"They dressed up two years ago."

"That they did."

"As Batman and Wonder Woman and then made out in front of like half the staff and campers." She glared at me. "We got complaints."

I grinned. "But it was the best, wasn't it?"

"Ugh, the best." She laughed. "Fine, do your little parent day, I'll send out the email this afternoon, you want it for the weekend or just overnight like previous years?"

"Let's do overnight, that way if things do go bad it's only a twenty-four-hour affliction.

"I hope you know what you're doing. The reason they didn't do parent day last year was because it distracted the campers and made them more homesick."

"They'll be fine." I shrugged. "Make it happen, Jen."

"Yes sir."

I squeezed her hand.

"Also," she said once she stood and let go of my hand. "You should know… she wants her chicken back."

"Tell her to come and get it."

Chapter SEVEN

Ray

I knocked on his cabin door twice.

It was late.

I knew he was in there because the light was on and because I always knew where he was — it was like my heart couldn't help it.

I wasn't okay.

I didn't know how to be.

I just knew I needed my stupid chicken.

I knocked again.

Finally, the screen door opened.

And there he was, my lawn boy, farm boy, my Wesley, my love. No shirt, so naturally all I saw was abs. Abs that I'd had my mouth on, skin I'd scratched, hips I'd wrapped my legs around. My vision lowered to the V I'd wanted to take picture of and save on my home screen.

He cleared his throat and crossed his arms.

"The chicken," I got out past the tightness in my throat. "He's mine."

"Is it a custody issue? Because he's been living with me for the past two weeks so…" He shrugged and then gave me an evil sneer that had me ready to strangle him. "Looks like your shit out of luck, maybe if you look hard enough you can find a turtle down by the beach."

"I want the chicken," I said through clenched teeth, taking a step toward him. "He's my pet."

"We voted, you lost, he likes it here better, plus isn't your cabin a bit drafty?" He tilted his head, his stupid silky hair fell over his forehead, and even though he was scowling he was beautiful, almost more beautiful angry than when he was in love, which seemed impossible but there it was.

"Marlo," I took another step toward him. He didn't move out of the way, but his breath hitched. I lifted my chin. "What do I have to do to take my chicken back?"

"Kiss me," he rasped. "Kiss me and you can take the chicken."

"Where?" I tried to keep the shaking out of my voice.

"Wherever you like." He towered over me. "Just one kiss, and you can take your pet home…"

"Fine." I dropped to my knees in front of him.

His expression went from confident and angry to extremely pissed off. He wanted a kiss? I'd give him a kiss all right.

I'd kiss him.

Moonlight flickered across his chest as I dragged my

fingernails down and then jerked his sweats down his hips and lowered my head.

"Ray—" His voice was angry, it was also disappointed, like I was doing something beneath me, like I was on the losing end instead of him.

Tears gathered in my eyes as I took him in my mouth, and then I parted with a kiss.

He didn't move, just stared down at me like I was a stranger.

Swiping at my eyes, I moved past him and grabbed Johnny. He was on the other bed, set up in a little nest of clothes and magazines that I'm sure Marlo left for him.

I had him in my arms and was walking by Marlo, when I was hauled back by the arm.

He kissed me then.

He kissed me so hard my mouth hurt, my teeth clanged with his, Johnny started flapping in my arms like he was getting smashed.

And then Marlo released me just as hard as he'd grabbed me.

"Don't be that girl," he said in a low voice. "Be better."

"I hate you."

"At least we have that in common," he responded. "Though I think you probably hate yourself a little bit more, don't you?"

"How dare you!" I about screeched as my tears began to flow freely. "You don't know me!"

"Whose fault is that, I wonder?" he fired back with a roar, slamming his hand against the screen door. "I'd give you everything and you'd still find a way to say it wasn't enough! I'm sorry I'm not rich enough for you. I'm sorry I'm not from the right family. I'm sorry I mowed lawns and grew up as a fucking servant. What else do you want from me. WHAT!? A lifetime full of apologies for not being enough?"

"I never said—" My voice cracked. "I never said it was you."

"It's the only thing that makes sense. Spoiled princess strikes again." He glared, his nostrils flaring as he drew fast, harsh breaths.

I slapped him.

I didn't mean to.

He grabbed my hand and then sighed as if he was relieved. "I'll take your hate if I can't have your love. Isn't it sick? I just want something passionate from you, whatever the cost."

"Remember, you'll always have both." I said, my face soaked with tears that were now dripping off my chin.

"One eventually has to win, Ray. And I won't wait forever. I'm done waiting. You love me, you hate me, you don't trust yourself, you don't trust me — find a way, because this—" he motioned between us. "—is over."

The door slammed in my face.

I wanted to kick it back open.

I wanted to scream and tell him he was wrong.

But he was right.

About everything.

Shame descended on me like a storm cloud as I walked back to my cabin, and no amount of tears could make it go away.

I wanted my mom.

I wanted my dad.

I wanted Kieran.

He would know what to do.

He'd died at such a young age, but he had been my best friend.

With shaking hands, I dug into my bag and pulled out the Polaroid I brought with me everywhere.

A dark-haired, dark-eyed Kieren. A light-haired, light-eyed me.

It was hard to remember the good times because the bad times so often overshadowed the good.

It was hard to remember a day where my parents said they loved me because it had been so long since they had.

Six years old.

We had only been six.

I hugged the stupid chicken, which managed not to move or get crushed in my arms, and I cried.

I cried for him.

For me.

For the prodigy that he was, the star he would have been, and I wondered if there was ever a time in my life when my parents hadn't wished it had been me instead of him.

Chapter EIGHT

Marlo

"Hey…" I knocked on Jackson's door and let myself in. I knew he was alone. I located a bottle of whiskey within thirty seconds, grabbed it, sat on his bed and took a long swig then laid back. "Tell me you have weed."

He was so quiet that I looked up to make sure he wasn't already passed out. He eyed me like he didn't know me anymore. Shit, if this was love, sign me up as a pass next time.

"I have weed," he finally blurted. "You can't have it, said it throws off your creative process, but I'll be happy to smoke it on your behalf."

I held out my hand.

He shook his head. "Aren't you the director of camp this year? Doesn't it state in the rule book that you won't do any drugs, legal or not?"

"Can't I fire your ass for possession?" I wondered out loud.

"You could, you won't." He grinned. "Also, you're weird when you're high. Last time you ate all of my food and then got pissed when we couldn't get pizza delivered."

"Dominos should deliver everywhere. That was bullshit, and you know it." I took another swig of whiskey, sat up and wiped my mouth. "I may have just taken five billion steps backward with Ray."

"How so?" He reached out, I handed him the bottle while he took his turn and handed it back.

"Oh, you know, lots of yelling, rage, asshole made an appearance and decided to stay after she sucked my dick rather than kissing me on the mouth, making it seem like a sexual favor rather than this personal thing I was trying to do to shake her up." I groaned into my hands. "I may have told her I hated her. Yeah, so basically all the things you can do wrong? I did in less than five minutes, and I can't apologize because she drives me so insane I can't help but just react."

"Huh," Jackson nodded. "This is why sex ruins things. You skip all the words and then realize that you're still just as fucked up as before you got naked, cheers."

"She won't let me in."

"You can't force yourself."

"If you could stop giving me good advice and just let me get high that would be fantastic." I groaned and drank more.

"And I'll take that." He jerked the bottle from my hand. "Look, this solves nothing, I would know, I mean look at me, I'm one bad decision away from going to prison at this point."

I rolled my eyes.

"It's true, trust me, just ask Jen, I'm kidnapping her later and putting her in my trunk, how long you think that will land me behind bars if I get caught?"

"Creepy looks creepy on you."

"You need more words between you. If she won't let you in and you can't force her, then guess what? She needs time, and you're not helping by asking for dick kisses."

"I didn't ask for a dick—" I shook my head. "The point is, I love her. Shouldn't that be enough?"

"What exactly did she say to you that day? We never got past the yelling and drunkenness on your part."

"She says she can't be with me if she doesn't love herself, but how the hell do I get her to love herself if she can't stand to be in the same room with the only guy willing to sell his soul to be with her?"

"That's your problem?" He burst out laughing.

I almost grabbed the bottle and hit him over the head with it.

"Bro, bro, listen up…" He grinned like he was already drunk, maybe he was. "Rumor mill i.e. Jen says she had a rough childhood right? And from the whole parent day thing happening this weekend, I can imagine that you're trying to parent trap her or something… If she doesn't love herself it's because she's never really known love and she doesn't feel worthy of it. So, you do the easy thing. You show her she is."

"I was showing her."

"No." Jackson tilted the bottle back. "You were fucking her. Big difference."

"That's not what I was—"

"That is exactly what you two were doing. That's not love."

"And you know this because?"

"I live by this." He rasped and looked down at the floor. "It's why I pissed Jen off, because I did things backward. Because I slept with her out of need, I took from her because I wanted her, and then afterward, when she was covering up her naked body, I knew I'd messed up — because she was insecure. And sex should never make a woman feel insecure, it should make her feel unstoppable, loved. So, I apologized because that's what a guy in love does when he messes up. Only she thought it was her. But it wasn't her. It was me. I messed up. She needed to know when we got to that place that it was about more than the physical, and she didn't. She assumed wrong and I tried to correct it — badly. You want her to know you really love her? Love her beyond all reason? You make her more important than you."

"She is."

"Prove it, because you've been walking around like a kicked, pissed-off puppy that never got a nice home. I know you have shit from your past, but you're Marlo Fucking Brandon, one of the most talented guys I know. Tell that little six-year-old shit self to shut the hell up and be a man. Now, if you'll excuse me, I'm going to drink the rest of this until I pass out and drown in my own puke."

I jerked the bottle from him. "No, you're not. I'm getting Jen."

"Oh good, she can kill me, thanks man."

Within minutes, I had Jen in the cabin.

She swayed toward him.

And then she was in his arms.

I left them staring at one another, hoping that she could at least anchor him and keep him from getting drunker.

I walked into my cabin, grabbed a pillow and a blanket, then made the trek up to Ray's cabin.

I knocked.

When she answered, she was sobbing.

Sobbing.

I did that.

I made her cry.

I pulled her into my arms and let her keep crying.

And then I gently tucked her into bed.

And put my pillow and blanket on the floor to set in for a very uncomfortable night next to a domesticated chicken.

Chapter
NINE

Ray

I woke up in the middle of the night and stared down at Marlo. I wanted him in my arms, in my bed. I wanted to tell him I hated him and I loved him and I was sorry.

I wanted him to know the truth.

That I hadn't felt like me in a really long time.

That he made me think I could be okay as long as I held his hand.

But what happened if he stopped?

It would break me.

I wouldn't survive having a love like his and losing it. It had nothing to do with self-sabotage and everything to do with growing up as if I was invisible and not wanting to return to that place.

How do you move past that feeling in your chest? The achy feeling paired with the words that say you are unlovable and you will never be enough to keep anyone's attention.

If you can't even keep your parents' attention?

How in the world can you keep him?

Perfect. Wonderful. Hateful. Him.

I reached down and touched his hair.

His hand immediately moved and grabbed mine, and then I was pulling him into my bed while he wrapped his muscular arms around me.

I pressed my head to his chest and listened to his heartbeat, and I wondered if it was selfish to wish that with every pulse it yearned for me the way mine yearned for his.

I squeezed my eyes shut and clung to him for dear life. I pushed away my worries, I pushed away my thoughts, and I inhaled him, drank him in, and just relaxed into his arms.

Morning would come too soon.

And along with that, I knew a line would divide us yet again.

If I could have him in my dreams, I could survive my day.

If I could have him in the moonlight, the sun wouldn't burn so bad.

He kissed my forehead.

"Sleep," he rasped.

So I did.

Because I was in his arms.

And I knew I was safe.

From the world.

From my nightmares.

Kieren would have liked him.

A lot.

I smiled as I drifted toward sleep with the picture of my twin in one hand, and the man I loved holding the other.

Chapter
TEN

Marlo

I woke up feeling like shit.

And when I turned and saw that Ray was still there, I felt even worse. She stared back at me like I was a stranger in her bed.

I didn't kiss her.

I held her next to me though.

I let out a dramatic sigh. "I'm sorry about the damn chicken."

Her lips pressed together in a firm line and then rose up at the sides. "It could have been worse, as in you could have eaten him."

I smiled wide. "Yeah that was in the plan, midnight fried chicken."

Johnny flapped into the air like he knew we were talking about him and then settled back in his spot on the bed.

I exhaled in relief. "I doubt I could have caught him anyway."

"Finally admitting that the chicken has more athletic ability?"

"I'm pretty sure that was never even on the table, but if it makes you feel better at night that the chicken can kick my ass — I'll give it to you." I stared into her hollow eyes.

I wanted to reach my hands into her body, to set loose her soul, I wanted her heart, I just wanted her to fly.

To be set free.

And no matter what I did.

Nothing worked.

I pulled.

She stayed.

And then like Cinderella at midnight — she lost the shoe, she retreated, she defaulted.

My mind went back to my conversation with Jackson. As much as I loathed what I was about to do, I said the words anyway. "I need you to know something, Ray."

"What?" Her face was worried, she chewed her lower lip and then inhaled a sharp breath like it was going to be bad news. Was she always expecting the negative? Never the positive?

"No matter what happens between us..." Kill me now. Someone stop me from dooming myself. "I want us to stay friends."

"Friends?" she repeated in a shocked voice. "What do you mean friends?"

I elbowed her in the side, then grabbed a pillow and

slammed it over her head. "You know the kind who have slumber parties and share secrets!"

"Ouch!" She tumbled away from me then grabbed the same pillow and chucked it at my face, I dove away only to have her jump onto my back and keep hitting. "You deserve this!"

I laughed so hard I had tears in my eyes as she lamely tried to muscle me back toward the mattress, I easily flipped her on her back and pinned her arms and legs. "Aw, you stuck?"

And since I was just taking the immaturity to an entire new low, I gripped her right foot and started to tickle.

She thrashed beneath me. "Noooooooooo!"

"Was it this spot?" I kept tickling. "Or was it the left foot that was more ticklish? I don't remember, it's been what… over twelve years so…"

"I'm KILLING YOU!" she shouted between huffs of laughter. "MARLO!"

"Keep screaming, only encourages!" I laughed and then dropped her feet when she tried kicking me in the face.

Ray let out a gasp and sat, hair wild, eyes alive with excitement like me tickling her was better than the best sex. "How do you remember?"

I licked my lips and tried to focus on the words, not the way I wanted to sink into her, the way I wanted to wrap my arms around her and make her promises I would keep, promises she deserved. "I remember everything about us back then, the late-night swimming, the campouts between our houses, you were always so sad, and then…"

She looked away. "You asked if you could be my friend."

"I was pretty lonely and dejected too," I admitted, giving

a half shrug. "I mean it wasn't as bad as asking my mom for a pet and then getting a rock, but…"

She winced. "Yeah that was a fun one, get a rock, dress it up, problem solved!"

"You had a lot of rocks." I grinned. "And then you had me."

"I didn't dress you up," she pointed out.

I let out a laugh. "Not for lack of trying!"

She smirked up at me. "You would have made a very pretty doll."

"I think the word you're looking for is creepy, and no. No, I would have looked like I belonged in a horror movie, trust me."

Tears welled in her eyes. "You were like this dark, angsty poet who hated everyone and everything."

"And you were this Ray of light who'd been pulled from the sky too many times, who'd started to dim because when you're pulled from your home — from your light, that's when darkness has no choice but to move in."

"Redemptive darkness," she whispered. "That's what you were to me."

"And now?"

"Now." She took a deep breath. "Now I just feel… like if I could just sit and touch you for the rest of my life and do nothing else — I would still feel unworthy of every second my skin touched yours."

I squeezed my eyes shut then opened them. "Funny, that we both feel the same way about each other — but not about ourselves."

"Easier said than done?" she asked with a nervous laugh.

"I want to start over," I confessed.

"What do you mean start over?"

"Well…" I moved to stand. "When we were kids, it was all about the words. I wasn't even sure what my dick was for other than peeing in your mom's fountain."

Ray's head fell back as she let out loud laugh. "Oh, she hated that."

"Also, why I found great joy in doing it." I crossed my arms. "We used to spend summer nights laying on the grass, watching the stars, making wishes. What did I promise you the summer before junior high?"

Her cheeks pinked. "You said I would be your first everything."

"First kiss, first sex, first love, first friend." I nodded. "And what did I do next?"

She looked down at her hands "You kissed me and said, two down, two to go. You said if other kisses don't feel like yours, then they aren't right for me, that you'd wait for me no matter the cost, and within two months, I was calling you lawn boy and making out with the point guard of our basketball team."

"He's in prison now."

"What!"

A laugh slipped out at the look of shock on her face. "Kidding, I was just trying to look better, give me that at least."

"You'll always look better." She gulped and stared down at my mouth.

See, normally this was where I would press her against the mattress, where I would ask her if I could taste her again.

This was where things would go south.

In a good way.

Don't go south.

Shit, this was going to be hard, because I'd already tasted, I'd already wanted again and again.

"I swore to you then I would be your first — and somehow I was able to follow through... Right?"

"Right," she whispered.

"Great, then hear me know... I will be your last Ray, your only, your forever, and I will wait that long if I have to. We have time, so be my friend today, so you can be my forever tomorrow." I held out my hand.

And surprisingly she took it. "What about yesterday and—"

"We're both stubborn, volatile, and dealing with our own shit, so we deal with it, together, without ripping each other's clothes off every time one of us gets too angry to see straight."

Her eyes widened. "Are you saying...?"

"Friends don't kiss, they also don't fuck every chance they get in the shower, on the bed, ground, against walls." It was going to be a long forever. I suddenly realized why Jackson looked so helpless. "I won't do any of those things — I won't kiss you until you ask me to."

"And what if I never do?"

"Then that's a risk I'm willing to take." I thumbed her lower lip and took a step back, wanting to kiss her so bad that I felt my hands start to shake at my sides. "Now, if you'll excuse me, I see at least a dozen cold showers in my future."

She laughed at that.

And I realized that this was one of the first times since she'd been here that we'd talked and not ended up naked.

And yet I felt high as I walked to the showers.

Even when I turned it on full blast and clenched my teeth against the cold water pelting my back, I smiled.

The high of sex wore off, didn't it?

The high of friendship on fire? Didn't.

And that was what we deserved. Friends and Lovers.

Chapter
ELEVEN

Ray

He kept his promise.

That was the first thing I thought every morning I woke up with him beside me. It's as if he wanted to be on my turf instead of his, he even started keeping clothes in my cabin. It wasn't until the weekend, when all the campers' parents were starting to drive in that it hit me.

We weren't having sex.

We were talking more than we'd ever talked in our adult lives.

And he was fulfilling something I didn't even realize I needed fulfilled.

Friendship.

I'd had that with Kieren when we were kids, and I'd felt so lost, and then this dirty, angry little boy told me we were going to be friends and I got a part of me back that day.

Not realizing how precious it was until I lost it, traded it in for what I thought would fulfill me, and only ended up being poison to my soul.

"I can feel you staring at me," Marlo said in a bored tone as he grabbed another case of bottled water and carried it over to the picnic table by the lake. We were hosting an outdoor barbecue before the dress rehearsal.

The campers were freaking out.

They knew they weren't ready but honestly this is what they needed in order to get their focus back, we only had three more weeks of camp, three more weeks to perfect what was a half-ass attempt at Dirty Dancing.

"I wasn't staring." I scoffed, "I was just wondering if the water was too heavy since you were grunting."

He tucked his chin and raised his eyebrows in a *"really?"* look before opening up a bottle and taking a few sips then holding it out to me.

I reached for it.

He jerked it back.

It was my turn to glare. "Are you twelve?"

"Are you sorry?"

"For insulting your big muscles?"

"And somehow that just seems more insulting when you say it that way?"

I laughed as he held out the water again. Then he was pulling it back with a teasing glint in his eyes.

"No!" I backed away. "Marlo, I just washed my hair!"

"I know, it's too pretty, we need to rough you up a bit."

He laughed and then chased. I stumbled and ran but he was faster, stronger, sexier — he was all the *"ers."* He caught me by the arm and pulled me against his chest. This is the part of the story where the girl and guy kiss passionately in front of everyone while the onlookers roll their eyes.

Instead, he sighed as he gazed at my mouth and then whispered. "Open."

I parted my lips as he dumped water into my mouth and muttered. "Never thought I'd be so fucking jealous of water, but I guess there's a first time for everything."

Heat flooded my cheeks. "Is it anything like being jealous of every single T-shirt that gets to wrap itself around your body?"

His gaze went from teasing to burning as his nostrils flared, pupils dilated. He swayed toward me and then released me and took a deep breath. "Maybe I should start meditating."

"Where'd that come from?"

"My unruly dick," he said plainly and then shook his head. "See that's where friendship gets us — honesty. Body and brain aren't really in sync right now."

"And what about your heart?"

"I have no idea." He shrugged and turned away.

Tears pricked my eyes and I blinked fiercely, determined not to let him see the hurt.

Without warning, he looked over his shoulder and winked. "You tell me... you're the one holding it in your hands. Careful, it's fragile."

I didn't have time to react because Jackson was nearing the table arguing with Jen over something to do with the set design while Brax trailed behind grumbling about all the parents hunting down staff members to ask about campers.

More and more cars pulled up.

And then Jen stiffened next to me while Jackson burst out laughing and did a slow clap. "Have I mentioned how awesome it's going to be when your dad's my father-in-law?"

She elbowed him in the ribs so hard he doubled over.

I turned around at the same time Marlo did.

And there they were. Probably the cutest adult couple I'd ever seen in my entire life—dressed as Johnny and Baby. And she was carrying a watermelon. "HI, HONEY!"

"Mom!" Jen did a half-hearted finger wave while Jackson ran toward her and grabbed the watermelon then kissed her on the cheek.

She pulled him in for a side hug while her dad gave him a high five, and I was stunned basically speechless.

Who were these unicorn parents?

Who dressed up and smiled all the time?

Who high fived the guy who slept with their daughter and looked at him like they saw potential when anyone else would run him over with a car?

And it just got worse as they made it through the crowd of staff members scrambling around them like they were celebrities. Even other parents trickled down to the lake and shouted at them in joy.

I didn't mean to stare so hard.

I also didn't mean to get so jealous that my chest hurt.

But how?

How was it possible to have something so wonderful like that? And how did someone get so lucky? The universe?

Music started pounding from the sound system around us as the BBQ kicked off, and still I stared in disbelief as happy campers hung out with their parents like it was normal.

I mean in high school everyone hated their parents in my circle, it was what brought us together.

But this?

Why did I feel like crying? Why was I getting so emotional over complete strangers? Yet the more hugging I saw and the more "I'm so proud of you," and "I love you," that I heard, the more I needed to bolt.

Because if I didn't, I was going to burst into tears.

I quickly turned on my heel only to run smack dab into Marlo's chest.

"Hey." He gripped my wrists with his hands. "You okay?"

"Uh, yeah," I lied, as tears filled my eyes.

"No lies."

"No," I said quickly. "I think I just need to go sit somewhere not here for a bit."

"Two minutes."

"What?"

"Give it two minutes."

"Give what two minutes?"

"Jen's parents were theater majors." He sighed, ignoring my question as Jen's parents started dancing around each other in perfect choreography. People clapped, laughed. Their joy was infectious, and it made me want to smile so bad — I wanted to laugh and join in, I would have, had my jealousy not been so severe.

And my sadness equally so.

"It shows," I finally managed to squeeze out over the emotions tightening my throat.

I had just exhaled and calmed down a bit when I felt Marlo stiffen next to me, his face was unreadable, but something happened. And I'd like to assume I knew him well enough to know that there was something wrong.

When I turned around it was to see my parents awkwardly standing next to the picnic table. Mom with her new Louis Vuitton purse, Dad with an expensive suit that had no business being worn in the woods, and of course she just had to wear Jimmy Choos. Her blond hair was pulled back into a low tight ponytail, her makeup flawless, and her white jumpsuit looked like it cost more than a car. Dad's hair was swept back, very clearly dyed a dark brown, and he had his ever-present Gucci sunglasses propped on his nose.

They stood out more than Jen's parents.

"Didn't I say wait two minutes?" Marlo wrapped an arm around me.

I dug my feet into the sand. "You did this?"

He nodded. "I'm also regretting this. Have I ever told you how much I detest your father? I think I'd rather the chicken do me in than speak one word to him, but here we go."

"For me?" I shook my head. "You did this for me?"

His eyes searched mine before he quietly answered. "I did it for us."

"I don't understand."

"You will. Hopefully." He started inching us toward them. My legs had filled with lead by the time we finally made it.

Mom blew me a kiss.

Like we were at the Hamptons and had just had a quick brunch.

I eyed her skeptically while my dad held out his hand.

Merciful God, was my own father trying to shake my hand?

I gripped it, he held it tight, then released it like I was a sickness.

Marlo held out his hand to him. "Sir."

"You." Dad barked out a laugh. "You've grown up into a handsome young man! Still mowing lawns?"

I clenched my teeth, while Marlo just smiled. "No, actually, I'm the camp director. And I'm sleeping with your daughter, but we'll touch on that later."

Dad sputtered while Mom let out a little gasp and looked behind her like people could hear that her daughter was living in sin.

"I'm going to make this really easy." Marlo cleared his throat. "I love her. You don't. But because you don't, she can't really love me, so I need you to clear the air. I need you to do the thing you should have done the day she was born and tell her how beautiful she is, how talented, how amazing. I need you to tell her she's all of those things. I need you to see her, really see her, see her hurt, her pain, I need you to see that this woman in front of you deserves more than a missed text on her birthday, a gift to replace your love. Think of it this way, you owe her a lifetime of apologies, and I'm giving you the chance to start now. It's your choice. Either way she's mine now, and I'll love her enough for both of you. I'll love her more than you could ever possibly comprehend." He bared his gritted teeth at my dad like he was ready to fight. "Be a man."

My dad reared back.

Oh no.

And then he pulled off his sunglasses.

It was a classic intimidation move. My heart pounded so hard in my chest that it felt like I couldn't breathe.

My mom wiped an errant tear from her perfect makeup then sniffled.

"Listen here, you little shit," Dad gnashed his teeth. "You clearly have no idea what I'm capable of doing to you, or will do to you if you ever disrespect me again!"

Marlo just smiled. "Joke's on you. You can't take anything away from me that I haven't already had taken. So go for it, I'm calling your bluff."

"You'll never get a job in town," he sneered.

"I'll just live off the land." Marlo laughed and then shrugged. "You don't get it. This isn't about me, this is about your daughter. Say what you want about me, but the only reason you're here is to fix something broken and that something broken is her."

I flinched and then opened my mouth. "We should…" I felt numb all over, like all of my worst nightmares were suddenly real. My parents in front of me, my parents walking away from me. I started to shake so uncontrollably that all I remember was Marlo reaching for me, and then almost falling to the ground as he caught me by the elbow and led me to the bench.

Mom didn't reach for me, not until she wiped off the bench with a few napkins then sat on more clean ones, then and only then did she touch my arm and smile. "Do you want some water, sweets?"

Marlo was already handing me some while my dad scowled in our direction like he was trying to find ways to plot his death.

"Thanks," I muttered, taking a swig that made my stomach curl.

Mom stared blankly at me, with her forced smile.

"Kieren!" someone yelled.

The blood seemed to drain from my entire body, and then I swayed.

Mom's face turned ghost white. And dad whipped his head around and paled.

A camper ran into what I assumed was his brother's arms and hugged him while I told my heart to start racing. It was as if the universe gave me that gift in that moment.

Or maybe just a stepping stone.

I opened my mouth.

Closed it.

Then finally took a deep breath and said. "I loved him too."

"Oh, honey." Mom waved me off with one perfectly manicured dismissive hand. "We don't need to talk about it."

"But that's the fucking problem!" I shouted, earning attention from at least half the campers near us. "We never talked about it because you were too sad! And then we never talked about it because I walked in on you and Dad crying and saying you wish it was me who had drowned!"

Marlo's eyes widened.

"That's enough!" Dad shouted.

"It's not enough!" I yelled, hugging my stomach. "Don't you see? You can't just say that in front of a six-year-old and expect them to recover! A six-year-old can't process things said in grief. It's why I did it, okay? It's why I did it!"

"Marlo…" Tears streamed down my mom's face.

"It's why I jumped in the deep end and screamed for you!" I nearly shrieked. My own tears flowed over my lips, I tasted salt. "Because at least then, you'd cry for me, you'd miss me, right? But all you did was scold me, all you did was tell me that I wanted attention!" I shook my head. "You damned a six-year-old to Hell, and the worst part is… you did it knowingly. And you never apologized for your lack of attention, for your lack of love, for your resentment that I had his nose, that I was never as talented or pretty."

"You weren't," Dad said. "You weren't him. You were twins, but you were… different."

My heart cracked in my chest. "Does that make me any less lovable?"

"That's not what I said." Dad shook his head. "You can't imagine losing a child only to turn around two days later and see your other child drowning!"

"But I LIVED!" I shouted.

"You died a long time ago," Mom whispered under her breath. "We all did."

With that, she stood and nodded to my father. They took each other's hands and then they stared at me like they didn't know me. Like I was the problem.

"This isn't the time or place to discuss family matters." Dad adjusted his tie. "When you come home, we'll all sit down." His smile was forced. "We'll talk this through, hire a psychiatrist, the very best to see you."

I let out an angry sigh. Yet again, they were missing the point. Ignoring the obvious. I wanted to shake them, but what good would it do? Nothing!

"I'm not coming back," I said in a strange voice that sounded stronger than I felt on the inside with my six-year-old heart sobbing all over the place, banging walls, throwing vases, cursing the universe. "I'm moving to California."

Dad just rolled his eyes. "Not this again. We said if you got an agent we'd allow you to give it a try, and the minute you got one through my connections, you dropped him.

See, this is why we struggle, you're irresponsible, you don't even know your own mind."

"I'm not coming back," I said it again, softer this time.

"The hell you won't. Find an agent or this discussion is over and from the looks of it — you'll probably get knocked up by the help before you even get a chance to live your life."

It was a low blow.

I charged.

Marlo snaked an arm around my waist and held me back.

And then I just completely lost my shit.

"Wanna know why I dropped my agent, Dad? Because he told me that he wanted to fuck me! And when I said no, he locked his door!"

Mom gasped while Marlo swore.

"So better to get knocked up by the help!" I roared. "I don't want to see you again. We're done here."

Mom started to full on cry. "Ray, you don't mean that."

"Leave," I said coldly. "Or I swear on Kieren's life I'll out every single one of your dirty secrets. And I know them all. I'd think long and hard about threatening the only person who knows what goes on behind closed doors."

It was Dad's turn to laugh. "You know nothing."

"I know you have a teenage son with Maria." I grinned, then instantly felt regret as my mom's face dropped.

"Fuck…" Marlo whispered under his breath still holding me.

Dad started to back away, his face pale, while Mom slowly charged after him. She hit him with her purse as they both made their way back to the car, the shouting started before the doors opened and continued as they swerved around the parking lot and left.

I was shaking like a leaf in Marlo's arms as something cold hit my palm. It was Jackson's flask. He just nodded and then started swearing right along with Marlo.

I drank it all.

And wrapped my arms around Marlo's neck and listened to the noise around me, the happy families, the laughter, the music. The smell of barbecue hit my nostrils, and it was almost bittersweet.

The happiest I'd ever been, was in my enemy's arms, smelling hot dogs and drinking cheap whiskey out of a flask.

I was drained.

But I was happy, because the only thing I could focus on, was that I didn't recognize myself in their eyes.

Which meant only one thing.

I wanted them.

But I didn't need them for me to be whole.

Which gave me hope that maybe I didn't need Kieren either.

Maybe all I needed was me.

And the person holding me, who said I was his forever.

He didn't know, though.

I'd always thought of him as my destiny.

Chapter

TWELVE

Marlo

The dress rehearsal went by smoothly, if smoothly meant nobody fell off the stage or forgot their lines and the parents enjoyed it, but we still had a shit ton of work to do, and I was completely worthless in that department because I was so concerned with Ray.

An hour after her parents left we had to get the campers ready for their performance.

Now everyone was either staying the night in the HQ lodge or had already headed back to the city.

I headed to the beach with enough alcohol to sedate an elephant, Jackson and Brax close behind. Jen and Ray were already by the lake lying on blankets placed around a bonfire on the beach.

It was just us.

"Thank God!" Jen ran toward us and grabbed a bottle of cheap rum from my box and then ran back to Ray. "Look! The universe provides!"

"Or I provide." Jackson winked.

She flipped him off.

"Good to see things are going well." I slapped him on the back and dropped the box next to one of the blankets then sat next to Ray. She hadn't said much since her parents left. Then again, it wasn't exactly like we'd been given time to say anything.

And what the hell was I supposed to say other than sorry? I'd had no idea? Do you want to talk about it? How is it that the princess in the golden tower'd had a worse childhood than me? At least I'd only suffered six years. She had suffered... a long time.

She was still suffering.

Funny how I always envied her, and she would have probably swapped places with me in no time. At least my foster mom loved me, truly loved me, and said so as many times as she could in a day.

How did a person even start that conversation? So, your twin — new news by the way — drowned at six and then you tried to kill yourself? Oh, and your dad's a cheating bastard, and sorry things didn't work out with that agent...?

I ran my hands through my hair and then exhaled. "So, I fucked up."

"Cheers." Jackson held up his flask while Brax knocked it with his red Solo cup. Jen nudged Ray, who sat up from her position.

"You were trying to do a good thing," she said softly. "And I love you for it."

Everyone went silent.

Crickets chirped a merry song.

My breath stalled in my throat, just about setting fire to my lungs. My body ached. I just wanted to love her in every human way possible over and over again.

"And…" She took a swig of rum and wiped her mouth. "I'm pretty sure we traumatized at least half the camp, including parents."

"Nah," Jen piped up, "Don't worry. The minute you all started yelling, my parents started a little strip tease. Mark my words, it's going to go viral by the morning."

"Her mom was wearing a bra, so no tits." Brax actually sounded disappointed. "But her dad had a thong on so… that's… special."

Jackson burst out laughing. "It was the best! I actually switched part of the video to slow-mo, you guys wanna see?"

"NO!" Everyone shouted in unison while he reached for a phone that I'm sure he'd probably had on him on a daily basis despite the staff rules. I was too exhausted to care.

"So…" Jen gave Ray a look, the prodding look, but I didn't know how to prod without sounding like a complete jackass. "You were a twin?"

I held my breath while Ray reached for my hand. I squeezed it. Dear God, let her just say something, anything.

"Yeah, we were inseparable from birth. I swear we even had our own language. And then we were swimming, it was summertime." Her voice cracked. "We had just eaten a huge lunch and Mom said not to go in the deep end, but we were really good swimmers and he was practicing diving, so he kept practicing and then, he started yelling that his leg hurt. I tried—" She bit down on her lower lip. "I tried to pull him to the side, see my mom had just run back inside. I screamed for her while water went into my lungs, while I tried to get him to the edge of the pool. It felt like forever. And then everything went black."

"What?" I squeezed her hand. "What do you mean everything went black?"

Tears dripped off her nose as she sniffed and took another long swig, all of us waited in silence.

"According to my mom when she came back out of the house, I'd somehow been shoved up onto the pool edge, and he was holding my hand floating next to me."

"Fuck me." Jackson swore breaking the silence.

"He saved my life. It should have been me. It's why my parents blame me, because that's just who he was, he was just... this selfless lovable brother who would do anything for anyone. He had the best voice, could play the piano by the age of three, he was just, every single thing that I wasn't. And then he was just... gone."

I pulled her into my arms. "You tried to save him, you can't blame yourself for that."

Jen started rubbing her back.

"I think it would be easier if my parents didn't blame me as well. You don't tell a six-year-old it's your fault. Two days after his funeral they were in his room sobbing, and my mom started screaming 'it should have been her, it should have been her. Why wasn't it her?'"

I was going to murder her parents. Plain and simple.

"And you guys know the rest. I ran outside, I wanted them to mourn me, to love me, to hug me. But they heard the splash, and the chasm between us cracked into something insurmountable to pass."

"No offense, Ray," Brax finally spoke. "But your parents are a bag of dicks, only worse, like I'm talking hairy, hairy—"

Jackson slapped a hand over his mouth. "Stop talking about yourself, it's gross man."

Brax shoved him while I just held her close, playing with her hair, trying to calm her as much as I possibly could.

"Is it time to get drunk now?" she asked, inches from my face.

I snorted out a laugh. "Yeah, I think if anyone deserves a night of drunkenness it's you."

"Yessss." Jackson did a fist pump. "Shots on me."

"Actually," broke in Jen. "The shots are compliments of the shady campers who thought it would be okay to bring alcohol."

"Amen," I muttered and then pulled Ray to her feet and twirled her around. "I'm so damn sorry."

She tilted her head and smiled, smiled so beautifully my chest ached. "Please don't ever apologize for loving me that much."

"But I—"

She licked her lips. I died a little inside. Hating that I was so close yet so far away from her touch. "You tried because you care, and you basically made my dad look like a dumb ass, so as far as I'm concerned, you're my hero."

"Should I ride in on a lawnmower next time?"

"Will you have theme music?"

"I'm confused. Is there any other way?"

She threw her head back and laughed. It was beautiful. "I'd never turn down a ride from you."

"Dirty!" Jackson shouted, lining up cups and pouring an ungodly amount of tequila into them. "And now, we party!"

He handed each of us a cup and the lifted it up to the sky. "To Ray!"

"To Ray!" we all yelled.

She took her shot, turned to me, and then pulled my head down until I could almost taste the tequila on her lips. I could tell we were about to kiss, about to do something that would change us yet again, would shift us.

"Hey!" Jackson's shout was accompanied by some mad scuffling in the sand between him and Jen.

She smacked his shoulder then gave him a shove that landed him on his ass. "Fuck off!"

Ray pulled back, the moment lost.

Jen launched herself and landed on Jackson before he had a chance to get up, straddling him and pressing open-mouthed kisses to his lips.

Brax made a show of covering his eyes, but when Jackson groaned and hauled Jen closer, Brax spread his fingers and peeked through.

Ray laughed and poured more shots. "Tequila, makes your clothes come off."

"Thank God!" Jackson said between kisses while Jen tugged at his T-shirt. He threw it over his head and drew a sharp breath when Jen dragged her nails along his chest. "Watch the claws!"

"I thought you liked it when I use my finer snails…" She frowned and giggled. "That came out wrong."

I glanced at Ray. "Finer snails?"

She snickered. "Some new sex challenge?"

"Might be erotic," I suggested. "Snail trails… Want to test it out?"

"On your dick?" she asked, offering a sweet smile.

"Because I'm thinking the odds of me touching a finer snail are up there with flying pigs."

Jen's shirt came off, revealing her sports bra beneath.

Brax whistled and crossed his arms. "Cool. Drinks and a show."

He patted the seat next to him, Ray laughed and sat.

"You guys are horrible friends!" Jackson said between kisses.

"We're the best, actually." Brax wrapped an arm around Ray, and I knew, that's exactly what she needed tonight. Laughter. Friendship. Love.

Chapter
THIRTEEN

Ray

"Never again." Marlo groaned from next to me.

I was afraid to open my eyes, why was I so hot? A sliver of pain ran down the back of my skull as I slowly moved to a sitting position.

Marlo was still moaning, rubbing his eyes with his hands, and cursing everything under the sun, but mainly Jackson and Tequila.

"Hey, you're the one who wanted to mix liquors." Jackson winced and then grinned at me like he had a reason to.

I frowned and then looked down by his side. Bra.

Underwear.

Clothes.

I grinned and then covered my face with my hands and gave my head a shake. "Jen? You feeling okay?"

"Ughhhh." The blanket moved, I saw part of her cropped head, and then she tried to get up.

"Bad idea." Jackson dangled her bra in front of her.

She grabbed it and turned bright pink.

"Next time we fight, I'm feeding you tequila. She scratched a map up and down my back with her fingernails." He laughed while Jen pulled the blanket over her head.

"Where's Brax?" Marlo's voice was sleep filled, deep. Chills washed over me. Why weren't we naked again? Why weren't we doing that thing?

Words. That's right.

And me.

My parents.

Brother.

Yet, when I thought about everything, that same sense of horror didn't wash over me. It wasn't gone. The pain was still there, but it felt like someone had invented ibuprofen for the heart and given it to me in the shape of four friends I had never expected to make — Marlo included.

Birds chirped around us while we all glanced at one another in confusion. We were still on the beach, all of us had crashed after a night full of drinking, laughter, and pranks. "Oh, no!"

"What?" Marlo whipped his head toward me then winced. "What's 'oh no' mean?"

"Pranks!" I stumbled to my feet and then ran down toward the shore and burst out laughing. I laughed so hard I had to hold my stomach, and a whole new slew of tears ran down my cheeks from the hilarious scene in front of me.

Brax in nothing but his boxers lying on a blow-up unicorn tied to the dock, with honey and bird seed on his chest.

Jackson and Marlo flanked me on both sides and joined in.

Brax's mouth was wide open as birds fed all over him.

Yeah, he wasn't going to wake up happy.

Jen joined us, having accomplished dressing herself, though her shirt was inside out. I figured it wasn't the time to tell her.

"I vaguely remember something about the bird seed and parent trap." Jackson rubbed his chin.

I wiped the tears of laugher from my achy cheeks. "Remember? He said he was going to attract a bear but would survive the night because he was in the water."

"All that damn bear had to do was pull the unicorn in." Marlo pointed out then frowned. "Would a bear even do that?"

"Still drunk?" Jackson asked.

Marlo moaned. "Yeah, think so."

Jackson jogged down the dock, Jen followed.

And then it was just me and Marlo.

I exhaled and turned.

He was staring at me.

His eyes burrowing into my soul.

Even hungover he was pretty.

It's like the messy hair and crooked smile paired with his gruff morning voice made him that much more sexy.

Words. Stop thinking about the physical.

"You're so pretty when you laugh," he whispered gruffly, and then he reached for my hand and kissed it.

I shivered.

His eyes zeroed in on my mouth.

I licked my lips and imagined them there.

If I closed my eyes, I could imagine his hands all over my body.

If I leaned in, I could have them.

"Son of a bitch!" Brax yelled, shattering the moment. The yelling was followed by a loud splash and more laughter from the dock.

I grinned and jogged down just in time to see Brax attempt to get back on the unicorn. The honey wasn't helping his case, and he just kept sliding right back off.

"He'll tire." Marlo burst out laughing while Jackson kept pulling the unicorn just far enough that Brax couldn't quite get fully on it.

"I hate all of you! ALL OF YOU!" he yelled and just gave up, held up two middle fingers, and then started swimming to the shore. Sideways.

"He's still drunk," Marlo pointed out.

"Nah, that's just Brax." Jackson chuckled "He can't even *walk* in straight lines. Why would we have high expectations of his swimming?"

"True." Marlo nodded.

Brax stumbled onto the beach, bent and scooped two handfuls of sand and then threw it in the air like he needed to show us how pissed he was. Without uttering a word, he plopped down half on and half off one of the blankets and held up both middle fingers again.

"Think he's mad?" I asked.

"He'll sleep it off," said Jackson, shrugging. "Besides, he should be happy! He won the bet!"

I froze. "The bet?"

"Yeah," Jackson grinned between me and Marlo. "He said if he survived the night you guys had to go on a date."

"A date?" I wondered out loud. "But we're at camp?"

"Yeah, you let me take care of that…." Jackson winked. "No backing out, you guys said yes!"

"Wait!" I tugged at his shirt to keep him from jogging off. "If we agreed to a date, what did you and Jen agree to?"

He patted my head like I was innocent then leaned in and whispered, "Three orgasms."

Next to me, Jen groaned like she wanted the earth to swallow her whole. Jackson wrapped his arm around her and pulled her close despite her constant hitting on his chest.

"And a gentleman never backs away from a bet." Jackson held her close. "Stop squirming, I'm the one who did all the work. Besides, you're the one who started it by doing a strip tease."

"I did?" Jen paled.

"Yeah, you asked me to call you Wonder Woman, and then I asked you to call me Batman, but in the Batman Dad voice, so hot…"

"I want to die," Jen grumbled.

"Chin up, buttercup." Jackson slapped her on the ass. Then his voice softened. "Let's go get you fed so you get your color back."

I couldn't help the smile that spread across my face as they walked away hand in hand leaving me with Marlo and a snoring Brax.

"So…" I didn't turn to look at him. I realized that sometimes I just liked being next to him, existing in his gravity. "A date huh?"

"A date." His hand found mine again.

We walked toward my cabin.

"We have two hours before breakfast." He slid his arm from my hand to my back as he let me go in first. "I say we sleep and then kill one of the campers and steal their Gatorade, you down?"

"Or we could just get it from the mess hall," I pointed out, slumping onto my bed.

"Where's your sense of adventure?"

"Out of prison, thanks." I grabbed my pillow.

He laughed and then joined me on my bed.

I didn't have to ask him to pull me into his arms.

He just did.

I didn't have to tell him I loved it when he played with my hair until I fell asleep.

He just did.

And when sleep finally did come, I could have sworn he said. "I love you."

Chapter

FOURTEEN

Marlo

Jackson said he would take care of the date, which meant it was back to business making sure that the staff was getting rehearsals underway.

I stopped by at noon and cringed when our Baby ran into Johnny's arms, screamed, and then backed away like she was scared he was going to drop her.

"Sara!" Jackson said from stage right. "You can't scream every time you run at him, you're not a banshee."

She gave him a confused look. "What's a banshee?"

Jackson clenched his teeth then shot me, a look that said, *I'm going to lose it*.

Brax waved his hands. "Let's try this scene again, and Sara at least try not to scream at Bryan, he's doing the best he can."

Bryan puffed out his nonexistent chest.

The scene started again.

And yet again, when it was time for her to leap into his arms.

A sharp scream.

Not as long.

Equally as loud.

Ray chose that moment to walk in with a group of background dancers. They stretched to the side.

I blew my whistle, gaining everyone's attention as the music stopped. "Bryan, Sara, I want you to watch how it's supposed to be done… RAY!"

Her eyes widened and then she shot me a glare.

Hah. Damn, I loved her glare almost as much as her smile. She walked toward the stage and joined me up front.

"Music," I called.

She shook her head at me. "You may never have sex again. I hope you're okay with using your—"

"Shhh!" Jackson grinned at us. "There are children present!"

"She was going to say 'hand.' Moving on," Bryan said in a bored tone. "Just show Sara how to do it right so we can break for lunch."

Sara scowled. "He's dropped me twice!"

"Because your screaming scares the shit out of me! I don't know if you're going to jump into my arms and let me do the lift or if you're going to nail me between the legs! You look possessed!"

Her eyes narrowed.

"Okay, then," Jackson nodded to us. "Go break a leg."

Ray grumbled something about killing me under her breath, and then we were on stage. The music started.

The background dancers weren't rehearsing with the lead roles yet, they had the entire afternoon to go through blocking. Fun times.

I nodded at Ray as I started dancing toward her. Technically, we were supposed to have dancers all around me, and then I pulled her into my arms as she threw her body back and did a circle around and lifted her left leg, I locked eyes with her and slid my hand up her thigh. I suffered for it. Because I hadn't touched her in what felt like years, so touching her now was like playing with a live electrical wire.

Blood pounded in my ears as she rocked her body against me, and then in sync she dipped her head back as I ran my fingertips down her chest. My breathing slowed when she turned and my knuckles grazed her ribs.

If I wasn't careful I was going to be giving all the campers a real show. Thank God I was in jeans.

I tried to squeeze my eyes shut and enjoy the music.

Instead, as the thumping rhythm filled the air around us, all I felt was her against me.

All I smelled was her skin.

All I wanted was to devour her whole and throw her over my shoulder, walk her to a sturdy object and ask her if I could please just rip her clothes off. On cue, we spun into a pause and locked gazes. We were supposed to act like we were about to kiss.

I wasn't acting.

The music shifted as we spun away from each other, and I performed a few spins and solo steps while she waited.

Then it was time for the lift.

I nodded at her.

She smiled and rolled her eyes at me, but I could tell she

was having fun, and with perfect grace she ran at me.

I lifted her with ease and did a small circle.

Applause erupted from the audience.

I was still smiling when I set her on her feet.

We didn't need to keep dancing.

The demonstration part was done.

Except that was what we did.

We kept dancing.

She waved the backup dancers over.

And suddenly we were skipping, blocking, and going straight on to another full rehearsal of the song.

Things clicked into place as campers danced around each other and laughed. Sara and Bryan even joined in.

Too soon, the music ended.

I pulled in Ray for a hug. "You were perfect."

"Thanks for not dropping me," she murmured against my shoulder.

I laughed. "Yeah, well, thanks for not running at me screaming. I think that tends to scare testosterone away for fear of sharp objects, kicking, losing testicles... that sort of thing."

"We wouldn't want that." She grinned up at me.

"No." I let out a rough sigh. "This is killing me, you know that right? You're so damn beautiful."

She ran her hands down my stomach.

I shuddered.

"Not playing fair," I said with a clenched jaw.

She just shrugged and then started to walk away. I grabbed her by the arm and tugged her back. "Are you flirting with me?"

"Yes." She seemed thrilled about it. "I figure it's like pre-date foreplay."

"Shit." I was about to maul her in front of the entire camp. "Keep talking like that and I'm going to get outed by a nerdy camper who likes rules and thinks it's wrong to get naked on stage with the love of his life."

Her expression changed. "Is that what I am?"

"What else, could you possibly be?" I countered.

Our gazes locked.

"So…" Jackson moved between us and separated us. "I know your juices are flowing and both of you want to just bang it all out, but save it for when young eyes aren't watching. One of the girls said if Director Marlo looked at her like that she'd sign over her dad's Ferrari." He nodded. "You up for it?"

"Hell no." I laughed.

"See! He loves you more than a car!" Jackson shook her by the shoulders. "Now, give them a thirty-minute break, so we can figure shit out, it's time to block. Good job, kids, now everyone knows what foreplay looks like via dancing… sex education, such a bitch."

And then he was gone.

Her eyes heated one last time in my direction, then Ray turned and flashed a smile to her backup dancers. "Get some lunch and make it fast, we need to go through blocking."

"Marlo!" Brax yelled.

"Until tonight," I said under my breath, knowing she wouldn't hear.

If I lasted that long.

Without combusting.

"Marlo!" he repeated.

"Coming!"

Chapter
FIFTEEN

Ray

"What are you wearing?" Jen asked from behind me.

I jumped a foot. "You scared the crap out of me!"

"Sorry, I was in stealth mode. Jackson's been trying to convince me to stay the night at his cabin. He said he wouldn't light any candles and that he'd let me pick a movie on his laptop while he painted my toes."

I frowned and kept walking toward my cabin, gravel crunching beneath my Nikes. "Wait, why is he painting your toes?"

"He claims he read it in Cosmo, he's trying to do things

right. Ergo, we need to watch a chick flick and pull out the nail polish."

"Men." I sighed and put my hands on my hips. "Why don't you just binge watch something on Netflix and let him touch your boobs?"

She burst out laughing. "Better plan and I think he'd actually prefer that, but he's trying to be good."

"That's still being good," I pointed out. "Ish."

"Right…" She shrugged. "Maybe I'll just make it too hard for him to say no, which brings us full circle. What are you wearing?"

I slumped like a deflating balloon. "I don't even know what we're doing so I'm not sure."

She wrapped an arm around me. "I'll help. Besides it will make Jackson more panicky, and he always kisses more aggressively when he thinks I'm pissed or gone."

"The games we play." I rolled my eyes.

I was nervous.

Why was I nervous?

I gave myself one last pep talk as I looked at my reflection in the long mirror on the far wall of my bare cabin.

"Are we sure about this?" I scrunched up my nose as I ran my hands down my black tank dress and tennis shoes. It was skin tight cotton that hugged every curve I had, which was why we paired it with the cute Nikes. I looked half tennis star, half *oh, I just woke up like this.*

My hair was pulled away from my face in a low ponytail, and I'd put on my Chanel earrings at the last minute.

"You look so hot," Jen said from her spot on the bed. "Seriously, if I was a guy…"

"You sound more and more like Jackson." I winked and

dodged the pillow she threw in my direction then blushed. Yeah, she had it bad.

"Your boobs look amazing, your skin has that nervous flush to it… Yeah, I highly doubt Mr. Camp Director is going to be able to keep his hands off of you."

"Is that what I want?" I wondered out loud, anxiety rippling through me in chaotic waves like I was my own personal hurricane.

"Look." Jen stood and grabbed me by the shoulders. "Him wanting you is never going to be a problem, he's obsessed with you, anyone can see that."

I didn't want obsession.

I wanted partnership.

Love.

I wanted to start over.

I sighed and then wrapped my arms around her. "It's going to be great."

She hugged me back; I got choked up when she patted my back and then whispered, "It's going to be amazing, just smile."

So I did.

I walked out of my cabin into the warm summer night and smiled my entire way down to the lake.

The only instruction I had been given was to go to the lake.

When I arrived, I found a giant picnic basket on the table. No Marlo, no Jackson, just a letter that read *open me.*

With a grin, I opened the letter.

And felt my soul weep in my body.

Dear Spoiled Princess,

You have to know I watch you.

You have to know I want you.

You have to know I hate you.

I love you.

Every time you drive by in your BMW, I wonder if you think about running me over with it as much as I think about running in front of it to get your attention. I would welcome your rage almost as much as your love.

Maybe that's the problem.

I will take whatever I can get.

I'll take your body if you just give me a taste.

I'll own your soul if you let it go.

I'll hold your heart if you hand it over.

And if all I get are the broken pieces, the ones that only bring you pain in your life, then I want those too.

Because I want you.

But you'll never know how much.

Because I'm your lawn boy.

Because we're from two different worlds.

Because I know that you care too much about your fake friends.

And because I know you're lonely.

I know you cry yourself to sleep at night — I
can hear you.

It's why I can't stay away.

Because pain recognizes pain.

And loneliness does the same thing.

It creates this chasm of want deep within us. It
begs to be filled by something other than the sound
of our own breathing, of our own fucking heartbeat.

I know the truth now. I know that if I fill you
with me, you'll still feel empty. I know if you give
yourself to me, you'll still feel the need to be loved
by someone other than the boy who mows your lawn.

So where does that leave us?

It leaves us here.

With a second chance.

With a crossroads.

We can own our pain.

Own the fact that we are too broken to be put
back together again.

Own that no matter what, we have a past that
we can't escape but a future together if we'd just
forgive the past.

Want to know why cars have giant windows in front and tiny rearview windows?

Because we aren't supposed to look back.

But I don't really agree with that, want to know why? Because I love looking back at those hot summer nights when I'd watch you skinny-dip, like I was some kind of creeper, and then punish myself for being the guy that lusts after the rich girl.

I love looking back on our first time with our teeth knocking, sweaty bodies gliding and grinding.

I love the scent of summer in your hair and the sunlight on your skin and the way you taste beneath my tongue.

So, I'm gonna look back, because even though the past is dark and riddled with pain — my sunlight was you.

I hate you.

I love you.

I need you.

Always yours,

Your lawn boy.

Marlo B.

Two teardrops dropped onto the handwritten page, and then I heard the sound of a lawn mower.

I looked up just in time to see Marlo coming down the dirt road shirtless, riding a lawnmower, and pumping his hand in the air to eighties music.

And I cried harder.

Because he had always seen me.

He got me.

He knew me.

All the ugly parts. All the parts I wanted to keep to myself.

He turned off the lawnmower and then sauntered toward me, his abs on perfect display, showing off, begging to be touched and tasted. His bulging biceps and triceps made his entire body look bigger. But my eyes wandered to where his low-slung jeans slid about on narrow hips.

I licked my lips.

And then he was in front of me, baseball cap backward, long hair tucked behind his ears, and crystal blue eyes searching mine with a grin that could melt hearts all over the world.

Too bad he already had mine.

Too bad I was making him keep it.

"I love you." I barely got out the last word before he leaned in and whispered his answer.

"I've loved you since I was six…"

"I was skinny and had frizzy hair when I was six," I pointed out.

"The frizzy hair was my favorite part, especially during the summers." He reached for my hair and ran his fingers through it.

I licked my lips as the music shifted. The sun was starting to set. I crooked my finger and grabbed the iPad off the lawnmower, then tucked my letter into the case.

We interlocked hands as we made our way down the trail to the other beach, the one he'd danced on so many nights ago.

With shaking hands, I placed the iPad near the tree then turned to face him.

He narrowed his eyes. "Is this where you tell me the date's over because you hated my note?"

"No." I took a deep breath. "This is where the spoiled princess makes her confession and finds her truth." I held out my hand to him. "But I'm going to need some help."

"Only you can let go."

"Only if you catch me."

He hauled me into his arms and whispered against my hair. "Even when I hated you, I was watching, waiting, your hero in every way, yours in every way, forever and always."

Chapter
SIXTEEN

Marlo

This was happening.

I was still in disbelief when she tossed off her Nikes and socks then turned to face me, her eyes searching mine for confidence maybe? I wasn't sure. All I knew was that my body buzzed with this keen awareness that something else was shifting between us.

For the better.

This was our fresh start.

This was our moment.

Everyone has one in their lifetimes, many of us ignore them, are too afraid to take that leap, fear keeps a lot of us paralyzed. I refused to be one more human of inaction when it came to taking a leap, especially for her.

Always for her.

Without question.

My answer would be yes.

The song started.

It was Zombie.

The same one I'd danced to a few weeks ago.

I narrowed my eyes. "You saw me dance?"

She nodded. "It was beautiful." And then she threw her hands over her head and started to dance, lifting her body effortlessly into the air as she twirled and bent around the sand.

I couldn't tear my eyes away as the sunlight kissed her skin, as her long neck stretched back, as she created fluidity with her body that was out of this world, and then she collapsed in on herself. Pain stabbed me in the chest as she rocked back and forth, then fell to her knees, and then forward onto her stomach. In almost one motion, she rolled then thrust her body up from the sand but holding back like it was weighing her down. She danced upward as though she was paralyzed by the heaviness of the ground trying to keep her from standing.

She'd said she needed help.

She'd said she needed me.

I shook my head in disbelief as I recognized my cue and covered her body with mine, then lifted her into the air with my feet and hands as she hovered over me in a perfect plank, her arms out. I brought her down over my body as her legs straddled me. She arched her back while I ran my hands up her bare thighs shoving her skirt to her hips as she kicked away from me, and followed with another high kick, and then another fall to the ground that shattered my heart and had me ready to release a primal scream into the warm night air.

This was her darkness.

This was her burden.

This was her letting go.

I moved toward her and stood, then tried to pull her into my arms from the ground, she gave way as her body went limp in mine, as I moved us away from the sand and held her close, cupping her ears trying to speak to her without words.

Don't listen to the noise, all you need is me, feel me.

She twirled under my arms and tried running for the sand, I jerked her back against my chest as the chorus started.

Our eyes locked as I lifted her into my arms, her legs wrapped around me briefly, and we whirled as I moved with her, perfectly in sync, and then she was rolling her hips against mine in perfect cadence to the music, driving me insane.

I let out a gasp as I clung to her shoulders, and then with my right hand, I grabbed her ass to keep her pressed against me as the music finally ended.

It was on repeat, and the music started up again.

I opened my eyes.

Tears streamed from her eyes, staining her cheeks as I whispered, "That was beautiful."

"Kiss me."

I slammed my mouth against hers, and I knew in that moment I wasn't just with the girl who had once gotten away.

I was home.

I was with my soul mate.

Her tongue slid past my lower lip as the music played on, and before I knew what I was doing, I was sliding my hands up her thighs and then gripping the material of her cotton dress and pulling it up over her hips. She wiggled out of her underwear in record time. Bracing a hand around my neck, she used the other to flick open the button on my jeans. I let out a hoarse growl as she slid her hand inside and grasped me.

I was already eager for her.

Had been for days.

Years.

My entire life.

I would never get enough of her.

She pumped her hand up and down.

I bit down on her bottom lip then pulled away and gritted my teeth as our bodies moved up and down, grinding against each other to the music.

"I've always needed you." She spoke against my mouth.

My eyes rolled in the back of my head when she thrust her hips against my cock and then moved her hand as she tugged my jeans down.

I dropped her to her feet and then walked her backward to the tree, the one hidden in the shadows, not that it mattered, I was taking her, having her, here, now, forever. Always.

I grabbed her hands and put them on the branch overhead. "Hold on."

"Are we really doing this?" Her eyes dilated in what looked like a mix of lust and shock.

I gripped her by the hips. "I would hold on."

She pulled her body up just as I grabbed myself and guided my tip into her. Her legs wrapped around me, sucking me into her core, holding me captive, as I moved inside her, slowly, passionately, giving her everything I had, and hoping she'd accept it, accept us.

My muscles strained to hold her in place while she

gripped the branch overhead using it for balance. I was so deep I never wanted to be saved from this place, from his moment between us.

"Marlo…" She let out a whimper. "It's almost too much."

"It should be more than too much — it should wreck you for life." I pulled almost completely out and then slammed into her. My right hand hit the tree as I scrambled for more to anchor us in place as my body pulsed with the need for release.

Her breath hitched. "I feel you everywhere."

"You're safe," I whispered against her neck before taking her mouth again as she bucked against me. Her walls constricted around me causing exquisite pain, sucking me dry as I chased the release she'd just had in my arms.

Chests heaving against one another, I finally opened my eyes, forgetting I'd closed them.

Her eyes were shining as she looked at me and then grinned. "We like foreign places."

"I couldn't wait," I admitted.

"Me neither."

Slowly, I pulled out of her and rolled down her dress, we were a hot mess, but I just wanted to do it again, and taste her longer, hold her closer.

"I love you, Marlo." She wrapped her arms around me, and then slowly pulled that same dress over her head and tossed it to the ground along with her bra. "And I loved your letter."

"I figured it would be easier for you to read it, then decide how you feel, where you want to go, how you want the date to go." I was rambling, but she was naked and I wasn't there yet and I wanted to be but I also didn't want to ruin this by just having sex with her every single waking moment of my life — no matter how good that sounded in my head.

"My turn." She gave me her back and then slowly waded into the chilly lake as the last remnants of sunlight disappeared and the moon showed its face on the horizon. She swam along and then turned back to me, treading water with a grin on her face. "You watching, lawn boy?"

"Lawn boy?" I crossed my arms and smiled. "When was I not watching?"

"Creeper."

"I'd like to think of myself as more of an opportunist." I shrugged.

She cackled out a laugh and then nodded. "I have a secret."

"Oh, yeah?" My fingers itched to pull my clothes from my body and join her, press a kiss against her neck and make love to her under the moonlight. "What's that?"

"I wanted you to see me. I skinny-dipped for you." She lifted one shoulder, let it fall. "I figured one day you'd crack and join me."

"Sadly, I never cracked." I inwardly berated my young stupid self and all his hatred and all his pain.

"So?" She tilted her head. "Join now?"

"But I'm just a lawn boy."

"No, you're not," she said quickly. "You're Marlo, my Marlo. Talented actor, dancer, choreographer, camp director, best friend, lover, but most importantly… you're mine."

I tripped over my own feet as I tried to pull off my shoes and jeans at the same time, sliding my boxers down so fast I was getting close to serious self-harm. I waded into the water and reached for her.

I was about to kiss her when she pulled back. "You've always been mine, and I want you to know I'm going to do better. From here on out, I'm going to look at myself that way, the way you're looking at me right now, as if I don't have black on my soul, as if I'm deserving when I know I'm not. I hate you. I love you. Forever and always, Marlo."

I devoured her next words as we treaded water under the moonlight, our limbs tangling within each other's.

And then she pulled back. "What was the date anyway?"

"Doesn't matter." I tried kissing her again.

She pulled back. "Marlo."

"Picnic under the stars," I answered. "Which we can do after we swim, after I taste you again, and after I take you at least three more times and get to see you come to life. And after that I want to dance, I want to dance under the moon and shout at the top of my lungs, I want to own you and brand you, and then I want to set you free just so I can chase you again. I love you, Ray."

Tears welled in her eyes as I pulled her in for a kiss.

This. This was the best kind of love.

Painful.

Aching.

Beautiful.

Scarred.

Chapter
SEVENTEEN

Ray

I was afraid to trust the moment as Marlo wrapped his arms around me, crushed me to his chest, and kissed my damp hair. In a tangle of arms and legs, we laid across blankets and towels.

Food gone.

Clothes still discarded.

We watched the moon and the stars.

And we breathed each other in.

I was afraid my voice would shatter this emotional silence as he ran his knuckles down my sides and breathed in and out, slowly, contentedly like he always knew it would be like this and was just waiting for me to get the memo.

"I miss fighting with you," he said in a low raspy voice that did insane things to my insides, making my stomach flutter and my heart beat a little faster.

"I'm stubborn," I said with a sigh. "There will always be a fight. Take, for example, the musical — the leads you picked suck."

"That, I actually agree with you on, but they're the only ones who know how to do the complicated moves and sing at the same time without bursting into tears or shitting themselves."

I smiled against his chest. "Romantic."

Marlo leaned up on his elbows causing me to look at him. "I'm not sure how things are going to go over during the final show. We have agents, managers, producers — important people coming to scout. What if it's horrible?"

I gave him a soft smile. "Then it won't be because of the choreography but because of your horrible casting?"

He glared. "You're asking to be dunked aren't you?"

"Why Marlo, I think I've waited since my freshman year of high school for you to jump naked into the water with me and take me down."

He bit down on his bottom lip then cupped my chin and whispered, "I'd fucking run if I were you."

Maybe it was the predatory way he said it.

The gleam in his eyes.

The hungry promise that it would be both good and bad if he caught me.

I jumped from his arms and stumbled down the beach, I could hear his footsteps behind me as I dove into the water and surfaced only to see him gone.

He wasn't on the beach.

And I couldn't see his body in the dark water.

I frowned and swam in a circle. "Marlo?"

Nothing.

Panic rose in my chest. "Marlo? This isn't funny!"

"Really?" he said from behind me like he'd been there the whole time. "Because there's nothing better than seeing a beautiful woman search for you with that sort of look in her eyes, like the reward of finding you will be so much better than you could possibly imagine."

I smacked him in the chest and tried to shove him down.

He just gripped my wrists with his hands and swam me back toward the dock then pinned me against the wood. "Does this mean I get to live out my high school fantasies?"

"You didn't already?" I teased.

He just shook his head and dove under the water.

I frowned. What? He wanted to dive for? Holy— "MARLO!"

He used my hips as an anchor as his tongue swirled around my core, sucked me in along with the water like he could survive off of my body alone.

I wasn't sure whether to be concerned he was going to drown or just let him — the pleasure was so intense I was having trouble not squirming against his mouth.

He surfaced slowly, panting. "I've always wondered what you would taste like under water, had vivid fantasies of taking you against the pool wall and then—" He grinned. "Let's go back to your cabin."

"My cabin?" I narrowed my eyes, my legs shook with unclenched desire. "What for?"

He just shrugged. "Follow me and find out, besides it's late, nobody's up, just wrap yourself in a towel and sprint."

With that, he was swimming toward the shore, and then his golden naked body was walking toward the towels and blankets, he hurriedly stuffed the blankets in the giant beach bag then grabbed a towel and wrapped it low around his hips.

I stared at him, slack jawed.

How was it possible to look that good after hours of conversation, food, sex, swimming? It was nearing midnight, and he looked like he'd just taken a quick jog and was invigorated by the water, whereas I probably looked bloated, exhausted, and haggard.

Every muscle stood at attention — along with everything else.

I tried not to stare too long, but it was nearly impossible; he was huge, warm, mine.

"You're staring again," he said huskily, crossing his arms.

"I like big things?" I offered.

He just licked his lips and looked down like he was embarrassment. "Yeah that's not helping the situation, and if I do see a camper on my way back to your cabin I'm going to have a lot of explaining to do. Mainly, why am I so turned on by the phrase, 'Hi, Director Marlo'?"

I burst out laughing and swam to shore, then grabbed the towel from his outstretched hand.

I loved how he stared at me.

Like I was perfect even though I knew I wasn't.

Like he wanted to taste me even though he already had.

I wondered if this was what it felt like to be accepted, to be loved despite all the reasons and reservations the person doing the loving should have.

It just simply… was.

Marlo was already making his way up the trail, grabbing the picnic basket and looking over his shoulder. "You coming?"

"Not yet." I angled my head and wiggled my eyebrows suggestively.

Fire flared in his eyes. "Yeah, you're going to pay for that comment."

"You won't hear me complain, though I may toss in a scream or two for your benefit." I winked.

He groaned and adjusted himself. "If I see any campers I'm telling them you seduced me and drugged me."

"I'd just own up to it," I said in a sing-song voice as I followed him up the trail.

He laughed as I joined him. And off we went, half jogging, half walking back to my cabin in the dark.

I couldn't wipe the grin from my face. I felt so free, and physically I was, since I had clothes bunched up in one hand while I held the towel to my body with the other.

My legs burned as I chased after him.

He was at the front door of the cabin before I even made it to the bottom stairs, and when I finally made it to the door, it was just in time to see Marlo drop his towel.

With a laugh, I followed suit.

He wiped his face with his hands. "You're too damn beautiful, it hurts my eyes."

"Are you complaining?"

"Absolutely." He grabbed me by the elbow and leaned down, meeting my mouth halfway, devouring my words, my breaths, my groans as he wrapped his arms around my waist and pulled me against his length. I could feel the heat of him pressed against my soft skin.

My heart pulsed with it.

My body demanded more.

The connection we'd had in high school was on fire, out of control, it was impossible to stop — and I never wanted it to go away.

I raked my fingernails down his back as he parted my lips with his tongue, sucking me dry, entering me so completely and with such a raw hunger that it was almost hard to kiss him back.

I'd seen every side of him — or so I thought.

Until now.

Without another word, he turned me around. "Hands on the bed."

My eyebrows shot up as I did what he said and looked over my shoulder. "What's this now? Lawn boy has some kink?"

He pressed his erection to my ass and then leaned over and whispered in my ear. "I'm sorry, are you complaining?"

I gulped. God, he felt good. Everywhere. I couldn't even find my voice as my body ached for his.

He ran a smooth hand down my ass. "Yeah that's what I thought."

My skin broke out into goose bumps as he nudged my legs apart.

I let out a gasp when I felt hard heat tease my entrance. Thighs quivering, I waited for him to do something.

He did nothing.

I looked over my shoulder.

"That's it," he said giving me a satisfied grin. "Watch."

He was inside me in one fluid thrust and I was arching my back against him trying not to come apart with each movement inside me.

"Don't stop!" Was that my voice? The one begging? Whimpering?

"Can't." He heaved. I had to grip the sheets and part of the mattress to keep from slamming into the closest wall. I clenched myself tightly around him, I squeezed my eyes closed, and I lost all control and awareness. All I had was him, all I needed was him.

His love.

His body.

His words.

"Ray—" He drove inside me one last time. I stayed in the same position, my body well and completely rocked as tiny little pulses exploded all around me.

"We're staying like this forever."

He chuckled. "Then we have some explaining to do with both parents and campers, not to mention the staff."

"Let them see." I yawned.

He drew away from me then.

I was dead on my feet.

He lugged a shirt over my head and then I felt the towel wipe down my legs, around every sensitive area before I was being tucked into bed.

He followed, lying down behind me, pulling me into his arms, kissing the back of my neck and whispering promises against my skin, I fell asleep to him saying. "Best first date ever."

"Last." I felt the words move across my lips. "Last first date."

"Last," he agreed.

I smiled as sleep took over.

Chapter
EIGHTEEN

Marlo

Three more weeks of torture.

Three more weeks where I lived and died by the fucking musical.

There wasn't enough time in the day to steal Ray away, to touch her, make her feel special, and I was so damn terrified that she'd feel like it was a competition, my job and responsibilities verses hers.

I hated it.

I hated all of it.

"Run away with me?" I whispered under my clipboard and giving Ray a pleading look as the leads yet again decided it would be a great idea to mess up the most pivotal part of the entire musical.

Everyone groaned, and a few cast members heaved frustrated sighs or walked in circles.

It wasn't that they couldn't do it; it was just that they both said they were feeling sick, which meant they were forgetting lines.

And we had everyone arriving in the morning for the final performance.

Ray gave me a stern look. "We can't just abandon them, look at them."

As if on cue, our Johnny tripped over his own feet and then started swaying and gave the crowd, mainly the staffers, a funny stare before puking all over himself.

I jumped to my feet. "Bryan!"

An odd look crossed Sara's face, and then she puked on Bryan.

So now, the stage had some funky looking puke from both our leads, and both wore guilty expressions on their faces.

Shit.

"Can we get some mops?" I called. "You guys okay?"

"I think I'm sick." Bryan groaned and clutched his stomach.

"You dick!" Sara roared. "You swore!"

"Am I missing something?" I threw my hands in the air. "What did you swear?"

"He swore he wasn't sick when I told him he had a fever yesterday, so of course I slept with him!"

My eyebrows shot up. "That's your natural conclusion when someone with a fever says they aren't sick?"

Sara glared. "Never mind. The point is—" She covered her mouth with her hands and then ran off the stage.

Bryan must have felt sick again too, because he followed

suit. I heard more puking and then yelling.

"We're fucked," Jackson announced to everyone.

"No we're not!" I shot him a warning glare. "We'll just…"
I eyed a wide-eyed Ray. "We'll do it."

"We?" Jackson repeated. "Sorry man, I haven't stretched."

"Me and Ray." I nodded to her. "We'll practice all night
if we need to."

"That what kids are calling it these days?" Brax said under
his breath while Jen sighed and looked between both me and
Ray like she hoped we could pull it off.

I groaned into my hands. "Everyone take ten while we
figure this out. No going to bed unless I say so. You go to
bed, you're off the cast, are we clear?"

My announcement was met with a shit ton of complaints,
"I'm hungry…"

"He's a monster…"

"…I'm exhausted."

I didn't care.

Because I was director this year, and I would not fail.

I couldn't.

Ray walked up to me and grabbed my hand. "Does the
lawn boy need saving from the rich spoiled princess?"

I smirked. "Yeah, I think he does."

"Good." She nudged me. "Because I've always wanted to
save you — maybe even more than you wanted to save me."

I frowned. "What makes you think I needed saving?"

"The look in your eyes every day I didn't do it," she said
softly.

I captured her mouth between my lips. I tasted her. I
kept her there. Kept us there in that moment as we touched
foreheads. "I love you."

"I love you too," she said simply. "So let's kick ass."

"Just like that, no stage fright?"

"Just don't drop me, and I think I'll be okay." Her smile sparkled.

It was like she was a new person.

And selfishly, I hoped that she was looking at herself differently because of me, because of what we'd been through, because of what our relationship meant to one another.

"I promise." And I meant it.

"Yeah, I know you do."

"All right!" Jackson clapped his hands. "The puke's cleaned up, it smells like bleach and last night's pizza, let's go from the last dance sequence right into the song."

I clenched my teeth, not used to getting ordered around.

Jackson flashed me a smile then held out his hand.

With a scowl, I handed him my clipboard and whistle.

"Feels so good…" He closed his eyes and sucked in a long, slow breath, like he was ready to have an orgasm, and then held up one hand. "Almost there… ahhhh yeah, there it is."

"Never using that whistle again," Ray said under her breath.

"Nope," I agreed.

"Places!" Jackson blew the whistle. I grabbed Ray's hands, kissed the backs of them, and winked.

"We've got this," she said as she took a deep breath.

"Maybe you'll get an agent," I offered, hoping that would at least put the excitement back in her eyes. Instead, you'd think I just snuffed out every light ever lit behind them. "Ray?"

That damn forced smile. "It's nothing."

"Nothing—"

"Marlo! Listen to orders as good as you give them!"
Jackson blew the damn whistle again, and I was escorted
stage right while she went to stage left.

We would have that conversation.

Even if it killed me.

I wanted nothing between us but skin.

No room for secrets, only us.

Chapter
NINETEEN

Ray

"All right, get some sleep!" Jackson called out at around four a.m. I was ready to strangle him, murder him, drown him, but I couldn't move my body, so I tried killing him with telepathy.

And when that didn't work, I glared.

"She having a stroke?" Jackson whispered to Jen.

I flipped him off. My hand didn't reach eye level, still counted though, right?

Jen tossed me a water bottle, and I batted it out of the air; that's how tired I was. The water bottle went sailing toward Marlo's head, but he ducked just in time for it to hit Brax in the stomach.

Brax looked down and sighed. "Do you guys have a

vendetta against me ever since the unicorn incident? Because if I remember correctly, I was victimized!"

"Drunk." Jackson grinned. "You were drunk." He looked around the empty outdoor auditorium and then pulled a flask from his pocket. "Speaking of…"

"It's four a.m.!" I screeched.

He held it closer.

"Yeah, okay," I took it, unscrewed the top, took a long swig, then handed it to Marlo, who had just sat down.

"Candy?" Jackson tossed me a pack of gummy bears.

I scrunched up my nose. "Candy sounds horrible."

Marlo made a strangled noise next to me.

"What?"

He just rolled his eyes. "That's not normal candy."

"Bullshit!" Jackson laughed. "It's the only kind."

Jen smacked him in the chest. "Stop trying to get everyone high just so you can find sick entertainment in it."

"Jackson!" I threw the bag back at him.

"What!" He lifted his hands into the air. "I remember a day not so long ago when this one came into my cabin and begged me to get him high."

"Thanks, man." Marlo took a swig, screwed the top, then tossed it to Brax, who was still rubbing his chin like he had something physically wrong with him when we all knew he was fine.

I ran a hand over Marlo's hair, and he turned his icy gaze on me, his impenetrable stare that made me both hot and cold. "It's time to skinny-dip."

"Yes!" Jackson was already peeling his shirt over his head.

"Again, it's four a.m.," I argued. "We have to be up at seven for breakfast, and everyone gets in at noon!"

"It's tradition," was all Marlo said as he stood then offered his hand. "You don't want to upset the theater gods, do you?"

Groaning, I put my hand in his. "Fine." I stumbled to my feet.

Marlo just shook his head. "Need a ride?"

I narrowed my eyes.

"On my back SP, not my dick."

Jackson roared with laughter while Brax grabbed the gummy bears and shoved two in his mouth.

"And there he is, king of poor choices, four hours man," Jackson shook his head. "You're going to wake up high still, bonus points if you can get the unicorn to fly!"

"Who needs a unicorn when Red Bull gives you wings?" Brax shouted as he ran from the auditorium straight down to the beach behind it.

Marlo jogged with me on his back like I wasn't useless dead weight overcome by exhaustion.

And when he set me down on my feet, he even pulled my clothes from my body with effortless ease.

"Done this before huh?" I teased.

"Once or twice." He shrugged with a smirk.

"Liar." I got up on my tiptoes. "I'd think by now you could undress me in seconds."

"Yeah, but a guy likes to take his time, especially with these," He cupped my breasts through my bra and leered. "Oh, and when I said skinny-dip I meant you keep your bra on, no chance in hell am I letting the guys see you naked."

I crossed my arms. "Just tell them to turn around."

"Yeah, because they're super honest, those guys." He rolled his eyes. "Fine. Jackson, Brax, get naked, get in the lake and turn around."

"Is he that dominant in the bedroom too?" Jackson chuckled as he waded in the water, all I saw was bare, white ass.

"Too bright to look away. It's like the moon but prettier," Jen pointed out. "All right Marlo, I know you see this one naked, but not me, so hurry along so the girls can play."

He blew me a kiss, turned and pulled down his jeans.

Jen let out a low whistle. "Praise God, they don't skip leg day."

"Amen." I high fived her as Marlo waded toward the guys.

"Game time!" I said as we both hurriedly pulled off our bras and underwear, set them neatly on the picnic table and ran toward the shore.

The water hit brisk like needles. And then I was underneath, diving toward the finest ass I'd ever seen.

Warm arms pulled me to the surface. "Snorkeling?"

I grinned at Marlo's smug expression. "Yeah I was looking for a sea snake but all the ones closest to me were so small!"

"That's it!" Jackson roared splashing toward me.

Marlo, the bastard, let me go, so I was left trying to swim away from someone who should be an Olympic swimmer!

"Jen! HELP!"

Jen jumped onto Jackson's back, wrapped her legs around him, then somehow meandered herself to the front of him and grinned. "Found one."

"My eyes!" Brax shouted and then stumbled under water, only to pop up and yell. "I'm fine!"

"He's high." Jackson laughed. "And thanks, Jen, for being the only woman strong enough to deal with the monsters below the surface."

"Monsters." Brax laughed even harder. "I'm friends with the Monster that's under my bed!"

And he was singing…

Jackson joined in, his voice going into a falsetto, and then he started rapping.

Of course he did.

I joined Marlo again, holding his hand below water as he slid his arms around me.

"We had a lot of shitty days back in high school," he whispered across my neck. "But we'll always have our summer nights."

"Always," I agreed with tears of wonder in my eyes as he looked at me like I was born for moments like this with him.

The moment was shattered when Brax started yelling about something touching his leg.

So our swimming was short lived.

But my night?

My night in Marlo's arms seemed to go on forever.

Just like the smile on my face.

Chapter
TWENTY

Marlo

I stretched my arms over my head while Ray scooted her ass into me, squirming against my body, making me so hot for her that I was already grasping her arm, flipping her onto her back, hovering over her.

Why did we even bother with clothes?

Her eyes were closed, but a brilliant smile dazzled her pretty face. It stunned me into silence, it stupefied, made a guy think about nothing and everything all at once. Like the way the sunshine cast a glow across those perfect lips, or the dusting of freckles across her nose that I wanted to suddenly name like a complete obsessed freak.

She was it for me.

The girl who had shared her ice cream cone when she was ten.

The girl who looked at my Nikes with the holes and said cool, I wish I had holes in my shoes, bet you could store things in them that way.

The girl who told me that it was okay to be tall that she wished she was tall too.

I squeezed my eyes shut against the onslaught of memory after memory of her laugh when we were kids.

Of the way she snuck me into her bedroom at night so I could watch cartoons in her bed.

And then the one night when she said I couldn't come over anymore.

That I was a boy.

She was a girl.

The lipstick.

The expensive clothes.

And the very distinctive change in her laughter. It used to be open amusement at the world whenever I was with her.

And then it was directed at me.

Not with me.

At me.

"Hey." Ray cupped my face with her hands. "I don't like it when you close your eyes."

"Why?" I wondered out loud.

"Because…" She swallowed slowly; I followed the motion with my eyes, drinking her in. "You've never hidden yourself, I'm not even sure you're capable of it. When I see your eyes, I know everything's going to be okay, because I see your love."

I shook my head and captured her lips between mine just

as someone sniffed and then said. "That was so beautiful!"

I jumped away from Ray and pulled the duvet to my hips to keep the familiar voice and body attached from seeing my growing erection. "Mom!"

"Nya!" Ray's wide eyes darted to mine as she very slowly pulled a pillow in front of her, like that was going to make the situation better, I swear I could still see nipples through the damn feathers.

"Oh!" My mom burst into tears.

"Mom?" I reached out to her.

She ran into my arms and hugged me, while I was still next to a semi-naked Ray, in bed, seconds away from ripping her clothes off with my teeth.

Awkward did not even begin to cover it.

"I'm so proud of you!" She pulled away and wiped under her eyes, she'd always been pretty, this tiny little Ukranian thing that had both bark and bite, but enough love to consume a person whole. "I knew you would finally see what I see."

"So you're… happy?" I squinted.

She slapped me on the shoulder.

"Ouch!"

"You have many muscles, you'll survive." She sniffed and then her gaze was completely on Ray. "I just knew this was meant to be, I've known for so long. I didn't mean to intrude, but I was searching for Marlo and someone named Jackson said you guys were up here studying…"

Jackson was dying tonight.

"Yeah…" Ray's laugh lacked humor. "Human anatomy, it's uh… for our role?"

"Did you tell her you got an A?" Mom just had to ask,

I could tell she was ready to start bragging because she got that took on her face, the very one I knew in my gut that Ray had never gotten from a parent, making my stomach clench yet again.

"It shows." Ray winked at me.

"Hilarious," I said under my breath while she started giggling.

Mom kept staring like she was afraid it wasn't real.

No, it's real Mom, I'm really naked with a girl. It finally happened.

I cleared my throat.

"Oh!" Mom clapped her hands together. "Yes, sorry, I was just going to drop this off for good luck for you both tonight, then I'll be on my way. Now Ray, I remembered that you used to always sneak his chocolate when I wasn't looking, and he always preferred the vanilla your parents had for you, so I made the cake with two different layers. Break a leg!" She leaned in and kissed me on the forehead then kissed Ray on the cheek. "Beautiful girl."

Ray's eyes filled with tears. "Love you, Nya."

"Oh, I love you too, both of you!" And then she leveled me with a glare. "Get her pregnant, and your father will stop speaking to you, young man."

I felt my entire body heat. "We're being…" I made a motion with my hands then looked to Ray for help.

"Surprise, you're going to be a grandma!" she shouted with laughter.

I grabbed the pillow and slammed it over her face just in time for my mom to recover and then join in the laughter. She set the pretty blue cake on the desk next to us and then shook her head. "See? Perfect for each other!"

The screen door slammed behind her, leaving me hovering over Ray with a pillow. "Give up!"

"NEVER!" she shouted, flailing her arms and legs, giving me a vision of her skin. I dropped the pillow, reached over for the cake, and swiped my finger across the frosting. "Mmmm, that chocolate tastes… incredible."

She gasped. "Monster!"

I winked and shot her a wicked grin. "I'll just eat your half."

She dipped her fingers into the vanilla part, not at all softly, mangling the frosting until it was half on her fingers half dangling over the clean mattress. She sucked one finger.

I gulped.

Another finger while she moaned.

And then she took her pointer finger and swiped it across my mouth, and captured my lips, sucking them dry, licking the sugar from the frosting and then returning that heated tongue to the corner of my mouth like she missed a spot.

My chest heaved. "I know she just dropped off the cake for us to eat, but it sort of feels like she just gave us a shiny new sex toy."

"I'll never look at cake the same again." Ray agreed, and then eyed the cake at about the same time I eyed it and wondered what it would be like to lick it from her thighs.

"We have at least an hour," I pointed out, already pulling her shorts from her body and her shirt from her head.

"At least!" She agreed, kissing me between clothes flying.

And then I was dipping my fingers in the frosting and drawing them down her thighs, following the dizzy blue trails with my tongue.

And she was bucking against me.

"I'm marking you," I said in a husky voice. "Drawing my name all over you, hope you don't think that's too caveman, but a guy gets nervous when a girl this pretty lets him see her naked."

Ray's eyebrows arched as she dipped her fingertips into the frosting and then wrote in giant blue letters across my chest, "*RAY.*"

"I like your name by my heart." I bit back a curse as she licked the R, then traced the A with her tongue and sucked her way down the Y. "I think I may like your tongue there even more than your name."

"I just like you." She kissed me again.

"HEY!" Jackson's voice neared. "I'm closing my eyes because I don't want to have to unsee some shit, but a few of the agents got here early and want to know where to set up." He opened the screen door with a hand over his eyes. "So, if you guys could stop all the laughing and what sounds like God knows what and…" He sniffed. "Hey, you have cake?"

Ray nodded to me just as we both grabbed a handful and slammed it against his chest, she was barely able to hold the blanket against her chest, and I didn't give two shits that I was naked.

In true Jackson form, he just nodded like he was expecting it, and then with one hand still over his eyes, reached down to his chest and took a chunk of cake off and ate it. "God, I love your mom's cake."

"He's impossible." Ray sighed.

Jackson flashed a smile to her. "All the compliments."

We both rolled our eyes as I turned him around and shoved him toward the door. "We'll be down in five minutes."

"Six," Ray coughed.

"And a half," I added for good measure.

"One day you'll get there!" Jackson called back.

He didn't see me flip him off.

Or the heated way Ray's stare devoured me as she dropped the blanket and crooked her sticky fingers at me.

Yeah, better make that seven, some things were meant to be savored.

Chapter
TWENTY-ONE

Ray

"Don't be nervous." Jen massaged my shoulders. "You guys got this, okay? Just let the chemistry speak for itself, and everything's going to be totally fine. Amazing even." She nodded at least five more times, cracked her knuckles, and then flashed me a forced smile.

I gave her a weak grimace. "What don't I know?"

"Nothing." She shook her head. "It's just… the expectation is around fifty industry professionals."

"And?"

"One hundred and twenty-five flew out. No idea why or how, other than we told everyone there was a change of casting at the last minute because of sickness. A few flew in from LA on the red-eye and there were a few others in New York that made the drive out."

"Fantastic," I said with clenched teeth. "And now I'm nervous."

"You're going to be great." She grinned wide. "I know it's overwhelming, but remember, they're here just as much for the campers as they are the staff members. It's why we join in on all of the big numbers."

"Right." I exhaled a sigh.

"Five minutes to curtain!" Brax called.

I locked eyes with Marlo across the stage. Jackson was massaging his shoulders, when he suddenly stepped back and slapped his ass.

I rolled my eyes about the same time Marlo mouthed. "Save me!"

And then I was calm.

All it took was Marlo and I was calm.

"I'll be right back," Jen whispered and then grabbed her walkie. "Go for J-Wow?"

I laughed at her nickname for herself over the coms while Jackson's voice boomed on the other end. "Juicy J has everything ready for a perfect performance."

"You look great, Ray," a deep voice sounded behind me.

Shivers of awareness and danger flashed through my body like I'd just been electrocuted. Slowly I turned.

And there he was.

In all his glory.

Deacon Tanningtom.

The blood drained from my face as he slowly eyed me from head to toe. "You'll be a great Baby, baby."

"Don't call me that," I said through clenched teeth.

He just rolled his eyes. "Look I think there's been a misunderstanding between us. Why don't we drive into the city after your performance? Have a drink? I'll put you and your friends up wherever you want to celebrate."

"Celebrate?"

"Signing with me of course." He shrugged. "I still think we're a perfect fit."

"I don't." I shook my head no. "I refuse to work with someone who would blackball me to the entire industry just because I refused to suck his dick for a favor!"

I didn't realize I was yelling.

Just like I didn't realize that my mic was hot.

His eyes bulged. "Listen, you bitch! You came on to me!"

"You locked your door!" I would not cry. He was the offending party. I was a victim. "You said you would sign me, but I had to get on my knees!"

"Bullshit! Are you trying to ruin me?"

"How many girls have you done that to?" I didn't know why I felt strong. I didn't know why I wasn't cowering, feeling worthless and alone. And then I saw Marlo running toward us across the stage.

And before I could do anything else, Marlo had Deacon by the collar and threw him onto the middle of the stage. "You sick fuck!"

"I hope you don't mind getting sued before your career even starts Mr. Brandon!"

"Fuck. You." Marlo snarled. "I'm sure all it will take is one woman coming forward and you're done. Oh look, we already have a willing woman." He held out his hand to me. "Did he sexually harass you with plans for representation if and only if you went through with his demands?"

I found my voice and stared down at the man on the ground bleeding. "Yes. He did."

The crowd gasped.

Marlo shrugged and then motioned to Brax with two fingers. "Call the police."

"What!" Deacon jumped to his feet, "You have no proof, you have no—"

A punch came out of nowhere.

I stumbled back in shock when my father shook his fist like the punch stung more than he'd thought it would. His eyes filled with tears and then he looked away and said under his breath. "I'll take care of this."

That was all he said.

I'll take care of this.

I'll take care of this.

And then he shook his head again and said. "I'll take care of this... so you don't have to."

My jaw dropped.

Marlo held out his hand to my dad.

And my dad stared at it.

Stared at it longer than what was comfortable for everyone in the audience watching, and for me to experience.

And then he took it and pulled Marlo in for a hug.

"Thank you," Dad said through clenched teeth. "Thank you for being her... thank you."

My dad wasn't a small man, he bent over and pulled Deacon to his feet and then escorted him toward the back of the audience while everyone stared at us with stunned expressions.

Well, they weren't going to forget our names any time soon!

I looked to Marlo.

He held my hand and kissed it then announced over his mic. "I love this woman."

Everyone cheered.

I leaped into his arms and kissed him amid the happy claps around the auditorium.

"Break a leg, Ray!" he said as we separated.

"You too, lover boy." I winked as the audience laughed again.

The lights went low.

And before I went out for my first scene, I looked toward the audience and saw Nya clutching my mom's hand with a smile of joy on her face.

"Thank you," I mouthed.

One single nod.

I don't know how she got them there.

What she did.

What she even said.

But that woman down there was more a mother to me than my own, and I owed her a lot more than I ever gave her credit for.

It was I who should be thanking her, for loving a lost little boy with no shoes and a fascination with acting to escape his own crappy childhood.

I should be thanking her for seeing below the surface.

For seeing him.

The way I saw him that first day I announced we were going to be friends.

Tears filled my eyes as Marlo's body filled the stage.

And then we were flying.

Together.

Dancing.

Singing.

And I was captivated by my Johnny as I walked in with a watermelon.

He moved across the stage, his eyes locking on mine. "What's she doing here?"

"I carried a watermelon." I squeezed my eyes shut as a real blush hit my cheeks.

He bit down on his lower lip.

I licked my lips in anticipation as he fired off his lines, everyone danced around us. I sighed to myself and tried to make my way past him when he grabbed my hand and thrust a leg against mine and rolled his hips. "Do you love me?" He sang as I danced awkwardly with him like I was supposed to.

And then too soon he was dancing with another camper, and I was staring after him with wonderment and lust in my eyes as the song ended.

"Better change your name, cuz you ain't a baby anymore," Marlo said, even though it wasn't supposed to be him delivering the line, it fit. Sexual tension rippled across the stage after another heated stare, and I knew, I would have never been able to this, without him.

Chapter
TWENTY-TWO

Marlo

Things were going perfect.

Seamless even.

Staff members and campers worked perfectly together, making it one of the best productions I'd ever been a part of.

I wanted to believe it was because Ray was so raw, so believable.

And the tension between us?

Not acting.

It was time for the love scene. It would be tasteful, but it still needed to convey this need, this hunger.

"...one last time, and I'll leave you alone," she whispered

her lines with a shaky voice as she went over and pretended to turn on the music, and then her hands were on my arms, pulling me to my feet, and we were dancing.

Flying.

I dipped her backward, pulled her against my chest.

Hooked her leg around my hips as our bodies moved in sync with one another. I shuddered when she moved behind me and kissed my back. Her fingers rippling down my muscles and then dancing again.

I was lost in her.

I didn't hear the music.

I didn't hear anything except for the erratic beating of my heart as I kissed down her neck and button by button undid her sweater, exposing her white bra.

Our mouths met as I slid her cardigan slowly off her shoulders, my mouth licking its way over her smooth skin.

I picked her up with both hands and carried her to the bed on stage, and then covered my body with hers as the music ended.

Both of our chests were heaving when the lights when low.

Applause like thunder rang my ears.

And still all I saw was her.

My Ray.

My Baby.

Mine.

Lights lit up stage left as we both ducked behind the bed and made our way backstage.

"Ray," I pulled her in for a kiss. "Almost there."

Her smile was wide. "This is fun."

"It's supposed to be fun," I said, smiling.

"With you." Her eyes darted to my mouth. "We would have been the hottest theater nerds ever in high school."

I burst out laughing. "Yeah except I'm pretty sure I had a six pack back then from lack of muscle, so not so sure you would have wanted to—"

She crushed her mouth to mine. "I wanted to. I did." And then she gave me her back and bumped her ass against me. "I tapped that."

Jackson swore. "Really guys? Give it a rest!"

"Aren't you supposed to be on stage?" I wondered out loud.

"Nope, but you are!" He double checked my mic to make sure it was hot again and then shoved me away from Ray.

Seconds passed, maybe another hour and we were at the final dance scene.

I felt my adrenaline spike when Time of My Life came on.

Ray winked at me.

She looked so fucking free I wanted to shout.

We made our way toward the middle of the stage amidst claps and yelling and then I opened my mouth to sing. "I've… had the time of my life…"

She joined in perfect harmony with a grin on her face that lit up the entire stage, that stole my heart and ran away with it.

Our friends danced around us.

Jackson and Jen in the background with Brax, the campers did their sequence, and then it was time for the staff part of the production. Staff members surrounded us and sang the chorus as we all did our huge dance number leading up to Ray jumping into my arms.

She ran across the stage and leaped, I held her high and twirled her, and she came down in my arms.

And kissed me.

She didn't even finish singing her part.

Just kissed me so hard and long that cheering and singing erupted around us with cat calls and cameras flashing.

I set her on her feet and kissed her back, I kissed her with everything in me, I claimed her on that stage under those stars, under that moon, I claimed that Ray of sunshine, and I swore I would keep it forever.

"We did it." She said against my lips. "Together."

"Together," I agreed as a standing ovation exploded around us, followed by roses getting thrown on stage.

And when she turned to smile at the crowd, it wasn't lost on me that my foster mom was sitting right next to Ray's mom — who was sobbing uncontrollably in her seat.

"He would have loved this, my brother," she said through tears as she squeezed my hand.

"He did love it." I pressed a hand to her chest. "Because he was here, with you, the entire time."

Tears filled her eyes as I wrapped an arm around her and then pulled her toward the front and bowed with her.

I recognized a few agents, a few industry professionals, and for the first time in a really long time, I didn't give a shit.

Because I already had my future in my right hand.

Chapter
TWENTY-THREE

Ray

I just wanted to celebrate with Marlo, with Jen, Jackson, even Brax, but I knew I needed to at least thank my mom for coming, though I assumed Nya had dragged her kicking and screaming.

Nya excused herself the minute I walked up, most likely to go in search of Marlo. The crowd was thick with bodies, laughter, industry chatter.

And then there was my mom and me.

Staring each other down.

"You," She cleared her throat. "You were magnificent."

I narrowed my eyes. "Thank you."

"Truly." She stared down at her pristine white heels with the red soles. "Everything was flawless. It seems that you've found your purpose."

"Maybe," I answered, as she swiped under her eyes.

"Your father and I…" She started and then glanced over her shoulder at my dad who was talking to a few police officers. I'd probably have to give a statement, press charges, do something, but for now, I wanted to think about Marlo, about the performance.

About being free.

"Your father and I…" She tried again. "Are going to try."

It wasn't what I wanted.

I wanted her to throw her arms around me and say how wrong she'd been.

But that wasn't them.

It would never be them, would it?

I nodded. "All right Mom, I'll try too."

She nodded and then held out her hand.

I wanted to be offended that my own mom wanted to shake my hand.

Instead, I shook her hand and breathed in the scent of Marlo behind me.

I turned. "You."

"Me." He breathed.

"You were perfect."

"You were the perfect one." He cupped my face. "And I'm so fucking proud of you."

That. That was what I needed.

"I'm proud of me too," I said. "Proud of us."

He tucked my arm into his side. "Excuse us."

We were walking at a fast pace toward the front of the stage again where a nice older gentleman was standing, talking on his phone. He gave us a nod, and then excused himself and hung up.

"Young lady." He shook his head, his eyes held wonder, the crinkles at the side made me think he smiled more than he scowled, and I liked that he was wearing a suit but already had the tie pulled and the buttons undone. "You were fantastic!"

"Thank you!" I beamed.

He held out a card. "I'd like to talk representation." He looked between us. "For both of you, actually."

"We'll be in touch," Marlo answered for me while I stared slack jawed at the card.

I had wrongly assumed it was just another agent with big promises and even bigger lies.

It wasn't just an agent.

It was the William Morris Agency.

"Close your mouth," Marlo whispered under his breath. "You earned this, and you also earned this…" He backed away and then spread his arms wide. "Ray, congratulations, you're finally starting to peak!"

I burst out laughing. "Yeah, yeah."

"She has boobs." This from a confused Jen.

"Party at the lake!" Brax shouted.

"That's going to end well," I mused while Marlo wrapped an arm around my shoulders and guided us toward the sparkling water.

"Whatever happens," Marlo said so only I could hear. "We'll always know, that it was the hot summer nights that got us to this place."

"And what place is that?" I stopped walking and looked up at him, his crystal blue eyes shone down on me with amusement, with happiness.

"Love." He leaned down and brushed a kiss across my lips. "Hate."

"Everything in between?" I wrapped my arms around his neck.

"All of it, Ray. All of it."

"Come on you guys!" Jackson was already pulling his shirt over his head.

"Run along, farm boy." I shoved Marlo.

He just laughed and started jogging toward the shore yelling, "As you wish!"

EPILOGUE

Marlo

Six Years Later

"You look beautiful," I whispered against her neck as we neared the building, our driver went to the back, as requested. "You're also fidgeting."

Ray pressed a hand to her stomach and gave me that death glare I found so damn attractive. "I'm allowed to be nervous."

"You're a movie star, kind of a big deal, you'd think that walking into a gymnasium would be cake." I winked.

She just scowled. "Look who's talking Mr. I have so many fangirls that movie theaters kept losing posters because high school girls were ripping them off the walls and running!"

I grinned to myself. "I can't help it. I have a nice ass."

She tilted her head and then licked her lips. "You know we could skip."

"Nope." The car came to a stop, our driver got out and then opened the door wide. "Out you go. Plus, this will be good for you! Think of it as your final moment."

"More like your final revenge," she grumbled to herself.

"Hey!" I stepped out, offered my hand, then pulled her against my chest. "I love you. I don't need revenge when I have you. Plus, we've been over this... we have each other."

Her eyes locked on mine. "I may be acting a bit more hormonal than usual." She bit down on her bottom lip as tears filled her eyes. "I'm pregnant!"

"What?" Breathless, I cupped her face as electrical charges surged through me. "Did you say you're pregnant?"

"I don't know how it happened!" She threw her hands into the air while I burst out laughing.

"Really? You don't? Because I can give you a list of how many ways and positions it could have happened in the last night alone..."

She smacked me. "It's just this whole... thing," She waved up at the gym. "Is making it worse."

"You're pregnant," I repeated with a sense of awe filling me. "My beautiful wife of two years is pregnant."

She wrapped her arms around my neck. "My sexy husband of two years, my boyfriend since I was six—"

"Are we suddenly not counting the hateful years?"

"Nope!" She popped the P and grinned. "Because I don't think we would be in this place had we not had those years of hatred. It boiled into something greater than that."

"It did," I whispered, then pressed a kiss to her mouth. "I can't believe you're pregnant."

"I found out this morning."

"This morning, this morning, when you cried over that

dog food commercial?" I wondered out loud earning another slap from her. "Ouch!"

"He was so hungry!" More tears came.

"Hell, let's get you inside."

Our security guard Mitch, the only security Ray allowed us to bring, opened the back door to the gymnasium as we slowly made our way inside hand-in-hand.

Music pumped through the sound system.

And I was immediately transported back to high school.

The nerd.

The unloved.

The guy stuffed in lockers pining after the prom queen.

Well, joke's on fucking them — I grinned so wide my face almost cracked. I was happy! Don't get me wrong, we were both extremely successful. Ray had a running sitcom that made the Big Bang Theory look like child's play, and I'd landed a few small roles before my big break as a vampire.

I was also never going to live that role down.

Not that I minded, since I genuinely liked it and was laughing all the way to the bank — or getting chased by teen girls, that too.

It was the perfect revenge from the universe.

Going from getting stuffed in lockers.

To being literally in every locker, as a vampire poster.

Hah!

A few whispers, cameras going off.

"May I have this dance?" I pulled Ray close as the rest of our graduating class watched. I danced with her in the middle of the floor, under the cheesy decorations next to the punch bowl.

I got my revenge in the best way.

I got the girl.

"I love you." I tilted her chin toward me.

She just smiled. "I love you too, lawn boy."

That got a laugh out of me as people watched us with adoring expressions and cameras out.

"See? Aren't you glad you came to your ten-year reunion? Told you it would be fun!"

"Yeah," She didn't pull her eyes away from me. "I'd rather take you behind the gymnasium like I should have my senior year."

I pressed a kiss to her ear. "What's stopping you?"

And that was all it took for her to grab my hand and drag me through the heavy crowd of iPhones lifted in the air.

And when the summer night air hit my face, I smiled. It always reminded me of camp.

Of my friends.

True friends.

True love.

Life.

A beautiful gift — you just have to love yourself enough to accept it, and then you have to fight like hell to keep it.

"Unbutton your pants," Ray barked.

"Is your whole pregnancy going to be like this?" I teased.

Apparently, I wasn't going fast enough.

"Remember how last year Jackson got me a Kama Sutra book and I opened it in front of everyone and then threw it at his face?"

I grinned as her hands worked my tucked shirt out of my trousers. "I think we all remember that, because it ended up hitting Brax in the face and Jen had to get him frozen peas."

"Well, I'm thinking, I have all this energy…" Her grin

was wicked. "So I'd hydrate if I were you." She jerked my pants open.

I bit back a curse as she shimmied her dress up past her thighs and settled a leg over my hips.

"Also, I'm not wearing underwear."

I sucked in a breath and gripped her hips with my hands. Digging my fingers into her tender flesh. "Damn, I'm so glad you said yes when I proposed to you next to the lawnmower."

She arched, then lowered herself onto me. "Maybe one day my dad will call you something other than 'kid.'"

I squeezed my eyes shut as I moved inside her. "Let's... not talk about your dad when I'm inside you, 'kay?"

We laughed. And then it was just us again.

Behind the gymnasium, where our old selves should have always been.

Loving each other.

Forever.

WANT MORE RVD?

Did you enjoy the Cruel Summer trilogy?
Then check out these other New Adult Romances!

Wingmen Inc.
The Matchmaker's Playbook (Ian & Blake's story)
The Matchmaker's Replacement (Lex & Gabi's story)

Bro Code
Co-Ed (Knox & Shawn's story)
Seducing Mrs. Robinson (Leo & Kora's story)
Avoiding Temptation (Slater & Tatum's story)
The Setup (Finn & Jillian's story)

Red Card
Risky Play (Slade & Mackenzie's story)
Kickin' It (Matt & Parker's story)

Players Game
Fraternize (Miller, Grant and Emerson's story)
Infraction (Miller & Kinsey's story)
M.V.P. (Jax & Harley's story)

Seaside Pictures
Capture (Lincoln & Dani's story)
Keep (Zane & Fallon's story)
Steal (Will & Angelica's story)
All Stars Fall (Trevor & Penelope's story)
Abandon (Ty & Abigail's story)
Provoke (Braden & Piper's story)
Surrender (Andrew & Bronte's story)

Single Titles
Office Hate (Mark & Olivia's story)
A Crown for Christmas (Fitz & Phillipa's story)

ACKNOWLEDGEMENTS

WOW, thank you guys so much for taking this journey with me! I'm so thankful to God that I get to do what I love on a daily basis! I'm fully aware I wouldn't be where I am today without my incredible family but also my readers! You guys are so awesome, thank you for taking a chance on this series, as I've said before it almost felt like coming home in a way, coming back to NA and all that angst and emotions and feelings. It was such a fun ride.

Thank you to my amazing publicist Nina for everything. Ian at iBooks you're my bro, no really you are. (I'm sure he's shaking his head right now and telling everyone he's never even met me, but that's cool I'll claim you haha). To all the bloggers and reviewers thanks again for being so supportive, this is an awesome community and I'm honored to be a part of it.

If you want to follow my shenanigans add me on insta @RachVD or you can join the friendliest reader group on Facebook: Rachel's New Rockin Readers, until next time, HUGS!

ABOUT THE AUTHOR

Rachel Van Dyken is the #1 *New York Times, Wall Street Journal,* and *USA Today* bestselling author of over 90 books ranging from contemporary romance to paranormal. With over four million copies sold, she's been featured in Forbes, US Weekly, and USA Today. Her books have been translated in more than 15 countries. She was one of the first romance authors to have a Kindle in Motion book through Amazon publishing and continues to strive to be on the cutting edge of the reader experience. She keeps her home in the Pacific Northwest with her husband, adorable sons, naked cat, and two dogs. For more information about her books and upcoming events, visit www.RachelVanDykenAuthor.com.

ALSO BY
RACHEL VAN DYKEN

Eagle Elite
Elite (Nixon & Trace's story)
Elect (Nixon & Trace's story)
Entice (Chase & Mil's story)
Elicit (Tex & Mo's story)
Bang Bang (Axel & Amy's story)
Enforce (Elite + from the boys POV)
Ember (Phoenix & Bee's story)
Elude (Sergio & Andi's story)
Empire (Sergio & Val's story)
Enrage (Dante & El's story)
Eulogy (Chase & Luciana's story)
Exposed (Dom & Tanit's story)
Envy (Vic & Renee's story)

Elite Bratva Brotherhood
RIP (Nikolai & Maya's story)
Debase (Andrei & Alice's story)

Mafia Royals Romances
Royal Bully (Asher & Claire's story)
Ruthless Princess (Serena & Junior's story
Scandalous Prince (Breaker & Violet's story)
Destructive King (Asher & Annie's story)
Mafia King (Tank & Kartini's story)
Fallen Royal (Maksim'& Izzy's story)
Broken Crown (King's story)

Rachel Van Dyken & M. Robinson
Mafia Casanova (Romeo & Eden's story)
Falling for the Villain (Juliet Sinacore's story)

Wingmen Inc.
The Matchmaker's Playbook (Ian & Blake's story)
The Matchmaker's Replacement (Lex & Gabi's story)

Bro Code
Co-Ed (Knox & Shawn's story)
Seducing Mrs. Robinson (Leo & Kora's story)
Avoiding Temptation (Slater & Tatum's story)
The Setup (Finn & Jillian's story)

Liars, Inc
Dirty Exes (Colin, Jessie & Blaire's story)
Dangerous Exes (Jessie & Isla's story))'

Cruel Summer Trilogy
Summer Heat (Marlon & Ray's story)
Summer Seduction (Marlon & Ray's story)
Summer Nights (Marlon & Ray's story)

Covet
Stealing Her (Bridge & Isobel's story)
Finding Him (Julian & Keaton's story)

The Dark Ones Saga
The Dark Ones (Ethan & Genesis's story)
Untouchable Darkness (Cassius & Stephanie's story)
Dark Surrender (Alex & Hope's story)
Darkest Temptation (Mason & Serenity's story)
Darkest Sinner (Timber & Kyra's story)

Curious Liaisons
Cheater (Lucas & Avery's story)
Cheater's Regret (Thatch & Austin's story)

Red Card
Risky Play (Slade & Mackenzie's story)
Kickin' It (Matt & Parker's story)

Players Game
Fraternize (Miller, Grant and Emerson's story)
Infraction (Miller & Kinsey's story)
M.V.P. (Jax & Harley's story)

The Consequence Series
The Consequence of Loving Colton (Colton & Milo's story)
The Consequence of Revenge (Max & Becca's story)
The Consequence of Seduction (Reid & Jordan's story)
The Consequence of Rejection (Jason & Maddy's story)

The Bet Series
The Bet (Travis & Kacey's story)
The Wager (Jake & Char Lynn's story)
The Dare (Jace & Beth Lynn's story)

The Bachelors of Arizona
The Bachelor Auction (Brock & Jane's story)
The Playboy Bachelor (Bentley & Margot's story)
The Bachelor Contract (Brant & Nikki's story)

Ruin Series
Ruin (Wes Michels & Kiersten's story)
Toxic (Gabe Hyde & Saylor's story)
Fearless (Wes Michels & Kiersten's story)
Shame (Tristan & Lisa's story)

Seaside Series
Tear (Alec, Demetri & Natalee's story)
Pull (Demetri & Alyssa's story)
Shatter (Alec & Natalee's story)
Forever (Alec & Natalee's story)
Fall (Jamie Jaymeson & Pricilla's story)
Strung (Tear + from the boys POV)
Eternal (Demetri & Alyssa's story)

Seaside Pictures
Capture (Lincoln & Dani's story)
Keep (Zane & Fallon's story)
Steal (Will & Angelica's story)
All Stars Fall (Trevor & Penelope's story)
Abandon (Ty & Abigail's story)
Provoke (Braden & Piper's story)
Surrender (Andrew & Bronte's story)

Kathy Ireland & Rachel Van Dyken
Fashion Jungle

Single Titles
Office Hate (Mark & Olivia's story)
A Crown for Christmas (Fitz & Phillipa's story)
Every Girl Does It (Preston & Amanda's story)
Compromising Kessen (Christian & Kessen's story)
Divine Uprising (Athena & Adonis's story)
The Parting Gift — written with Leah Sanders (Blaine and Mara's story)

Waltzing With The Wallflower — written with Leah Sanders

Waltzing with the Wallflower (Ambrose & Cordelia)
Beguiling Bridget (Anthony & Bridget's story)
Taming Wilde (Colin & Gemma's story)

London Fairy Tales

Upon a Midnight Dream (Stefan & Rosalind's story)
Whispered Music (Dominique & Isabelle's story)
The Wolf's Pursuit (Hunter & Gwendolyn's story)
When Ash Falls (Ashton & Sofia's story)

Renwick House

The Ugly Duckling Debutante (Nicholas & Sara's story)
The Seduction of Sebastian St. James (Sebastian & Emma's story)
The Redemption of Lord Rawlings (Phillip & Abigail's story)
An Unlikely Alliance (Royce & Evelyn's story)
The Devil Duke Takes a Bride (Benedict & Katherine's story)

www.rachelvandykenauthor.com